JOHN HENRY CLAY

The Lion and the Lamb

HODDER

First published in Great Britain in 2013 by Hodder & Stoughton
An Hachette UK company

This paperback edition first published in 2014

1

A CIP catalogue record for this title is available from the British Library

ISBN 978 1 444 76134 4

Printed and bound by Clays Ltd, St Ives plc

Hodder & Stoughton policy is to use papers that are natural, renewable
and recyclable products and made from wood grown in sustainable forests.
The logging and manufacturing processes are expected to conform to the
environmental regulations of the country of origin.

Hodder & Stoughton Ltd
338 Euston Road
London NW1 3BH

www.hodder.co.uk

For Mum and Dad

CONTENTS

The Four Provinces
of
BRITANNIA

c. AD 366

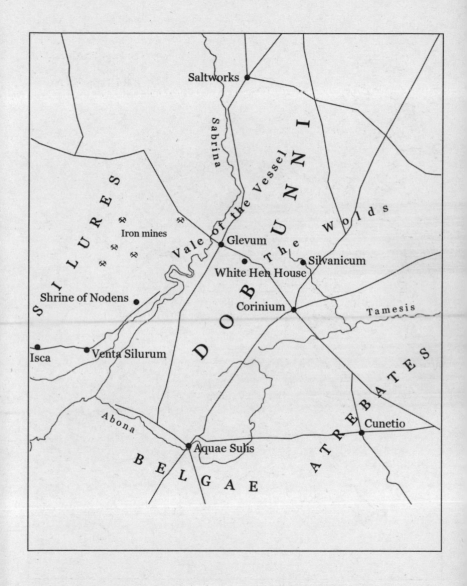

Saltworks

Sabrina

S I L U R E S

Iron mines

Vale of the Vessel

Glevum

D O B U N N I

The Wolds

Silvanicum

White Hen House

Shrine of Nodens

Corinium

Tamesis

Isca

Venta Silurum

Abona

A T R E B A T E S

Cunetio

Aquae Sulis

B E L G A E

THE FOUR PROVINCES OF
BRITANNIA, AD 362

One Thousand One Hundred and Fifteen Years
Since the Founding of Rome

Three Hundred and Sixteen Years
Since the Conquest

Five Years Before the
Great Barbarian Conspiracy

Prologue

Consider the sunlight as it glints on the edge of the blade. The sword is silent and sharp, and steady: the point hovers one short thrust from your face. Its wielder stares at you, but with the sun behind him and his face in shadow he has no identity. You hear his breathing and your own and the sound of the river in which you lie. You do not know who the man is, or where he came from. He has you here, and in a moment he will kill you.

Paul lay in the forest stream on his back, naked, his head and shoulders raised on his elbows above the churning water, and waited for the man who stood before him, rough trousers soaked to the knees and sword held at arm's length, to finish it. The stones of the streambed dug painfully into Paul's bare flesh. His teeth chattered and his limbs shook from fear and from the freezing water, which had already sucked all heat from his body.

Do not beg, Paul told himself beneath the thumping of his heart. Death is nothing to you now. Consider the justice of your end, and accept it. All the workings of the godless world have brought you here. You began your life naked and screaming: you can at least end it with what little of your dignity remains.

Paul did not beg, but nor did he stop shaking, and though he tried to close his eyes he could not move his stare from the gleam of the blade. He awaited its next move, a jab to his throat, and oblivion awaited him.

In the final moment he thought with sadness of his sister. Despite everything, he wished he had said goodbye.

The blade did not move. Paul heard a dull thud, and he saw the man's chest jolt strangely. The man staggered, still holding his sword, and almost fell. He veered left, sloshed clumsily through the water like a drunkard, came to the bank, began to crawl onto the turf, and there collapsed.

The man lay on his front with the sword at his side. Embedded deep in his back was the shaft of an arrow, its goose-feather flights shining white in the sun.

Paul stayed where he was, quiet amidst the waters, and stared into the darkness of the trees beyond the riverbank, but he saw no movement, and heard nothing beyond the rushing of the stream and the nearby song of a blackbird. The arrow might have flown from Heaven itself. When he decided to rise, it took painful effort to force movement and life into his frozen limbs. Slowly, stiffly, he climbed to his feet. His chest was heaving, blood pulsating in his neck. Instinctively he felt to check that his seal ring was still on his finger. It was.

He steadied his mouth enough to fling out two short words: 'Who's there?'

A single figure emerged from the trees. He looked about the same age as Paul, sixteen or so; he wore peasant's clothing, a travelling cloak and satchel, a cloth cap and quiver of arrows, and in his right hand he carried a hunting bow. His face was long, his mouth broad. He was smiling to himself, and did not look at Paul as he came down to the bank.

'Thank you, friend,' Paul said, wishing that his voice was stronger. His body was still shivering as though it wanted to shake itself apart. Shortly before, his would-be murderer had come across him bathing in this forest stream, and had taken his clothes from the bank and flung them downstream before advancing upon him. Its water was shallow, but the current was thick and strong, swollen by the spring rains, and it had carried Paul's tunic, cloak and undergarments some distance to a willow overhanging the bank, where they had become snagged.

The young peasant had reached the body. He nudged it with his toe. Satisfied that the man was dead, he twisted the arrow from his back and looked at Paul for the first time. He seemed amused by his nakedness, and when he noticed the golden ring on Paul's finger, and then the clothes caught downstream in the willow – the deep, dark red of Paul's cloak, the tunic with its fine gold-threaded border, the costly linen underwear – slowly his smile became an open grin, and then a chuckle, and suddenly he was laughing so hard that he bent over and shut his eyes.

Moments ago Paul had thought himself prepared to meet death calmly. Now he felt ridiculous, standing naked in the river before the mockery of a peasant. The fact that he owed the peasant his life only deepened his humiliation. Angrily he tried to ignore the laughter and began to wade with the current towards his clothes. He took two steps before his foot slipped on a mossy stone and he stumbled face-first into the stream. He scrambled to his feet, shook the water from his ears, took another step and slipped again. As he once more rose he looked over his shoulder and saw that the peasant was now lying on his side, still laughing, as though he were reclining at a feast and Paul were a clown prancing for his amusement. Paul swore, forgot all pretence of dignity, and clambered messily on all fours to the willow, from which he violently snatched his clothes, wrestling his trousers free with such force that he tore them where they had caught on a bough.

Paul staggered to the bank and heaved himself onto the grass, exhausted. He took only a moment to catch his breath before he spotted a thick branch lying in the undergrowth. It looked damp and rotten, but he did not have the patience to look for another, and so he snatched it up, brandished it at his side and advanced on the peasant, who was still laughing like a madman. Even as Paul raised the branch and brought it down in fury, the peasant did not stop; he shielded himself with his arm and with the first strike the branch broke in two.

The rest of the branch was useless. Paul flung it into the stream. He would have kicked the peasant in the ribs, or thrust a heel in his eyes, but instinct prevented him; it was demeaning to beat inferiors by hand – with whips and canes, yes, but never with one's own fists or feet. And he was still naked, his clothes lying in a sodden heap on the bank. The peasant could wait.

Paul returned to his clothes and untangled his trousers. He had managed to rip them near the top and they would be useless until stitched. His woollen tunic and cloak, heavy and cold with water, would never dry before sunset. What would he do until then, with the chill of evening already seeping into the forest air?

Something dark landed on the ground beside him. It was a pair of boots.

'Put them on, lord.'

Paul turned to see that the peasant was now on his feet, tugging the trousers from the legs of the corpse. When he had removed them, he tossed them over.

Paul looked at the trousers distastefully. They were coarse, poorly stitched, and were no doubt uncomfortable. He bent down to pick them up. They still carried the warmth of their last owner. 'I won't wear the clothes of a dead man,' he said.

The young peasant laughed again. 'We're all dead men, lord.'

By the time Paul had dressed, the peasant had dragged the body into the undergrowth and left it for the wolves. He returned to the stream to collect his satchel, quiver and bow. Paul noticed that the dead man's sword now hung from his belt. It was illegal for peasants to carry such weapons; a sword marked a man as an outlaw, and he could be executed in the public forum merely for possessing one. But Paul was now far from the cities with their law courts and judges. He thought better of mentioning it.

'I was going to make camp some way downstream,' the peasant said. He bowed to a sarcastic depth. 'If my lord desires food and warmth, I would be honoured by his company.'

Paul nodded, containing his irritation, gathered his damp clothes and followed the peasant, a member of the local Cornovian tribe to judge from his speech, along a forest track. The dead man's tunic and cloak fitted him poorly, but they were at least dry. And he was alive; were it not for this boy, *his* naked corpse would now be food for wolves. For the first time it struck Paul how easily the peasant could have killed him, too, had he wanted to, with a swift second arrow that would have won him a golden ring. Few men lived in these woods, and Paul had been utterly defenceless. Instead, the peasant had saved his life. As they continued, although the itchiness of the rough tunic kept Paul's mood from calming, he began to feel some grudging gratitude towards his saviour. 'Do you have a name, peasant?'

'Victor.'

Paul waited for the peasant to ask his name in turn. When he did not, Paul asked, 'Are you a hunter?'

The Cornovian snorted. 'The hunted.'

He did not elaborate, and neither spoke again until shortly before dusk, when they made camp in a clearing not far above the river. Paul had been journeying through these forests for several days and knew how to build a fire, but now it seemed proper to let the peasant do it while he stood to one side. Only when the fire was blazing, by which time the clear sky was turning a deep blue and stars were beginning to appear, did Paul come to sit beside it. He watched the peasant pull a hare from his satchel and set about cutting the hide from the back legs with a hunting knife.

'My name is Gaius Cironius Agnus Paulus,' said Paul.

Victor gave a brief nod, intent on skinning the animal. Treading on the hare's back feet to keep them in place, he smoothly tugged the hide up to the neck, turning it inside out. The naked muscles shimmered purple in the firelight. He cut through the neck with his knife and tossed skin and head aside. 'Honoured,' he said.

'My father,' Paul said patiently, 'is senator Gaius Cironius Agnus of the Dobunni.'

At these words the peasant glanced up. 'Now, I think I've heard of the Dobunni.'

Paul realised that he was being mocked. Of course a Cornovian would have heard of the Dobunni, the neighbouring tribe to the south. He must also have heard of the Cironii, one of the wealthiest and most powerful families in Britannia, descended from an ancient line of tribal kings whose princely blood flowed through Paul's own veins. Paul watched the peasant closely, and saw a faint smile curl his lips. He was teasing Paul, wanting to humble him into explaining his own noble pedigree. The very thought was infuriating. Paul had never before met someone who did not already know who he was, let alone someone who pretended not to know.

'You're a long way from home, Gaius Cironius Agnus Paulus,' said Victor. 'You lost?'

It was an impudent question that deserved no answer. The best demeanour for now, Paul decided, was a dignified silence. This peasant would realise his mistake when they were out of the woods, when they had returned to the civilised world . . .

He stopped that thought. *You cannot return, you fool. Have you forgotten that already?*

Today's narrow escape from death had shaken him, and he had settled back into his old habits. But now the memory of his crime once more crept to the front of his mind like a raven. He felt its wings darken his thoughts. It cloaked his pride in the blackest of shadows. *Why are you in these woods?* it asked of him. His heart began to thump. A sickening weakness spread through his limbs. *You have poisoned the blood of the Cironii. You have no right to claim their name as your own. You are nothing but a wandering wretch without honour.*

You should have died in the stream.

He should have died – for the crime he had committed, by natural law he should have died. Fate had been ready to take vengeance through the steel of the bandit. Paul had not pleaded for his life, nor appealed against his sentence. He had been ready to die. And yet he still lived.

At this thought the darkness receded; not entirely, but enough for a brief glimpse of light, maybe even hope. Why had he been spared?

The peasant pushed a spit into the hare's neck, and forced it the length of the body. 'These things are hardly worth the effort, skinny little bastards,' he said with a chuckle. With one hand he held it over the fire. With the other he removed his cap to reveal a bald head. He had been freshly and messily shaved, his scalp left patterned with razor cuts.

Such cuts could only mean one thing. Paul was not the only fugitive in these woods. He cleared his throat. 'You're a deserter,' he said.

'No.' Victor showed Paul his right wrist, which did not bear the tattoo of military service. 'I was drafted from my lord's estate a couple of days ago, that's when they shaved me. But this morning I ran for it before they made me take the oath. Not a soldier, not a deserter.'

'But you're running from both your lord and the army.'

'I never swore an oath to my lord, either. I'm not a slave, but I was born on his land, and he treated me like one. He was ready enough to hand me over to the army. Why should I give him my loyalty? I owe him nothing, and the army nothing. I have no family. I'm as much a Roman citizen as anyone.'

That was true in part. Since the days of Emperor Caracalla every freeborn man within the empire was technically a citizen of Rome. But that also meant being subject to Roman laws, among them loyalty to one's lord. 'You're an outlaw.'

Victor shrugged. His smile never seemed to leave his face.

He did not look like an outlaw to Paul. Despite his skill with the bow, despite the coolness with which he had killed the man earlier, there was a gentleness to Victor's eyes that did not seem suited to that sort of life. When they had made camp, Victor had unbuckled the illegal sword, had casually left it lying on the grass near the edge of the clearing, and had evidently forgotten about it since. He had made no threats or demands for a reward, seemed to have no intention of holding Paul to ransom. If he was an outlaw, he was not a very good one.

Paul thought about this, about how the peasant seemed to have fallen into a role for which he was despairingly ill-suited, and then thought about himself, and for the first time imagined how he must have first appeared to Victor: a young noble, stark naked, standing shivering in the middle of a forest stream with his black hair matted to his head and his fancy clothes snagged in a willow tree. And now here they sat, the pair of them, cooking a miserable scrap of meat in the depths of the barren woods, one with a shorn head and the other in the clothes of a dead man. It was all so absurd.

For the first time in many days, Paul began to laugh.

★ ★ ★

'Wake up.'

Paul was roused by a hand shaking his shoulder. He opened his eyes to see the peasant leaning over him. 'What is it?'

Victor spoke urgently. 'We need to go. Quick.'

Paul sat up. Dawn had just broken with a yellow glare in an open sky, and the forest was alive with birdcalls. He was beside the dead remnants of the campfire, across which he and the peasant had talked until well into the night. Though Paul had not told Victor his reason for running from home, never before had he been so familiar with someone of such low rank. He had found it strangely agreeable. 'What's wrong?'

Victor was already on his feet with his satchel and bow. 'The fucking army. Can you hear the dogs?'

Paul rose, grabbing the cloak he had worn as a blanket. He listened carefully. Through the trees he could hear a pack of yapping hounds. His chest tightened in sudden panic. He had once seen an army press gang chase a fugitive across his father's estate. They had scattered flocks, torn through fences and terrorised the tenant farmers, caring nothing for who their lord was, until they finally ran down their prey.

'I thought I'd lost them yesterday, but they must've picked up our scent downwind. Just my luck. Come on!'

Victor set off at a run into the trees, down towards the river. Paul was about to follow him when he noticed the sword still lying on the edge of the clearing. 'Wait – the sword!'

'Leave it!' called Victor. 'I don't want to be caught with it. Now come on, run!'

They stumbled through the undergrowth down to the water, and then sloshed across the stream to the opposite bank. Paul followed, with no idea where Victor was hoping to escape to. The barks were becoming louder, and now Paul could also hear the cries of men behind them, the voices of a press gang closing on its quarry. He and Victor could run as hard as devils, but they would never outrun dogs in the forest, and would quickly be caught by mounted men in the open.

The trees ended and they found themselves in a rough pasture of grass and scrub. Mist hugged the flat, boggy ground, which stretched into the distance, interrupted only by a few thick clumps of coppiced wood. Victor pointed towards the nearest large copse. 'There, run! With luck the dogs lost us at the river.'

They sprinted across the open ground to the copse. The trees were coppiced hazel, and the pair pushed between the thick, mature spines, half crawling their way deep inside. At the gloomy heart of the copse they crouched and remained still. Paul could no longer hear the dogs, or the voices of men. 'Maybe we lost them,' he said.

'Shh.' Victor's eyes were squinted in concentration as he cocked his ear to listen. 'They might've seen us.'

They waited, motionless. There was no sound except the birdsong and the rustling of animals in the undergrowth, and their own strained breathing.

After a while Victor, coming to a sudden realisation, looked at Paul with wide eyes and said, 'You can tell them to leave me alone.'

'What?'

'I saved your life, didn't I? You can tell them to let me go. You're noble. You can tell them!'

Paul shook his head. 'That's not my place. You have your own lord. I can't just—'

'I saved your fucking life!' Victor lunged forwards, grabbing Paul's throat and forcing him onto his back. 'Fucking *tell them*!' he spat as they grappled on the ground. He let go with one hand for an instant, but only to snatch the hunting knife from his belt, which he quickly brought up against Paul's jugular.

At the touch of the sharp iron blade on his skin, Paul stopped struggling. It was hard to speak with one hand still crushing his throat, but he stared intently at Victor and forced words out. 'Yesterday you save my life and share your fire, this morning you cut my throat?'

Somehow Paul knew that Victor would not cut his throat in cold blood. He was right. Victor did not release him at once, but his brow slowly relaxed, the frantic flaring of his nostrils eased, and the long line of his mouth and his thick lips turned from anger to desperation; then he removed his hand and the blade.

Paul sat up, coughing air back into his throat. Victor was sitting in a ball, his arms wrapped around his knees, his head low and face hidden.

A voice came from outside the copse. 'Peasants! Come out or we'll burn you out!'

Their pursuers must have seen them enter the trees. If he and Victor stayed in the copse, Paul did not doubt that the press gang would set fire to it.

'Come out, you rats!'

Paul tried desperately to clear his thoughts. By imperial law, all vagrants could be forced into the military or into slavery. If he went out and pretended to be a commoner, he would share Victor's fate. On the other hand, if the army learned of his true identity they would send him back to his father, and he would have to answer for his crime. Perhaps he would not be condemned. Perhaps if he returned and pleaded publicly for forgiveness, his father would be obliged to offer it. He could live out his days in disgrace, but also in comfort and safety.

The voice came again from outside: 'This is your last chance!'

It was no good. His gut recoiled even at the thought of going home. It was not just shame: he was sick with fear. He could already see the fury in his father's eyes, the contempt in the face of his mother, the stark coldness of the criminal tribunal in the basilica of Corinium. There would never be forgiveness. If fate took vengeance on him, he would not defy it; but he did not have the courage to walk home and face judgement. Not yet.

He crawled over to Victor and shook his shoulder. Victor raised his terrified eyes. 'I owe you my life, that's true,' Paul said. 'And I promise I'll repay you. But I can't let them know who I am, not yet. So I ask you for one more favour – don't tell them anything. Let me be drafted with you, don't tell them, and I swear that when I'm ready to go home, when I decide to leave the army and they have to let me go, I'll take you with me.'

Victor looked doubtful. 'How long?'

'I don't know. Weeks, months.'

'Swear it on the gods.'

'I don't believe in the gods. I swear it on the life of my mother.'

Victor thought it over for a few moments. 'All right.'

'Good.' He twisted his head in the direction of the outside voice, and shouted in his best rustic accent: 'We're coming out!'

The pair clambered through the branches until they emerged into the meadow. Five mounted men awaited them, wearing caps and long brown cloaks. Press gangs preferred to remain as inconspicuous as possible. Paul would have mistaken them for civilians were it not for the bronze trappings of their harnesses and their broad, army-issued leather belts. A few yards away three dogs were chewing happily on bones, watched over by their unmounted handler, who also wore a hooded civilian cloak. There was no mistaking, however, the demeanour of their leader: despite a non-regulation beard his face bore the hard lines of a veteran biarchus, a squad commander. It was he who had demanded their surrender and threatened to burn them out, and now he looked at Paul and Victor with all the satisfaction of a victorious huntsman. 'We lost one, and we find two!' he said, to the amusement of his men. He extended a birch rod towards Paul. 'Name yourself, peasant.'

'Paul of the Dobunni.'

'Who's your lord? What're you doing in Cornovian country?'

Paul said nothing. He had spent long enough in the company of workers on the family estates to imitate the Dobunnic dialect of the British tongue, but he knew that a peasant voice was not enough. He hung his head low, sagged his shoulders, and forced himself to feign the humble bearing of a commoner faced by an angry superior.

'That ring,' said the biarchus. 'Where'd you get it?'

Paul's heart jolted in his chest. He had forgotten to take off his gold ring, which bore the senatorial seal of the Cironii. Now he slipped it off his finger. Still looking down at the ground, he said, 'I found it.'

'You stole it.'

'No.'

'Give it to me.'

The biarchus took the ring, holding it up to the light and scrutinising it carefully. Before he could speak there was an approaching rumble of horses' hooves. All present turned and saw a group of about a dozen horsemen come into view from behind the copse. In contrast to the dull, waxed cloaks of the biarchus and his men, these newcomers shimmered like jewels; the sunlight glittered on their red-plumed helmets, on the bands and scales of their body armour and on the sheets of iron that hung over the horses' flanks. The press gang's light-footed mounts shifted nervously at their approach. Paul had seen such horsemen before: they were cataphracts, ironclads, the heavy cavalry of the field army.

The junior officer leading the cataphracts raised his arm, signalling his men to stop some way distant, while he continued at a heavy trot towards the press gang. He rode into their midst and came to a stop in front of the biarchus. On his massive warhorse he dwarfed the riders around him; its great hooves stamped and scuffed the soft turf; it threw its head back in a gesture of dominance, clouds of steam bursting through the iron grills that covered its snout.

Paul looked up at the officer, at the young, harsh expression framed by the cheekpieces of his helmet, and quickly turned away. A name had come to him at once: Flavius Agrius Rufus.

Rufus was the son of a rival family. Four years ago he and Paul had been schoolboys in Londinium. Paul remembered little about him except that they had once found themselves on opposing sides of a student brawl: Gauls versus Britons. There were a great many Gauls in the government offices of Londinium, including Rufus's father, who sent their boys to local schools, and scraps between their sons and the sons of British families had been common. This one had been particularly bad, Paul remembered. It had left him with a bleeding ear, and the main city market in ruins. At some point in the fight he had given Rufus, two years older than himself, a nosebleed. Soon afterwards

Rufus had left Londinium, and Paul had not seen or heard of him since. Now he prayed that he was not recognised.

Rufus addressed the biarchus in his Gallic-inflected Latin, seeming not to have noticed Paul. He asked the biarchus to identify himself, and explain his presence on imperial land. The biarchus replied haltingly, uncomfortable with the Latin tongue, the language of officers and administrators. He told Rufus that he was chasing down two draft-dodgers.

Paul stared at his own feet, trying his best to hide his face.

There was a pause, then he heard Rufus say: 'Carry on.'

Rufus turned and rode back to his men. To Paul's relief they fell into formation, and Rufus led them across the pasture out of sight.

'Posers,' muttered the biarchus. His men laughed. 'You're a thief,' he continued, looking at Paul, 'and a runaway. You should lose your hand, but the gods are smiling on you today. Like your friend here, you can make good your past mistakes by serving his Divine Excellency Julian Augustus.' He swept his right hand outwards in mocking imitation of an orator. 'The enemies of Rome lurk in the shadows, my brothers, waiting to strike against us. The Picts regather their strength beyond the Wall. The Irish and the Saxons prowl our shores like wolves. We need brave men, noble warriors, to guard Britannia, to tend the watch-fires so our children may sleep soundly in their beds. What do you say, peasants? Will you answer the emperor's call?'

Paul glanced at the biarchus, then at the other horsemen. On every face he saw a sadistic smile that was a promise of what lay in store for him and Victor, and for that he hated each of them. But he would bear it. He had bought himself some time, and bound himself by oath to return home, even though he did not know how he would ever find the courage to do so.

Until he did, he would steel himself for the judgement of fate.

FOUR YEARS LATER

One Year Before the
Great Barbarian Conspiracy

I

Our yearning anticipates landfall,
throws hope as an anchor towards the shore.
St Augustine of Hippo

She was free.

Eachna clambered over the bramble hedge of the farmstead, tumbled into the ditch beyond and clawed her way up the opposite slope. She paused for a heartbeat to glance back at the compound. Her master was still down on his knees in the dirt, both hands clutching his bleeding face. The dogs were running wildly around him, savage and frantic, almost drowning out his roar. Other shouts began to arise from across the enclosure, from the vegetable field, from the spinning huts.

Eachna saw this all in a moment that seemed to hang outside time. She felt it burn itself into her memory like the image of a flickering fire snatched in a blink, and it stayed before her eyes even as she turned and ran across the scrubland towards the forest.

She was free.

She fled down curling valleys smothered by forest and laced with mumbling rivers. She scrambled over rocks; she squeezed between the trunks of trees, the image of her master and his fury always behind her, beneath arches thrown overhead by their limbs as they grappled and wrestled, into a darkness of scuffles and howls that she did not believe would ever end. She sniffed the air and through the fractured crown of the forest, whose blooming oak branches hung heavy and dark over her head, she watched the sky for traces of smoke.

She could not hear anyone following her, but that meant nothing. Her master was small, wiry, and could slip through the forest like a ghost, and even though her rock had struck home and surely left him half blind he had spent enough nights roaming the forest to hardly need his eyes. Several times she saw a shape in the shadows that took his form – those high shoulders, the head held low like a boar's – but it was only his spirit, if it was him at all.

Let him stumble upon me, she thought. I will tear out his throat with my teeth.

For days she continued, not knowing how far or how long she had travelled or what lay ahead. One night she dreamed that he crashed through the branches upon her and began tearing at her eyes. She awoke with a jump to find the fingers of a tree scratching her face. She panicked and struck at the skeletal hand, gripped the branch, twisted and tore it from the trunk and with a scream hurled the broken limb into the undergrowth. The trees had grown around her overnight and tried to smother her in her sleep. This time they had failed, but they were becoming more treacherous the deeper she sank into the woods, the further she went from the taming prayers and offerings of men.

She needed to escape the trees, which imprisoned her now as the barbed hedge of the farmstead had imprisoned her for four years. She forced her way upwards, climbing towards the breeze and the promising sky of early summer. By late afternoon, weary with the pain of hunger and fatigue, she had reached the crest of a hill with an open view. Looking to the west, she could see a long, narrow lake. Beyond the lake rose more forested hills, but to the south the hills sank towards the coast and the fine blue line of the sea.

She had not seen the sea since the day the pirates had taken her across it, the day her master had bought her and dragged her into the mountains with her wrists bound to the dirt-stiff tail of a mule. Beyond that sea was her home. She remembered, many years before, walking from the shore with an apron full of mussels, gleaming black with foam; sipping warm broth while wrapped in a sheepskin rug; the dog that whined as it slept by the hearth – what was its name?

She smothered the memories as she always did. For all she knew, this was a different sea, facing the other end of the world. She told herself that the place she had known as a child, from which she had been wrenched and thrown across the ocean, was as distant and dreamlike now as the Otherworld.

When the pirates had taken her she had been on the brink of womanhood. She had had her first bleeding in captivity, alone, unwatched and uncared for. She had not been washed in the holy stream by her mother and grandmother as was required; she had not had the prayers and offerings that brought every child through the second birth into adulthood. She was left a child's soul in a woman's body, an aberration, an obscenity.

She had not been strong enough to resist her master the first time he heaved himself onto her, though she had tried, and in the pain and desecration of that moment she had lost something that could never be replaced. Even if, by some magic of the gods, she were to be carried on the clouds to her family, she would inspire only shame and revulsion. Her father would no more offer her to a neighbour in marriage than he would offer his guest a lump of meat that had been dropped in the midden and chewed on by the dogs.

She looked down at her bare feet, filth and dried blood plastered on white skin, at her numb soles, deeply cut and scratched, callused lumps of unfeeling flesh carrying her to an empty death. One day soon her body would stumble from hunger, too weak to go on, and she would die in the belly of these woods, known only to the wild animals who would pick apart her corpse, and the spirits who would watch her passing without concern.

Sorrow and bitterness tugged a burning feeling up her throat. The great open sky looked down on her with scorn. She felt its weight press her back into the arms of the forest, into the snagging, spiny embrace where she belonged.

Her knees buckled. She closed her eyes so tightly that the blackness behind her eyelids was soon flooded with pain. She began to run down the hill. She fell almost immediately, rolled over trunks and leaves, climbed to her feet and continued, her eyes still closed. She did not want to see the world and its sights. She threw herself blindly into the forest and kept running. She let its punishments flood over her, a struck shin, the sole of her foot stabbed on a splintered log, her hand shredded on rocks, and a final fall into an ocean of barbs and nettles. She writhed and cried, absorbed by pain until she could feel nothing else, until her entire body was alive with fire.

She turned on her stomach, buried her face in her arms and wept, and did not move from the place until night had fallen and she passed finally into an oblivious sleep.

Eachna woke with the smell of cooked fish tickling her nostrils. The sun was newly risen, and she heard voices nearby. She was no longer surrounded by brambles. Twisting where she lay, she looked across a small grassy clearing to where a group of four men was cooking a breakfast of roasted salmon. They were kneeling around a small fire, each holding his arms before him, palms upward, chanting in a language she had not heard before. Her instinct was to scurry back into the bushes, but she realised that someone had lain a woollen blanket over her. Of course they already knew she was here.

The men finished chanting and sat down, and one of them saw her. Like the others, he was wearing a long tunic, tied with a thick cord at the waist. He held out a piece of fish. 'Hungry?' he said. When she did not reply, he continued, 'We tried to rouse you, but you were sleeping like the dead.' By now the other men were looking at her. 'What's your name?' another asked.

The dialect was strange to Eachna, but she understood them. 'Eachna,' she said.

'Ah,' said the third man. 'Irish, yes? Who are your people?'

'Delbhna.'

Now the fourth man spoke, tasting her name on a foreign tongue: '*Ak-na?*' He did not look like the others. His skin was dark, his hair and eyes jet black. He was a little older than his companions, perhaps forty, and where their heads and faces were thick with hair he was almost bald and wore only a thin beard. They seemed to respect him as their leader, for at his voice they had fallen silent. Then he looked at Eachna and said to her directly: 'You are a slave.'

The suddenness of his words frightened Eachna, and she could not muster a reply.

'Don't fear us,' he said. 'We don't want to hurt you.' He held out another piece of fish, and Eachna's stomach yawned. Saliva moistened her dry mouth. Cautiously she rose, keeping the blanket wrapped tightly around herself to cover her left arm, which ended in a stump at the wrist, and edged forwards. She took the fish from his outstretched hand, returned to a safe distance, crouched and stuffed the fish into her mouth.

'Where are you travelling to?' asked one of the other men.

Eachna waved vaguely to the south. This was a nameless country to her.

'To the coast, perhaps?'

She nodded.

'We're going to Luguvalium,' he said. 'Perhaps we can travel together. A girl shouldn't be alone in the hills.'

'Shouldn't be alone,' agreed another. 'We thought you were dead when we saw you.'

'No,' said Eachna. 'I need to go quickly.'

'Well, our feet move lightly enough over this ground. The people around here know us. We won't be troubled, and we can escort you home.'

'No.'

'It's better to travel with company, little sister. Where is your home? Among Herne's people?'

'I need to move on,' said Eachna, chewing the last of the fish. She licked her fingers and stood, letting the blanket fall away.

'We're travelling to the coast, and east by boat to Luguvalium,' said the man closest to her, rising. 'We could carry you as far as you need, if you're going that way.' Eachna shook her head. As she started to walk away the man grabbed her arm. 'Where's your master, girl?' he snarled. 'Where have you come from?' He tugged her closer, so their bodies were touching. Eachna struggled, but she did not have a shred of strength against his. 'Tell us, or we'll punish you for him!'

The dark man, who had been watching the exchange in silence, now jumped to his feet. '*Nol' illae obstare!*' he shouted, and his companion released Eachna's arm. '*In nomine Dei—*' continued the foreigner, and went on to berate the other in a tongue Eachna had never before heard. His broad, round face was flushed as though about to burst. Eachna did not wait, but slipped away, following the stream to lower ground, into the forest.

She had not gone far when a voice came after her. 'Girl! Wait!' It was the dark man, panting as he raced to catch up with her. 'If you go on alone, you will die!'

Eachna paid him no heed. He overtook her and tried to block her path, his short legs moving clumsily through the bracken. 'We shall protect you,' he said. 'My companion – he has much to learn. He is sorry for his act. Please stop; I want to speak with you for a moment, that is all.'

She halted, seeing that he would pester her for a good while yet before giving in. 'I need to keep moving,' she said. 'I can't stay with people. I have to return home to my father—'

'You're afraid,' he said, seeing through her lies as though she had not spoken them. 'You do not know why you are here. You don't know this country, or where you should go. Your name was Eachna, yes? My name is Ludo.' He paused, giving her the chance to reply. When she did not, he went on, 'I feel I know, Eachna, why you are here. Of course you do not have faith in me. But if you come with us – I can save you.'

Eachna pushed past him. He could save her? She had escaped by herself; she had survived so far by herself; she needed nobody, least of all a foreigner. The only foreigners she had ever known had been robbers and slavers, greedy and cruel to their fingertips: the arrogant men who used to take their food for tribute when she was a child, the pirates who had stolen her, the farmer who had dragged her into the hills.

'If you continue, you shall die,' Ludo said, relentless. 'The lands south of here are full of people. Perhaps you'll last a few more days as a walking corpse. If you even live out the summer, you'll freeze in the winter, and if you don't starve first, you'll be slain like a wild dog by anyone who sees you. There's little pity to be found in this country.'

Those words brought her to a stop. She turned to face him. 'Pity is for sick children and cripples.'

'You are a cripple,' said Ludo, nodding at her handless left arm. 'And you seem to me to be just a child. But I don't mean the pity you think of – there is a greater sort, which brings neither shame nor dishonour.' He stepped closer. 'Do not take my pity, then, since you don't understand it. But take my food, and my companionship. Come with us to the city of Luguvalium. I can promise you freedom. By the holy waters of baptism you can be reborn. Our Lord Christ can wash away the cruelty and ignorance of this world, and show you the light that is offered to every tribe in every land. He will embrace each of us, Eachna, if only we listen to his call.'

Ludo held out his hand. Eachna looked at it. She glanced down the stream, and in the tangled depths of the trees saw cold and nameless death awaiting her, a shadowy place where she would wander in eternal grief, never able to reach the Otherworld. This man's accent was strange, but his voice, gentle as it was, carried the tone of one accustomed to being obeyed. Eachna had never before heard anyone talk like this. He had promised rebirth through water, and this spoke to her; and in the stranger's lined face, beseeching, tireless, kind, she saw, if only for a moment, an answer to the unreasoned wretchedness of the world.

The moment passed, but Ludo's hand remained.

Eachna travelled on with Ludo and his companions, the men carrying their own light shoulder sacks, walking south to the coast along forest paths before breaking out beneath an overcast sky. In a gesture she did not quite understand, Ludo had given Eachna his own cloak and shoes, seeming content to go barefoot. She was glad for the rare comfort. The party did not talk to her, but for much of the time sang songs in that same alien tongue that Ludo had used earlier in anger. This time it lilted and danced lightly in the air, sounding so different from the mournful ballads of British and the guttural grate of Pictish. Eachna listened carefully, trying to pick through the inflections and stresses, and thought she heard some mentions of Ludo's Lord Christ, but she understood nothing more.

By dusk the party had reached a fishing village at the mouth of an estuary. The four men, Ludo in particular, seemed to be well known and liked here, for they were warmly welcomed by the locals. Ludo introduced Eachna as a lost northern girl whom they were taking to Luguvalium, and she too was suddenly surrounded by a gaggle of smiling women, almost tearful with joy, who raised their voices and hands into the air in praise of Christ. Eachna, exhausted and weak, straining to see clearly in the fading light, felt as though she had slipped into a dream, lost among so many faces that shifted through the red glow of torches, chattering, singing.

The next day brought a sky of broken clouds and a fine wind to the east. After breakfast, Ludo and his group boarded a light fishing vessel with a local man to act as pilot, and set sail along the coast. Eachna sat at the prow of the little boat as it rolled through the water. She watched the masses of seagulls circling overhead, filling the air with a harsh chorus. Warm limbs and a full stomach, those most unfamiliar sensations, brought a smile of elation and defiance to her lips, and she decided that she would not be afraid of the fair-haired goddess Clíona, queen of the Land of Promise, the protector who had turned betrayer and let her fall into slavery. Clíona's realm broke upon the shores of distant Ériu, not here. Even as the boat churned its way to the east, Eachna felt the grip of the goddess weakening.

'I am from a place called Massilia,' came a voice, shouting to be heard above the wind and waves, the creaking of the boat and the flapping of its sail. Ludo sat himself at the prow next to her. 'The ocean is blue there,' he said. 'And clear, like the sky. I never thought the ocean could be so grey.' He pointed at the sky, and the sea. 'Grey above, grey below. Cold, wind, mist.' He shook his head and shivered. 'And is your country different from this?'

Eachna did not know the names of the gods who lived in what men called the empire of Rome, apart from the lord called Christ, who she assumed was Ludo's father-god. Without knowing them, it was difficult to understand the moods and turns of the weather. Hers was a country where the voices of other gods rushed across the sky. 'Some days,' she said, 'the Dagda comes from the south, bringing walls of rain from the endless ocean. The next day Morrígu, his raven-queen, will come from the north, pushing mountains of cloud before her. She is kindest in the summer. They bring glorious rainbows.'

'We are both foreigners here. A strange country is a difficult skin to wear. And when one is alone . . . it can be a great trial.' He smiled, showing his fine, even teeth. 'But when one has faith, and hope, no trial is too great. Do you not agree, Eachna?'

'Yes,' she said, though this was a new idea to her. She wondered about this man's kin, and why he claimed to be alone. Perhaps he was an exile.

'I am a messenger,' he said. 'The Lord sent me here, across mountains and oceans, to the very edge of the empire, with a gift for all men of every nation, every clan. It is not a gift of gold or power or things of this world, for the Lord is not a lord of this world. It is the gift of eternal life, unending joy. He will offer this, and asks for nothing in return but your faith.'

'Your lord,' said Eachna cautiously, 'he is a child of the goddess Danu?'

'No, no!' Ludo shook his head. 'The gods you know are not gods at all, but demons. They lie and trick you into offering them sacrifices without worth. Eachna, they have fooled your people into believing in their power.'

Eachna looked away in puzzled silence. How could Dagda father-god, who ruled the seasons on the strings of his harp, have no power? Without Lugh, how could the breasts of girls, the bellies of mothers-to-be, the ripening fields of summer, swell to bring forth new life? How did the sun shine, if not from the radiance of his face?

'Those houses where we stayed last night,' Ludo continued. 'The people there, most of them, they have opened their eyes and ears and embraced the message of Christ. They have entered the cleansing waters of baptism. They have been reborn. Now they see the old gods for what they are: cruel demons who demand the blood of blameless victims, who delight in ignorance and darkness. The way of Christ is the way of love and light. Those people see the truth, and now the light is within them. Did you not feel it last night, when they took us in? Our Lord, when he walked this world, commanded us to feed the hungry, to give drink to the thirsty, to clothe the naked, to care for the sick. Each of those things they did, Eachna, because they feel the fire of Christ burning within them – and no demon, no demon can stand against that!'

The sea spray had by now soaked them both. Ludo's dark face glistened with water, but he no longer seemed to feel the cold. Eachna thought of the previous night, the kindness of the villagers, the food and comfort they had given a nameless, lowly slave without question or payment, and felt only bemusement. She did not understand why they had acted in such a way any more than she had understood the cruelty of her old master.

'I believe, Eachna,' said Ludo, and clasped her hand, 'that you have been sent here by the Lord, just as I have. I have wondered all my life at the mystery of his call. Now, at last, I see the truth. The Lord is the maker of the Otherworld and of this world, and of the sea, and of everything in them. It is written that he defends the cause of the oppressed and feeds the hungry. He frees the captive, lifts up those who are bowed down. He loves those who have good in their heart. He watches over the foreigner and protects the fatherless. You were called to that glade, Eachna, just as we were, though none of us knew why. The Lord is calling you home. He is bringing you on a path to end your travels. And he has called me here to be your guide. You will see – you will see.'

He left her alone, moving down the craft to his fellows. Eachna looked over to the coastline as it slipped past, taking with it huts, corrals, fishermen, silent forests and dullish banks of sand. She was moved by a glimpse of truth, but it was uncertain, flickering like sunlight on the crest of a wave.

Only yesterday she had been lost and alone in the woods, broken, ready for death, violated and corrupt. Now she found herself in the care of a stranger who was promising a new kind of rebirth through the water of a different god. For a strange moment she wondered whether she was in a dream, or had passed through to the Otherworld. But with a steep rise and fall of the prow, her stomach lurched and a salty slap of seawater hit her face; and everything seemed solid, more solid and real than she had ever known.

She could never go back to her family: she knew that. Her old life was lost to her. With this man and his curious god, in the place called Luguvalium, perhaps she could find a new one.

II

The idea of fighting is agreeable to those who are strangers to it.
Vegetius, *Concerning Military Matters*

They knew something was wrong as soon as they came to the village. Bear was the first to pick up on it, and his hesitation was enough to alert Paul and the others. Bear was the biarchus, the leader of their eight-man squad, and a veteran of twenty years with more experience than the rest of them combined. He had fought in the last war six years earlier, when the Master of Soldiers Lupicinus himself, commander-in-chief of the imperial field army, had marched north and crushed the Picts. There was not a valley or farmstead within a day's march of the Wall that Bear did not know. So when he paused on the track overlooking the village and watched it suspiciously, his squad paused with him and waited for him to speak.

Paul had never been to this valley before, but he saw nothing unusual. There was a stone-built enclosure wall containing a dozen thatched round huts, a grid of animal paddocks and fields that ran in narrow strips towards the river. The peasants had already fled into their huts, as peasants always did when soldiers approached. The only figure to remain in the open was a tall, thick-bearded man, likely the chief, who was looking at the Romans and smiling to them in welcome.

'Biarchus, why have we stopped?' It was the tax assessor, sitting on his pony. He was the only mounted member of the party. Since leaving the Wall that morning he had remained in the middle of the squad, four soldiers walking in front, four behind.

Being the sort of man who tried to mask fear with babble, he had hardly stopped talking. Paul was sick of listening to his voice.

'We should move on,' said Bear.

The tax assessor waved his leather satchel. 'No – no! We're here now, and I'm not coming back a second time. Why have we stopped? I can see the chief there!'

Paul glanced at Victor, who shook his head with disdain. All taxmen hated coming north of the Wall, but tax assessors most of all; the collectors of tax always had the benefit of a fully armoured century behind them, whereas mere assessors were given just a single light squad. They were hated in turn, too, both by the peasants who suffered their demands and by the soldiers who had to protect them.

'I know that chief,' said Bear. 'I've been bringing your type here for years. Never once have I seen him smile at a taxman. It doesn't feel right.'

'It doesn't *feel* right?' laughed the tax assessor. He was a dark-skinned, wiry man, nervous. Most taxmen were nervous when brought beyond the Wall. It was clear that the only thing that frightened him more than being here now was the thought of coming back later. 'Biarchus, I am your superior. Take me down there, or I'll be making a full report to your tribune!'

Bear ignored him. He barked commands for the squad to turn about. Moving to the front, he led the squad at a quick pace away from the village, back along the track to the south. The taxman kept his place in the formation, complaining bitterly.

Paul had no sympathy. Naturally the official would be punished for failing to complete the tax assessment of his allotted district, but Bear's instinct could not be ignored. Their biarchus was no coward, that much was certain: if he sensed danger, it was real. Paul was starting to feel it too, and he became increasingly uneasy as they marched down the open valley away from the village. He felt exposed here, half a day's march from the safety of the Wall, with neither mail shirt nor helmet. His cloth cap and tunic would be of little use if they were attacked. He and Victor had spent the last few days grumbling to one another that the garrison tribune, despite Bear's request, had refused to authorise a double-strength combat escort in place of the regular light patrol. Everyone knew that the tribes were restless, that there were rumblings of rebellion among the Selgovae and even the Votadini, and that the Pictish King Keocher was banding the northern peoples together into a new confederation. Weeks ago there had been a rumour that Keocher's son Talorg, a youth of fifteen, had cut out the eyes of two Selgovan chieftains who had refused to join his father. It was a bad time to be escorting a Roman taxman north of the Wall.

Paul's nervousness only deepened as they followed the track to the bottom of the valley, where the babbling river entered a wood. If they were to be ambushed anywhere, it would be in those trees.

Before they reached the wood Bear called them to a halt. 'Sling your shields,' he ordered. His squad hesitated; the order was to put their shields on their backs instead of carrying them. It was the opposite of what should be done in hostile territory. 'Are you deaf? Do it!'

The squad jumped to obey. There was a quick bustle as spears were stuck in the ground and shields were strapped over shoulders, and in moments the squad was ready to move again.

'Now keep tight,' Bear said. 'And be ready.'

They followed the biarchus down to the riverbank and entered the dark shade of the wood. The track was narrow here. On their left side was the river, on their right a steep, almost vertical rise of trees, moss and broken rock. Straight ahead, between river and rise, continued the path, with barely enough room for the taxman and his pony. The opposite bank of the river rose in a much gentler slope, the trees giving way after a few yards to rough pasture.

The moment the attack came, Bear was ready for it.

It began with a fierce cry from the steep slope above. Instantly Bear was yelling for them to get across the river and make for the pasture. This time nobody hesitated to obey, not even the taxman, who twisted his startled mount and plunged it into the water. Paul jumped in after him, Victor and the rest of the squad close behind; the water was cold, but not deep, and using their spears for support they swiftly waded through the strong current to the opposite bank. As Paul gripped onto an exposed root to pull himself out of the water, he felt the sharp crack of a sling stone against the shield on his back. More stones ricocheted off tree trunks, hit the water, thudded into the ground. The trees behind them were alive with savages.

Paul, terrified, fumbled as he tried to haul himself out. Victor was beside him and their comrades were already running up the meadow. Bear, who was still in the water, put a hand on Paul's buttock and with a hefty shove sent him scrambling onto the riverbank; Paul turned around, offered Bear his hand and pulled him out, and together they sprinted to join the rest of the squad.

'Shields free, form up!' Bear was already shouting. 'Single line, combat spacing! Right foot forward! Faster, come on! Keep those shields up, guard your heads!' They fell into line three feet apart, hoisted their oval shields, readied spears and formed the shield wall.

Fifty yards away, the trees were quiet. There were no more voices, no more sling stones. They might have been attacked by the forest itself. On either side and behind them were the lower slopes of the valley, nothing but grass, rock and scrub.

The taxman had dismounted and was cowering behind them, both hands clutching the reins of his frantic pony. 'Biarchus, how many are they?'

'Only a handful,' said Bear. 'Now we'll see if they really want to fight.'

There was no movement from the trees, but Paul, in the middle of the line with Victor to his left, felt the eyes watching them. In the six years since the last war there had been little trouble on the frontier, little chance for new soldiers to put their training to the test. It would be Paul's first taste of real combat. After a while he started to feel the weight of the shield and the dryness of his throat. His thumping heart slowly began to calm. His eye was caught by the curl of a falcon's flight against the grey sky.

At that moment the enemy erupted from the wood. They were fewer than Paul had thought, no more than a dozen. They had begun their charge too early. Bear unsheathed his sword and barked his commands. 'Make ready! Take the charge on your shields, boys! For the emperor!'

The attackers looked like mountain folk from the north, dressed in thick boots and coats of animal hide, their powerful thighs naked, their hair greased white and beards braided; Paul noticed little else before he braced himself for the charge. A gleaming axe came sweeping from above. He ducked behind his shield, absorbed the blow of the axe and the force of the man's weight, then pushed him back and in one smooth motion jabbed his spear forwards; the mountain man, eyes ferocious, dodged the spear and grabbed the rim of Paul's shield, pulling it aside and raising his axe for a second swing towards Paul's exposed head.

For an instant Paul realised that there was nothing he could do. The man was too close, and there was no time.

Suddenly the man froze, his mouth hung wide open, and his arm stopped in mid-swing. The axe fell from his fingers. He folded to the ground as Victor tugged the spear from his side.

'Thank you, brother,' gasped Paul.

The barbarians had broken off the attack and were fleeing back towards the trees. A couple were hobbling, apparently wounded, but the only kill was Victor's. The soldiers jeered, calling them women and cowards.

They held the shield wall until the barbarians had vanished from view. Bear knelt beside the corpse as the squad gathered round. 'Pict,' he said, turning the man's face to show the faint spirals tattooed on his clean-shaven neck. 'A killer, too. Well done, soldier. This was the only real fighter of the lot. Just a bunch of young lads looking for adventure. Reckless.'

'But Picts, this far south?' said Victor. He was still in the flush of his first combat kill, pleased by the rare praise from their biarchus.

Bear rose, looking north up the valley. 'Like I said, reckless, but a sign of what's coming.' He pointed at the body. 'This is a lesson. Know what the enemy is going to do and you can beat him. If they were going to attack us anywhere, it was going to be down by the river, from the high ground, where we wouldn't see them. I ordered you to sling your shields so we could cross the river quick and safe. If you're ever ambushed, the first thing you do is *try to get out*. In any ambush you can guarantee that the enemy has the best position. If you can't escape outright, get to the high ground and make a stand.'

The taxman, who had already mounted his pony, cleared his throat. 'I give you my thanks, biarchus, and I'll be sure to mention this astonishing act of courage in my report to the Minister of Finance.' His voice was exuberant, his hand waving frantically. He was on the edge of hysteria. 'Perhaps even the Count of the Sacred Largesses will hear of it! But maybe we should leave before the savages return?'

'You're right. We should get back to the Wall. Form up to march, shields free.' While the squad shuffled into formation, Bear drew his dagger and crouched by the corpse. Swiftly and skilfully he dug out each of the man's eyes and flung them into the scrub. He wiped his hands and his knife on the man's coat and got to his feet. 'They hate it when we do that,' he said. 'Picts need their eyes to get to the Otherworld.'

Even as they began the ten-mile march back home, Paul could tell something was not right with the biarchus. His voice had sounded strained, as though he had been winded, and Paul thought he had seen a look of intense pain flash across Bear's face as he had risen from the corpse. But Bear took his place at the head of the column and led it without incident back to the old military road, and within three hours they were within sight of the Wall. The sight of this great stone ribbon across the landscape, the fine lines of its coursework gleaming even on a cloudy day such as this, was a relief to everyone, not least the taxman, and there was a fresh energy in their step as they took a track across open country to their home garrison of Vercovicium.

The fort was built into the Wall itself, its battlements and towers rising defiantly from a rocky bluff that overlooked the grasslands of the north. Light flashed on the helmets of sentries as they paced along its ramparts. The road split, one way leading to the civilian gate in the Wall below the bluff, the other climbing up an earth ramp to the fort's northern gate. They had barely begun to take this second track when Bear collapsed.

He fell to his knees, letting go of his shield, and clutched his chest as he rolled onto his side, his face twisted in agony. Paul, who was closest, rushed to help him. 'Fuckers hit my chest,' gasped Bear. Paul forced Bear's hands aside and tore open the front of his tunic. A great black and purple bruise had spread across his chest. He must have taken a sling stone while getting them across the river.

'Help me lift him!' shouted Paul, and with the aid of Victor he raised Bear to his feet. 'Come on, old man, we'll get you to the surgeon.'

They carried Bear up the steep track to the fort, through the gatehouse and past the granaries. By the time they reached the hospital the medicus had been alerted and was waiting at the main door. He ushered them inside, leading them to the surgery, where they lifted Bear onto the operating table.

Bear's face was twisted, his eyes red-shot and panicked as he struggled to breathe. Sweat flooded in streams down his thick neck and blood was beginning to ooze from his mouth. Suddenly he tried to sit up; Bear was a big man, a famed wrestler in his younger days, and it took both Paul and Victor to force him back down.

'What happened?' asked the medicus.

'Ambush,' said Paul. 'A few hours ago. A stone hit him.'

The medicus pressed his fingertips gently on the bruise. Bear grimaced, teeth clenched. The medicus shook his head. 'I can't help him. Too much internal damage. I'm amazed he lasted this long.'

Bear twisted his head and through the haze of pain saw Victor. He gripped his tunic to pull him close. 'Look after my girl,' he said through trembling lips. 'Do you hear me, boy? She's yours now.' He released Victor and began to cough violently, blood now erupting from his mouth; his limbs shuddered and convulsed, and with a final, slow gargle as he drowned in his own fluids, he lay still.

Paul and Victor stood in shocked silence, their hands still holding the biarchus. The rest of the squad, along with the taxman, was standing at the surgery door.

The medicus was the first to speak. 'I'm sorry.'

Paul left Victor and the corpse of their biarchus and escaped the choking air of the room. He walked across the small hospital courtyard to an empty infirmary. In the quiet, cleaner air of this room he washed his face in a basin set below a window, then stood and felt the passive breeze brush against his cheeks.

It was almost evening, but the air still carried some warmth. Beneath the clanging din of the smithy came the steady tramp of feet on the drill ground, the drillmaster's barks, the rhythmic chant of the soldiers almost a lullaby in the red glow of the west. Sheep and cattle called lazily beyond the ramparts, driven from pasture to paddock with a symphony of bells. The horn for the twelfth hour, the last hour before night watch, droned across the fort. Another day was ending.

Their biarchus was dead.

Victor's voice came from the doorway. 'He told me to look after Rosa; you heard him, didn't you?'

'I did, brother.' Bear's wife had died some years ago, but he still had a daughter, Rosa, who lived in the village outside the fortress. She was sixteen and Victor's sweetheart. It was not normally tolerated for a mere *pedes*, an unranked soldier, to court the daughter of a biarchus, but Bear, never one to stick to rules whose value he could not see, had made an exception for Victor. The girl had no other male relatives. With her father gone she would need to be protected.

'I'm going down to the village,' Victor said. 'Someone should tell her. You want to come?'

Paul shook his head. 'The old man would want you to do it.'

Victor left him alone. Bear's death was like a cavern that had opened beneath Paul's feet, and he felt the beginning of the hollow plunge into grief. He returned to the surgery, where the centenarius, their century commander, was interrogating the taxman and Bear's second-in-command, semissalis Motius. The taxman was weeping with the emotional exuberance typical of easterners. He could not praise highly enough Bear's valiant service to the emperor. Paul stood by, confirming or adding details when asked, staring at the body. It was unreal. He remained where he was after the centenarius and the others had gone. The medicus offered him a stool and a cup of water, both of which he accepted, and left him alone. Paul sat and watched as a group of Bear's fellow biarchi came to the hospital, washed the corpse where it lay, wrapped it in a linen shroud, leaving only the face exposed, and placed it gently onto a ceremonial bier of knotted yew. Two of the biarchi then lifted the bier and carried it out of the hospital, the others following.

They would take Bear down to the village posthouse. His comrades would stay with him and drink until dawn, as was traditional, supposedly to help his passage into the next life. Paul did not believe in such superstitions, but nor did he intend to sleep that night. He would drink with the others, and in the morning they would return to barracks to grab a few short hours of sleep. At noon they would be taken to the principia and accused before the tribune of shirking their morning fatigues, and the tribune would sentence them all to a lashing; the punishment officer would then brush the fronds of the lash gently over their shoulders, pronounce the punishment complete and officially recorded, and they would return to normal duties.

After four years, these traditions no longer seemed odd to Paul. He was by now used to the peculiar military logic that steered a course between brutality and comradeship, and that meant that he now felt such pain at the passing of the man who had beaten him more harshly and more often than any other in his life.

Paul was occupied by these thoughts as he finally left the hospital some time later, and in the lane outside he accidentally collided with another biarchus named Braxus. Even as he apologised, he knew it would do him no good. Braxus was known as the most bitter-hearted of all the garrison biarchi, an old rival of Bear's, and it was his custom to prowl the fort at this time of day in search of inferiors to terrorise. When he recognised Paul, a rotten grin spread across his wide, thick featured face. 'Report to the granary, soldier. You've earned yourself an hour with a broom.'

'I was heading to the wake at the posthouse—'

That got Paul a stinging, back-handed slap across the face. He staggered from the blow, and touched his nose. Braxus had drawn blood.

'The granary,' snarled Braxus. 'Before I break your fucking legs.' As Paul set off to collect a broom from his barracks, Braxus called after him: 'That poor girl!'

The granary was empty but for a clerk of the quartermaster, who instructed Paul to clean the floor around the large mounted querns. He set to work, less bothered by the labour and the nosebleed than by Braxus's parting comment. It was well known that Braxus had lusted after Bear's daughter for some time, despite his forty years and the drunken violence that had driven his wife to flee to the safety of her family in Arbeia last winter. While Bear was alive Braxus had not dared do anything but talk, just as he would never have dared lay a finger on any of Bear's squad. Now that was changing. Paul knew that the slap across the face had been a test, and a warning.

Once released from the granary, Paul took his evening pass and headed for the southern gate. Immediately south of the fort, so close that the nearest buildings almost touched it, was the civilian settlement: a busy jumble of streets, animal pens, and stone and timber buildings that clung to the steep slope of the bluff as though afraid to leave the shadow of the Wall. It was now long after sunset. The open market area outside the south gate was busier than usual for so late in the day, and Paul had to push his way through the crowd of villagers and off-duty soldiers to the home Bear had shared with his daughter.

It was down one of the market side streets, a modest pair of rooms above a shoemaker's shop, reached by an outside staircase. When he reached the door Paul could hear a low, soft singing within: a funeral lament, sung by a group of older women. This, too, was part of the tradition; the women would stay apart and sing while the men drank with the body, and at dawn the body would change hands. Slowly Paul opened the door. The room was blazing with candles set on every shelf and table. Rosa stood in the centre, surrounded by the other women. Seeing her there, without Bear's bulk looming beside her or taking her in a great hug, with a look of such loss on her young face, Paul felt a surge of pity. Candlelight glinted in her moist eyes and on the tracks of tears down her cheeks, still round with the puppy fat of child-hood.

Paul remained at the threshold. 'I grieve with you,' he said.

Rosa came over to him, taking hold of his hands as the women continued their lament. 'Thank you, Paul. Sometimes he spoke of you and Victor as his sons.'

Her voice was strong despite the pain in her eyes. Since maturing, Rosa had attracted the attention of many young men of the village and garrison, especially Victor, and Paul understood why. Her dark hair was as tough as a thicket, her face could not be called especially pretty, and she was growing into a stout and rather shapeless woman. Yet despite this she had a certain bright-ness born of an inner fire, the sort that warmed all those who came near it and burned for a lifetime. Rosa made people feel good, and they loved her for it.

Paul did not stay with Rosa and the other women for long, since that would have been against custom. Though he was worried about Braxus he said nothing to her. For a few days, at least, she would be protected enough by the pall of bereavement.

Military wakes were not sober affairs. When Paul returned to the marketplace he saw the soft light spilling from the windows of the posthouse, and heard music that seemed to shake it on its foundations. It was gloomy inside, for this large open room, despite the blazing hearth against one wall and the torches fastened high on metal mounts, was so busy that it was thronged with shadows and silhouettes. Soldiers wove between tables and the wooden posts that rose into the dark, smoky heights of the timber roof. Bear lay in their midst, placed on a trestle table in his shroud, half-buried under wreaths of oak leaves and twisted myrtle that had been laced with flowers – foxglove for sorrow, rattle for joy.

Paul felt his skin begin to prickle in the thick heat of the room. He searched for Victor and saw him in a group of dancers, his arms around the shoulders of two other members of their squad, the remains of a crooked wreath on his head. Paul shouldered his way across the room, taking knocks and careless footsteps as he went, his shoes sticking to patches of stale beer spilled over the flagstones and dragging along little clumps of straw.

'Brother, will you dance?' cried Victor when he saw Paul, and pulled him into the group.

The pipes played and drums throbbed, the soldiers clung to one another and the floorboards shook under their feet. When the song ended, and the dancing packs stumbled to a breathless halt, whoops and clapping filled the room with a music of their own.

Paul detached himself from the group and found a vacant bench by the wall. He did not feel himself, and was not in the mood for dancing. As he sat and watched he became aware of a tension in the room, a desperate edge to the revelry that went beyond grief at Bear's death. A tax assessor attacked, a biarchus killed – and by Picts, who had not ventured so far south for six years.

There would have to be some retribution for this. It was a matter of honour for the entire garrison. They had missed the chance to go to war two years ago, when the Picts had attacked the Votadini tribe, Rome's strongest allies beyond the Wall. The chief of the Votadini had sent an embassy to the *dux Britanniarum* Fullobaudes, who commanded all frontier forces in the Four Provinces of Britannia, begging for military support. Paul remembered how he and Victor and the other young soldiers, the ones who had never seen war, had prayed that Duke Fullobaudes would send the Tungrians north. But he had not. Instead he had raised an irregular force of barbarian mercenaries and condemned criminals and sent them to reoccupy an old abandoned fort three days north of Vercovicium. That sorry excuse for a garrison was supposed to be keeping the Picts away from the Wall. They were not doing a very good job. It was time some proper soldiers were sent north to teach the Picts a lesson.

A man joined Paul on the bench, nodding in greeting. He was not dressed as a soldier, but wore a traveller's cloak of wool over a tunic, with coarse trousers and tall leather boots. His thick beard was plaited in the fashion of barbarians beyond the Wall.

Paul did not know the man's name, but recognised him as one of the arcani who sometimes passed through the fort. He had no time for the arcani. They were nothing but untrustworthy spies, northerners in the pay of Rome who acted as traders while gathering intelligence among the far northern kingdoms. This arcanus was well known and disliked in the fort. He would emerge from his secret conference with tribune Bauto, clutching his payment of a shiny gold solidus – enough to feed a large family for a month – and swagger down to the posthouse, where he would drink and gamble and try to sell made-up secrets for a jug of mead.

'Grim business,' said the arcanus.

Paul ignored him. The man had no right to be at Bear's wake. Were he not known to be protected by the tribune, he would not have been allowed in.

'Grim business, aye,' repeated the arcanus with a sigh, as though taking Paul's silence for agreement. 'Heard you were on the patrol.'

Paul grunted in acknowledgement. He fought the urge to grab the arcanus and drag him across the room to the door.

'When I was at King Keocher's court last month,' the arcanus continued, 'there were some lads boasting they wanted to come south for raiding. Must have been them did this. I'd say they've learned their lesson. That's the Picts for you. All mouth, no guts.'

Victor came and sat on Paul's other side with a drunken laugh, a mug of beer in his hand. 'War's coming,' he said. 'I can feel it.'

The arcanus leaned forward and looked across to Victor. 'Don't get your hopes up, lad,' he said. 'Picts don't have the stomach for a fight.'

Victor raised his mug. 'I'll drink to that! Jus' like a Pict to skulk in the trees. Hiding in the shadows like a rat. Get 'em on the open ground, they don't last long. The First Cohort of Tungrians'll sort 'em out. Won't we, brother?' He gripped Paul's shoulder. He raised his mug and yelled, 'To the Tungrians!'

The cry was taken up by the soldiers standing around them. Victor looked at Paul, offended that he had not joined in. He stood up, dragging Paul with him. 'I said, *to the Tungrians!*' The room repeated the cry, and this time Paul was with them. Victor lifted his mug a final time and screamed his throat hoarse: '*The Tungrians!*'

The room shook with the response. Paul and Victor collapsed back on the bench, laughing.

'You and me, brother!' Victor shouted in his ear. 'Let the barbarians come!' He leaned over to the arcanus, who had remained seated throughout. 'Will you not join us in a toast to the Tungrians, stranger?'

The arcanus shrugged awkwardly. He began to speak, but Victor cut him off.

'Oh, I see, you have no drink! Well, we should fix that. Why don't you go up and get yourself one? Every man should have a drink in his hand at a wake.' He wrapped one arm around Paul's shoulders. 'You can get one for my quiet brother here while you're at it.'

Paul was trying hard not to laugh. He knew Victor's game.

'In fact,' Victor went on, 'why don't you get drinks for the house? Put some money on the bar. One of those precious solidi of yours, that should keep us going.' He brought his mug to his lips and messily gulped down the last of the beer. He tossed the mug aside, wiped his mouth and guffawed. 'For an hour or two at least, am I right, brother? Here, listen,' he went on, beckoning to the arcanus, who was beginning to shift uncomfortably. 'Let us see one. Let's see one of them solidi. I don't think I've ever seen one close up. Does it have old Valentinian's head on it? I want to see the excellent rascal.'

'I don't think I have any,' the arcanus said. He was trying to sound good-humoured, but Paul could hear the nervousness in his voice.

''Course you do!' said Victor. 'C'mon. Let's see it. I just want to touch it. What, d'you think you're not safe here? Don't you think the Tungrians will protect you and your gold?'

Reluctantly, the arcanus reached into the folds of his cloak and fumbled in a purse. Casting a quick glance over his shoulder, he held out a cupped hand to Paul and Victor. In his palm lay a single gold solidus. Despite the darkness of the room, it seemed to capture the torchlight and hold it with a radiant glow.

'Can I hold it, friend?' Victor asked. Without waiting for a reply, he reached out and delicately plucked the coin between two fingers. He studied it closely, running a finger over the profile of the emperor. 'There he is,' he muttered. He turned the coin to examine the reverse side. Valentinian was depicted in the old-fashioned imperial garb of bronze breastplate and short tunic, holding a Christian battle-standard in his right hand, and a victory globe in his left. Victor squinted at the lettering that encircled the image. 'What's it say, brother?'

'*Restitutor rei publicae*,' said Paul. 'Restorer of the Republic.'

Victor grinned at the arcanus. 'Impressed, eh? Let me borrow this, friend.' He rose, coin grasped tightly in his fist, and pushed his way through the crowd. The arcanus looked after him anxiously and started to get up, but a firm hand from Paul restrained him.

'He'll be back, don't worry,' Paul said.

The arcanus settled uneasily on the bench. He stared into the drunken throng, anxiously holding his thin neck high to get a better view. He reminded Paul of a goose. Eventually, unable to spot Victor, he half turned to Paul and forced a companionable smile. 'You can read?' he said. 'I rarely meet a soldier who can read. Officers, yes, but . . .' He trailed off when he saw Victor emerge from the crowd. He was carrying two mugs of beer, and gave one to Paul as he rejoined them on the bench.

'Cheers, comrade,' said Paul.

There was a cough from the arcanus. He held out a beseeching hand. 'Might I . . .'

Victor looked at the hand, affecting brief confusion. Then he said, 'Of course, your solidus. I didn't buy these drinks with it, don't worry. A gold coin for two drinks, imagine that! No, never buy your drinks with another man's coin.'

The arcanus seemed to be edging closer to panic. 'Where's my gold, soldier?'

'It's safe and sound,' said Victor reassuringly. 'Outside, in the gutter. If you hurry, you might find it before someone else does.'

Almost immediately the arcanus was out of view, shoving through the soldiers towards the door. Paul and Victor broke into laughter.

Once they had recovered, Victor raised his mug. 'To the old bastard.'

'To Bear,' said Paul.

They said little else but watched as the hours wore on. The musicians played until they were too drunk or too exhausted to continue. After they left, the soldiers amused themselves with jokes and stories, some about Bear, some that stretched back through two hundred and fifty years of Tungrian history, to when the unit was first stationed on the Wall. Soldiers stood up one after the other, each drunker than the last, and recounted these tales, drawing applause, laughter or argument from the audience. Paul and Victor had heard them many times before: the legend of Flaccus the Cooper, who had escaped a druidic circle and brought about the downfall of a mountain tyrant; of Old Asinius, the retired soldier who had taken a horse and a fire-poker and single-handedly rescued his young wife from a band of raiders; of Consa the Hornblower, who, during the Severan War, had defended the unit's standard until he was standing on a mountain of dead Picts, and afterwards had joked: 'Fuck the flag – I thought they were after my wine ration!'

Paul listened to the stories, was reassured by them, and drank and let the weariness and the alcohol slowly deaden his senses in a pleasant fog. He watched grey-black smoke curl around the crooked lamp hanging from the rafters. He chuckled as he thought of the arcanus scrabbling about in the pitch-black mud outside. Victor would not have made the solidus too hard to find; just hard enough that the arcanus would end up covered in filth and reminded that neither he nor his gold was welcome at a soldier's wake.

It had been a long time since Paul had been so close to a solidus. That was a strange thought. The last gold coins he had seen had borne the face of a different emperor, and had filled the reinforced chest in the strongroom at Silvanicum, the ancestral family seat of the Cironii. That estate alone had brought in almost four thousand solidi per year. And now the sight of a single solidus was a marvel.

He buried the memory with accustomed swiftness. Those days were nothing to him now. His life had begun the moment he took the military oath with Victor, and through their training in the Brigantian hills they had grown close as brothers.

There they had been taught to fight, to obey orders and to forget themselves. Somehow they had survived those hellish months of drills and beatings, when others had not. With their unexpected posting to the First Cohort of Tungrians at Vercovicium had come the promise of a new family, a leakless roof, dry beds, hot food, regular baths and – most important of all – the village with its posthouse, women and all the unpredictable wonders of civilian life: there, they knew, a soldier did not have to live like an animal. They had embraced this new life. They became two of the countless pieces of flotsam that washed up on the northern frontier, lumps of deadwood with no past.

Paul had not forgotten the promise he had made to Victor on the day of their capture, but they had not spoken of it for a long time. Why should he go home? Had he not done penance for his crime? He had given up everything – the wealth of his family, the comforts and privileges of his birth, his noble name. In the last four years he had endured enough misery and beatings to last a lifetime. And yet never in the classrooms of his old school or in the columned basilicas and churches of Londinium had Paul found such contentment as he felt here, in a posthouse tavern filled with common soldiers. Soldiers bickered and fought all the time, but at least they did so openly; and although the ranks included Dobunni, Cornovii, Brigantes, Atrebates and men from half a dozen other British tribes, here they were united: they were the First Cohort of Tungrians, and this made them brothers. Paul knew that he belonged here. You do good here, he told himself. You are loved and protected. That is as much as a man can hope for in this world.

It was well past midnight when Braxus turned up. The room hushed as it became aware of his presence; stories and laughter stopped, mugs were lowered, and at the doorway a space formed in front of him and the three men who entered with him. Every man present knew of the old and bitter rivalry that had existed between Braxus and Bear. Paul rose to see more clearly, swaying as he felt the rush of blood and alcohol to his head.

Braxus came slowly towards the bier, trying to conceal the unsteadiness of his feet. He was blind drunk. His gang waited at the door. They were biarchi like him, weak-minded and cruel, and Paul had often seen them follow Braxus around like puppies, lapping up his cruelty with glee and later inflicting it on their own men. They stood back, watching their leader and the crowd warily. There were several other biarchi present, friends of Bear, but no higher-ranking officers, who had paid their respects early in the evening and then left. The night belonged to the enlisted men.

Braxus stood at Bear's feet. He stared at the corpse for a long moment, blinking as though fighting sleep. The room waited for him to speak.

He said nothing. Instead he hitched up his tunic, fumbled with the front of his trousers, and began to piss on the floor.

The dull, steady trickle of urine on rushes was quickly followed by a bitter tang that seeped through the air of the room like a curse. At first nobody moved. Even Bear's oldest friends, the veteran biarchi who were standing closest to his body, looked too stunned to react. When one of them did move, it was only the beginning of a gesture, an instinct, quickly restrained because a wake was no place to start a brawl, no matter the provocation. They held back from laying hands on Braxus to throw him out. He was left in peace to finish his business, rearrange his clothes, wipe his hands on his tunic, and then stagger calmly out of the posthouse with his followers.

At first the room stayed quiet and still. Finally murmuring arose, then movement, then the revellers released their anger in an explosion of arguments, accusations, threats of revenge. Paul sat back down on the bench beside Victor, his drunkenness forgotten. He felt a hatred the depth of which he could not fully comprehend. There were no words to describe what Braxus had done. The stench of the piss was still overpowering the stale smell of beer and sweat, an acrid reminder of the insult. Were it not for the fury now convulsing dangerously in the room all around him, Paul would have thought he had imagined it. What kind of a man would do such a thing? Not even Braxus, surely, drunk or not. But he had done it. Piety, honour, respect for the dead – none of this meant anything to him. He was an animal. A fucking animal.

Victor gripped his arm. 'Rosa,' he said.

At once the pair rose and pushed their way through the bickering crowd. They reached the door and came out into the cold, sobering night air. The marketplace was black and empty beneath the heavens, with no other light except from the shuttered windows of the posthouse. They set off at a run to Rosa's house. Paul wanted to throw up. What would they do if Braxus and his friends were there? The two of them against four biarchi! They should have gathered the rest of the squad first, Paul knew, or any of the other men in the posthouse, but this had occurred to neither of them and now it was too late: their love for the old man propelled them down the darkened street, trampling reason, and Paul no longer had control of where his legs took him.

They came to Rosa's house and clambered up the staircase, Victor leading the way. When they reached the door Paul gripped Victor's sleeve to hold him back for a moment, just long enough so they could listen for voices within. There was no singing, as there should have been, only the trace of a woman's voice, followed by the deeper growl of a man. At that, Victor burst through the door.

They saw Braxus standing with his broad back to them, Rosa standing beyond him. The rest of the women were huddled at the far end of the room. The other biarchi were nowhere to be seen. Braxus half turned to look at Paul and Victor. His eyes were bloodshot and bleary, his fat lower lip hanging stupidly, as it always did when he had nothing to say. He swung his head back to Rosa, briefly, then again to Paul and Victor, too drunk to decide what to do.

Rosa took a determined step towards him, planted two hands in his chest, and gave him a powerful push. 'I said, *get out!*' Braxus staggered backwards and lost his balance, Paul moved aside to let him land heavily, the floorboards shuddering with his weight.

The biarchus lay there, blinking. 'Fucking whore,' he slurred. 'I'll fuck you on your daddy's corpse.' Clumsily he raised himself on his hands and climbed to his feet, and with a vague lunge, hardly aware of what he was doing, he grabbed hold of Paul's tunic.

Paul was seized by revulsion at his touch. He already hated Braxus for his cruelty, but now he looked at him with contempt for his weakness, for the way he had disgraced himself and the honour of the dead, for all those qualities he lacked that Bear, their old man, had embodied. With rage filling his mind, Paul took hold of Braxus and dragged him to the open door, onto the staircase, and hurled him down. The biarchus flung out his limbs and came to a stop halfway down, one hand grabbing onto a wooden step. Paul came to him and stamped a hobnailed boot on Braxus's fingers. Braxus yelped, let go, and Paul kicked him solidly in the side of the head, sending him tumbling the rest of the way.

The biarchus lay sprawled in the dirt, groaning. Moments later Paul was on top of him and pulling him to his feet, with a vicious snarl in his ear: 'Get up and *fight!*' He held the biarchus from behind while Victor, screaming, landed two heavy punches in his stomach. Braxus doubled up in pain, but Paul lifted him again to expose his face, which Victor struck with a single clean punch. His head snapped back, his eyes fluttered and closed, and his body went limp.

Paul dumped Braxus on the ground. He and Victor stood over the unconscious body, breathing heavily. Now that his blood had risen and the fire of violence was coursing through his arms and legs, that clean, liberating feeling, Paul felt the urge to continue the punishment. He wanted nothing more than to break and pound the biarchus into pieces, to tear him apart. Only weariness and slowly encroaching reason held him back.

'The filthy rat,' muttered Victor in a sobbing voice. Soldier or not, it took a great deal to provoke Victor to such violence. Paul had never seen him lose his temper like this.

The reality of what they had done was gradually taking form before them. Striking a biarchus was a serious offence. They exchanged looks. 'Let's get back to barracks,' said Paul.

Victor nodded, and together they walked hurriedly down the lane to the marketplace, leaving Braxus where he lay, and up to the south gate of the fortress. The sentries checked their passes and let them in, but Paul could feel the suspicion in their stares as they passed through the gatehouse and walked hurriedly up the lane towards their bunkroom.

Paul lay awake for a long time, running through what had happened, obsessively recalling every last detail. There had been no witnesses who would speak out on Braxus's behalf, nobody but Rosa and the other women. If they were lucky perhaps Braxus himself would not even remember who had beaten him.

* * *

They were not lucky. Paul felt as though he had barely fallen asleep when he was awoken by the splash of freezing water on his face. As he came to his senses and wiped his eyes dry, he saw a familiar, unfriendly face leering above his bunk. This was one of Braxus's gang, a biarchus called Trenico. 'Get up.'

Paul twisted to sit on the edge of his bunk, blinking in the fresh morning light. His head throbbed, and his mouth felt like a dried-out riverbed. Victor was already awake, climbing out of the opposite bunk. The other members of the squad, hung over from the previous night, watched with semi-awareness.

'Both of you,' said Trenico. 'You're under arrest for assaulting a superior.' He was holding a birch cane, his hand twitching with impatience to use it. No doubt he was also hoping to wield the lash used to punish them later.

As soon as they had dressed, Trenico led them from the barrack block down the steep central lane of the fortress to the principia. It was a blue-skied morning, and the dawn light lay warmly across the land to the south. Columns of hearth smoke were already rising from the roofs of the village. The garrison was busily waking as soldiers headed to fatigues, stretched and relieved themselves in buckets outside their barracks, tramped past in columns towards the drill field. Paul and Victor attracted glances as they went: some sympathetic, most amused. Soldiers were always happy to see men from other squads being punished.

The principia, the place of administration and justice, stood in the very heart of the fort. They went through its double gates, through a small courtyard surrounded by offices, into the high, open space of the assembly hall, already busy with passing administrative staff. Directly opposite was the open arch of the military chapel, where the Tungrian battle standards stood surrounded by candles and busts of Valentinian Augustus and the imperial family.

'Here,' commanded Trenico, and brought them to stand in front of the tribunal at the north end of the hall. Braxus was already waiting there, a fierce bruise across his jaw, and he ignored them as they stood next to him. On top of the raised stone platform was a vacant chair, the tribune's seat, from which he would dispense the justice of the military. Paul and Victor waited before the tribunal, saying nothing, beneath the grey light filtering through the windows and the sounds of voices and footsteps echoing in the rafters.

It was half an hour before tribune Bauto appeared. Trenico barked a command, and Paul and Victor snapped to attention. Bauto climbed the steps of the tribunal and took his seat. He was flanked by a notary bearing a writing tablet and the primicerius, his second-in-command, who whispered something in his ear. Bauto nodded and turned his eyes on the three figures standing before him.

Even sitting, tribune Bauto was an impressive figure: huge-shouldered, with a neck of solid muscle, a wide jaw and a long, flat nose that almost touched his upper lip, and above this a pair of cold blue eyes. Most commanders sought to earn both the fear and respect of their men; Bauto relied on fear alone. He was a Frank, and behind his back soldiers cursed him as a half-literate savage from a Rhineland bog, a mercenary without culture who had climbed his way up the ranks by virtue of the barbarism that suited the army so well. Paul liked to think that he feared no man, but now, standing in Bauto's power as he never had before, gripped by that pale stare, he could not help but be afraid.

'The tribunal of the First Cohort of Tungrians is in session by the authority of his Divine Excellency Valentinian Augustus and Duke Fullobaudes of the British provinces,' began the primicerius, reading from a tablet in a rapid Latin drone. The notary scribbled to record his words. 'The kalends of May in the year of the consulships of Flavius Gratianus and Dagalaif. First case. Pedites Paul and Victor of first squad, second century, are accused of assaulting biarchus Braxus of fifth squad, second century, and leaving him unconscious. The assault happened during the fourth hour of last night in the civilian settlement. It was unprovoked.'

Paul prickled at that last statement. Braxus and Victor did not react. Like most of the lower ranks on the northern frontier they spoke only the crudest provincial Latin, and the Italian primicerius was making no effort to be intelligible. 'It *was* provoked, tribune,' said Paul.

Not wanting to give away his educated upbringing, Paul had used the common rustic Latin of the south, but it was enough to surprise the primicerius. He looked up and snapped, 'It is not your place to speak, soldier.'

Paul raised his chin. 'If the tribune is to make a wise and just decision, should he not have all the facts?'

The officer was about to reply, but fell silent at a gesture from the tribune. 'We have the testimony of the biarchus,' Bauto said. His voice was deep, rasping, strangely quiet for a man of his size. 'Do you wish to deny the accusation?'

'No, tribune. But—'

'What else happened or didn't happen in the village is of no interest to me. This was a breach of Roman military discipline and the facts are clear.' He raised his hand in the gesture of passing judgement. 'One month solitary confinement on prison rations.'

Braxus began to utter a curse; the primicerius hesitated and bent down to whisper in the tribune's ear; Paul and Victor exchanged confused glances. This was not right. A soldier who struck a superior officer should suffer the lash. It was meant to be swift, savage, and public, a humiliating punishment that left a man scarred for life. Next to the lash, even a month in prison was lenient. The notary was surely attempting to explain this to the tribune, but Bauto was unmoved. He nodded, shook his head, waved his hand, and dismissed the objections.

The primicerius shrugged and cleared his throat. 'Let it be recorded in the name of his Divine Excellency Valentinian Augustus that pedites Paul and Victor will be punished with one month solitary confinement apiece, on prison rations, to begin at once. With the blessing of God and the emperor, judgement has been given. Next case.'

Still bemused, Paul and Victor were manacled by prison guards and pushed out of the basilica. Paul caught sight of Braxus's face as they passed. At first the biarchus had looked angered by the merciful sentence of imprisonment, but now, having realised that Paul and Victor would be out of his way for a month, he was grinning. He winked at them, and Paul, with a sickening lurch in his stomach, understood.

That poor girl, Braxus was saying.

III

The weary shepherd with his languid flock
Seeks out the stream and the thickets
Of wild Silvanus, where silent banks
Lie untroubled by the wandering wind.

Horace, *Odes*

Amanda brought her horse to a halt and looked across the valley towards home. It was called Silvanicum, the haunt of the forest god, and was widely acknowledged as one of the finest villas in all of the Four Provinces of Britannia.

It was certainly the finest in this valley. Summertime travellers fortunate enough to pass it while riding along the riverside track were often taken unawares by its sudden appearance on the wooded slopes to their side. They would observe how pleasantly it was situated, nestling comfortably at the top of the combe, its white-painted facade stretching from slope to slope and standing imperiously above an industrious clutter of barns and workshops. But only if they crossed the Colona, the small river that flowed below it, and took the track up the opposite high ground would they truly appreciate its seclusion. It was a pearl set in a sylvan glade, half cast in shade even at the height of summer, a pocket of tranquility facing the cool air of the east.

'God, let me die here,' Amanda whispered.

She was torn from her thoughts by Lucas, who bolted past with a whoop, the hooves of his mount thundering up the uneven slope. To her alarm he almost lost his balance as he reached the crest of the meadow, but he righted himself and let out a triumphant yell.

He and his mount were still out of breath when Amanda reached him. 'You shouldn't bolt up like that,' she said. 'The ground's treacherous here.'

Lucas laughed. 'I said I'd beat you up to the top, sister!' His mount was panting and restless, and he twisted in the saddle to take in a complete view of the country. He looked almost handsome as he ran a hand through his dark hair, sweat glistening on his brow. The sun was high, the surrounding pastures and pockets of wood subdued by the torpid numbness of an unusually warm May afternoon. A dull breeze brushed over the ridge, carrying the wild smell from the meadow ground of the estate – buttercup, yellow rattle and sorrel; from the cropfields below, a living mosaic of dusty spurrey, corn cockle and violet. 'I've missed this place,' he said.

'You always seem so happy to leave it,' Amanda replied.

'Not true!' He grinned mischievously, and said in a low voice, 'I've got big plans for Silvanicum; I'm just waiting for my inheritance. You'll see.'

Amanda smiled and said nothing. Lucas was two years her senior, but even she was nervous at the thought of Silvanicum falling under his care. A vision came to her: pastures strangled with scrub, flocks wild and unguarded, the slate roofs of the villa crumbling. Lucas was not in the vision, but his gleeful cries carried over the hundreds of miles from the imperial capital of Treveris, echoing down the weed-strewn corridors. A sudden gust brought a shiver to Amanda's shoulders, and the vision dissolved. She wanted this place never to change.

'All right, then,' said Lucas, 'since you don't seem in the least bit curious, I'll take you home.' They turned and took the path down the meadow towards the bridge over the Colona. 'Anyway, forget this place,' he continued with a smile. 'Treveris is much more exciting. If you're good, perhaps Father will let me take you there.'

'What about the barbarians?' Treveris, the imperial capital in

Gallia, lay close to the frontier with Germania, and Lucas had already told Amanda about the savage barbarian invasions earlier that year. He had seemed almost amused by the anxiety it had caused her.

'I already told you, barbarians never bother themselves with cities; they don't have the patience, or the catapults. Besides, our generals taught them a lesson they won't forget in a hurry. Don't worry about them. I'll show you the theatre, the imperial palace . . . cruising down the Mosella, the riverbanks thick with vineyards . . .' He winked. 'And who knows? Perhaps by then you'll have a wedding ring on your finger.'

Amanda blushed at that thought. 'I don't see that happening,' she muttered. At twelve years old she had been betrothed to the eldest son of an equestrian family, but within a year her father had cancelled the engagement without telling her why. She had not been upset; her betrothed had been ten years her senior, pallid and unimpressive, and she was relieved not to be marrying him. She had once asked her father what had happened, but he had not replied. It had been a peculiar kind of silence: stiff, expressionless, forbidding. She had learned not to question those silences.

Since then her father had never hinted at another marriage. She was almost sixteen, when most girls of her status were already married, or at least betrothed. Each passing summer made Amanda less eligible. She told herself that she did not mind this, for marriage would mean leaving home, and she was happy where she was. Her mother and Ecdicius, the household steward, were teaching her domestic account-keeping. She enjoyed visiting the chief groom, Brico, when new mounts were brought to the villa stables. On fine days she rode with Lucas or her handmaiden Pinta across the meadows of the estate, and when it rained she could sit at her loom or in her father's library as the mood took her.

Yet her brother's stories of Treveris did touch something within her, barbarians or not. She could also picture herself not in Silvanicum, but walking with the most noble men and women of Rome in the great palace of Treveris where the emperor held court, her gown rustling on the marble floor, the sunlight glinting on a thousand gilded statues . . .

'I'm sure Father will put you on a boat when the time is right,' Lucas said eventually. 'I've been tasked with finding you a suitable match, did you know that? Someone old and fat, and *rich*.' Lucas saw the look of horror on Amanda's face and he laughed, leaning over to tug playfully at her sun hat. 'Have no fear, sister, just teasing! No fat old ogre for you; the imperial court is bursting with virile young senators. I've got my eye on one or two in particular.'

Amanda felt an indignant flush as she rearranged her hat. 'I've no intention of marrying,' she said.

'Of course you have. What, d'you want to live like a monk your whole life? You'll end up like cousin Julian.'

'And what's wrong with cousin Julian?'

'What's wrong with Julian?' cried Lucas. 'God, Julian! I bumped into him back in Londinium, and he was still the spotty little prude I remembered. D'you know he's become a deacon?'

'Of course I know! You shouldn't mock him just because he never wanted to join in your stupid schoolboy games.'

'Dear sister, there are two ways to smother the fun out of someone: wrap him in either a military uniform or a religious habit. And poor Julian was never much fun to start with.'

'He came to my baptism last Easter,' Amanda said, adding firmly: 'I don't think I've ever met a happier or kinder person in my life.'

'Happy!' scoffed Lucas. 'Do you know why he was in Londinium? He was begging the bishop to let him go to the Wall. He actually *wanted* to go. The bishop was all for keeping him in Londinium, or even sending him to Gallia, but Julian pestered him for weeks so he could go to the darkest and dampest piece of rock in the empire. Pious rubbish. Mark my words, he'll realise his mistake. He'll come back south and become chaplain to some rich family, and one day he'll turn into Father Arcadius. How is it a priest gets to be so fat, I ask you? Priests are always the worst bunch of hangers-on at the imperial court. You see them skulking in the shadows and wagging their fingers, when everyone really knows they'd prefer to be sticking them in the pie like everyone else. God, Julian would fit right in with them!'

Amanda pulled sharply on the reins and came to a stop. She was used to Lucas being provocative, teasing, disrespectful. She was even used to him sneering at poor Arcadius, the kind-hearted family chaplain who had taught her to read and write. But this was different. She could not listen to him mock Julian, who had become a deacon in the face of his father's objections, and had inspired her so deeply with his selfless piety. Julian was everything Lucas was not: modest and humble, never thinking of himself. Amanda had received a letter from him saying that Bishop Gregory of Londinium had finally granted him permission to go to the Wall. Ever since then she had been sure to remember him in her daily prayers.

And now to hear Lucas speak of him in such a way . . . she had hoped that a year of studying rhetoric at the famous school in Treveris would have matured her brother, but had only been disappointed when he'd returned six weeks ago as frivolous as ever, spending his days hunting when he was not in Corinium drinking and gambling with his friends. She knew how deeply his behaviour vexed their father, even the way he had let his hair grow into a disordered brown mop, the affectation of a poet and dreamer. Their father would return this afternoon after his long business trip to Londinium. It would be the first time in over a year that the whole family had been together: herself, Lucas, and Mother and Father. She was anxious that the reunion went smoothly.

When Lucas, wiping tears of laughter from his eyes, finally noticed that Amanda had fallen behind, he stopped and twisted in his saddle. 'Amanda?' The smile melted from his face and was replaced by a frown, but even the frown was insincere. 'You're angry at me, aren't you? All right, I'll be quiet. Not another word,' and he moved his hands as though stitching his lips shut.

She did not reply. They were now directly below the villa. A

path led from the riverside track up the slope of the combe to
the main gate; directly ahead, the track continued for a hundred
yards until it was swallowed by the gloom of a forest. She rarely
went riding in the forest; there was not much to see from the
main track, and its depths were infested with wild boar that could
easily startle a horse. But neither did she want to take the path
up to the villa. She knew she would arrive home in a sullen and
irritable mood because of Lucas. Her mother would sense it, and
know that Lucas was to blame; then Mother would tell Father
when he returned, he would argue with Lucas, and his homecoming would be spoiled and the whole atmosphere of the villa
soured.

Amanda needed time to cool her temper, and the forest offered
respite from the sun, at least. She rode past Lucas, making a
point of ignoring him when he called after her. Let him abandon
her in the forest, she thought, or let him follow. She did not care.

Before long Lucas stopped calling, but when she entered the
shade of the trees and turned her head slightly, Amanda could
hear the clip-clop of hooves a short distance behind. He was
trailing her, knowing that he would pay dearly if he left her to
ride through the woods unescorted. Amanda felt some satisfaction. She would not look back; she did not want to see his face.
She would continue until her mood had calmed and she considered him sufficiently chastened. It was another mile or so to the
far edge of the forest and the boundary of their estate. That
would suffice.

After a quarter of an hour, her mood calmed, she came again
into the heavy warmth of the sunlight. Away to her side the river
emerged from the trees and continued along its winding course
through open pastures.

Lucas appeared at her side. 'Ready to go home?' he muttered.

But Amanda had spotted something. A few hundred yards
distant, behind a copse by a bend in the river, was the villa of
old Caecina, abandoned since her death five years before. Amanda
thought she could see people streaming towards it along the lanes.
'Lucas, look down there, all those people down at the villa.'

'That's odd,' said Lucas, shielding his eyes from the sun. 'What's going on?'

Caecina had died leaving no heirs and no will, and her modest lands had been left in the stewardship of Amanda's father until the ownership could be resolved. Many fists had been shaken in the council chambers of Corinium over who was entitled to them, as year by year her old home was left to crumble. 'Poor Caecina,' said Amanda. 'I remember her coming to my sixth birthday party. She gave me a jet medallion, and afterwards Father made fun of her because the handwriting on her birthday note was so atrocious. She couldn't afford to keep a scribe by then, I suppose.'

'I don't know how you remember things like that.'

'We should go and see what's happening. Father will want to know about it.'

Lucas glanced hesitantly back into the woods. 'I don't know, Amanda. I don't think we should get involved without Formosus. He's the foreman, this is his business more than ours. And the old bat's still dead, isn't she?'

'Oh, come on!' She urged her mare forwards. 'And you'd better not call her an old bat when we get there. Her ghost will haunt you.'

As they neared the crossing point over the Colona, Amanda saw that the gathering crowd was composed of tenant farmers, perhaps a hundred in all. They were congregating immediately below the single-storey villa, which looked down on them, glum and gap-toothed, most of the boards having been torn from its small windows, its front yard unkempt and overgrown after so many years of neglect. The crowd was clearly waiting for someone to emerge from the villa. As Amanda came closer she saw that some of them were carrying farm tools – spades, mattocks, pitchforks.

'Wait here,' said Lucas once they had crossed the bridge.

'Lucas—'

'I mean it, Amanda! Stay down here. I'll go and see what the trouble is.' He dug his heels into his horse's flanks and cantered irritably towards the crowd. They spotted him as he came near and parted to let him pass through, drawing together to close the gap behind him. Amanda saw him approach a man at the front, who appeared to be the leader of the peasants. She was too far away to hear what they said to one another, but the peasant was obviously angry and did not seem willing to listen. Lucas raised his voice to address the entire crowd, loud enough for Amanda to hear. 'All of you, go home! Leave now, or suffer for your disobedience!'

The men in front began pressing towards him, unsettling his mount and forcing it to retreat into the yard. Bitter voices rose. Amanda sensed the mob come to life like an animal slowly climbing to its feet and baring its teeth. She was frozen to the spot, cut off from Lucas by this rising beast, entirely forgotten.

The front doors of the villa swung open and half a dozen young men ran out, grey-cloaked and wielding clubs. They were bucellarii, the armed household retainers of some powerful lord, though Amanda did not recognise them. They surrounded Lucas as a protective shield while he steadied his horse. The chief bucellarius yelled at the farmers to keep their distance unless they wanted to end up on the gallows. The mob hesitated, but only for a moment. It continued to push Lucas and his small band of protectors back towards the door of the villa. They were now so tightly pressed that Lucas dismounted, and with a slap sent his horse galloping in a panic around the side of the villa. The farmers let it go. One peasant yelled out for someone to fetch some fire.

They were going to force Lucas and these other men into the villa and burn them alive. The unreality of the scene froze Amanda. She felt powerless, robbed even of her own voice.

At that moment a horn sounded from across the river. Amanda turned to see a new group of riders galloping out of the forest. Relief flooded through her as she saw the green cloaks of her family's retainers. Her father, Agnus, was in front, followed by his secretary Alypius and a number of their household bucellarii. Amanda recognised Peter, captain of the bucellarii, blasting his horn as they came clattering across the bridge and thundered up the grass to the villa. Agnus came immediately to his daughter, drawing his mount close to take her hand. 'Are you all right?'

She nodded, her throat tight, and looked to where Lucas was besieged at the door of the villa.

Alypius had already reached the rear of the crowd, supported by four mounted bucellarii. Amanda was fond of the Greek secretary, who was wise, loyal and always had a smile for her; but his wide, good-humoured brown eyes could easily narrow to severity, as they did now, and his gentle voice take on a toughness that could not be ignored. 'The next person to raise a hand against any nobleman here will pay with his life!' At his words the people quietened and lowered their makeshift weapons. He now had their full attention. 'Make a path for senator Cironius!'

Cironius Agnus dismounted with a swiftness that belied his fifty-six years. He had evidently only just arrived home, and had not yet changed from the senatorial dress he always wore when travelling: a deep red tunic with elaborate purple and yellow roundels, the badges of his rank, sewn above the hem; a broad belt of leather and brass to signify his career in imperial service; and, most impressive of all, his chlamys, a heavy, deep-green cloak fastened at his right shoulder with a gleaming golden brooch. The farmers parted hurriedly as he walked through them, his cloak billowing in his wake. Amanda, still at the rear of the crowd, watched as he stood at the villa entrance and surveyed the scores of peasants waiting in expectant, fearful silence. 'Explain the meaning of this gathering,' he demanded. He spoke in British, the language of rustics, instead of Latin.

One of the leaders, a tall, bearded man of advanced years, stepped forwards and fell stiffly to his knees. 'The son of Agrius Leo is inside, my lord,' he said. 'We meant no disrespect to you, or to your son. We only wanted to defend your land while you were gone.'

'I was a steward of old Caecina's lands,' Agnus replied, 'not their owner. I've just returned from Corinium, where I was told of the sale and saw the charter. That man inside, the noble you're besieging, is now your lord, not I. In the eyes of the law,' he continued, raising his voice to be sure that all could hear, 'this is a revolt against your rightful master. If you leave now, I will try to temper his fury and you may escape punishment!'

The people were subdued, uncertain. Some were already leaving, shaking their heads. Their leader was not yet placated. 'He came with a tax assessor. Land tax, poll tax, on top of our rent – how are we to feed our families?'

'That is no longer my concern. Your loyalty is to your legal master, and your appeals must be to him. I suggest in future that you make them with words, not with clubs and pitchforks. Now, I say one last time: return to your homes.'

As the bucellarii encouraged the crowd to disperse, Amanda rode to join her father and Lucas at the front of the villa. She wanted to ask about Agrius Leo, whose name she knew only from her father's tirades against him. He was a powerful and wealthy member of the Corinium aristocracy, an arrogant man of Gallic origin, bullying, devious and greedy. He was said to imprison and torture tenants who failed to meet his ruthless demands for imperial tax, even cast them into slavery; then, having high friends in the Ministry of Finance in Londinium, he would keep some of the tax for himself. Such tactics had brought him immense wealth. Amanda had never met him, but she could not pass up the opportunity to see his son in the flesh.

Her father had other ideas. 'Stay outside,' he commanded as soon as she came near, and he entered the building with Lucas and Alypius.

Amanda waited reluctantly with the bucellarii. These were young men hand-picked by Peter and her father from the estate families for their size and strength. Even though they were forbidden to address her without good reason, she had always been intimidated by them, by the aggressive looseness of their limbs, their deep voices and the way they lounged and prowled about like a pack of wolves. She tried to ignore them, and wondered angrily why the new owner, if he had been waiting inside, had not emerged and confronted the rabble even when her brother was being threatened. It was the behaviour of a coward.

There was no reason for her to wait out here. She had been the first to notice the crowd. She had a right to see the coward for herself, even if it meant disobeying her father.

She dismounted and went after the others into the building. The air behind the boarded-up windows was stale and gloomy. Leaves and dirt were strewn across the floor. Following voices, she came to what had once been the dining room, now little more than a cold shell, and peered inside. Her father and brother and Alypius were standing in the room. In front of them, sitting on wicker chairs next to a small table, were two men. One was young, not much older than Lucas, his eyes hidden in the shadow of a deep brow, his dark hair chaotic, his tight lips and square jaw fixed in an expression of contempt. He was examining Agnus, Lucas and Alypius, but had not risen, as he should have in the presence of a senator, and did not notice Amanda. The second man was on his feet. He wore the tunic and belt of an imperial agent; the tax assessor, Amanda presumed.

'Wait outside until I send for you,' the seated man said. He had a Gallic accent, and his voice was like a kitchen knife – a succession of short, sharp cuts. The tax agent bowed and shuffled out of another door.

'Agrius Rufus, son of equestrian Agrius Leo,' Agnus said. 'God be with you. I dare say you already know my son, Gaius Cironius Lucas.'

Rufus acknowledged Lucas with the briefest of nods.

That nod infuriated Amanda. This Rufus had no right to sit here, in old Caecina's house, and show the Cironii such disrespect. 'How brave of you, Agrius Rufus,' she snapped from the doorway, keeping the sarcasm sharp in her voice, 'to sit safely inside while my brother was trying to protect you from a raging mob.'

Agnus turned and noticed her for the first time. 'Peace, daughter!' he snapped.

She said nothing more, but she had got the attention of Rufus, who was glaring at her with an intensity she could not return.

Instead her eyes fell on his hand, which was illuminated by a splash of sunlight from a window. He was clutching the rim of the chair with powerful fingers, the ridge of his knuckles bleached almost white.

'I expected to find your father here, not you,' Agnus said.

'He sent me ahead to take custody of the villa,' replied Rufus. 'And to meet the locals.'

'And it did not occur to you that on his first encounter with new tenants, a new lord might choose a more pleasing companion than a taxman?'

'My father's instructions,' said Rufus coldly. 'These lands haven't paid tax for years.'

'Yes, because they've been under my stewardship, and I will not have imperial bloodsuckers harassing my people.'

'Intestate lands belong by right to the emperor. As steward, you had an obligation to collect taxes on his behalf.'

'I've seen the charter in Corinium, Agrius Rufus. I do not dispute your father's purchase of the land from the emperor. I only regret that the matter was transacted while I was absent in Londinium.' His tone was hardening. Amanda sensed the anger he was attempting to control. 'When this land was sold I had a right to be involved in the arrangements. One might indeed suspect that I was deliberately excluded. Tell me, Agrius Rufus, as your father's immediate representative – would such a suspicion be justified?'

Rufus stared at him with something close to contempt. 'As my father's representative,' he said slowly, 'I can say that you would have to ask my father.'

For a long moment nobody moved or spoke. Agnus stood with fists clenched at his side. Amanda waited in awkward silence at the door. Rufus sat in his chair, arrogant even in his stillness.

Suddenly Agnus turned and left. Lucas, Alypius and Amanda followed him, leaving Rufus sitting alone in the shadows. 'I refuse to waste another breath on that Gallic pagan,' Agnus muttered as they came out into the yard. 'His father is a vulture. He bought the seat of the Governor of Corinium for his idiot cousin, and now the two of them are wreaking havoc. Half the land they own in this province once belonged to Britons falsely accused of treason. Many of them good friends of mine.' He let out a long, slow breath as he surveyed the pastures, the winding line of trees that marked the Colona's course, the stretches of cornfields in the distance. 'We're going home. There's nothing more to do here.'

Amanda rode with her father and brother on either side, their escort a short distance behind. None spoke until they had withdrawn from the open air into the woods, back onto their own lands. 'Caecina was a Christian, and proud of it,' Agnus said at last as they rode slowly along the path. 'When I became steward of her land, I swore in her memory that no heathen would set foot in this valley. He has the name of a lion, but he acts with the cunning of a fox, pouncing on the land while I was away. I've been trying to buy it from the government since she died. He and his cronies in Corinium stopped me every time. Now his cousin is governor, and suddenly the land is sold.' He laughed to himself grimly. 'One thing's for sure: some pockets at the crown treasury are a great deal heavier than they were a month ago.'

'That soggy scrap of land doesn't belong to us, Father,' said Lucas. 'It never has. What do we care who owns it?'

Amanda tensed at the lightness of his words. She knew it was a deliberate provocation.

Agnus said, 'Lucas, how long have you been home?'

'Six weeks, Father.'

'Six weeks. Have you been to Corinium?'

'Yes, Father.'

'And during how many of those visits did you grace the council chambers, or the offices of the governor, or visit the bishop?'

'You know I haven't, Father.'

'You're right. I realised that when I visited the council chambers myself yesterday morning and was presented with this welcome news. Obviously I wished to Heaven that I had someone at home who could have kept his nose in Corinium in order to

sniff out this sort of plot; and then I remembered that my very
own son was in just such a position. I realise, of course, that your
interests lie elsewhere. Since you missed this raging lion
approaching our threshold, perhaps you could tell me of any
conspiracies you have detected among the hounds and the hares
with whom I gather you prefer to spend most of your time?'

Amanda bit her lip. Surely her family had a common enemy
in Agrius Leo; why must they fight one another?

Lucas said, 'You left me no instructions to keep vigil in
Corinium.'

'Heaven forbid you should perform your duty to the family
without explicit instructions! Should I write a note reminding
you not to burn down the villa each morning?'

'My apologies, Father. In future I will attempt to anticipate
your unspoken desires.'

They rode for the next few minutes without saying a word.
The sounds of the forest continued peacefully around them.
Sunlight flickered through the branches overhead.

At last Agnus spoke. 'You should know better than to let your
sister ride out under the noon sun. She looks as red as a washer-
woman. And then to expose her unprotected before that mob
– that was foolish even by your impressive standards.'

Amanda shrank into herself. She did not wish to become a
gaming piece in this contest between father and son. 'Father,' she
said hesitantly, 'it was my idea to go down to the villa Caecina
when we saw the crowd. Lucas had nothing to do with it; in fact
he suggested we go home.'

'I see,' said Agnus. 'So the one useful and courageous thing I
thought he did today – trying, however ineptly, to deal with the
villa Caecina – was actually down to his little sister.'

Lucas pulled sharply on his reins and veered down a beaten
track into the forest.

'Boy, return here!' roared Agnus. 'I command you!' Lucas
seemed deaf to the voice of his father, and did not pause or turn
back. 'You test me, Lucas – go back to acting the minion with
your friends in Treveris! Let Agrius Leo break the back of this

province! Wait and see how you break the heart of your own mother, and ruin the name of your family. Everything you touch, boy, you corrupt!'

Amanda watched her brother withdraw into the trees, her throat tight. She wanted to close the hundred yards between them and smash her hands against his shoulders, batter some sense, some natural feeling of respect into him. But it was too late. He was out of sight.

She rode home beside her father, while he muttered half to himself. She knew better than to offer her own thoughts while he was in such a mood; at these times he simply needed someone to listen in passive sympathy, and it mattered little whether it was his wife or his daughter. Perhaps he did not realise how much he had taught Amanda since she had grown old enough to understand what he was talking about. By now she had a keen sense of the political world in which her father had spent his life. In her mind she saw the empire as a brilliant constellation that stretched across the night sky, with each city a star, and the emperor a wandering planet, brilliant in his distant splendour. But their star, their ancestral city of Corinium, was fading. Men like Agrius Leo wanted to snuff it out and take its wealth for themselves. Amanda did not understand why anyone would want to do this. She longed to understand; she wanted to help and advise her father where Lucas would not. Yet this was not her part in life. She was to marry, and produce children, and listen in silent composure, as she was doing now, to the affairs of men.

They left the forest and took the path up the combe to the villa, whose high white walls shone in the sun. A small crowd of clients waited outside the gatehouse, as they always did when Agnus was home. They were tenants and smallholders eager to declare their loyalty to the family in return for protection and legal support. Today, however, Agnus was in no mood to receive petitions, and rode through their midst in silence. As soon as they had passed through the outer gatehouse into the lower courtyard with its stables, workshops and labourers' huts, Agnus leapt from his horse and shouted for the baths to be made ready.

He stalked up the tree-lined path to the upper courtyard, Alypius at his side.

Peter was supervising the bucellarii as they dismounted, getting them into line with deft sweeps of his horsewhip. They were still boisterous, excited from having had the rare chance to wield weapons in anger. Peter was the largest man Amanda knew, and the fiercest looking. The sun gleamed on his bald head, and on the scar that ran from his left temple almost to his chin. Keeping her shoulders firm and her head high, Amanda approached him. 'Captain, please send two men to find my brother.'

He clutched the whip in two huge hands and bowed to her. 'With a message, my lady?'

'Tell him that my mother will expect him at luncheon.'

Leaving Peter to choose his men, Amanda walked to the upper courtyard, the private part of the villa. Her father had already gone to his quarters. She passed directly through the orchard garden, where the scent of roses and foxgloves drifted in the air and the wooded slopes of the combe rose on three sides, into the ivy-smothered colonnade at the rear wing of the villa, and finally into her own bedroom. Once there, having closed the door, she fell face down on her bed and let the tears emerge. All she had wanted was a peaceful reunion.

Presently there was a faint purr behind her. It was her mother's cat, creeping inquisitively into the room. Amanda's mother Fausta stood at the door. Amanda sat up and composed herself, dragging the rough fabric of her sleeve across her wet cheeks, as her mother quietly closed the door behind her and drifted to a wicker chair facing the bed. Fausta lowered herself into the chair and sat with her back straight, her hands folded delicately in her lap. Her face was thin and pale, barely recovered from her last fever, her skin smooth but for some creases at the corners of her eyes and the wrinkles of a sympathetic frown across her forehead.

The cat jumped onto Amanda's lap and nuzzled against her hand. 'I'm sorry, Mother,' said Amanda, stroking the cat and trying to force some degree of dignity into her sitting posture. 'Lucas offended Father, and he's furious about the Caecina estate.

I went there with Lucas, there was a huge mob, and then Father accused Lucas of taking me there, when it was my idea all along. I didn't know what would happen . . .' Her voice cracked and failed her. She was not sure what she was saying.

'Lucas will learn. All young men rebel against their fathers at his age.' Fausta rose from the chair and sat next to her daughter, putting an arm around her shoulders. Amanda leaned into her and closed her eyes. 'Left to themselves,' Fausta said, 'men would tear this world to pieces. You've read enough history to know that. And many of the worst wars in history are down to the squabbles of father and son. Imagine now if your father and your brother had armies at their command – what a mess they'd make of this valley!'

Amanda watched the darkness behind her eyelids. She took comfort from the steady purring of the cat in her hands. Her mother's words seemed to pour into and fill the emptiness, giving it substance and purpose.

'Think of Livia Drusilla, wife to Caesar Augustus,' Fausta said, 'or his sister Octavia. Remember how Augustus, Antony and Lepidus were driving Rome to ruin with their wars and intrigues until everyone decided that Antony should marry Octavia, for they knew that a woman of such dignity, such intelligence and beauty, was *exactly* what Rome needed to save it from total destruction. She isn't known as the "marvel of womankind" for nothing, is she? And think of what she had to contend with! That shallow vixen Cleopatra, who wanted to steal her husband and plunge the whole world into chaos. Be thankful Cleopatra isn't here to make matters worse! Can you imagine what she'd do to a poor impressionable soul like your brother?'

Amanda could well imagine it. The absurd fantasy brought a smile to her lips.

Fausta squeezed Amanda tightly, then released her. 'Fortune has not been kind to our family. Do you remember the Winter of Grief? Of course you don't, you were scarcely a child. But you know the stories. You know how you lost your uncles and grandfather. You know that to survive, we must be united; and never doubt that a determined wife and mother, with honour to shield her, can have the strength of an army. This worry about the Caecina estate will pass, once your father is resigned to it. But first he must bluster and blow, and your brother must sulk, and after they are wearied of fighting, we'll be there to reconcile them.'

'I understand,' said Amanda.

'Of course you do. Watch me later at supper when I sow the seeds of peace between them – without them even realising it: that is important. Always keep the most edifying models of history and literature in mind, use them as your guide, and you'll be the very image of matronly virtue; admired by all and treasured by one very, very fortunate husband.'

Her mother's words brought only temporary calm. Octavia, Amanda remembered grimly, had failed to save Mark Antony from the clutches of the Egyptian queen. And she tried and failed to imagine how the noble Octavia would have restored peace to this troubled family, whose problems ran far deeper than the occasional heated row. Amanda was no longer a child; she knew the truth of her mother's words. But the family would never be reunited until its lost son returned.

Paul. He had disappeared over four years ago, at the same time that Faustus, the eldest of her brothers, had been killed. Amanda had not fully understood what had happened, and she had not since asked. She knew only that Paul had argued with their parents, and fled the house; Faustus had gone after him, but somewhere in the wild woods they had been attacked by brigands, and Faustus had been killed. Paul's body was never found.

Faustus had been buried outside Corinium with all the honour due to the heir of the Cironii. But the pain of losing Paul was such that Amanda had never heard her mother or father mention his name again. It was as though the earth had swallowed him whole, or he had vanished in a puff of Persian dust. Amanda did not know if they blamed him for the death of Faustus. She did not know if Paul had fled or had been taken into slavery; she did not even know – though she prayed for him almost every day – whether or not he still lived.

She remembered only fragments of the night Paul had left, that night when raised male voices thundered over the dining table, when the merciless wind had torn through the combe and ripped slates from the roof and hurled them into the surging black treetops. Amanda, then only eleven, had been ordered to her room, where she had prayed long and hard for the raging air to calm.

God, in his unknowable wisdom, partly answered her prayers. The storm did calm. But by then Paul and Faustus had already left the house. The next afternoon her mother came to her room and said that Faustus had been found dead, and Paul was lost. 'Pray for your brothers, Amanda,' she had said.

Almost every morning, from that day to this, Amanda had prayed for Paul to return. He still had not. And even if he did one day appear at the gates of the villa, what if that was not for many years? He had been gone so long already; he might be in deepest Sinae by now, at the far eastern end of the world, or wandering the deserts of Africa, or lost amidst the icy wastelands of Thule. By the time he returned, if he did, Amanda could be married and living across the sea.

The daunting thought of marriage tempered her old childish fancy that Paul might stroll into Silvanicum at any moment. She should not hold on to that dream. Four years had passed already. Faustus and Paul were lost, and Lucas, however much Amanda loved him, was not fit to lead the family. That left only her to maintain the honour of the Cironii, and if marriage was the only way to do it, then she would marry.

She picked up a hand mirror that lay on her desk and inspected her reflection. If she was growing into a woman, surely she should be able to see it, and as she turned her chin first one way, then the other, she thought she could; in the polished copper surface, which softened her face and gave it a warm, golden hue, there was a new definition to the lines of her cheeks and jaw. She looked deeply into her own eyes, which appeared a hazel in the copper, though from her mother's glass mirror she knew that they were actually a more ambiguous grey. Her nose was long and narrow – a good Cironian nose, as her father said – her forehead tall, and her brown hair had such natural fullness that she usually left it unstyled. When she tested a smile she was pleased by the way her eyebrows rose, giving her expression an openness that she imagined could not fail to charm, and the neatness of her teeth reassured her that daily cleansing with that sour-tasting powder was, after all, worth it.

Amanda laid the mirror on the table. She was not only growing into a woman, but a beautiful one.

To the lunch table that afternoon she would bring a light mood and pleasant countenance, say little, and observe the behaviour of her mother most closely. Amanda did not need the model of long-dead Octavia as a guide when she had such a living ideal of womankind before her.

Amanda went to the luncheon room when summoned by a servant. Her father was waiting there alone, relaxing in a cushioned chair. He was dressed in a light tunic and smelled of fragrant oils. 'Wait,' he said, holding up a hand to stop her from kneeling before him. 'Stay there for a moment.' She stood while he inspected her. His mouth stretched into a smile. 'There, I thought so. Even prettier than I remembered. That's good!' He held out his hands. She took them and bent down so that he could kiss her. 'Now, honoured daughter, I'm afraid your foolish old father was not in the finest mood earlier, and for that he apologises.'

'Don't apologise, Father,' Amanda smiled.

'Tch! It was cruel of me after so long an absence to become wrapped up in business like that. If you can find it in your heart to forgive me, I shall consider myself the luckiest and most unworthy of fathers.'

'Very well, Father,' said Amanda, the restoration of his usual humour filling her with warmth. 'You are forgiven.'

'Good. Now, sit down next to me. I've been waiting for someone so I could start to eat. My stomach is turning about itself like a dizzy chicken.' He leaned towards the low table before them, set with plates of cold meat, cheese, fruits, bread and salad, and took a slice of pear. 'Tell me how your mother has been – truthfully now. She never lets me worry. When I heard of her fever last month, it was all I could do not to rush back home from Londinium that day – only the reassurances of the doctor's letter kept me where I was.'

'The doctor was quite right, Father. Her fever wasn't too heavy; she was in bed only a day or two, then up and about again as though nothing had happened.'

'I'm glad to hear it. And since we have nothing but truth between us, tell me how useful – or otherwise – your brother has been making himself since his return.'

Amanda swallowed, considering her answer. How to sweeten the truth without smothering it completely? She glanced towards the door. She hoped that her mother would appear soon. 'He's been finding it rather quiet after Treveris, I think,' she ventured. 'He spends a lot of time out on the estate though. Every day, in fact.' She did not mention that these were hunting expeditions, and not due to Lucas's meagre interest in agricultural matters. Her father would already have gathered as much from Formosus, the estate foreman.

Agnus grunted and helped himself to a chicken leg. He tore off a lump of flesh and popped it in his mouth, chewing as he spoke. 'Your brother is the last hope for this family, and he drives us to a final ruin.'

Amanda could think of no suitable response. As daughter, there were limits to what she could say. She was relieved when she heard footsteps in the corridor and a shape appeared at the door. But it was Sulicena, her mother's handmaiden, and her face was distraught.

At once Amanda knew that something terrible had happened. She sprang to her feet as her father was asking urgently what was wrong; not stopping to put on her slippers, she sped past Sulicena, reaching the main corridor before she realised that she did not know where to go. She set off at a run towards her parents' quarters before Sulicena's voice came behind her: 'Lady Amanda, not that way!' Amanda slid to a clumsy stop on the polished floor, turned in time to see her father rushing into the orchard garden. She hastened after him, and followed to where Sulicena was leading.

There, in a quiet corner of the garden, half hidden in the grass at the gnarled foot of an apple tree, lay a still body in a white dress. It was Fausta. She was on her side, curled up like an infant. Agnus was the first to reach her, dropping to his knees and turning her onto her back. He clasped her cheeks in his palms and put his face close to hers, repeating her name over and over again. Her eyelids flickered and opened.

Amanda dropped into the grass on Fausta's other side, taking a firm hold of her hand and pressing it to her lips. She felt the warmth of her flesh, pressed two fingers against her thin wrist to feel her pulse. She was alive; the light was still in her eyes; the black horror of the moment, that terrible void, had receded.

'Sulicena,' said Agnus, 'fetch Alypius. Tell him to send for the doctor at once. Quickly, go!' Sulicena nodded and ran into the villa, tears streaming down her face. Agnus looked closely into his wife's eyes. 'Can you hear me, Fausta? Say so if you can.'

Fausta looked at Agnus unsteadily, swung her gaze to Amanda, then let her head fall back and closed her eyes with an expression of great weariness. A groan crawled from her throat. Agnus lifted her in his arms and, cradling her gently, walked from the orchard to their chambers. Amanda was at his side, keeping her mother's hand tightly in her own. A servant was ready to swing open the bedroom door as they approached, another stood waiting with a bowl of cool water and a flannel draped over her shoulder. Agnus lowered Fausta onto her bed, where she lay limply, her eyes still closed and her chest rising and softly sinking. 'Leave the water on the table there,' Agnus instructed the servant girl. 'Then leave us, she needs peace.'

A trembling voice came from the door. 'Is she hurt?' It was Lucas.

Agnus did not look up. 'You are not needed here.'

Lucas hovered for a moment, watching his mother. His lips tightened. With a final glance at his semi-conscious mother and at Amanda, with the pain of injustice burning across his face, he slowly left the room.

Taking the flannel and dipping one corner into the water, Amanda perched at the head of the bed and moistened her mother's forehead. Agnus brushed a finger across Fausta's white cheek.

Her lips parted, and a single word came out, barely audible, half formed, as though coming from the mouth of a dreamer. 'Paul . . .'

IV

You are a spirit bearing the weight of a dead body,
as Epictetus used to say.
Marcus Aurelius, *Meditations*

Eachna had overheard stories of the men of the south and the empire of Rome, of its stone cities surrounded by walls, but her imagination had not prepared her for Luguvalium. From the river dock she went with Ludo and his brethren up the road to the gates of the city. She kept her eyes on the ground before her and tried not to attract attention. The few upward glances she took confronted her with such alien sights that she quickly looked down again. Not in her childhood home of Ériu across the sea, nor in the northern hills of Britannia where she had endured slavery, had she seen such a place. As they passed through the cool air of the gates, Eachna felt as though she were a fly crawling into a great spider's web of stone – straight roads spun off in every direction, and everywhere swarmed crowds of people, scores or hundreds, converging on Ludo and competing noisily for his attention. She saw hands clapping sharply and tugging at his tunic, one man kneeling and kissing his naked feet as though he were a king.

Eachna stayed close, followed Ludo deeper into the web and avoided the eyes she felt all over her. They came to a compound with a high wooden fence, and Eachna was guided by one of the brethren through its gates. She found herself in a small paved courtyard with a well and a few apple trees. One side was fenced off from the street, the other three sides enclosed by stone buildings. She turned around so she was facing the double gates, which a brother was now bolting shut, with the buildings looming behind her and to either side. The late sun had dipped behind a roof, and the only remaining sunlight touched the upper branches of the apple trees. It was almost like a man-made cave. She believed she could feel safe here.

Ludo led her into one of the buildings and showed her the small room she was to call her own. He gave her new clothes, had a new bed brought for her, and a tub to clean herself daily, and told her in strict terms that when she was hungry she must eat, when she was dirty she must wash, and when she was tired she must rest. She was to be under his ownership, but by serving him she served Christ; and by serving Christ she served herself.

As well as working daily in the kitchen and around the house and yard, Eachna had the task of rising before dawn each morning to sit with Ludo as he prayed. After prayer, a young deacon named Julian took her into Ludo's room and taught her Latin for half of the morning, leaving her to practise what she had learned until noon, when she resumed her normal household duties, and revising it with her by oil lamp in the evening. He showed her how Latin could be drawn using symbols, and how the words of ancient men had been recorded on parchment using them. If she progressed well with the tongue, he said, he would teach her to write.

There was a distance between Eachna and Ludo, as there should be between a slave and her master, especially a master of such authority, but in Julian Eachna saw something close to a friend. He was not like other men she had known. He was gentle in his mannerisms, almost womanlike, but in his restraint she could detect a deep inner strength fed by the love of Christ. She liked the way he disregarded the mess of red hair that sprouted from his narrow head, and the way his green eyes were friendly and attentive amidst the acne that scarred most of his face. When he spoke, she listened, and his lessons became the best part of her new life.

One night, while in bed, Eachna suddenly found herself awake.

She was surrounded by darkness, the room thick with shadows and silence, which seemed to oppress her where she lay. She could not move. Objects slowly took form around her, emerging from the gloom: the table by the window, the torch cradle on the wall. The door was open. In the doorway, a black shape against the faint glow of the corridor, stood a hunched figure.

She knew it was her old master. He had found her. She tried to rise, but her limbs would not obey, and she could not cry out. He began to limp across the room softly, careful not to make a sound. From behind his back he drew a meat cleaver.

Now he was close. He leaned over her. She recognised the old stench. She felt drops fall from his face to hers, and saw that it was blood from a terrible wound where his left eye had once been. He said nothing, but reached down with his free hand and pulled the blanket away from her. He gripped her bare ankle. He raised the cleaver and brought it down in a swift chop, severing her foot like a cut of meat.

She screamed, but there was still no sound. She could not move.

Slowly, almost tenderly, he took hold of her other ankle. Again he raised the cleaver, and brought it down. The blade sliced through flesh and bone.

He took hold of her right wrist and pressed it down into the mattress. He rested the blade edge carefully on her skin. She felt the cold, sharp metal, wet with her own blood. She tried to beg for mercy. She summoned every ounce of will to move her hand, but her numb flesh did not listen.

Her old master stared at her with his dull eye and raised the cleaver.

The door swung open and a new figure hurried into the room. At the same instant Eachna's old master disappeared, and she lurched upright in her bed, still covered by her blanket. She heard the breath escape from her mouth in heavy gasps. She was shaking and damp with sweat.

The figure came to her bedside. It was Julian. 'Rest, sister,' he said. 'You're safe. I could hear your breathing from outside.'

'He was here.'

'You're alone. You were dreaming.'

She could still feel his presence close to them. 'I want light.'

Julian rose and went to the door, where a house servant was standing. He asked her to bring a lamp, and then came back to sit on the edge of the bed. 'Who did you see?' he asked.

'My master.'

'It was a dream, Eachna.'

'No. I was awake.'

The servant returned with a burning lamp. Julian told her to set it on a stool next to the bed, and dismissed her. Eachna climbed out of bed and took the lamp. She raised it above her head and used it to examine every corner of the small room. There was nobody else here, and no way he could have escaped. Finally she replaced the lamp on the stool and returned to the bed.

'Keep the lamp by your bedside,' said Julian. 'I'll sit and pray over you tonight. It was an illusion of the mind, nothing more.'

She closed her eyes, but she did not dare sleep again that night. Her old master must have found a witch who had agreed to turn him into a ghost. It had taken him days to find her, but now he knew where she was, he would surely return.

The following night he did. This time he was not interrupted, and she lay helpless as he removed her feet and her remaining hand. He withdrew quietly from the room, leaving her lying in the blackness, dumb and paralysed, blood pouring from her wrist and ankles into the mattress straw, until the dawn light crept through her window.

Finally life returned to her body. She still had her feet and hand. The mattress was dry. She rolled over onto her side and covered her face with the blanket.

The next night she lay awake in bed until the entire compound had retired, and then she left her room, trod softly down the corridor and eased open the door to the courtyard. She sat on the flagstones with her back leaning on the well, a blanket wrapped tightly against the chill, the walls of the courtyard a shell against the world beyond. She listened to the strange night noises of the city, the calls of dogs, drunks and infants, through the sound of the breeze in the apple trees. Above her head, bats flitted against a field of stars. As long as her thoughts were guarded, she knew her master could find no entry.

The following day Ludo left with a large company to journey the length of the Wall and preach and administer to the Christians who lived along it. He would be gone for two weeks, and he took with him Julian, along with other deacons and priests and believers. Eachna was to remain behind, perform her daily chores and practise the Latin she had learned.

She went with the other household slaves to watch the bishop's procession leave the city. It was the festival of Beltane, the first day of May, and the people had decorated the eaves of their houses with hawthorn and rowan, and lit a pair of bonfires on either side of the city gates in order to purify all those travellers who passed between them. Ludo had publicly denounced these superstitions, but not even his own congregation had listened. When he led the procession through the gates, he paused between the bonfires and called upon Christ to subdue them and kindle the fire of belief in the hearts of the common folk. The flames ignored him, as had the people.

Eachna watched the procession set out on the eastern road, the priests sweating in their heavy cassocks, half hidden in the clouds of incense that spilled from their swinging censers and curled around them, followed by the deacons, Julian among them, who sang psalms and carried a banner of white cloth embroidered with a black chi-rho, the symbol of Christ. After them came the faithful: men, women, old and young together, wearing shoes and bearing staffs, with tokens of devotion around their necks. Finally came the penitents, atoning for their sins through public suffering. Some walked with shoes but without staffs to bear their weight, some with neither shoes nor staff, and the very last to pass through the gates were three pathetic figures in torn and filthy clothes, whose feet were already blackened by blood and dust, their limbs emaciated and their red-rimmed eyes hollow, whose cries, wordless pleas for the deliverance of mankind, rose into the heavens with the smoke of the bonfires.

Ludo had left, and Julian with him. Eachna's heart sank. If they could not protect her when they were here, what chance would she have now that they were gone? She went through the day weary and withdrawn, fearful that she would sooner or later have to sleep and suffer another visit. She worked through the day in the kitchen and again spent the night secretly in the cold air of the courtyard. When she returned to her room she lay on her bed, exhausted, and fought to keep her eyes open. She splashed her face with basin water and pinched her arm until the pain brought tears. It was clear that she could not stay here. She had no choice but to run until she had escaped him for good.

It was still early, with only the first glow of dawn in the east. The servants had not yet risen. She had seen where the cook kept a spare key for the front gate of the compound. Creeping to the kitchen, treading lightly to avoid notice, she found the key and went to the main gate. She fumbled with the unfamiliar instrument, finally working out how to insert it into the lock that held the wooden bar of the gate in place. She removed the lock, gently lifted the bar and pulled the door open.

In the lane outside, like an apparition, stood Julian. He wore a hooded cloak, held a travelling staff in his right hand and had a bag slung over his shoulder.

'Sister,' he said, surprised.

She did not move. Would he catch her if she tried to run? If he did, how would she be punished?

'Are you still haunted at night?' he asked, keeping his distance.

'I can't stay here,' she said.

'I know you haven't slept. I know you've been coming to the courtyard each night. But running won't help. Whatever troubles you here will follow you elsewhere.'

'Not if I run far enough.'

'Stay,' he said, stepping closer to the gate. 'Let us fight it together. If this is an evil spell, there is no better place to overcome it than here.'

'He's already found me,' she said, her voice weak. 'I can only run.'

'Let me try,' Julian urged. 'I give you my word that if I fail, you can leave. I'll even give you clothes, money and help you leave myself, and tell no one. But it won't come to that, Eachna. I spoke to the bishop about this last night. He believes it may be a demon torturing you because it knows you've been chosen by God. He told me to return at once and pray with you every night until you are free. I can rejoin him later. Faith, Eachna – faith will be your shield. We'll pray together tonight, and I'll sit vigil over you. I swear: no demon will harm you.'

His words and her weariness drained her of the will to escape. She did not know if she even had the strength to run a single step. Never had she been so tired.

That night she lay in bed while Julian knelt at her side and prayed. He called upon Christ to protect this poor innocent, who was suffering under a demon invoked by the heathens. In the name of the Trinity he forbade any evil spirits entry into the room, or into the compound, or into the city. The shadow of death, beyond which no demon could set foot, was to retreat back into the darkness of the north. He fortified the prayers by flicking holy water into every corner of the room, but especially on the door-frame. He left a boat of burning incense hanging on the wall in order to banish evil spirits from the air.

Once the ceremony was complete, Julian extinguished the lamp and knelt again at her bedside. In the darkness, the sweet smell of incense drifting around her, she listened to the soft murmur of his prayers.

Her master did not return that night, or any other night.

V

Each man tries to flee from himself,
But that self, from whom he cannot escape,
He clings to and comes to hate;
And the patient is truly sick
Who cannot grasp the cause of his own illness.
Lucretius, *On the Nature of Things*

Paul had hoped that he and Victor would be imprisoned in the southern gatehouse of the fort. There all the sights and sounds of the village would have been laid out before them. They could have peered through the windows and followed the comings and goings of civilians and soldiers, the drunken midnight arguments outside the posthouse, the traders and travellers and taxmen moving along the military road to the south. They might have been able to talk to one another from their separate cells, perhaps even shout down to the world below without reproach. On bright days the sun would have slanted into their little cells, granting them warmth and light.

But they had taken Victor to the southern gatehouse, and Paul to the northern gatehouse. Its walls were damp, the air between them never touched by the sun, stale and cold. The windows were little more than defensive slits through which Paul could glimpse no settlements, no signs of human life except an occasional wisp of smoke from a hearth deep in the hills, or a trader or patrol on the road to the north. The only sounds he heard were the muffled voices of sentries below who refused to speak to him, the scrabbling of vermin and insects in the straw, and the wind speaking through the windows. Even when the sky was still, the windows never ceased to whisper; their delicate sigh sometimes rose to a hiss, or to a screeching, open-mouthed lament when the clouds piled high above the far edge of the world and came rolling across the wilderness. Once he saw a small convoy, two ox-pulled wagons followed by a squad of foot soldiers and four chained men, heading into the hills. The chained men would be condemned vagrants, thieves and murderers who had been offered the chance to join the northern war in place of death or slavery in the tin mines. Over the last two years Paul had seen many such men trudging north. Each time the sight had reminded him how lucky he was to have been posted to Vercovicium.

He could not understand why the tribune had given them this punishment instead of a whipping. If it was an act of mercy – from Bauto, of all people! – it was misjudged, because even as the cell door was closed behind him Paul could think only of Rosa, and he knew that she would rule his troubled thoughts for the next month.

Paul had never been chained to the punishment post in the drill ground, never been lashed, but he had seen it done to others. He had seen those men cry and buckle at the knees as their backs were ripped open, beg for mercy, pass out; he knew what a torment it was. But he had also seen them recover. A beating was not fatal. Even with flesh hanging off their backs Paul and Victor would have been able to protect Rosa. Imprisoned, they could do nothing. Paul could not forget the way Braxus had winked. As long as Paul and Victor were imprisoned, with Bear dead, there was nobody to stop him doing as he willed.

Each day the guards brought Paul a bowl of porridge, a chunk of bread, sometimes a piece of fruit. He had a bucket that they filled with water, and when the bucket was empty he urinated and defecated into it. His waste became a daily feast for cockroaches, his body their plaything. He forgot about Rosa only when he was too hungry to think at all, and when this happened he stuffed the meagre rations into his mouth like an animal. At night he watched the stars pass the keyhole slits of his windows.

These became the fixed poles of his existence: mealtime and stars. Otherwise time became a grey, arbitrary thing that stretched or collapsed itself beyond his comprehension, hours passing in what felt like moments, or a few heartbeats seeming to last an eternity.

But the days did pass. In the final week of his sentence Paul was visited in his cell by someone he had not seen for over four years, and had not expected ever to see again.

It was late in the morning and the cell was as bright as it ever got, but even in the gloom Paul could tell that the newcomer was wearing the long, rough habit of a Christian cleric. Paul remained where he was, sitting in a corner of the cell beneath one of the windows, and said nothing. He knew that clerics from the bishop's staff in Luguvalium sometimes passed through Vercovicium and often made a pious show of visiting downtrodden prisoners. He had no desire to be a vessel of their charity.

The door closed behind the cleric and he stood there, his sleeve covering his mouth and nose against the stench, searching the darkness. At last he spotted Paul, lowered his sleeve and came halfway across the cell. He squatted on the floor. 'What is your name, brother?' he asked. The voice sounded younger than Paul had expected. It still bore the uncertain tones of adolescence. 'My name is Julian. I've been sent here by Bishop Ludo. Are you a Christian?'

Paul looked at him. As his eyes traced the features of the cleric's face, he suddenly felt as though he were at the centre of a great swell: the walls of the cell ebbed and withdrew, and he plunged into a great gap between them, at the centre of which, as immovable as rock, was a pair of familiar green eyes.

The cleric unfastened a gourd from his belt. 'Here,' he said. 'Take some wine.'

Paul reached for the gourd almost by reflex and brought it to his lips. Only by the sweetness of the wine, by the slow sensation of that strange, vivid taste, could he convince himself that this was no dream. He studied the messy red hair covering the cleric's brow; the thin, hollow cheeks. Years ago he had known it as the face of a quiet, oddly pious schoolboy, and was not surprised to see it now beneath a cowl.

Paul's next impulse was to lower his gaze and cover his face as best he could; but it was too late. He felt his cousin staring closely at him. At the moment of recognition Julian breathed in sharply, and swallowed.

'Paul?' he said.

Reluctantly Paul met his stare. 'Julian.'

Julian stood and went to the furthest window as though needing fresh air. He closed his eyes and the grey morning light fell across his face. Paul noticed his lips move quickly in silent prayer. Finally he opened his eyes and studied Paul. He began to speak, but clamped his mouth shut, stifling a threatened outbreak of tears. After a deep breath, he said, 'In the name of God, I have never stopped praying for you, Paul, these past four years. I knew in my heart that you still lived. I feared you had been taken for ransom, even enslaved. But to see you cast down in a dungeon like this . . .' Again he paused as he searched for words. He strode back across the cell and crouched before Paul, then he spoke quickly, in hushed tones: 'I knew there was some purpose – I knew there was *something* that drew me north. If I were pure in heart, I would walk you from this place, and the guards would fall before us and the locks and gates open of their own accord, as when the Lord freed Saint Peter from the dungeon of Herod! I know I'm unworthy of such a miracle, but God will free you through me, Paul, through the miracle of words and the power of men's hearts – but quietly, it must be done quietly; I'll return to Luguvalium and tell my bishop I found you, and write to Bishops Gregory and Martin, and to your father, and we'll have you freed from whoever put you here. We shall bring you home!'

Paul was unable to listen to any more. His cousin had adopted not only the habit of a churchman, but also the attitude – emotional, hand-wringing, forever ready to push out tears and sing praises into the sky. He seemed to think that Paul had been in this cell for the last four years. And he was claiming this chance encounter as divine providence! Paul did not need his help. He did not want to go home. He rose weakly to his feet, Julian rising with him. 'Save your prayers,' Paul said. 'In three days they let me out.'

Julian was puzzled. He looked around the fetid cell. 'In three days? Then why . . .'

'I'm a soldier, cousin. I'm in here for beating up a superior. This fort is my home now. Go back to your bishop. God didn't send you here. Forget you found me, please. Just go.'

Julian did not move. His brow was creased in a deep frown. 'But – I don't understand. What about your family?'

'My family is here.'

'Your real family, Paul. Your father and mother. Amanda and Lucas. Have you forgotten them already?'

'They're better off without me. What kind of son would I be if I returned now?'

'A son who was lost, and then found. One who has been missed and mourned by those who love him, by Amanda most of all. You know she still prays for you. But she doesn't know whether she should pray for your life, or your soul. How can you choose to let her suffer like that?'

Paul had no answer. Of everything he had left behind, he missed his little sister most of all. She had been only eleven at the time. He could well remember her innocence, her clever smile, the way they used to tease their siblings and pull faces at one another in church. It was painful to remember all this, to think of how deeply he must have hurt her, and so he had taught himself not to remember. With time he had found it easy not to think of such things. But now he tried to banish the thought of her from his mind, and found it impossible with Julian standing there.

A flood of other memories, long hidden, rose to confront him. They clung to him still, images of the cultured world of the southern cities, of the wealthy men who had used to come to the villa at Silvanicum, or to their townhouses in Corinium and Londinium, dangling whips at their sides and stepping around puddles in their fine black shoes. He remembered his former tutors, long-faced statues who rarely spoke but with the words of ancient men; he remembered how he had swapped the cane of the grammar teacher for the birch rod of a drillmaster, and the feather pillow of his home for one of straw.

'And what of your duty as heir?' Julian demanded.

Paul gasped in sudden surprise, bringing on a fit of coughing. He doubled up, waiting for the spasms in his chest to calm. 'My duty as *heir*?' he said. 'Look at me, cousin. You think I should be heir, after what happened?'

Julian looked at him in earnest sympathy. 'What happened to Faustus . . .' He shook his head. 'I can see you carry the guilt for his death, Paul. But you mustn't. Your father would never blame you for it. He would rejoice to have you back.'

Here was another delusion of Julian's faith, Paul thought. His father would not rejoice to see him return. He would curse his name and cast him from the gates of the villa. And Paul would deserve nothing better.

'God knows the blood of Faustus isn't on your hands,' Julian insisted. 'His murderers carry the weight of their own sin. You mustn't carry it for them. Has that kept you away all these years? You must not blame yourself, just because you survived.'

'Because I survived . . .' Paul muttered. He did not understand. 'My brother's murderers?'

'The brigands,' Julian said. 'Your father sent men after them, but they were never caught. They only found the body of Faustus at the old barrow. Everyone thought you would be held to ransom. Nobody ever dreamed you had escaped with your life. You must come home, cousin, do you see?'

The bitter truth dawned on Paul. Julian was mistaken. There had been no brigands at the old barrow, only Paul and Faustus. Nobody else had seen what happened that morning. Afterwards Paul had fled north, and not stopped for days.

Paul turned from Julian and went to the nearest window, resting his palms on either side of the slit. He closed his eyes to think.

He had always assumed that the truth of his crime was known to everyone at home. He had not attempted to hide the body, had never intended to deny it if caught. Yet thinking back, he remembered that a gang of bandits from the western mountains had been raiding nearby farmsteads at the time. It would have been natural for people to assume that they were responsible.

You can go home, a voice told Paul. *No one need ever know.*

For the briefest of moments he was seduced by the thought – there would be no condemnation, no public shame. He might go home and claim his birthright. But it was followed by a tightening of his gut that almost made him vomit, a sickening shudder that ran the length of his body, and he knew that he would never be able to live with such a lie.

He opened his eyes. In four years Paul had not seen anyone from his old life, nor even heard their names spoken, and he had slowly willed them to fade into his memory like phantoms, along with everything else. Julian's physical presence had conjured them again to life. Paul turned to look at his cousin, and could almost see his parents standing there, with Amanda and Lucas next to them; and there was Alypius, and Formosus and portly Arcadius; and taking form behind them, a dark shadow in the gloom, was the last member of his family he had ever seen.

He could not go home and live a life of deceit; but his life in the army was also based on a lie. There had only ever been one path to truth. He had tried to ignore it for four years.

It was time to fulfil his promise to Victor and face judgement for the murder of his brother.

He faced Julian, who was waiting in patient silence. 'I'll come home,' Paul said.

At that instant the guard outside hammered on the door. Through the thick planks of oak came a muffled shout: 'Time!'

'I must go,' Julian said. He reached out and took hold of Paul's shoulders, pulling him into a tight embrace. 'God protect you, cousin. We'll talk again. Send me a message in Luguvalium, and we can make arrangements. Shall I write to your father?'

'Not yet,' Paul said. Before they went any further Julian needed to know the truth, but now there was no time. 'I'll send word, and try to get leave in Luguvalium as soon as I can. Then we can talk more. But keep this a secret for now, cousin. Can you do that?'

'Of course.'

The door swung open. Julian, looking at Paul one final time, turned and walked out. The guard closed and bolted the door, and Paul was alone again. He leaned his back against the wall and slid to the floor.

It was done. He had sworn to return home. Somehow Julian had given him the courage he had lacked for the past four years. He had fancied himself courageous and strong because he served under a military standard, because he had taken an oath to fight and die for an emperor he had never seen. It was all nothing: he had stayed here out of fear. He had only ever been fleeing from himself.

It would not be easy to get a discharge from the army, but an appeal from his father to the duke, and a few judicious gifts in the right places, would do it. They would need to obtain a discharge for Victor, too, which would be even harder. It might take months to arrange everything, and cost hundreds of solidi.

In any case, it was done. He was committed to confessing his crime. He might be condemned to exile, spurned by his father, despised by his peers. But he would face it without complaint, and with as much honour as a man like him could still claim.

Three days later Paul was released. Marcus, another soldier from his squad, was waiting for him outside the cell. Only as he began to take the staircase down to the ground floor of the gatehouse did Paul realise how weak he had become over the last month, and he would have fallen were it not for Marcus's arm around him. The pair walked through the fort, past the granary and hospital, to their barrack block. By the time they reached their bunkroom, Paul felt some strength returning to his legs.

Victor had also been released and was already in the barrack room, leaning against one of the bunks talking to Bear's former second-in-command, Motius. Victor looked worn out, weak, with a thick growth of facial hair. When he saw Paul he smiled, but his bloodshot eyes contained only a spark of their old humour.

'Right,' said Motius, looking Paul up and down critically. 'To the bath house, the pair of you. I've blagged a couple of passes and fresh tunics. Get yourselves cleaned up.' He handed Paul and Victor each a folded tunic and a small wooden chip.

'Thank you, semissalis,' said Paul.

'Biarchus now,' Motius corrected him, pointing at the round badges newly stitched onto the shoulders of his tunic. 'I don't know if they told you, but we've got a new tribune, too.'

'What happened to Bauto?'

'Arrested for corruption. The new tribune is Paulinus Maximus. You remember that mutiny by the Twentieth Legion in Deva last year? Well, Paulinus was the man Duke Fullobaudes sent to punish the ringleaders. Most of them ended up in the arena. I'd advise you to do what the rest of us are doing, and keep your noses clean.'

Wordlessly Paul and Victor fell into step as they walked through the fort to the east gate, beyond which, down a track at the foot of the bluff, stood the bath complex. Its furnaces burned through the day, fed by the firewood that was stacked as high as a man against its walls. Even the thought of a warm bath and shave did not distract Paul from his other concerns. He wanted to ask Victor what he knew about Rosa and Braxus.

They were halfway down the slope before Victor muttered, almost as though he did not want Paul to hear him, 'I'm going to cut his throat.'

Paul did not know what to say. His comrade's words and tone had told him all he needed to know: Braxus had taken Rosa and dishonoured her, and nobody had tried to stop him. Victor had never expressed his anger so clearly as he did now, through an unnatural silence.

Paul felt his own anger begin to rise. He cursed Braxus, but cursed himself, too, for the drunken bravado that had put him and Victor in prison and left an innocent girl unprotected. He cursed the village and the rest of the garrison for looking the other way and doing nothing to preserve either the girl's honour or her father's memory. What kind of community would let such a thing happen?

They reached the baths, showed their chips to the attendant and undressed in the changing room. It was painful to peel off clothes that clung to flesh in a thick matte of hair and sweat. They took oil and strigils and put on wooden sandals. In the warm room they exercised and stretched their stiff muscles in silence, their gaunt, bearded faces observed with passing interest by the other soldiers using the baths. The hot room was thick with steam. They sat together on a wooden bench and rubbed oil over their limbs and torsos, and into one another's backs and shoulders, and with the strigils scraped themselves free of sweat and grime.

Only for a little while did they have the room to themselves, which was when Victor said, 'He forced her to marry him. He didn't give her any choice. I could hear it from my cell.'

'I didn't think he was divorced from his last wife.'

'He's not. He says he is, but he's not. The other biarchi are scared of him, the officers don't care. He's even sold his old shack and taken Bear's rooms. What could Rosa do? Nothing. It's not her fault.'

At that point another pair of soldiers came in, and Victor said nothing more. When he and Paul were clean they climbed into the hot bath. The skin of Paul's hands had cracked and bled several times from the cold of his cell, and his palms felt as though they were on fire when he sank himself into the steaming water.

After shaving and dressing they walked back up to the east gate. 'Brother,' Paul said, 'we shouldn't do anything rash.'

'Cutting his throat isn't rash. It's justice.'

'Listen. While I was in prison someone came to me, a Christian.'

'You too? I told mine to fuck off.'

'This one knew me. He was my cousin. You remember my promise, brother, that one day I would leave the army to go home, and take you with me?'

'I remember.'

'Now I'm ready to fulfil that promise. I'm going to leave, and you can come with me.'

Victor stopped in his tracks. They were standing among the animal paddocks that lay outside the east wall of the fort. He cocked his head to one side and looked at Paul, obviously only half believing him, and still thinking of Rosa.

Paul had always shared in his friend's happiness, and he would not deprive him of it now. 'Rosa can come with us.'

For the first time that day, Victor's face broke into his old, full grin. 'You can arrange that?'

'My father has influence enough to get us both an honourable discharge, and Braxus will be like an insect to him. And if Braxus has committed bigamy, the marriage isn't even valid. He has no legal power over Rosa.'

Victor laughed, and gripped Paul's shoulders. 'May the gods you don't believe in bless you, brother!'

That evening Paul was placed under secondment to the hospital. There had been another ambush in the north during which a soldier had been wounded, and Paul had been told to scrub the flagstone floor clean after his surgery. The rest of the room was deserted, the hospital building quiet. He was exhausted, looking forward to the end of the hour and the promise of warm broth and a game of dice in the bunkroom, and the chance to write his letter to Julian. He would be careful in what he said, in case Julian's bishop should read the letter. He would certainly write nothing about his crime. That confession could wait until they met again in person.

It could not happen too soon. Already Paul could sense that life in the garrison had changed since the death of Bear. Motius, though a good soldier, had never had the courage to keep Braxus in his place. Even the centenarius, the commander of their century, was intimidated by him. Braxus was now the senior biarchus and had become more overbearing and arrogant than ever. The other soldiers said that he drank more and gave out harsher punishments. They seemed confident that his attention would now turn to Paul and Victor. The tribune would not notice, or care. A new commander would not be interested in how discipline was maintained, so long as it was.

As though his thoughts had been a premonition, Paul heard the door of the hospital porch open and close, and moments later Victor came into the surgery. He was out of breath and his eyes were wide, desperate. 'He's after me,' he gasped.

'What happened?'

'I'm sorry, brother, but I saw Rosa in the marketplace – she had a cut on her lip, and a bruise the size of a hand on her collarbone; she tried to cover it with her hair but I saw it. It made me want to hunt him down and strangle him.'

'Did you tell her anything?'

'All I did was promise that things would get better, nothing more. She looked at me like I was a coward! So I left her, but Braxus saw us. He says he's going to beat me to death just for talking to her.'

The porch door crashed open. Paul began to move, but too late: even before he and Victor reached the doorway of the surgery they found it blocked.

It was Braxus. He was alone. There was no other way out of the room. They backed away and he advanced on them, one lumbering step at a time, his mouth a twisted smile. He was laughing to himself in a series of nasal snorts that flared his nostrils and were punctuated by animal growls from his throat. In his hands was a whip. It consisted of a short wooden handle from which hung a bunch of knotted leather tails, flayed at the tips. He twisted the tails around his fist, pulling them taut, as his gaze settled on Victor. 'Fresh out of prison and I find you talking to my wife – I'll fucking tear you open!'

'Biarchus,' said Paul, knowing it was useless, 'you have no right. We'll make a formal complaint to the centenarius—'

Braxus raised his whip suddenly, and Paul instinctively cowered. This delighted the biarchus. He made a couple more threatening jerks with his arm, as though about to bring the whip down on Paul's head, and laughed as Paul scurried around the operating table beyond his reach. He then turned on Victor, who had backed up against a wall. Braxus brought the whip up, and with a snarl brought it down on Victor, who had raised his naked forearms in defence; the leather nails snapped viciously on his skin, and he screamed in pain. Victor crouched on the floor, turning away from the whip, bunching himself into a protective ball, burying his face in his arms, and Braxus struck him again.

Paul looked around desperately for anything he could use, and saw a broom leaning against the wall. He grabbed it, wielding it like a staff, and came around the table behind Braxus. 'Let him go!'

Braxus twisted his head to look back at Paul. He was no longer laughing. He brought the whip around in a sudden sideways swipe, but he misjudged and struck the broom handle. Angrily he turned fully to face Paul, raising the whip. This time Paul did not cower or back away, but stood his ground. 'I don't want to fight you,' he said. 'Just leave us alone.'

Hatred burned in Braxus's face. 'After what you did to me?' he roared. 'Jumping me in the alley, a pair of rats! No prison for you! I'll flay you alive! I'll rip every last fucking scrap of flesh from your bones!'

Braxus struck out with the whip; again Paul deflected it with the broom. Braxus screamed and stepped closer. He was beserk, unsteady on his feet, almost delirious. One last time he swung, putting all his strength into the blow, and the whip struck Paul's upper arm. Pain seared his flesh, flooded his mind. But rage and the force of the swing had made Braxus lose his balance; his boots found no purchase on the wet floor and he toppled backwards, flailing his arms hopelessly, and his skull cracked against the flagstones.

Paul and Victor stood and looked at the biarchus. He lay on his back, still gripping the whip in his right hand. His eyes were open, but there was no life in his stare. From the back of his head a pool of blood started to spread across the floor.

There were footsteps, and Paul saw two of the other hospital staff at the door. Moments later a junior officer appeared, along with a pair of armed sentries.

The officer looked at the dead biarchus, and at Paul and Victor. 'Take them to the tribune,' he said.

The new tribune, a Gallic career officer, was not inclined to mercy. He did not want to hear the testimony of Paul or Victor. He knew only that he had lost an experienced biarchus in a brawl involving two soldiers fresh out of prison, and such a breach of discipline demanded the harshest punishment. Where normally this would have meant death, for Paul and Victor it meant exile. God was smiling on them, announced the tribune as he passed sentence. Duke Fullobaudes, the commander-in-chief of Rome's forces in Britannia, needed soldiers in the north, and he was not fussy about where he got them from.

They were kept in a cell for two days until the next party for the north came by the fort, when they were given caps and hooded cloaks and were brought down to the postern gate on the Wall below the fort, their necks and hands fastened with rope. Awaiting them were a dozen recruits led by a dull-eyed biarchus, a veteran of the north. His men were young and frightened looking, obviously unwanted farmworkers who had failed to escape the draft levied on their landlords. They had no armour, carried spears but no swords or shields, and on their feet they wore the cheap leather shoes of peasants. When they saw Paul and Victor they stared enviously at their strong military boots, the only good pieces of kit they had been allowed to keep.

As the convoy was about to pass through the postern gate onto the northern road, Motius came hastening down the track from the fort, carrying a satchel. He placed the strap around Victor's shoulder. 'A few rations,' he said. 'Some salted pork I scrounged.' He gave them both a firm stare. 'Look, boys. Everyone knows Braxus got what he deserved, nobody thinks it was your fault. Me and the rest are going to petition the centenarius; we'll get the tribune to change his mind, bring you home. We'll look after

Bear's girl, too. But you've got to hold on. Keep Tungrian honour alive. Do you hear me?'

They nodded.

The rain started as soon as they passed through the postern gate. Great clouds pushed up from the mountainous country of the Picts, crawling their way over a skyline that lay twisted like the spine of a slumbering monster. Soon a downpour beat upon the ragged column as it crept along the old north road, its broken, grassy surface shimmering almost black in the rain. Paul, at the rear of the column, could feel the wretched spirits of those around him. He occasionally tried to look up from his boots, but the rain blinded him and he dipped his head and concentrated instead on the uneven road beneath his feet, trying with each pace not to slip. His cloak was sodden and heavy, every inch of his body was wet, and water was leaking through a small tear in his hood, running in a constant, irritating stream down the side of his face.

At the end of the first day they reached the first of the old abandoned forts, set on a ridge not far from the road. Its worn battlements loomed in the fading light. A causeway led the soldiers through the southern gate, or what had once been the southern gate, for there was a yawning hole where formerly had been a pair of wooden doors. The great hinges that had supported them still remained, embedded deep in the stonework. A single crow perched on the gatehouse watched them pass with a sidelong gaze.

Everything was wet, everything was cold and dark, and even the air seemed to hold itself still as though asleep, subdued by the hammering rain. They followed the biarchus into the nearest block that still had a tiled roof. Inside was some basic furniture and slowly rotting hay. Quietly, gloomily, the soldiers ate their damp rations in front of a fire and prepared themselves for the night.

The biarchus cut their bonds. Paul collapsed on the hay, exhausted. He dreamed that night that he was back in the post-house at Vercovicium. Julian was with him, surrounded by drunken soldiers. Paul was trying to tell him the truth about

Faustus. He screamed as loud as he could over the sounds of revelry, but Julian could not hear him.

He awoke to a cold and comfortless morning, the rising sun pale and half lost in the mist. Their destination was still two long days away. Paul remembered Motius's parting promise to appeal against their sentence. It had been an honourable thought, but it was bound to fail. No matter. Once at Trimontium Paul would somehow send a letter to Julian in Luguvalium, explaining what had happened. Surely his father's influence could reach him and Victor even in this barbarian wilderness. He only hoped that they would survive long enough.

VI

Beauty when unadorned is adorned the most.

St Jerome

Amanda walked along the colonnade that looked out on the upper courtyard of Silvanicum. The cool air of the early August morning drifted around her, and she pulled up her shawl where it had slipped from her shoulders. The house was hectic with preparations for her birthday party later that day: she heard the bubbling of stew from the kitchen and the clattering of dishes and utensils as the feast was prepared; servants busied themselves preparing decorations in the orchard; from the rear of the villa came the sound of wood being unloaded for the bath hypocausts. Surrounding it all, the combe rushed and breathed with a western wind, a threat of approaching rain.

Even before Amanda reached the room she smelled the nauseating cloud of mustard and poppy scent, lingering traces of the hopeless attempts at saving her mother; and, fainter yet, wormwood and diluted honey, the now-familiar smell of a bewildered and defeated physician. She entered the room quietly, easing open the door, and saw that her mother was sleeping. Three months had passed since Fausta's collapse. Her sickness was always most severe early in the day, when she was rarely able to talk or keep food down, and her speech had become slurred, her movements lethargic. The doctor whom Alypius had fetched from the village had returned on infrequent visits. A blockage of phlegm in the brain, he had pronounced sadly, shaking his head. Yesterday he had arrived and departed for probably the last time.

Amanda sat on a wicker chair at her mother's bedside, and prayed long and hard that God would find some mercy for a woman who deserved life more than any other. She prayed that he would show compassion towards a daughter who would be lost without her mother's example. She begged that God would not leave to ruin a family who had striven so hard to keep a faithful Christian life.

This was her birthday, and never had she felt less ready to smile or accept the good cheer of friends.

Amanda left her mother and returned to her bedchamber, where her handmaiden Pinta was waiting to help her prepare for the party.

'Is your mother well, mistress?' Pinta asked as Amanda entered.

'I think she's a little stronger today,' replied Amanda, though she thought no such thing. Pinta had been in Amanda's service for five years, and was precisely the same age, having been born on the same day. She was a sweet girl, quiet and well spoken, and Amanda was very fond of her. It did not seem right to cloud Pinta's day with her own worries. 'You can leave me alone until later,' Amanda said. 'I can prepare myself. It's your birthday too, after all.'

'Are you sure, mistress?'

'Of course. I'll need you when we go to the baths, but until then you can do as you like.'

Once Pinta had gone Amanda inspected herself in the mirror. Today she would have no elegant coiffure, no bone pins holding a mass of coiled hair that could tumble loose with a quick turn of the head. She would have her dark hair knotted simply at the nape of her neck, and let those party guests who looked on her with the vulgar eyes of the city think what they liked. A touch of foundation; a necklace of golden links inlaid with dark beads that had belonged to her grandmother, a pair of jet earrings, a single bracelet on her left wrist and a gilded brooch to fasten the shoulder of her gown: these ornaments she would suffer.

The first guests began to arrive around noon, by which time the skies had long cleared and the sun dried the orchard grass.

Amanda was stirred from composing her poem of birthday thanks by a cry for attention from the upper courtyard, and a good-humoured demand to see the master of the house. She came into the orchard in time to see her father already approaching the newcomers, the family of Censorinus from further up the valley, laughing and sweeping his arms wide.

'Happy birthday, my dear!' said Censorinus when he saw Amanda. He took her in a solid embrace. 'See, I told you,' he said, making way for his wife. 'She grows more radiant with every season.' He at once began to praise the decoration of the garden, especially the garlands of laurel and white roses that had been suspended from the orchard trees and the colonnades, and the ivy-wrapped stands, mounted with copper boats of burning incense, and it was a while before Agnus could fix him in a debate on the advantages of Siluran over Cornovian greyhounds.

Other guests began to arrive. Aunt Fuscina, who had journeyed for two days from Aquae Sulis, was wearing a black mourning gown and veil, as always. She had been married to Amanda's uncle, Viventiolus, until his arrest and execution during the Winter of Grief. She graced Amanda with a rare smile. Most other guests were landowners from the valley, or at least from this side of Corinium, and soon the orchard garden was filling up. The men stood under trees, their parents and wives sat on couches arranged in the shade, and the children played in the grass under the attentive eyes of their nursemaids. Amanda spoke to all, and received warm congratulations and praise, and smiled and laughed until her jaw ached.

'You must come up and see us before the summer is over,' Flidaia, the teenage daughter of Censorinus, was telling her, 'or else before autumn gets too cold – we noticed on the way down that part of the road was slipping, just past the bend at the end of your father's land – look, there's Alypius again! But still no Lucas – it was slipping down into the river, so Father said he'd have to get some men to re-cut it all before the rainy weeks. Imagine if the road slipped away in the autumn! We'd be stuck up there until spring at least; who knows what we'd do if we had to come down, we'd have to go over to Glevum or somewhere, and the road down that side of the hill isn't much better . . .'

At this point the announcement of new guests interrupted her. Amanda rose from the couch, trying to disguise her weariness behind a welcoming face.

Flidaia also rose. 'It's your cousin Patricia,' she exclaimed, and put a hand to her mouth.

All conversations in the orchard had stopped. Patricia was now standing between her parents at the entrance of the courtyard, and had already attracted the attention of every pair of eyes in the garden.

Beautiful Patricia, who, with her willowy figure, had always made Amanda feel so short and graceless, had been away in Gallia with Lucas the previous year. Amanda had not seen her since her return, nor had she wanted to. Her time in the imperial capital had only increased her beauty. She was wearing a long, light purple tunic, more finely cut than any Amanda had ever seen, with its hem left to trail at the back and gathered at the front to give a glimpse of a pair of red slippers decorated with silver swirls. Over her shoulders and head she wore a translucent silk veil embroidered with gold thread, fastened somehow to waves of red hair, which had been arranged with exquisite precision. The bracelets on her slender, sleeveless arms glittered in the afternoon sun, and flashes of light played on her necklace and earrings as she bowed to receive her host.

Agnus took Patricia by the hand and led her towards Amanda, who was still standing beside the speechless Flidaia. Patricia seemed to glide noiselessly along the gravel path and grass, her slim form moving with all the grace of Queen Dido, her hand raised delicately in her uncle's, her long neck dipped forward with the perfect degree of modesty. It all served to perfect the natural beauty of high cheekbones that tapered to a delicate chin, of a dimpled smile and expressive moon-shaped eyes that could entrance with a single look. Friendly greetings followed, but even as Amanda accepted the compliments of Patricia and her parents, she felt that all attention was on Patricia, not her.

When the arrival of servants bearing refreshments provided a break in conversation, Amanda excused herself and returned to her chambers. There she washed her hot face and neck with a damp cloth, and positioned herself before the mirror. She was flushed from the heat, and thought her nose was a little burned. Why could she not have Patricia's complexion, which was as fine as the smoothest marble, and was never touched by the heat except to bring a delicate flush to her cheeks? The simplicity and taste of Amanda's preparations in the morning had faded to nothing: now her necklace was clunky and garish, her jet earrings common, her hair dull and inelegant. She had not reckoned on having the height of Gallic fashion as competition.

It was not right that she should be upstaged on her own birthday. Patricia should know better. Cousin or not, she was only from an equestrian family. Amanda's father had served one year as consul-governor of Belgica Secunda, a post that had brought him the rank of *vir clarissimus*, the first senatorial grade. It was rare for Britons to rise so high in the imperial service, and few had earned such an honour. It meant that the Cironii, already ennobled among the Dobunni by their ancient princely blood, could also stand with pride alongside the aristocrats of the empire, as cultured and worthy as any of them. If the two of them were to go to Treveris, Amanda would receive the better seat in the theatre and be given precedence at any social gathering, not Patricia.

And yet was not this all her father's fault? He had always kept Amanda away from city society except for obligatory winters in Corinium, and had taught her that true elegance was to be found in modesty and simplicity. Yet *he* had taken Patricia's fine fingers to lead her across the grass, and all that time in Treveris had clearly not undermined her decorum or modesty. Suddenly the attraction of the city was bitterly clear. Amanda looked at her reflection steadily and now, for the first time, saw herself as she must appear to others. A dark, inelegant country girl, dressed in her grandmother's finery and, for all her aristocratic blood, too uncultured even to have her hair set properly for her own birthday.

She was no better than Flidaia or any other girl from a semi-impoverished family.

She opened her make-up box, determined that improvements had to be made before she could show her face outside, but no sooner had she raised the pencil to her eyebrows than she threw it to the floor. Pride forbade her to alter her appearance. People would notice, and remark that she was trying to compete with Patricia, and think her vain and petty for doing so. She would have to stay as she was, dwelling in the shadows cast by the radiance of another, and endure the humiliation.

Shortly afterwards Ecdicius, the house steward, announced that the bath houses were ready. The men went to share a bath in the north wing, and the women in the west, while the children were left outside under the supervision of servants. The smaller size of the western baths required the women to bathe in three parties, and following some confusion it was determined that Amanda and her two young friends should enter first.

Amanda undressed in silence with Patricia and Flidaia, attended by servants who followed them barefoot into the neighbouring warm room to apply thick, fragrant oils to their skin. Then came the hot plunge bath, while the attendants waited in the cold room, and it was in this newfound privacy, cloaked by the noise of the furnace outside and the writhing clouds of steam around them, that Patricia began to speak. 'Your figure has improved so much since I last saw you, Amanda,' she said, smiling as she sank to her chin in the water. 'You've gained a true womanly form. I can think of twelve dozen men in Treveris who'd drool into their bejewelled goblets if you were to walk past.'

Amanda responded only with a half-smile and closed her eyes. She did not want to look at Patricia's face, which remained a picture of naked perfection, glowing with unaccountable grace even while Amanda's and Flidaia's were violent with sweat.

'Now, I've been looking forward to seeing you especially because I heard about the latest scandal in your valley – that the villain of Corinium, the infamous Lion, has bought an estate next to yours and installed his son there. Tell me – is it true?'

'Yes,' Amanda said in a tone that she hoped would make her lack of interest clear.

'And that son of his, Rufus, have you met him yet?'

'Briefly. He was rude and tedious.'

'Oh, he's a scoundrel like his father! He was in Treveris for a while last year, and we found ourselves thrown together once or twice. Now *there's* a stud who'd have had his pick of the bored wives of the court if he'd bothered looking at any of them twice. Such a serious, moping face on him! Do you not think, Amanda?' She laughed to herself, and swept her long limbs through the water with a sigh of pleasure. 'He always reminded me of Orpheus, when he returned from Hades heartbroken, and wouldn't even think of women for three years. And you know what else they say about Orpheus:

> 'Many women, burning with desire,
> Yoked themselves to the bard,
> And many lamented their rejection;
> Aye, it was he who taught the men of Thrace
> To turn their love to tender boys,
> To pluck the brief springtime buds of youth.'

Patricia laughed again to herself, while Flidaia, only her eyes peering above the surface of the water, observed her cautiously. Amanda pretended to have heard nothing. It was better to ignore such indecency – that Patricia had no right to talk in such a vulgar way about a near stranger, even an enemy of her family, Amanda knew with righteous certainty; it was offensive to her and to all those of modest disposition, and Amanda felt especially angry that Flidaia should be subjected to it.

Patricia again broke the silence. 'I'm sorry I said that. It was wicked of me. I'm afraid I've become too used to city conversations – in Treveris such comments are rarely given any weight.'

The girls said nothing more until they stepped from the hot bath, and nothing in the next room except subdued gasps as they lowered themselves into the cold pool. Once the three were freshly dressed they went to Amanda's room to be readied for the dinner gathering. Amanda politely but stubbornly refused Patricia's advice and her offer of a touch of Attican foundation, instructing Pinta to apply as little make-up as necessary, and she kept her hair free and straight as before.

After Flidaia went to find her mother and left them alone, Amanda turned to Patricia, who was still applying eyeliner with the concentration of an artist. 'You shouldn't have spoken as you did in front of Flidaia,' Amanda said.

'What do you mean?' asked Patricia distantly, finishing one eye and moving on to the other.

'What you said about Agrius Rufus and Orpheus. It was indecent of you, cousin. You know your mother wouldn't approve.'

'Amanda, you have grown! Besides, I apologised, didn't I?'

'Just be mindful of how you speak,' said Amanda. She added, failing to hide a touch of bitterness: 'You're not in Treveris now.'

Patricia placed her make-up on the dressing table and turned to Amanda. She laughed suddenly. 'Envy, dear cousin? Why, do I detect a flaw in your noble senatorial bearing? Perhaps if I had *your* pedigree, might I too be permitted the occasional foible?'

Amanda did not reply. Eventually a servant came and beckoned them to the large, new dining room at the far end of the north wing, where the others were already settled. It was only on special occasions that this dining suite was used, and for this particular dinner it had been decorated with rare splendour. Warm, green-tinted afternoon sunlight splashed through the high windows, gleaming on the purple-painted walls and the trellises of ivy arranged around the room; lamps suspended from candelabra of twisted bronze cast a glow upon the polished mosaics and on the deep red arms of the dining couches; a soft scent drifted from rose petals scattered on the floor, from bunches of rosemary hung from the ceiling, and from a smoking incense burner beside the door.

All families present had been assigned their places according to conventions of hierarchy, and Amanda, amidst clapping and wishes for her health, was led to the place of honour beside her father and Lucas on the highest couch, on a raised dais at the far end of the room. Agnus rose and welcomed each guest by name and title, raising a glass of wine to their health, and wishing Amanda a happy and prosperous birthday, to the ready agreement of all. His chaplain, Arcadius, a portly, bearded man, gave a prayer of thanks for God's grace. Then came the gifts, brought in by servants and offered by the heads of each family. Censorinus and his wife presented a set of three silver spoons, one engraved with Amanda's name and the remaining two with their own. From Patricia came a pair of bracelets inlaid with precious stones. Other guests had brought Capuan perfumes, an ivory hairpin box, a silk shawl, and more besides, all of which Amanda received with grateful thanks. After the gifts had been circulated for the admiration of all those present, they were arranged on a table at the far end of the room. Finally the food was brought in to the sound of music, layers of light gleaming on the reddish rims of copper bowls overflowing with oysters and boiled mussels, on the sparkling silvery sheen of fattened snails on pewter, and the dull green glass of flagons filled with Hispanian wine.

Despite the grandeur and good spirits around her, despite her simmering irritation at her cousin, Amanda's thoughts returned to her mother, who at this moment was lying in her bed at the far end of the wing, no doubt hearing the distant sounds of celebration. Amanda wished that she had insisted on having her mother brought to lie on a couch on the dais, regardless of what people would think. Those who loved her would understand that she had been struck down on a whim of fate, not by the hand of God.

When it was time for neighbours to make their way home within the few hours of sunlight remaining, the guests and hosts went to the orchard garden for final partings. Once this was over, Amanda escorted Patricia and her parents to the guest chambers, since the fifteen miles across the wolds to their home required them to stay until tomorrow.

Finally she went to her mother and sat by her side. Fausta managed a smile and forced out a few syllables that Amanda heard as birthday congratulations. Amanda gripped her mother's hands tightly, and told her all about the events of the day, the news of relations, the presents she had received, and how sorely she had missed her throughout. Eventually she wished her mother a peaceful rest and made her way down the corridor to her own rooms.

Her father emerged from the library as she came near. 'Amanda,' he said, smiling. 'How is your mother?'

'She's awake,' she said.

'Has she been speaking to you?'

'A little. Not much. A few words. I told her about the day.'

Agnus took her shoulders gently. 'You are a treasure to this family. I'm afraid some urgent business will take me to Corinium at first light tomorrow, and I shan't be back for a week or so. Alypius and Arcadius will be with me, as usual. While I'm gone, watch over your mother and brother for me, won't you?'

'Of course, Father.'

Despite her best intentions, Amanda rose too late the next morning to see her father off. Instead she acted hostess to Patricia and her parents, who made ready to leave after breakfast. Lucas, as usual, went out onto the estate with the foreman, Formosus, but Amanda knew that before long he would ride away alone into the woods or across the meadows, his hounds bounding close behind. It was typical of him, Amanda thought sourly, that he should disappear without saying goodbye to their guests.

Shortly before her departure Patricia asked Amanda to take a stroll with her through the orchard. This time Patricia's hair was pulled back and set in a chignon with a subtlety that must have taken an hour to perfect, and was far beyond Pinta's provincial talents. Such effort on one's personal appearance so early in the day, Amanda told herself irritably, particularly when one was going from an empty villa to another empty villa in a covered wagon with one's own family, was the height of vanity.

'It's a week to the Ides, isn't it?' Patricia said with an affected air of weariness. 'I'm sorry we have to leave so soon. Father can't bear to be away from the farm for long at this time of year, what with the harvest and the taxes. That's the rotten thing about August birthdays, I suppose.'

'I think some peace will be better for my mother anyway.'

'True. It's probably the most boring time of year.'

They paced between the laden apple trees for a minute or two in silence before Patricia continued, her voice more quiet and cautious than usual, 'Cousin, I honestly am sorry about what I said in the baths yesterday. About Agrius Rufus, I mean. It would be better if you didn't think of him at all.'

'I don't,' said Amanda truthfully. She had scarcely thought of Rufus since first seeing him three months ago.

'I'm sure you don't; but I think I ought to warn you about him, just in case he tries to take advantage of the situation. What I said about him taking pains to avoid women wasn't completely true. There was one woman in Treveris, a very rich widow, who was quite enamoured with him, and there were rumours – I can't pretend any more than that – rumours that he seduced her and convinced her to part with a great deal of money. I don't doubt that it's true, but it's all hearsay, you know, and I'm only telling you because – well, he's hardly two miles away from you, after all.'

'Thank you for your concern, Patricia, but I have nothing to do with him. He probably came to organise the estate at the start of summer, and he might be here to supervise the harvest, but for all I know his father will have more use for him elsewhere.'

'Well, I don't suppose he's much use for anything these days, not after his fall.'

'What fall?'

'Didn't I mention it yesterday? Yes, he fell from his horse last winter and broke his leg or his hip or something; in any case, he hasn't been able to walk since. He gets carried about everywhere in a litter, I heard. Not quite the dashing cavalry officer he once was.'

That explained why he had failed to rise from his chair when she saw him in the villa, Amanda realised. But it was probably no more punishment than he deserved if Patricia's gossip was true. 'I don't want to talk about him any more, Patricia. You needn't worry about me. Even if he is at the villa, I won't be crossing into *that* estate again, and Father would sooner invite a Pictish cannibal to dinner than Rufus.'

'Good,' said Patricia, giving a sigh of relief. She took Amanda's hands in her own. 'You've always been the most sensible girl I know, Amanda. I am sorry about our little spat yesterday; it was your birthday, after all, and I behaved like a brat. And now I want you to take this.' She released Amanda's hands to unfasten a silver pendant from around her neck. 'I bought this one day at the theatre in Treveris, and I want you to have it as a token of our sisterhood. We don't have blood sisters of our own, after all, do we? Here, let me put it on you.'

Amanda, dipping her head and gathering up the hair from the base of her neck, accepted the gift reluctantly. She was able to tolerate Patricia as first cousin for Julian's sake; accepting her as a sister, with all the confidence and love that that implied, was more than she would wish to bear. Her only reassurance was that this gesture was probably no more sincere than most of Patricia's expressions of affection, and would soon be forgotten.

Amanda escorted Patricia and her parents to their wagon, bidding them a safe journey. Patricia was the last to climb aboard. As she kissed Amanda on the cheek, she paused to whisper in her ear: 'Remember, cousin: he is dangerous.'

VII

The lion has emerged from his lair, the destroyer of nations
approaches; he has left his home to make your land desolate;
your cities shall be laid waste, and no one shall remain.
So put on sackcloth, and lament, and wail;
for the fury of the Lord is upon you still.
Jeremiah 4:7–8

The hot August weather finally broke and brought a heavy storm from the south. It battered the parched earth with rain, while fierce winds ripped through the streets and howled along the ramparts of Luguvalium. The next day the sky was filled with thick clouds, a low, heavy roof that oppressed the air and obscured the sun, and gave the city a stillness that seemed to Eachna almost like the half-death of the shadow world. She at first read the turn in the weather with fear, thinking that perhaps the old gods had sent it as a warning. But the storm had come from the south, she told herself, not from the west, and so could not be the fury of the Dagda, or of any god she knew except Christ. Ludo and Julian had left the city on another visitation, this time along the western shores, and she would have to wait for their return if she wanted to know what it meant.

Eachna was kept awake for much of that night by the screams of a woman in labour in a nearby house. Shortly before dawn the screams reached their worst as the birth took place, and were joined by the shrieking of a newborn child, and then by the group of other women and girls present at the birth: screams not of pain, but of horror. Voices spilled out of the house, bringing people running frantically onto the streets. Eachna heard feet rushing by her room and voices in the courtyard. She rose, pulled on her cloak and cautiously followed the other servants out through the gates of the compound.

It was almost light, and the street was filled with rushing, half-lit shapes. People raced past them towards the source of the outcry. Eachna came to the nearest junction, peered around the corner and saw a dark mass of figures outside a house. Some of them were holding blazing torches above their heads. The great mass began to move, shuffling like a single creature, away from the house and towards Eachna. Near the front she saw a woman holding high an infant, which gleamed with blood and afterbirth in the torchlight, and split the air with its screams; as it came close she saw that the child was misshapen, horribly so, its limbs twisted almost beyond recognition, its face and hands mere lumps of flesh without form. She drew back quickly, pressing herself against the wall of a building as the crowd passed her and headed down the main street towards the gate.

When they came to the city gate the guards, panicked by the hysterical mob coming towards them, unbolted the doors and heaved them open, even though this was forbidden before dawn. Eachna followed the crowd down to the river, but it did not stop there. It went further downstream, beyond the place where people bathed and where the fishing boats were moored, as far as it could go before the bank was made impassable by thick reeds and bushes. There, with their frenzied screams filling the air, they hurled the wailing creature into the waters.

The Christian and pagan communities of Luguvalium rarely found much to agree on, but on this occasion everyone seemed to accept that the child had been sent as an omen. The meaning of this omen was less clear. Among Eachna's people such a terrible birth would be the result of a curse on the mother. Curses could call down blight upon crops and livestock if not countered, and only the most bitter curse, invoked by a powerful witch, could blight a child while in the womb. Yet the child's mother was the wife of a farrier, quiet and inoffensive, and though a Christian, was well liked even by the pagan people of the city. Eachna could not think why anyone would have held so violent a grudge against her. She considered the matter a great deal but could find no answer, and eventually decided to wait to hear Ludo's opinion. There was much about her new life that she did not yet understand, and his guidance would surely bring clarity.

Ludo and the others returned one late afternoon a few days later. A mass was celebrated straight away to give thanks for their safe arrival. As usual, Eachna stood in the crowded porch of the chapel with the other catechumens, before leaving when the mass reached those sacred mysteries that they were not yet entitled to witness. She returned to her room and studied some simple lines of the Gospels, impatient to learn from Ludo what the cursed childbirth could mean.

She heard his voice before she saw him. He was outside on the street, and when she sensed the anger in his tone she at once rose to find him. Many others nearby had already gathered before him where he stood, just outside the gates of the compound, and even more were being drawn by the volume and fury of his words.

Eachna could scarcely believe that he was the same person. His face was flushed a deep, violent red by his anger. She had not seen him like this since their first meeting in the forest, when he had reprimanded his companion. Now his veins bulged in his neck as he shouted over the heads of the audience. His hands flashed and arced with the fury of his words.

His anger was not with the woman who had borne the child, for she had played no part in its killing. Nor was it with the pagans who had led the crowd and pronounced the child a curse, and who had murdered it in the river, for they were ignorant and by the rejection of the message of Christ had already doomed themselves in the eyes of God. His anger – relentless, bitter – was hurled at those Christians who had done nothing to prevent the killing – and much worse, who had joined the devilish parade and with their senseless howls had submitted to the execution of one of God's children. Christ had commanded that the children be brought unto him, for each child born to a woman, regardless of its bodily form, housed a soul that was sacred to God. Where Christ opened his arms to the children, the wicked people of Luguvalium hurled them into death; where Christ demanded that they be brought into his father's kingdom by baptism, they threw them in the river to drown. By this act they would provoke the wrath of God. 'Listen now, you fools!' he roared. 'Can you not hear the trumpets of war? King Keocher of the Picts, destroyer of nations, raids the coasts, butchering men and women in heaps, casting their children into fetters. His son Talorg burns the herding lands of the Votadini. The Lord brings this wrath upon us, this evil from the north! Yes, the ragged black sails of the Verturians have been seen in the western ocean!'

Unrest rippled through the crowd. Eachna had already been told that the Verturians, the fiercest tribe of all the Picts, had attacked the city six years ago. The citizens had been betrayed, the barbarians had attacked while most of the soldiers were away, and the people who lived in the houses outside the city had been slaughtered or taken into slavery.

'In the storm that is approaching, the fires of your pagan gods will be snuffed out like candles, the idols will be blown apart like dust. Do you soldiers believe that Mithras will rise from his cave on your behalf? Did he or the old spirits of Luguvalium rise up when the savages last came here? Rather, I promise you, the children of Britannia will be scattered across the country, lost and doomed!' By now Ludo was struggling to have his voice heard over the noise of the crowd. 'Therefore listen! The light of God has favoured Rome since the time of your grandfathers. It is his will that we spread his message to every corner of the Earth, even into the dark valleys of the barbarians. I have been among the Novantae and the Selgovae. There are people among them who have listened to the Word and have seen the light. If barbarians are worthy in the sight of God, how much more worthy are you citizens of Rome? How much more eagerly should you throw yourselves on his mercy, and accept his protection?

Discard all superstition, I urge you, and embrace the light of Christ!'

Ludo turned away from the crowd, leaving it seething with unrest.

Eachna had wanted Ludo's guidance, and now she had it. After three months of Christian instruction, how could she have been so foolish as to witness the murder of one of God's children without any thought that it was wrong? How could she have been so cowardly as not to stand against the crowd? She could have spoken out, or tried to – even the attempt would have been an act of faith and love. Had the teachings of Ludo fallen on such barren ground?

Ludo commanded that every Christian in the city do penance, fasting on bread and water for ten days, and praying seven times a day to God; this would include himself, along with his companions on the road and all those who claimed ignorance of the murder. They were a family, and together they must beg God's mercy for their brothers and sisters as for themselves, or together they must face the terror of his judgement.

After this event Eachna could not look at Ludo in the same way. It was not merely his anger, which she could now well understand, but the intensity and suddenness with which it had been unleashed. Where before she had seen the love of Christ behind his smiles and in his happiness when she did well, now she saw the desperation of a servant so fearful that his master's will be done that he was prepared to smile at anything that gave him relief. She became nervous around him, afraid that she would make more mistakes as her lessons became more difficult – and that one day, if she should make a mistake he could not forgive, his fear of God would swing him towards anger, not patience. She noticed, too, that he was becoming less gentle with his congregation. Under the gathering shadow of war he would no longer tolerate minor misunderstandings or compromises as he had done.

One evening Ludo joined Eachna's Latin lesson with Julian, sitting in silence, watching her. Eachna recited psalms from memory, carefully and quietly, pausing every few lines to allow Julian to correct or approve of her pronunciation, trying not to show how nervous Ludo's presence made her.

Near the end of the lesson, as he rose suddenly to leave, Ludo announced, 'There are some who believe that wisdom lies in restraint. They say that the message of the Lord must advance step by step – sometimes even taking a step backwards – if it is ever to conquer the mount of devilishness and ignorance. I thought so myself. But now I see the folly in that. If a vine is diseased at the root, Julian, it cannot be pruned into health, but must be ripped from the ground. So it must be with these people. Ignorance, superstition, wickedness – these faults are in their blood.'

Eachna stared at the floor. She felt Ludo watching her every move.

Once Ludo had left, Julian said quietly, 'What he said about tainted blood – he doesn't mean you, sister. Sometimes, in his passion, our bishop says such things. He's very proud of you. I think you give him hope where he would otherwise despair.'

Eachna placed her pen on the desk. 'I'm afraid his doubts are growing,' she said.

'Not concerning you. One would hardly believe that a few months ago you'd never seen a pen. I've known boys from the noblest of Latin-speaking families who took twice as long to learn their alphabet as you did, and moaned and sulked with every letter.' Julian smiled gently. 'Has our bishop mentioned to you that Bishop Gregory of Londinium will be visiting us after the summer?'

'No.'

'Well, there's no harm in my telling you. Gregory is our bishop's master and has been watching his work with great interest. Bishop Ludo is trying to persuade him to send more men of God among the barbarians of Hibernia and Caledonia, believing that the word of Christ might pacify them where three hundred years of the sword have not. A year ago Gregory might have listened. Now, with what's been happening in the north . . .' Julian shook his head. 'Gregory would never risk his priests if he thought they or their converts would be killed.'

'Our bishop spoke of the Lord sending evil from the north. Will there be war?'

Julian made a tidy pile of the tablets and pens. 'I believe so.'

VIII

What madness drives a man to seek dark death in war
When death with silent foot forever stalks his door?
Below he'll find no fields or vines, but fearsome
Cerberus, gloomy waters of the Styx;
And, with hollow cheeks and cindered hair,
The ghostly host which wanders through his lair.
Albius Tibullus, *The Elegies*

From a distance it looked like any other farmstead in these northern valleys: two stone-built roundhouses with thatched roofs, a grain store, a small paddock containing a fat hog lazing in the dust, all encircled by a low palisade. An old woman standing outside the gates looked up, saw the watching soldiers, and hurriedly ushered a pair of children into the enclosure.

Paul and Victor stood with the rest of the squad on the opposite slope of the valley. Their biarchus, Caratoc, was observing every movement within the compound. No men emerged; there were only the children and the old woman, who now pulled the compound gates shut and waited for the soldiers to approach.

'The menfolk'll be in the next valley with the cattle,' Caratoc said, gripping the hilt of his sword. The men of his squad, all except Paul and Victor, shuffled and grinned in anticipation. No men would mean easy pickings. Paul prayed that this was a good thing, that the Selgovan woman and the children would not try to resist, that this time there would be no violence.

The sky was heavy with clouds that seemed to suck all colour from the sea of heather and scrub. Paul's skin prickled in the humid air. With a short grunt that passed for an order, Caratoc began to lead the squad across the valley towards the farmstead. They hardly looked like Roman soldiers to Paul. Half of his comrades wore simple cloth sandals instead of boots, and caps instead of metal helmets, their tunics were tattered and patched, and a couple lacked even their standard-issue wide leather belts. There was not a single piece of body armour between them. Only Caratoc had a sword; the remainder carried spears. Their broad oval shields were not painted with any unit emblem. The garrison at Trimontium had no emblem. They might have been a band of brigands.

The old woman was waiting defiantly behind the gate of woven branches, her broad shoulders firmly set. She stared at the approaching soldiers with eyes of black steel. The two children, a boy and girl no older than ten, hid behind her. Two hounds had begun to bark ferociously, jamming their noses through the narrow gaps in the palisade.

Caratoc called the squad to a halt in front of the compound. 'His Excellency the Divine Valentinian Augustus demands his tribute,' he shouted over the noise of the dogs.

The woman scoffed. 'Then he can come and get it himself!'

'His Excellency demands your hog! Bring it out to us!'

'Our only lord is King Keocher. Go and argue with my sons, if you have the courage to face men!'

Paul and Victor had seen this scene half a dozen times by now. It was what the soldiers at Trimontium called a reaping patrol. They would visit remote farmsteads deep in Selgovan country, when they knew the men were up on the high summer pastures. They would claim tribute in the name of the emperor even though the country this far from the Wall was not tributary to Rome. These hill folk were herders, and had little enough worth taking; pigs and goats, some bushels of wheat or the occasional scrap of fine metalwork. It was theft and extortion, nothing more. But lately the Selgovae had been resisting, and the commander of Trimontium had ordered the patrols to start burning rebellious farmsteads. It was madness, Paul thought. The Selgovae had never been friendly to Rome, but they had at least been quiet. Now the soldiers of Trimontium would drive them into the arms of the Pictish King Keocher and his son Talorg, and their ever-stronger alliance of northern barbarians.

Biarchus Caratoc cared nothing about such things. He was interested only in the hog. It would be a rich prize to take back to camp, and their prefect would reward him for it, perhaps even let him join the feast when it was roasted. He turned to face his squad. 'You two,' he said, pointing to the closest pair, 'break down the gate and keep watch outside. You other three take care of the hag and the kids. If they won't keep quiet, knock them down. No bloodshed unless they ask for it. You,' he said finally, looking at Paul and Victor. 'Search the huts.'

The semissalis, Caratoc's second-in-command, walked to the gate and kicked it open. Three soldiers rushed in. The first had barely crossed the threshold before the old woman threw herself on him, tugged off his cap and clamped her teeth on his ear. He screamed in pain, ramming the woman against a fence post. His companions tried to pull her loose at the same time as keeping the two children off their own backs. Caratoc pushed through the entrance, but strayed too close to one of the tethered dogs, which leapt up and clamped its jaw on his sword arm. He cried out and hammered the dog's head with the edge of his shield while the semissalis rushed to his aid.

Paul watched the farce in disgust, then nodded to Victor and gathered his nerves. Caratoc had given them the most dangerous job, as usual; it was better to get it over with, do what they had to do, and leave. The two of them went to the nearest roundhouse, stooping to peer into the darkness, seeing nothing. This time it was Paul's turn to go first. These huts had no windows, and one always entered them blind. He kept his shield high and took one step forward. If there were men in the compound, they would be hiding in here, waiting for him to enter and pouncing on him from the shadows.

Paul took four slow steps inside, his heart thumping. Nothing happened. He looked around as his eyes adjusted to the gloom.

Between the beams of its conical roof the air was dense with smoke and shadows, pungent with human smell, but empty. 'It's clear,' he called.

Victor entered, and they began a swift search of the hut while the confusion of screams and barks continued outside. In a pile of clothes Paul saw the glint of a silver brooch. It was a rare and precious find, no doubt a prized possession of some family member. He slipped it into his belt pouch.

The air was suddenly punctured by a shrill squeal. It was fierce, inhuman, gargling, and at once drew Paul and Victor running from the hut.

The old woman and the boy had retreated to stand behind the dogs, who were still tethered to their post, snapping at the soldiers who stood just beyond reach, their shields raised. Another soldier was crouched at the gate, pressing the blood-soaked hem of his cloak to what remained of his ear. Paul could not see Caratoc or the girl. Then they emerged from behind the second roundhouse: Caratoc first, cursing, blood streaming from his mauled forearm, dragging the girl behind him.

'This little bitch has destroyed the emperor's property,' Caratoc growled. His voice shook with pain and anger. 'She cut the hog's throat. That makes her a thief.' He flung the girl at the semissalis, who grabbed hold of her, pinning her arms behind her back. Caratoc spat, then wiped his clean arm across his mouth. From his belt he drew a blood-soaked butchery knife, the one the girl must have used to kill the hog. He tossed it to the ground in front of Paul. 'You,' he said. 'Cut her throat.'

Paul stared at the girl. She was calm, not struggling or making a sound. She stared back at him, her clear, watery eyes shining through a curtain of tangled blonde hair.

'Don't stand there like a damn mute. I gave you an order.' Caratoc took three steps forward and picked up the knife. He pressed the hilt against Paul's chest, breathing heavily. 'Cut her throat.' His breath was unbearably foul.

Hatred twisted Paul's gut. On the very day he and Victor had arrived at Trimontium and been assigned to Caratoc's squad, their new biarchus had stolen their bag of salted pork, the one comfort they had brought with them. When they had objected, Caratoc had dislocated Victor's jaw and walked away without a word, the bag slung over his shoulder. His was not the casual sadism of Braxus; it was sharper, more cunning, almost dispassionate.

Paul looked at the knife, felt the pressure of the hilt in his chest. 'I refuse,' he said.

'All right,' said Caratoc. He walked calmly to the girl and gripped a handful of her hair, pulling her head back to expose her throat. He dug the edge of the knife below one of her ears, and with a swift, clean stroke cut her throat. There was a convulsive gargling, and her eyelids fluttered. The semissalis let go of her shuddering limbs, letting her collapse on the ground.

The old woman screamed a tortured lament into the heavens. The boy wrapped his arms around her and wept.

Caratoc wiped the knife clean on the girl's clothes and thrust it in his belt. 'Fire the huts,' he told the semissalis. Then, to the soldiers guarding the woman and boy, he said, 'Get rid of them. The dogs, too.'

As his men carried out their orders, the biarchus looked finally at Paul. It was like being fixed in the gaze of a wolf. In those eyes Paul saw a grey emptiness that chilled him.

It was dusk by the time they approached the fort of Trimontium. First they saw the hills that gave the place its name: three looming mountains, crouched together like beasts, casting a grave shadow across the river below. It was said that these hills had once been a place of the gods. They were still called the Holy Hills by the Selgovae, whose chiefs had gathered here for their great summer feasts since ancient times. That had changed two years ago, when the Romans had reoccupied the old fort.

Trimontium cowered below the hills, near the bank of the river. From this distance it looked like any other Roman fort, with its regular battlements enclosing a huddle of buildings, the clusters of civilian homes outside the gates.

But as they marched nearer, the truth was revealed. Before Duke Fullobaudes had sent his ragtag cohort of rejects and criminals north to reoccupy it, this place had been abandoned for a hundred years. The enclosures that had once contained bustling villages had long been abandoned to wind and weeds, their stone foundations lying broken and scattered amidst scrub. Beyond this vast civilian graveyard the battlements of the fort were scarcely recognisable as such; in places they had crumbled and been clumsily patched with mortar and rubble. Its towers were for the most part piles of half-collapsed masonry.

They were waved through the northern gatehouse by a bored-looking sentry. Inside were no orderly lines of barrack blocks, but the jagged remnants of walls that had been patched with wooden boards and roped with stretches of canvas. Open midden pits and smouldering fires filled the ash-thick air with stench, drifting between worn clothes drying on lines; piles of mossy debris had been pushed aside to make open patches of ground where miserable-looking men stoked porridge on braziers and threw dice and drank beer; crooked stalls of starved cattle and goats observed Paul and the others with half-maddened stares. Beyond the barracks and pens, in the centre of the fort, rose a large stone building, an old cavalry basilica whose broken tiled roof had been replaced with thatch.

Paul noticed a group of soldiers unloading a large ox-pulled wagon that stood outside the main doors. Good, he thought. The arcanus would still be here.

'I'll see you back at the barracks,' Paul said to Victor.

'Don't take too long, brother.'

As Caratoc led his squad down a side lane to their barracks, Paul slipped quietly away and continued down the main road to the cavalry basilica. He took up position about a dozen yards from the wagon, watching the fort primicerius, a huge Saxon, supervise a group of soldiers as they carried its cargo through the open doors. There were several small kegs and amphorae, sacks of grain, some bundles of cloaks, boots and leather. Last of all came the crates, nailed tightly shut, each needing two men to carry it. Paul saw white letters stamped on the first crate: RM G LEG VI EBOR. It contained swords from the imperial factory at Remis, intended for the Sixth Legion at Eboracum. Another crate followed of mail shirts from Augustodunum.

Since arriving at Trimontium, Paul had learned that Duke Fullobaudes had originally been ordered to reoccupy and rebuild the fort with a detachment from the Sixth. The duke had refused to send any of his experienced men so deep into the wilderness for what he saw as no good reason. Instead, he had raised this cheap, unwanted rabble, and sent them here to be commanded by a disgraced prefect. But some clerk on the duke's staff, colluding with the prefect at Trimontium, had found a way to divert occasional shipments of brand new, good quality imperial weaponry north. It looked legitimate in the records, since the garrison at Trimontium was officially part of the Sixth. But once in the fort, the sealed crates were carried into the basilica, their contents never seen by the ordinary soldiers. Everyone knew that the prefect was selling them to the Picts in return for silver and slaves.

The soldiers of Trimontium loathed the prefect, whom they rarely saw. They despised watching cartloads of good quality imperial weaponry and clothing pass into the hands of barbarians when their own swords were rusting, their shields rotten and their boots falling apart. They hated being given the meanest rations while he sat in his cushioned hall and took his pick of the captive women and girls. The air was poisoned with talk of murder and mutiny. But fear and distrust ran so deep in the ranks that it was nothing more than talk.

This was not why Paul was watching the wagon. When he returned home, perhaps he might have a chance to report the prefect and see him brought to final justice. The idea certainly gave him some satisfaction. First, though, he needed to get home, and that meant finding the arcanus, who always arrived with the supply wagon, pulling a mule laden with baskets of fine pottery. Under the guise of a trader, the arcanus would range north into Pictish country, returning a couple of weeks later and joining the next supply wagon from Trimontium back to the Wall. Paid enough, he could obtain small things for the soldiers: a decent pair of shoes, a new blanket, candles or packets of salt.

Paul had been the first soldier to approach the arcanus and ask him to carry a letter. It was the same arcanus Victor had sent crawling in the gutters outside the posthouse for his solidus, and he had recognised Paul straight away. That had not helped, nor had the fact that the arcanus could sense his desperation.

Almost anything could be exchanged, gambled or stolen in Trimontium. Paul had already given his leather boots to the prefect's secretary in return for pen, ink and tablets, and had suffered two weeks of bloodied and infected feet. The only thing the arcanus cared for was precious metal. Eventually Paul had collected – stolen – two bronze brooches and a small silver ingot from Selgovan farmsteads, and the arcanus had agreed to take his letter to Luguvalium. The next time he had passed through Trimontium, he had assured Paul that he had delivered the letter; bringing back the reply, however, was another matter. Luguvalium was inconvenient, he had said, far from his accustomed route. He would need more payment.

Paul slipped a finger into his pouch to check that the silver brooch was still there. If this did not finally get results, he might have to find a less gentle form of persuasion.

The soldiers had finished unloading the wagon when Paul saw the arcanus walk out of the basilica. He did not know what business the arcanus always had with the prefect, and did not want to know. Only one thing mattered.

Paul walked casually across the lane towards him. The arcanus saw him and smiled, spreading his arms in welcome. 'Good to see you, friend! Let me save you the trouble of asking, and tell you that I've still not managed to go west along the Wall. It's not my usual route, inconvenient. All this talk of war is bad for men like me. It's all hot air, but it hurts business. If only I had some reason . . .'

Paul knew well enough that this arcanus often travelled west as far as Luguvalium, and he did not have the patience to listen to his lies. He reached into his pouch and drew out the silver brooch.

When the arcanus saw the brooch he stopped talking. He bent forward to inspect it. 'Very nice,' he muttered. 'Worth a few nummi, anyway.'

'It's all you'll get,' said Paul. 'Bring me a reply from Luguvalium, and it's yours.'

The arcanus chuckled. 'Expenses, friend! Not to mention insurance. What if I go all the way to Luguvalium and back, only to find you dead, gods forbid?'

Paul slipped the brooch back into the pouch. He gripped two handfuls of the arcanus's cloak and pulled him close. 'You'll get it when I have my reply,' he said quietly. 'Or I'll give you something much worse.'

'Of course, friend! But you must give me time. Another month at least. I head north tomorrow, then south again, and then it's a long road to the west. Give me a month, and you'll have your reply – if there is one.'

Paul released the arcanus, having nothing more to say to him, and went to find Victor. Their barrack block, like everything else at Trimontium, was a crumbling ruin, but at least it was not crowded. The entire garrison numbered fewer than three hundred soldiers, in a fort built for five times that number. Most of the squads were clustered in the blocks surrounding the old basilica. Paul came to the room he shared with Victor, a space intended for an entire squad. It was missing the wall facing the lane, along with its roof, but they had managed to secure a canvas sheet above the surviving three walls to provide some shelter from the rain and sun. This was their refuge from their comrades, with whom they had as little to do as possible. The squad across the lane was the worst. They were Saxons, recruited from one of Rome's client tribes in Germania. Their capacity for drink and violence horrified Paul, despite the four years he had already spent in the army. It was a rare night that did not see a pair of yellow-haired Saxons tumble into the lane in a sudden bout of drunken wrestling. When they were not fighting, they were bellowing at one another in their throaty, barbaric language.

Paul entered the hovel to find Victor stirring a pot of porridge set on a brazier. He looked up when Paul entered. 'Did you find him?'

Paul sat on the pile of straw that passed for his bed. 'Yes. One more month.'

'And then?'

'We'll see.'

'Ha,' Victor laughed. Then he said, 'There's always the other way.'

He meant desertion. The two of them had considered it very soon after arriving and seeing the conditions here. For a while they thought they might brave the dangers of crossing an unknown country infested with hostile tribes. Surely it was possible.

Luckily for them, another soldier had tried it first. As soon as his desertion was discovered, the primicerius had led a group of mounted soldiers and hunting dogs to bring him back. Paul and Victor had expected them to return with the deserter in chains. They had not expected them to return with him slung from a pole like a hunting trophy, naked and bloody, and then to see his body thrown to the pigs.

Since then, they had rarely discussed desertion. But each time Paul spoke to the arcanus, the less he trusted him. He had no guarantee that Julian had even received the letter. Desertion may yet prove to be their last means of escape.

A crash followed by riotous laughter erupted from the Saxon squad across the lane. Victor winced and looked up at Paul. 'D'you know why they always fight so much? It's because even they can't understand a fucking word they say to each other. So they talk with their fists instead.'

'I can believe it.' Paul thought back to Vercovicium, where they had known a group of Saxon veterans who lived in the village and spent most of their time gambling with soldiers in the post-house. Paul had tried to learn their tongue, mainly to improve his chances of beating them at dice, but had never got far with it.

'Trust me,' said Victor. 'I've been studying them for weeks. If you want to say, "Time to get up," it's a kick in the face. "Good night" is a punch on the nose.'

'What about "You're the son of a whore"?'

Victor thought for a moment. 'I think that's when you press a man's face into the mud until he chokes to death. Could be wrong. It's a subtle language. Full of poetry.'

Paul laughed. Victor's jokes were one of the few reminders he had left of their old home. Trimontium was not the army life Paul had known. Drills were rare, inspections rarer, and the only duties seemed to be keeping sentry, clearing out latrine pits and re-digging the old defensive ditches, but none of them was imposed with much conviction by the biarchi. Most of the time was filled with drinking, gaming and grumbling, or sleeping. The more time you slept, one soldier had told them when they first arrived, the less time you spent here before you died.

And soldiers did die. Dysentry was rampant, and Paul and Victor had both been struck down with it during their hellish first week. Too sick to eat or walk far, untreated, ignored by their comrades, they had gone hungry through those days. They had recovered, unlike another new arrival, and had survived so far. By now they were familiar with the lethargy that hung over the fort like a low cloud, the glare of the three mountains pressing spirits ever deeper into the mud. Paul clung to the hope of his letter reaching Julian, but did not think beyond that. He did not allow himself to think of home, and what might await him there.

The chill of night was creeping into their hovel when Caratoc appeared in the lane outside. 'You,' he said, pointing at Paul. 'Come with me.'

Paul had known this would come. He had disobeyed a biarchus in front of his men, and the punishment would be a public lashing with a birch rod. There was no point resisting it. He rose grimly from his straw bed, motioning to Victor to remain where he was, and walked out into the lane.

Caratoc, however, did not intend to punish him in the lane. 'Come with me,' he said, and led Paul into his own quarters, a simple shed at the end of the barrack block. It was dark inside, the only light coming from a single candle set on a barrel. Two large men were waiting on either side of the door, and as Paul entered they moved behind him to close the door and block his escape. They were Caratoc's semissalis and the primicerius, the prefect's right-hand man.

Next to the candle was a folded writing tablet. Caratoc picked it up. 'This is yours?'

Paul's heart sank. He should never have trusted the arcanus.

Caratoc snapped the tablet in two and tossed it aside. 'Attempted desertion,' he said.

The semissalis grabbed Paul's arms from behind. Before he even had a chance to struggle, Caratoc had landed a powerful punch in his gut. Paul doubled up in agony.

'You still want to leave,' Caratoc growled. 'That's why you're weak.'

Paul straightened himself with difficulty, coughing. 'Biarchus . . .' he began.

He said nothing more. He saw Caratoc's fist flying towards his eyes, and he was knocked unconscious for the first time.

IX

Tell yourself: the body is the garment of the soul.
Keep it pure, then, for it is innocent.

Sextus

In the days after her birthday party, with her father away in the city, quietness returned once more to Silvanicum. Amanda had barely settled back into the usual routine of household management, sitting by her mother, daily prayers and quiet evening meals, when Pinta brought her a late birthday present. 'It didn't come with a note,' she said, handing Amanda a finely carved trinket box. 'A man brought it on horseback but wouldn't say who it was from.'

Amanda dismissed Pinta and sat at her desk, placing the casket before her. It was well made, though hardly new; the sort of gift one might find by rummaging around in the back of an old cupboard. She lifted the lid. There was a note inside, a small folded tablet, tied with string and sealed with an anonymous lump of wax. Carefully she broke the seal and opened the letter. She did not recognise the script, inelegant yet carefully written.

When she read the name of the sender she almost laughed.

To Cironia Amanda, daughter of Gaius Cironius Agnus,
Flavius Agrius Rufus sends greetings . . .

She lowered the letter and looked to the window. It was amusing that Patricia's fears should be proven correct with such swiftness, as though she had known that the gift was coming. Still, Amanda reminded herself, one casket did not equal a conspiracy, and such a present was a correct gesture of respect towards one's neighbour, despite coming several days late, and from someone who had so recently offended her father. Perhaps Agrius Rufus was capable of feeling guilt, after all.

She continued reading the letter.

> *It is only after thinking for a long time that I write to you. First I wish to assure you that neither my father nor anyone else knows that I am doing this. I have written this note in my own hand, and the bucellarius who has delivered it to you is sworn to secrecy.*
>
> *I have news of your brother Paul. He is alive. It is urgent that I speak to you.*
>
> *There is an ash tree next to the crossroads at the northern edge of your father's land. I will be there through the third hour after dawn every day for the next five days. Meeting there will attract no suspicion and you will be safe. People will think we are just exchanging pleasantries. It is important that you mention this to nobody, not even your father.*
>
> *I beg your forgiveness for the rustic style of this letter.*
> *Farewell.*

Amanda felt like snapping the letter in two. Even without Patricia's warning, so crude an attempt to ensnare her would have failed. Her father leaves for Corinium and days later this invitation appears: did the son of Agrius Leo, assuming that Agrius Leo himself was not behind the letter, truly think that Amanda would not notice this strange coincidence? Did he imagine that without her father's restraining hand she would rush to meet the first stranger who so much as mentioned Paul's name? It was absurd; it was offensive. And his clumsy, awkward writing showed him for the ill-educated dullard he was.

She put the letter aside and set about brushing her hair. Her father, when he returned, would know what to do about this.

Yet the letter could be hidden from her eyes more easily than from her mind, and it rarely escaped her thoughts over the following days. The reference to Paul had made her heart seize for a moment when she first read it, and she felt the same desperate grip every time those words stubbornly repeated themselves in her head. *I have news of your brother Paul . . . He is alive . . .* What if that much was true? She knew that the letter and its writer could not be trusted, but suppose that Rufus, like all good schemers, had mixed a truth into a broth of lies? Could she not play along and take this opportunity to discover how much he knew, exploiting his trust as he had hoped to exploit hers?

It was a tempting, exciting notion that Amanda mused upon, swinging first one way then the other. As the days passed she slowly came to accept that meeting Rufus would be too dangerous. Better to wait for her father to return.

But on the fourth day after receiving Rufus's letter, Amanda had her mother brought to the orchard garden in her cushioned chair. Amanda sat with her and read poetry, and watched for flickers in her sleeping eyes, but she could not keep her mind on the words. Instead she stared at her mother and thought of how she had saved the family during the Winter of Grief. Had she not shown that moment of boldness, what would have become of the Cironii? Amanda had been an infant at the time, too young to remember, but she knew the story and could picture it perfectly.

It had been thirteen years ago, a time of persecution. The British rebel Magnentius had just been crushed, and the emperor had sent a special inquisition to root out his supporters. The inquisition was headed by a sadistic agent known as Paul the Chain. Paranoia and treachery poisoned the air. Accusations flew across the island as men took the opportunity to settle old scores and be rid of their rivals. Some of these accusations, false as they were, landed on the Cironii. Amanda's grandfather, Cironius Bonus, along with his three adult sons, had been accused of giving property to the usurper. He and his two elder boys were arrested in Corinium. The last son – Amanda's father – was in this very villa when the soldiers came for him.

They were met at the gates not by a squad of his bucellarii, but by his wife. Noble and fearless, Fausta alone had blocked their entry. Amanda had heard half a dozen accounts of what had happened next, but in her favourite account, her mother had said this:

'I am Lady Bodena Fausta, eldest daughter of Marcus Bodenus Faustus. Two years ago, when this island was riven with traitors, my father spoke out against the usurper and paid with his life. By his death he sanctified my family in the name of the emperor. Now you dare accuse my husband of treachery. If you will take him, if you will harm my children, know that you must first take out your swords and strike me down where I stand.'

Fausta was defiant. The soldiers, like everyone, knew that her father had indeed been murdered by the usurper. They hesitated, unwilling to violate her dignity. Then they retreated. Agnus was saved.

But she had not been able to save her husband's father and brothers. All three – Amanda's kindly grandfather Bonus, Uncle Maximus and Uncle Viventiolus – had been dragged to Londinium in chains, tortured by imperial agents and executed. Even thinking of their fate brought bitter tears to Amanda's eyes. Only her father had survived to continue the princely line of the Cironii.

Of course Mother never spoke of what she had done. Amanda had learned of it one time from Father, and had heard different versions from Sulicena and the other house servants, and they had said little enough: it had been an evil time, everyone agreed, and it was better to remember it in silence than talk of it. But Amanda had seen the affection and wonder in Father's eyes when he spoke of Mother's courage.

'But for your mother,' he had told her, 'I would be dead, and you would be nothing. Never forget that.'

And now, with her mother struck down, her father away, and both brothers as good as exiled, who was left to defend the family? Rufus was no secret imperial agent. He was merely an idle, crippled young man. He was not besieging the villa with armed men. There was no risk of torture and death. It would be one single meeting on the edge of the estate, with plenty of witnesses. If Amanda had so much as an ounce of her mother's blood in her, why was she even hesitating?

It was the last chance to act. Amanda knew what she had to do, and shortly afterwards she instructed the stable steward to have her riding horse saddled and ready for the morning.

The following day was cool with an early taste of autumn in the westerly breeze. Pale, insubstantial tufts of cloud glided smoothly across the top of the sky. Amanda was glad for the fair weather, as it made her announcement that she wished to take a ride all the way to the top of the estate more plausible, and Pinta expressed her approval of the idea. 'An early-morning ride will do your spirits a world of good, mistress,' she said cheerfully as she brought out Amanda's riding boots and sun hat.

They reached the crossroads near to the end of the third hour, as Amanda had planned, half hoping that Rufus would have given up and gone home, thereby proving his insincerity. But she saw his litter resting in the meadow next to the road, his litter-bearers and bucellarii lounging nearby. Rufus was already at the cross-roads. He was standing by himself, leaning heavily on a walking stick and staring up at the half-rotted head of a sheep thief, which had been impaled on a tall post. Pinta had spotted him too, for she said urgently, 'Mistress, that's the son of Agrius Leo ahead. Would you like to return home?'

'No,' said Amanda with, she hoped, a convincing degree of nonchalance. 'My father's land reaches up to the crossroads, does it not? I have as much right to be here as he does.'

Now Rufus turned and saw her. He left the road and hobbled across the grass towards the ash tree. He was at the tree by the time Amanda reached the crossroads, clearly waiting for her to go to him; he had chosen a spot just sufficiently removed from the crossroads and from his own servants that low voices would not be overheard, but not so far as to make any encounter seem clandestine. By now Amanda's heart was beating furiously. It was not too late to return home and forget the whole thing, she told herself. That would be the proper thing to do, and nobody would gossip except to say how properly the daughter of Gaius Cironius Agnus had behaved by openly snubbing the pagan interloper at the crossroads.

That much was true, she admitted. But it would be unworthy of her mother's daughter. 'I'm going over to speak to him,' she told Pinta, her mouth suddenly dry.

'Mistress, I don't think your father would approve.'

'I don't like the way he's lingering there like a bandit. Wait here; I shan't be long.'

She rode slowly to Rufus. He had a dark, heavy look in his eyes, a sullen turn to his mouth. Coming closer, she noticed that his tunic and cloak, which had looked fine and expensive from a distance, were in fact a little threadbare, and that his black hair was the thick, wavy sort that did not take kindly to the comb. His skin was pale and unhealthy-looking. This dishevelled appearance, unbecoming the scion of such a powerful family as his, strengthened Amanda's own confidence as he bowed slowly and respectfully to her.

'Say what you have to say,' she announced.

'I'm pleased you decided to meet me at last.'

'I will not stay long,' she said impatiently. 'I happened to be surveying this corner of the estate today anyway, so you needn't presume that I've made any special effort because of you. If you have news of my brother, as you so arrogantly and disrespectfully claim, I insist that you inform me at once, in order that I can relate it to my father, the senator, when he returns – an act that your honour should have led you to in the first place.'

That should do it, Amanda thought, gratified by the effect that her words were having on Rufus, who now cast his gaze downward in an expression that might have been shame. He took a step forwards, but froze, wincing and letting out a sharp gasp of pain. When the pain subsided he looked up at Amanda. 'I've seen your brother,' he said.

'Where?'

'Near Viriconium,' he added, somewhat reluctantly. 'It was four years ago.'

'Four years ago!' Amanda exclaimed. Is *this* all he had to tell her?

'He'd been caught by a press gang on an imperial estate,

pretending to be a commoner. I didn't even recognise him at first, but later I saw a ring they confiscated from him – your family's seal. That's when I knew who he was.'

'And you said nothing.'

Rufus lowered his face again. He let out a long, slow breath, a regretful and guilty sound.

'I don't believe you,' Amanda continued. 'Do you at least have his ring as proof?'

'I gave it to my father,' he said. 'My father has friends in the army. He arranged for Paul to be sent north, to a quiet and safe place on the Wall called Vercovicium.'

'Well, that was kind of him. Of course, an even kinder gesture would have been to tell my father that Paul was still alive and well.'

Now Rufus met her eyes steadily, and said: 'He did.'

For a moment Amanda was lost for words. It was impossible that her father knew Paul was still alive. 'I don't understand,' she said, her voice faltering. When Rufus did not reply, she gathered her wits and said in a stronger voice, 'I don't understand how you can make such an absurd comment and expect me to believe it.' Over her shoulder Amanda saw Pinta waiting obediently and nervously at the crossroads.

'It's the truth.'

'Oh, spare me! I've been warned about your scheming. I know all about that poor widow in Treveris, what you did to her.'

'Who told you about that?' he demanded, anger edging into his voice.

'Did you think the daughter of Cironius Agnus was a simpleton? You've said what you had to say and proven that you're a liar; my father will hear all about how you tried to ensnare me, and I'm sure it won't sit well with those decurions of Corinium who still have a sense of honour. Goodbye, Flavius Agrius Rufus.'

Amanda pulled sharply on her reins and her horse twisted to leave. Rufus lunged forwards and grabbed onto the bridle. A yell of alarm came from Pinta, but Amanda called for her to be calm, and turned to Rufus. 'Release me before I whip you to the ground,' she hissed.

Rufus let go of the bridle. 'Listen to me. Paul's disappeared from Vercovicium. My father has told me to send men to track him down. I intend to do so, my lady, but only to bring him home safely to you.'

Amanda hardly paused long enough to listen. She urged her mount with a swift, dignified trot back to the crossroads, where Pinta awaited her anxiously. 'Did he hurt you, mistress?'

'Of course not,' snapped Amanda. 'He's nothing, just a rude little toad. You were right, I shouldn't have wasted my time on him.'

Not wanting it to seem as though the encounter at the crossroads had been the sole purpose of the excursion, Amanda took Pinta on a circuitous route around the northern half of the estate. They did not return to the villa until shortly before noon, by which time they were both thirsty and saddle sore and Amanda was still in a tempestuous mood.

She had been able to dismiss Rufus's letter as a bundle of lies with perhaps one simple truth, but now, having met him properly, she did not know where the deceit ended and the truth began. She believed, or she wanted to believe, that Paul had escaped the bandits and was still alive, and she was even prepared to accept that Rufus had seen him four years ago. But was it true that Rufus had handed the family ring over to Agrius Leo, who had arranged to have Paul sent to the Wall? That much was also plausible. But why would he do it? If he was for some reason acting in Paul's interests, why not have him exposed, discharged from the army and returned to his family? Or, if not, why not simply have him murdered? And what was Rufus hoping to gain by telling her all this?

This, Amanda noted, was where Rufus's fiction unravelled – happily, before it got to the part where he claimed that her father knew of Paul's whereabouts. For that was one lie she could not, would not swallow. Lucas, the last remaining son, seemed content to squander the family name and fortune. Under such circumstances, it was unthinkable that her father would not do everything he could to bring Paul home. Anyway, a senator's son was not allowed to serve as a common soldier, and so if their father knew that Paul was in the ranks, he would be legally obliged to report it and have him discharged. Paul might lose part of his legacy in fines for trying to shirk his senatorial inheritance, but even that would be preferable to having the entire estate turn to ruin in the hands of Lucas.

The only moment in their meeting that brought a secret smile to Amanda's lips was when she remembered how Rufus had grabbed the bridle and she had threatened to set about him with her horsewhip. How proud her mother would have been to see it. This thought brought some freshness and energy to her stride as she walked from the stables to the upper courtyard. There she heard a quiet voice through the rustling of the trees, and found her mother and Sulicena in one corner of the garden. Fausta was dozing in a wicker chair in the shade of an apple tree, while Sulicena recited poetry from a small codex. Hanging from a branch of the tree was a birdcage housing a nightingale.

Amanda dismissed Pinta and Sulicena, and once alone she touched the back of her hand gently to her mother's forehead. She was glad to find the skin cool and dry. She sat by her mother's side and took up the codex, and when she saw it was one of her favourite fables, she decided to recite it from the beginning.

Diana, goddess of the hunt, was bathing in a forest pool, attended to by her nymphs, when mortal Actaeon, seeking refreshment after the day's hunt, stumbled across her. The nymphs clambered to cover the chaste goddess's naked body; Diana was outraged, and struck Actaeon with a curse: she caused antlers to sprout from his head, stretched his neck, turned his hands and feet to hooves and made fur burst over his body. Actaeon, terrified, fled into the trees, bounding across logs and streams in the form of a stag, until he was hunted down by his own pack of hounds and torn apart while his hunting companions looked on, laughing and calling their lost friend's name into the depths of the forest. *And not until his life through countless wounds was ended was the wrath, they say, of the huntress Diana sated . . .*

Amanda found herself smiling at these closing lines, her heartbeat quickened by the rushing chase through the forest and Actaeon's terrible death. A moment later she realised that she had unwittingly given Actaeon the face of Agrius Rufus, and Diana her own, and the scene and pursuit had taken place between the spring-fed pool at the back of this very villa and the forest down by the river. She had even pictured Actaeon's hunting pack as her father's. This realisation thrilled and troubled her, and her breathing came short as the images ran again through her mind in new detail: Rufus's eyes widening at seeing Amanda's glistening, pale body in the secluded glade; the high screech of her curse; his desperately straining flanks pierced by the jaws of the first hound; his tumble and gradual evisceration while he threw his head from side to side and screamed his name in the helpless wail of a fallen stag . . .

A groan from her mother recalled Amanda to herself, and she closed the codex with a sudden flush of guilt. Those were not proper thoughts for a Christian girl. She took a deep, steady breath to fortify herself against their return. Perhaps this was the danger of pagan literature to which her father sometimes alluded, but which she had never truly understood: they were not just amusing old stories, but fierce and dangerous to an unguarded mind such as hers. She looked at her mother sleeping beside her, and the lingering images caused her such deep shame that she called Pinta to fetch her book of psalms, and after reading them for half an hour felt almost worthy to be called her parents' daughter once again.

'The damn arrogance!'

Amanda shuddered at her father's outburst. He was pacing furiously to and fro between his desk and the shelves of his library. After his breathing had subsided, he stopped at the desk, picked up Rufus's letter, read through it for the third time and once again slammed it down. He rested his balled fists on either side of the letter. 'By Christ,' he growled, 'the next time I see him or his father in the city they'll need every friend they can buy to keep me from throttling the pair of them.'

'I know I did wrong, Father,' Amanda said.

'Oh, Amanda,' he replied, his face distraught, and beckoned to her. He took her in his arms. 'Amanda, it's my fault; you have the same spirit as your mother. I knew I should have forbidden you to speak to that scoundrel, but I didn't even want to mention his name. I've tried so hard to keep you out of the rotten world of politics! But this latest outrage has pushed things too far. My daughter, my daughter!'

Amanda had already told him several times that she had never been in any real danger, that she had met Rufus very briefly in a public place where he could do her no harm and there would be no room for scandal, but he had waved these assurances aside. For him there was only the central fact that the son of Agrius Leo had attempted to hoodwink, even seduce, his daughter the minute he had left the estate, and whether he blamed Rufus or himself more for this, Amanda could not tell.

'In God's name, I would give my right arm to have Paul back home, Amanda. You know I would. If I knew where he was I'd do everything I could to bring him home. But I don't, Amanda, I simply don't.' The emotion was so thick in his voice that it smothered any more words. He grasped Amanda's head in both hands and kissed her brow, his warm tears running into her hair.

'Then, Father,' she said, fighting to keep the words steady, 'if there was a strand of truth in there, the bait to draw me in, perhaps Paul did escape the bandits and end up in the army. Maybe you could write a letter to someone who could help you find out. Perhaps someone in Londinium? Or the church, Father – Julian is on the Wall! I write to him often already; I could ask him if he knew anything. He could even go to the fort Agrius Rufus mentioned. There would be no harm in trying.'

'That's true,' said Agnus. He half released Amanda from his embrace in order to look closely into her face. 'If only your brothers had a fraction of your good sense.'

Amanda could not help but give a melancholy laugh at that. 'Then I'll write to Julian,' she said. 'He might be able to ask the bishop to help him. I'm sure they could find out easily enough if Paul was in one single fort. And even if he has been sent north of the Wall, you can write to have him brought back.'

'Write the letter, Amanda. But impress upon Julian that the matter must be kept completely confidential – including, I'm sorry to say, from his parents and sister, and if possible from his bishop. It must remain entirely between you and him.'

'Of course, Father. This shall be our own little intrigue.'

Agnus smiled and pulled her close. 'Don't get a taste for politics quite yet, daughter,' he said. 'It's an ugly world, and not one for a good Christian girl.'

'I promise, Father.'

'In the meantime, it seems to me that you'd be best away from here for a short while. I need to go back to Londinium, and I'll be taking Lucas with me. I don't want you left here alone.'

'Where would I go, Father? The household doesn't move to Corinium for more than a month.'

Agnus inspected the brass faces of his water clocks thoughtfully. The room was silent but for their steady dripping. 'It might be best,' he said at last, 'if you go to stay at White Hen House until winter.'

White Hen House was the home of Julian and Patricia's family. Amanda's first dreary thought was that she would have to endure the company of Patricia for so many weeks. This was quickly and guiltily buried by the realisation that she would be leaving her mother.

Agnus anticipated the more noble of her worries. 'Your mother can go with you,' he said. 'We couldn't possibly leave her alone here. You can take the servants you need; the journey won't be too much for her. I'll be busy in Londinium and elsewhere, but I'll try to visit. You haven't been to stay with Uncle Pertinax and Aunt Tertia for at least two years, and of course there's your cousin Patricia to keep you company. The weeks until winter will fly by. And who knows, perhaps the change in air will do your mother some good.'

So it was decided, and Amanda did not resist. She had no desire to stay in Silvanicum now that Agrius Rufus had cast his dangerous shadow upon it, and the notion that fresh scenery and company might stimulate her mother made the plan even more attractive. As for Patricia – Amanda tried to imagine that they might warm to one another given enough time, though this was something of a desperate hope. Patricia's parents had never inspired much affection in her either, despite the bond of blood.

Three days later everything had been arranged. The small group of servants was assembled, the carriage had been hauled out from its shed and scrubbed clean, its interior packed with cushions for the comfort of Fausta, who was carefully carried down to the lower courtyard in a sedan chair. Once she had been safely installed within the carriage, Agnus embraced Amanda tightly, and asked, his voice soft with affection, that she give his love to their relations. Amanda promised that she would.

Now that it had come to it, the thought of being away from Silvanicum before the end of the summer was causing her pangs of sorrow – she would miss her father, the servants, the rustling of the combe, the sloping meadows and the stream below – she would miss even Lucas, who had risen especially early to see her off. She climbed into the awaiting carriage with Pinta, who carried the protesting cat in her arms.

It would only be a few weeks, Amanda told herself, and forced a smile as she waved goodbye to her father. The carriage creaked with its escort through the gatehouse and onto the riverside path, dull brown beneath a grey sky. She had already written to Julian, and hopefully his reply would arrive before the winter. Until then she could only pray that Paul was safe. With faith and devotion, all would be well in the end.

But her final regret, a feeling that rose within her, sudden and unexpected, was that she would not see Agrius Rufus again.

X

Through one man sin entered into the world, and through sin
came death; and thus death comes to every man,
for every man is a sinner.

Romans 5:12

'Perhaps I can come with you,' said Eachna.

'No,' said Julian. He did not raise his eyes from the letter he was writing.

Eachna bent her neck and finished scratching the Lord's Prayer into her tablet. *Ne nos inducas in tentationem, sed libera nos a malo* . . . She wrote a tidy *Amen* at the bottom of the tablet and looked over her work. Her handwriting was improving, though she suspected that her distracted mind had let one or two spelling mistakes creep in.

'I've been away before,' continued Julian, folding his completed letter. There was a hint of irritation in his voice. 'This time won't be any different.'

'But Bishop Gregory will be here in a fortnight. What if you're not back?'

'If the bishop has any doubts that God brought you here, he won't once he sees your command of Latin.'

This was a reassurance that Julian frequently gave her, but it did little to ease Eachna's worries. She had no idea how quickly one was supposed to pick up another language. She had learned to decipher the Pictish growls of her old master within the first few weeks of her slavery, and she had mastered the British dialect of Luguvalium just as rapidly. Had God helped her with those pagan languages too? Or was she a dunce for stumbling so frequently over Latin letter shapes, the pen clutched awkwardly between her fingers?

Over the last week Julian had become ever more distracted and increasingly short with her. Whenever she had asked what the matter was, he had either given no answer or said that it was something he could not discuss. It had started when he had received a letter from the south, she knew that much. She had watched him open it, and had seen the concern in his eyes as he read it, before he had risen suddenly and walked out of the room.

Since then he would say only that he was going along the Wall, alone. She was hurt that he no longer felt able to confide in her. It did not help that talk of omens and judgement from Heaven had only deepened since the birth of the monstrous child over a month before. Only last week traders had brought word that a rain of blood had fallen upon Londinium. Ludo had refused to believe them until he received a letter with the same story from Bishop Gregory, who had witnessed the terrible event himself along with his entire congregation.

Eachna wished she could go with Julian, both to avoid the terrible judgement of the Bishop of Londinium and to be of some comfort and use; but she knew that this was impossible. Instead she bade him a sad goodbye when he left, and awaited the arrival of Gregory with trepidation.

Ludo carefully explained to her the purpose of Bishop Gregory's visit. He was the most senior of Britannia's bishops and Ludo's immediate master, and each year he made a round of his subordinate bishoprics to look into the spiritual health of the Christian communities. He was a kind of high priest, Eachna concluded, higher even than Ludo, and the idea of meeting such an exalted figure while still unbaptised was her greatest source of worry. She longed for the holy water of Christ to be poured over her, to cleanse her pagan spirit and her soiled flesh, but Ludo insisted that this rite could only be performed on adults at Easter, and that she must wait until next year like all the other catechumens.

Her mind was crowded with the meticulous protocol Ludo had commanded her to learn for her audience with Bishop Gregory. When she saw him surrounded by his priests and deacons she was to greet him alone by bowing; he would extend his ring finger, but she was only to lower her head, not kiss it, for she was not yet worthy to touch him; she was to speak first: *o reverentissime domine Gregorie, episcope Londiniensis, indignissima serva Eachna sum* – most reverend Lord Gregory, Bishop of Londinium, I am your most humble servant Eachna, as she repeated to herself hundreds of times.

Two weeks went by, the afternoon of Gregory's arrival came and Julian had still not returned. Eachna had spent the morning in her room rehearsing her movements and words, trying to distract herself from worrying about her tutor. She had already bathed and was wearing a coarse brown tunic that symbolised the darkness of her unsaved soul, its sleeves stitched up to the elbows in order to make clear that she was also a cripple, and deserving of pity. Ludo had promised her a fine, long-sleeved tunic of white linen once she was baptised.

Eachna waited in her room and listened to the cheers and psalms of the crowd outside as they welcomed Bishop Gregory. When a deacon finally came and requested that she follow him to the presence of the bishop, Eachna thought her heart was going to thump out of her chest. She followed the deacon from the compound down the street and into the church precinct, almost halting when she saw that they were to enter the church basilica itself. She had never been further inside than the porch, the flagstones of which could be touched by her profane feet without being polluted. The sacred space of the nave was another matter, but it was here that the deacon was leading her, and she shrank in fear as they passed through the heavy, smoke-laden curtains that separated it from the porch.

There, at the far end of the nave, just in front of the altar itself, sat Bishop Gregory. Eachna allowed herself only the briefest glance before lowering her eyes. There was a crowd standing behind and on either side of him, all wearing the long gowns of churchmen. Ludo was to Gregory's left.

She halted, unsure whether or not to approach. The deacon took her arm and gently pulled her forwards. She went with him, treading softly as though the weight of her pagan soul would crack the floor and plunge her into the underworld. She stopped two yards in front of Gregory, who had raised his ringed hand. She bowed deeply and spoke her greeting; if she made a mistake, her thoughts were too tumultuous to notice it.

She waited for a response. 'Look up at us, daughter,' the bishop said in Latin.

She did so, only for a moment. She had never seen so old a man. He smiled at her benevolently, then looked at Ludo. 'We see she understands us,' he said in his wheezing, rasping voice. Ludo nodded but was silent. 'Good daughter,' Gregory continued slowly, 'your master, the most reverend Bishop Ludo, tells us you are from Hibernia. We have a question we hope you can answer. The ancient authors assert that the pasture in your country is so lush that cows will eat it until they burst if left unwatched. Is that the case?'

'I have never seen it happen, my lord.'

'Then perhaps it is a myth after all. And what about the curious claim of some sailors that parts of your island are all but overrun by werewolves, and that some of these beasts even become kings?'

'We have werewolves, my lord,' she said, 'but I have never seen one, and I have never heard of a werewolf king.'

'No bursting cattle; no werewolf kings. This is a lesson not to believe the ravings of old seadogs, can we not conclude?'

There was a murmur of humour from the clerics. Eachna dared to meet Gregory's eyes. She said, 'In my country we say that sailors spend so long listening to the whispering of the ocean that they start to talk like it; and the ocean is known to be a terrible deceiver.' Her translation of the poetic saying, Eachna thought, was rather awkward, and she was not sure that Gregory had understood her meaning.

But he clapped his hands and exclaimed, 'My word! A real Hibernian proverb. We must remember it! And so beautifully rendered. Your lord bishop had mentioned that you had achieved some competence in Latin, but now we believe he was understating the case.'

Gregory was no longer moderating his speech, and had even lapsed into his natural dialect of Latin. Was he trying to test her, Eachna thought? 'I have a fine teacher, my lord,' she said.

'So I see. And how long have you been in our country, daughter?'

'Since April, my lord.'

'And do many of your people speak Latin?'

'I had never heard it before Bishop Ludo brought me here, my lord.'

He looked incredulous. 'You've learned to speak our tongue like this in . . . what, not even six months?'

'I have much trouble writing it, my lord.'

Gregory creased his brow. He looked at Ludo. 'She's learning to read and write, too?'

'Quite masterfully, and with remarkable speed, my lord,' said Ludo, bowing respectfully.

'Astonishing,' Gregory mumbled, stroking the thin wisps of growth on his chin. 'Perhaps it is as you say. God not only whistled for her to come to you, but is teaching her tricks, too.'

Those words made Eachna flush. She was sure she had not misheard. Was the bishop comparing her to a dog?

'God's will does appear to be at work here, my lord,' said Ludo.

'Perhaps. We hope that he also directs her hands – her hand, I should say – to do his good work. Her skill in Latin is impressive, I grant you, but we shall see if you can train her to think like a Christian as well as talk like one.'

Eachna felt her skin prickle with humiliation. Bishop Gregory seemed to regard her as a beast who behaved only by training and instinct. Despite the awful sacrality of the audience she could not stay silent. 'My lord,' she ventured, 'surely an animal that must be trained to follow Christ cannot be thought good because of it.'

Ludo chuckled, a little too loudly, and began to speak, but Gregory silenced him with a raised hand. 'Go on, daughter of Hibernia,' he said.

She had not prepared an argument in her head, much less considered how to phrase it in a foreign tongue, and had no idea what to say. But the bishop stared at her, the clerics around him stared, Ludo stared, and the intensity of their attention drew words from her mouth. 'You said, my lord, that Christ whistled to me like a man might whistle to a dog. I believe he did, though it took me a long time to understand his call. But when I did, I chose to follow. A dog doesn't think. It obeys its master without thinking. I remember the very moment when I made the choice. That is all I mean.'

'Wouldn't you call an obedient dog a good dog?'

'Yes, my lord,' she said. 'But that is a dog.'

'And you are a barbarian and a slave,' said Gregory. 'Without the grace of God no man, not even the wisest, can perform good deeds. Your people, stuck on their wet little island, lack the natural reason of civilised races. What hope will you have of attaining Heaven if you are not trained to it like slaves and dogs, as you have been? How else do you expect to expunge your corrupt souls of the sin of Adam?'

'I know the story of Adam,' she said, not sure of where her speech would take her, 'and I feel sorry for what he did, because he angered God and was expelled from paradise for it. But why would God allow that to happen, so that everyone was born cursed? Could it not be that Adam disobeyed God as an example to us, a bad example, and Christ came to Judea and preached peace and died on the cross as a good example, and each of us is given the reason to follow whichever example we choose?'

'You mean, daughter of Hibernia, that baptism is useless?'

'No, my lord,' she said hurriedly. 'Baptism is rebirth in Christ.

It allows God to work his grace more easily within us, to help us along the right path, and the priests and bishops can help us too.'

Gregory snorted. 'So you don't mean to deny the authority of the church. Well, that's something. I do wonder, though, why the barbarians, if their reason is as bounteous as the verdant meadows of Hibernia, as you seem to claim, have not worked all this out and do not already have an empire and church of their own.'

'My people are ignorant of Christ, my lord, only because they live at the edge of the world, and we fear the power of the druids. But we are not an island of fools, nor of dogs. I was not born a slave, and I am crippled only because I refused to act like one.' She thrust her handless arm forwards. 'My lord, this is the badge of my reason and free will.'

There was a long, still silence, during which Gregory eyed her and her stump with an expression of bemusement. Then he said to himself, quietly: 'Not even six months . . .'

The audience ended abruptly after that. Eachna was led by the deacon back to her room. She was consumed by trying to recall what exactly she had said. Very little came back to her. She had spoken her mind, that much she knew, but could not quite remember which answers had followed which questions, how Gregory had reacted to them, or, most worryingly of all, what Ludo would now think of her. She should have stayed silent; she had no right challenging a bishop on the nature of a religion that was still so strange to her. But how could she have said nothing when he compared her to a dumb beast?

In any case, it was done. She could only wait and see. She missed Julian sorely. *He* would have agreed with everything she said, she was sure. He would know how to reassure her now.

The bishop left with his retinue three days later, and there was still no word or sight of Julian. Eachna began to worry. She was soon given an even more immediate cause for unhappiness when Ludo summoned her to his chambers the day after Gregory's departure. She went to him nervously, afraid that he had received bad news about Julian. It was late September, and he had been gone almost three weeks. He would have sent a message by now if all were well.

But Ludo did not intend to talk about Julian. As soon as Eachna entered his room, he said, 'His reverence has determined that your lessons should come to an end.'

Eachna, her thoughts still full of her teacher, was too confused to respond, and stared at Ludo dumbly.

'I'm sorry, my daughter. But I cannot go against his command.'

'Did I anger him?'

Ludo rubbed one hand over his bald head. 'Anger, no, of course not. His judgement in these matters is guided by the will of God, Eachna; you should know that and accept it.'

'But I want to know why.'

'*Why* is not important for you. You're also to move to the slave dormitory at once.'

Being denied her lessons was bad enough, but being sent to sleep with the other slaves could only mean she was being punished. Her throat was painfully tight as she asked, 'What did I do?'

Ludo sighed deeply. His face was lifeless and tired, as though he sorely needed sleep. 'His reverence . . . quite simply, the situation in the north is far too unsettled for a mission at the moment, and he has advised greater caution on my part.'

This was unthinkable. How would she bear it? Even if her legal status would not change, under the drudgery and anonymity of domestic slavery she might as well be back in the Pictish hills. There she had yearned and fought every day for her freedom, had suffered for it, had won it; here, she had taken on the challenge of a new life and a new language, where every mistake she made with her pen or her tongue was the same as tripping on the roots of the northern forests: she had picked herself up, hardened her brow with new determination and pushed on, first chasing the light of freedom, then the light of Christ, and now . . . without her lessons she would have nothing to fight for. This loss of purpose horrified her more than anything. It was her fuel; without it she would smoulder to nothing. 'I beg you, my lord,' she said, 'let me have a writing pen and tablets, if nothing else.'

'Bishop Gregory was clear,' he said. Then he added, this time in British, 'Leave, sister, and take your things to the slave quarters.'

XI

They are few in number, fearful in their ignorance; this sky,
the forests, the waters: they look about themselves and
everything is foreign. The gods have handed them over to us,
trapped and defeated.

Tacitus, *Agricola*

By late September Paul had been beaten almost daily for a
month. After the third or fourth time, as always in the evening
when he was deeply drunk, Caratoc was joined by two other
biarchi. Paul did not know why he had attracted such hatred
from them. They often laughed as they kicked him across the
floor, but their laughter was so ruptured and tearful that at times
Paul could not tell it apart from crying. Other times they set
upon him with almost sober dedication, telling him that they had
to toughen him up for his own good, for otherwise he would be
driven mad or to suicide as the three peaks sucked out his soul
bit by bit. Better to have it beaten out, they said, to become as
cold and hard as the rocks of the north. Better that than to die.

Eventually Paul had forgotten what it was like to be without
the constant throbbing pain of bruised flesh and broken bones.
He stopped talking even to Victor, at first because speaking was
painful through swollen gums, and finally because there was
nothing to say.

During one especially drawn-out session, Paul lost track of
time until it became too dark for Caratoc and the rest to see
what they were doing, when even the sharp gleam of moonlight
through the cracks of the decayed roof was not enough for eyes

and hands as unsteady as theirs. Eventually, once their attempts to punish the shadowy form of Paul was causing them more irritation than amusement, they grew bored and threw him out into the lane behind the barracks.

Movement caused agony, so Paul stayed motionless. When it began to rain, he lay in the dark and let the rain wash the blood from his broken nose and teeth.

Pain enshrouded him. Fate had never intended to lead him back to Silvanicum, to truth and life, but to death: his own death, and the death of others.

There was movement in the shadows, which Paul felt more than saw: a shape coming towards him, standing over him, watching him. It bent forwards and its face came into the moonlight. It was the girl from the farmstead, the one whose throat Caratoc had slit. She looked at Paul curiously, her eyes glittering silver, her chaotic hair bound by a rag that dripped blood. It was not the first time he had seen her shade, the part of her that had followed him to Trimontium, had joined its shadows and slipped into this crack between worlds. How many more had gone the same way? Slowly, though his neck had become as stiff as iron, Paul looked around and sensed others creeping out of the shadows and crowding around, all the hundreds of souls who dwelled beyond sight in the ruins. They came closer, bunching together until they were pressing against his aching torso and limbs, smothering the pain. He could no longer feel his body, and welcomed the void.

He was about to pass into the blackness when a new voice came, clear and light above the murmuring of the spirits. 'Paul?'

He strained to see the source of the voice, tried to push away the bodies burying him, his hands pushing through them as though they were steam. He glimpsed a slight form standing a few yards distant – it was a girl, no older than the girl in the farmstead but wearing a long white dress that shone through the wall of rain, with her dark hair tied neatly behind her head.

'Amanda,' Paul croaked, reaching out uselessly. He wanted to cry for her to get away from this place, to run out of the fort, over the hills of the north, through the Wall and across the province to Silvanicum, not to stop until she was safely back home.

She watched him with affection in her eyes. 'A long exile awaits you, Paul, and a wide sea to be crossed.' She paused, and smiled. 'But you will come to the lands of the west, where Colona flows amidst fruitful meadows, and a gentle flock of humanity.'

'Home?'

'Home.' Her smile faded. Worry filled her eyes. 'Don't go into the hills, Paul. You must not go into the hills.'

There was a sudden jolt: Paul's shoulders lifted from the ground, his legs staggered into place to support his weight. It was Victor, his arm wrapped around him, raising him from the mud. 'Let's get you somewhere dry, comrade,' he said.

Paul looked around, desperate to find Amanda, but she had vanished along with the ghosts. The lane was deserted but for Paul, Victor and the rain. Paul called out his sister's name hopelessly.

'They truly fucked you up this time,' muttered Victor as he helped his friend back to their room.

Paul was awoken by a kick in the stomach. Caratoc was working through the barracks, waking the soldiers who were to go on the patrol that day. Across the lane, the biarchus of the neighbouring squad was rousing his own men. This was to be a patrol in force: Caratoc's squad and the Saxon squad sent on a three-day march to visit a group of uncooperative farmsteads. Their only objective was to cause terror.

Paul opened his eyes but remained lying on his back. The air was clear and bright, already busy with the sounds of the waking garrison. He remembered the vision of Amanda from the previous night, recalled the fretful crease in her brow, the love in her warm eyes. She had looked the age he last remembered her, had even been wearing the same clothes. She had spoken a prophecy of exile and return.

If he went into the hills today he would die. The fear that

seized him was like nothing he had felt before. It was a vice that held him fast and overpowered every atom of his being.

The shadow of Caratoc loomed over him. 'Get up, soldier.'

Paul lay on the ground, his hands trembling.

The biarchus of the Saxon squad appeared next to Caratoc. He looked down at Paul and laughed. 'Looks like you broke him the wrong way.'

Caratoc grunted and left. Paul's first thought was: *Thank God*. He lay in darkness, surrounded by the bustling noises of two squads rushing to ready themselves.

Caratoc was calling his men to assemble by the northern gate when Paul felt a hand shake him. 'Rest and get your strength back, brother,' Victor said. 'When I'm back, we'll find a way to get out of here.' A final, furious call to assembly came from a distant Caratoc.

Paul tried to smile but could not. Victor jumped to his feet, grabbed his shield and raced out of the barracks.

The fourth morning came, and still the two squads had not returned.

Their disappearance could only mean an ambush, and the garrison was in uproar. A group of biarchi had already demanded of their superiors that they head out to burn the Selgovan country from one end to the other. The prefect was refusing to take any action.

Paul had not slept the previous night, nor could he bring himself to eat without vomiting. It was as though half of his being was now lost out in the hills. He hated himself for the cowardice that had kept him curled up on his straw.

Around noon Paul, the only remaining member of his squad, noticed that the other soldiers from his century were congregating at the prefect's hall. He got up and joined them. Outside the hall was the supply wagon that had arrived that morning from the south. Pushing to the front of the crowd, Paul saw that the wagon contained crates of mail, helmets, shields, spears. The four drivers were standing in front of their vehicle, swords drawn, as angry soldiers surrounded them.

Centenarius Corfidius was confronting the drivers. He was a dark-skinned veteran from North Africa, the commander of Paul's century. He was also one of the few soldiers in the fort who still preserved a trace of military honour. 'You'll let your Roman brothers die out there in the hills?' he was shouting. 'Open the crates!'

The drivers were loyal to the prefect, who rewarded them well for their part in his treasonable racket, and they were not about to back down. At that moment the prefect himself emerged from the hall, followed by the primicerius and campidoctor, his two senior subordinates. By now the prefect hardly looked like an officer, or even like a Roman. He still wore the boots and the belt of his old uniform, but his pale tunic was of expensive cotton, though soiled, and over his shoulders was draped a heavy bear-skin cloak. He was fat, slovenly in his movements, full-bearded. He stood between the wagon and Corfidius, mere feet from Paul. 'Get back to barracks!'

Corfidius stood his ground. 'Prefect, two of my squads are missing. Let us take these weapons and find them!'

'These weapons are not yours! Cover them up, cover them up!' The prefect waved frantically at the drivers, who pulled the canvas sheeting back over their cargo. 'This is mutiny! Any man who doesn't return to duties at once will be flogged!'

The massive primicerius stepped forward, brandishing his birch cane and casting hard eyes over the crowd of soldiers. 'Obey your commander, dogs,' he growled.

Corfidius hesitated and looked away, swearing under his breath. Paul could feel the will of the soldiers give way. The ambush had awakened an old sense of comradeship in them, but their spirits were too weak, their morale too drained, to sustain it in the face of the prefect. He ruled their souls as he ruled their bodies. He was the only thing stopping them, and stopping Paul from finding Victor.

He hardly needed to think it through. Slipping his hand discreetly to his belt, Paul grasped the handle of his long dagger. In a few swift paces he had reached the prefect and had drawn the dagger; a moment later he had grabbed hold of his fur cloak and had thrust the blade up through his ribs and into the softness of his heart.

Nobody had time to react. They merely stood and watched as Paul withdrew his dagger and let the convulsing body of their commander collapse onto the ground.

Even after that, nobody moved. The prefect had lain still for what seemed like an age before Corfidius said, 'Biarchi, kit your men out, collect rations. I want six squads ready to patrol in force within the hour.' The primicerius and the wagon drivers stood aside. The soldiers clambered onto the wagon and began tearing open the crates.

Paul was not thanked or congratulated for his action. The other soldiers watched him warily as they unloaded the armour and weapons and distributed them amongst the squads. He asked Corfidius if he could join the patrol, and the centenarius agreed.

Fifty soldiers, all the remaining able-bodied men of Corfidius's century, left Trimontium that afternoon. The column headed up the valley and past the farmstead Paul had visited before. Like many of the settlements along the valley, it was now a burned-out ruin. They camped on a patch of open ground beside the river, and the next day marched deeper into barbarian country, following the supposed course of the first patrol. Still they saw not a single person. It was as though the farmers of these valleys had become ghosts. They entered a forest and picked their way along the overgrown path, and the air became cold and still. The autumn sky was filtered into patches and dapples of sharp light, and as his eyes adjusted to the gloom Paul thought that the shadows of the trees were unnaturally deep. They marched on, slipping into single file, silent but for an occasional snapped order from a biarchus, or the curse of a man after he slipped or caught his foot in brambles.

Finally they came to a clearing beside a river. The subdued sounds of the forest were drowned here by the churning water and the furious cackling of the crows that sailed overhead and nestled in the roof of the forest. Paul felt the sharp tang of ash in his nostrils, and the lingering smell of burned meat. The column had come to a disorganised stop. Some men were gathering around a large oak on the other side of the clearing. Paul, one of the last men, edged around the group until he had a clear view.

At the base of the oak was a large mound of ash covering a collapsed bier of charred wood and bone, splintered and bleached white. Wisps of smoke rose from the pile. Paul could make out ribcages and long bones in the jumble, which he realised belonged to men. He could see no skulls, and when, following the stares of every other man present, he looked up into the branches of the tree, he saw why.

There were a dozen heads hanging high in the branches, fixed by lengths of cloth nailed into the skulls. Their mouths lolled open, the tongues bulging out of some. Their eye sockets were rimmed with bone where the flesh had been pecked away, and the pale skin of each was ripped and bloody. They swayed to and fro in the breeze.

Among them Paul recognised Victor's ruined face.

'Demons,' muttered one soldier. The men began to whisper to one another, and the whispers turned into a babble of voices: angry, desperate, fearful, rising above the chatter of crows and the rushing of the river. Paul heard every word distinctly, felt every shifting human tone. The breathing crowd of soldiers around him, the gleam of sunlight on leather straps and bruised steel helmets, a bead of sweat crawling down the back of a man's neck with extraordinary slowness – every detail struck Paul with sudden clarity. He observed the scene around him in total calm.

Corfidius was bellowing for silence, but some of the men ignored him, or did not hear. 'Group your squads!' he cried, and the biarchi began to shove and yell their squads into orderly shape. 'Biarchus Minicius – your men cut down those heads!'

'Centenarius, another man is alive!'

Two soldiers had found a survivor from the patrol, naked, his skin a pale, deathly white, fastened by his raised arms to a nearby tree. His feet were crooked on the ground, his legs sagging. They cut the rope and he collapsed to the base of the tree like a discarded doll. It was one of the Saxons from the barracks opposite Paul's. He had been flayed, and Paul saw the fine lines of a scourge cutting across his white skin, as pale and tight as a linen shroud.

'Give him room!' said Corfidius, and went closer. 'What's your name, soldier?' The soldier moved his head, lolling it weakly from side to side, and with some effort raised his bloodshot eyes. His parched mouth opened, and a single rasping sound came out: '*Lic . . .*'

'I can't understand. Who can talk with this man?'

'*Dynne – Dynne!*' cried another soldier, rushing forwards. Paul recognised him as Duddo, a Saxon from another squad. He went to the survivor and knelt before him. He took his gourd and gave the man a sip of beer. '*Dynne – hyrest thu mec?*'

Dynne let his head drop, and shook it slowly. '*Tha lic,*' he gasped. '*Deade mannas . . .*'

'What's he saying?' demanded Corfidius.

'I'm not sure,' said Duddo. 'He's making no sense – something about the dead, but—'

'Just find out what happened.'

Duddo moved his face close to Dynne's. Several squads had already been called away to check the surrounding trees, but those men who remained crowded as close as they dared. Paul tried to follow the meaning from the little Saxon he knew.

'*Dynne, hwæt belamp thec?*' But Dynne remained silent, and so still that Paul thought for a moment he had died. Duddo put a hand under his chin and gently raised it, until their faces were close. '*Hit is Duddo, thin brothor. Miht thu nu sprecan?*'

Dynne's wavering eyes fixed briefly on Duddo, and narrowed. '*Ic geseah hund deadra manna, ac hie onsteppon . . .*'

'*Dynne!*' Duddo now held his brother's face between his palms, fixing his gaze. '*Dynne, hwa dyde this?*'

A smile came to Dynne's cracked lips, but it was weak, like the smile of a man in the grip of fever. '*Duddo, min brothor,*' he said, as though recognising him for the first time. Duddo released his hands, and Dynne's head turned unsteadily towards the trees, beyond the charred, smoking remains of Victor and the others. '*Hie cwomon fram beamas*,' he said with great effort. But his face broke apart, held in the grip of a terrible remembrance, and tears squeezed out from his anguished eyes. '*Hie eodon Talorg æthelinge to . . . we ne mihton us sylf aweardian, brothor*,' he croaked, struggling to hold his voice together. '*We ne mihton . . .*'

His brother embraced him, and held his head against his chest. '*Ne, ne*,' he said quietly. '*Thu wærest thonne cene.*' He looked at Corfidius. 'We shouldn't stay here.'

'What did he say?'

'It was Talorg, son of King Keocher. He must have come south with his Pictish warband. We should leave.'

The soldiers glanced nervously at the forest surrounding them. Paul saw nothing in the darkness between the trees.

'Get him some clothes,' said Corfidius. 'We'll bring him back with us.' He pointed at the heads hanging silently from the oak. 'We're not going anywhere yet – those are our boys, I won't leave them up there for the crows. I ordered you to cut them down! You men, clean this place up – now, move!'

One squad began the difficult task of scaling the oak to recover the heads, while the rest of the men searched the clearing for detritus. Clothes were scattered everywhere – shoes, cloaks, tunics, breeches, blankets. They were picked up and thrown on the smouldering pyre beneath the oak. The murdered patrol's bags had been torn open, the contents scattered in the grass. Helmets, belts, shields and weapons were nowhere to be found. Dynne sat at the foot of the smouldering heap, staring at it with empty eyes.

Paul looked about himself, anywhere but at Victor's face. He appeared to have been forgotten in the general commotion. Standing before the heap of ash, he remembered a bonfire behind the woodshed at Silvanicum, how the acrid smell had tickled his nostrils. Faustus had been there, watching him poke a stick into the fire. Paul had wanted to show him how close he could keep his hand before the pain defeated him. Suddenly the breeze shifted and the smoke of the present fire wafted into his face, and the memory dissolved.

It must have taken half an hour for all of the heads to be cut down, but Paul was scarcely aware of time passing. He heard the command to reform the column and prepare for a quick march home, and his body obligingly took its position close to the rear. As they began the march, Paul looked over his shoulder to the naked branch of the oak, still touched by smoke from the smouldering pyre.

The clarity he had felt when they had first entered the grove was now fading into a dreamlike haze. He walked on through the snares of the forest floor and out into the afternoon sunlight, rough ground juddering his helmeted skull, in the silent despair that he knew would come before a fall into nothingness. Words danced in his head, words of the poet Virgil that years ago had carried meaning, but which were now empty and taunting:

'Remember, O Roman, that you must impose empire
upon the Earth!
For these shall be your arts:
You must impose the habit of peace;
You must spare the vanquished;
You must grind down the proud in war.'

Over and over again, a mantra in perfectly constructed Latin metre, measured by the pace of the march and the steady rhythm of his breathing, burrowing into his head until it seemed that its syllables were the only things holding his lifeless body together.

He was dead. He had hardly believed that death could strike directly at the soul.

They reached Trimontium that evening, and Paul went straight to the barracks, dumping his kit in the mud and collapsing on his pile of straw. Time passed; he heard the call to assembly somewhere in the distance. Voices spoke his name, but he did not listen to them.

The door flap was thrown open, strong hands gripped him, and he was dragged out into the open. He was screamed at, thrown on the ground, kicked and punched. His arms rose to cover his face and were pulled away, and fists pummelled him. Eventually it finished, and he was lying with his face sinking sideways into a puddle of slime and blood. His entire body was beating like one gigantic heart.

XII

In friendship there is no feigning, no pretence; and, as far as it goes, it is both true and willing.
Cicero, *On Friendship*

Amanda sat on a stone bench at the top of the gardens of White Hen House. Sunset was approaching, and the gardens had already fallen into shadow. She closed the small codex and rested it on her lap. She looked over the tidily descending terraces of flowerbeds and ponds, over the red-tiled roof of the villa, through the haze of smoke from the kitchens. A mile away, beyond the stubbled cropfields of the valley, rose the western scarp of the wolds, its ridge catching the last rays of the sun. The leaves were turning, and many of the trees had begun to shed their summer coat. Clinking from the workshops drifted over the roof of the villa, the crying of cattle and sheep from the crest of the slope behind her.

This was Amanda's favourite part of the day. Since arriving here with her mother last month, she had taken to sitting at the top terrace of the garden during the late afternoon, with her mother in a wicker chair beside her. Amanda would read aloud, embroider, or sometimes just talk, always watching out for some response. She knew from her mother's occasional smiles that she liked to listen, though her tired eyes were often closed and she could hardly speak a word in reply.

Soon the peaceful hour would be over. It was almost time for Uncle Pertinax to return. He owned most of the land Amanda could see, a large estate that lay at the foot of the wolds. A retired soldier, for as long as Amanda could remember he had brought military energy and discipline to the role of landowner, working his property from dawn till dusk, riding from meadow to coppice, fishpond to granary, brandishing a horsewhip to terrify his tenants, while his wife Tertia stayed at the house to receive guests and petitioners and manage the estate finances. His homecoming always brought an end to the tranquility of the afternoon.

A single mounted figure caught her eye, approaching on the road that led up the valley. It was not Uncle Pertinax, who would be accompanied by his bailiffs and his pack of hounds. Amanda squinted, and as the rider came nearer she recognised him as one of her father's bucellarii, a letter-bearer from Silvanicum. Her spirits rose.

She had written to Julian after her encounter with Agrius Rufus. She had known that a reply would take at least two weeks, but waiting even that long had been difficult. Six weeks had by now passed. She watched as the rider came to the front gates of the villa and out of view. She would not torture herself by going all the way down to the courtyard to greet him; if there was a letter for her, Pinta would bring it up. Even so, she whispered a quiet prayer.

A few minutes later, Pinta appeared at the foot of the garden. She climbed the terraces with hasty steps, one hand lifting the front of her dress so she would not trip, the other holding the letter. She handed it to Amanda with a quick bow.

Amanda looked at the return address on the back of the letter. It was from Julian in Luguvalium. 'Make sure the rider has quarters here for the night,' she said to Pinta, 'and give him a silver coin for his trouble.' As soon as Pinta had left, Amanda hurriedly broke the wax seal, untying the cord that bound the folded wooden tablets together.

> *To Cironia Amanda, Lollius Julianus, unworthy servant of Christ, sends greetings in Christ.*
> *When I received your letter, dearest cousin, my heart leapt*

*that you had remembered my unworthy self here in the
northern lands of the barbarians.*

*The son of Agrius Leo told you the truth: your brother lives.
Before the summer I myself discovered him at Vercovicium.
Forgive me, cousin, for not telling you, but we thought it better
to keep it secret until we arranged his discharge. I saw him
only once, briefly. I wrote him letters, which went unanswered,
and then I discovered that he was no longer at Vercovicium. I
have heard a rumour that he was sent north. If this is true, I
fear for him. There is incessant talk of war. The barbarians
beyond the Wall are restless, and people say that Duke
Fullobaudes is preparing to march in the spring.*

*I can learn nothing more from Luguvalium. Therefore I am
about to go to Vercovicium and discover his fate. In the meantime I urge you to obey your father and avoid any further
contact with Agrius Rufus. Any interest the Agrii have in
Paul cannot be to his benefit.*

*I pray that my next letter will be happier than this.
Farewell, dear cousin, and sister in Christ.*

Amanda closed the letter, tying the cord into a tight knot, and
placed it on the bench beside her. She felt like a puppet character
of a Greek tragedy, as though the gods were playing cruel tricks
on her by revealing a glimpse of her long-lost brother in one
scene, and plunging him into battle in the next. Nothing she had
learned boded well. Paul had been found, and now was lost again;
he had been sent north, where a war was brewing; brave Julian
was risking his life searching for him: what if she lost Julian, too?
And she still did not understand why Agrius Leo had sent Paul
to the Wall in the first place, or why Rufus would want to bring
him home.

Forbidden by her father to speak of the affair with anyone,
even Lucas and her mother, trapped in a strange villa with relatives in whom she could not confide, Amanda had never felt so
alone.

Her troubled thoughts were interrupted by the blast of a horn from the valley, heralding the return of her uncle. It was a signal for the kitchen staff to begin preparing the evening meal, and for the bath house furnaces to be fired. She spotted her uncle approaching on the distant road, three other riders behind him, his dogs on either side. There were yells from the house below as servants hastened to receive their lord.

Amanda usually preferred to remain in the garden until she was sure her uncle had gone to the bath house. Then she would have her mother carried to her room, and would wait with her until she was called to dinner. The evening meal at White Hen House was always stiff and awkward, something to be endured more than enjoyed.

Amanda saw Patricia emerge from the rear of the villa and begin ascending the garden. The two cousins had not grown much closer over the last six weeks. Some days they went riding together, or played a board game, but there was not much common sentiment between them. Amanda was an early riser, loving the brightness of the morning, whereas Patricia slept late and rarely bothered with breakfast. Patricia had little patience for any task that involved sitting in one place for too long, such as embroidery or reading. Given the slightest chance, she would talk and talk about Treveris. Amanda had learned a great deal she had never wanted to know about life in the imperial capital.

Patricia bothered to climb only halfway up the garden. 'My father wants to talk to you,' she called. There was obvious irritation in her voice. 'He didn't say why, but I'm no use, apparently.'

Amanda had no idea why Uncle Pertinax would want to see her. He usually showed less interest in her than in his own daughter, and considerably less in his daughter than in his hunting hounds. Amanda glanced at her mother, who seemed to be sleeping. She did not want to leave her sitting up here alone. 'Would you look after my mother?' Amanda asked, rising from the bench.

'Of course,' snapped Patricia. She continued up the garden. 'I may as well be useful to someone, after all.'

Amanda found her uncle still inside the courtyard at the front of the villa, arguing with a petitioner. His estate manager and three more of his men waited to one side while his two dogs ambled around the yard, tails wagging. 'Go on!' Pertinax yelled at the petitioner, waving him towards the gate. 'Stop wasting my time!'

As the petitioner scurried away, Pertinax turned and noticed his niece. He was wearing the rough cloak of a common labourer, and his working boots were thick with mud, his face windburned and his hair disordered. He laughed. 'What a sight! Pardon my appearance, niece; my wife is used to me coming home looking like an overheated pig this late in the day, and has learned to stay away. Come on, you can help an old soldier make himself look fit for civilised company.'

He brushed past her, beckoning, and she followed him across the courtyard, intimidated by his powerful, sure-footed gait, and by the authority with which he dominated everything and everyone around him. Pertinax shouted for his personal attendants to ready his clothes and to prepare the bath, his voice carrying an uncultured bluntness. He was a man who had fought to attain his position in life. Amanda knew that many years ago he had saved the life of a general during some war, and had been richly rewarded with the gift of this villa and estate. His humble origins had ill prepared him for such wealth, and he knew of no other way to maintain it but through fear and strength. Amanda, too, was afraid of him, of his turbulent temper and of the power that she did not believe he had the breeding to exercise with compassion and reason.

They climbed the wooden staircase to the main corridor at the front of the villa and passed through a pair of double doors to their right, into the room he used as an audience hall. He led her through another door to his chambers, leaving a trail of mud on the mosaic floor. In his bedroom he tugged off his cloak and gave it to an awaiting attendant, who hurriedly folded it and deposited it on a side table. He sat on a chair while the servant unlaced his boots. 'My secretary claims to be sick, or at least he's refusing to get out of bed. So you can take down a letter for me. I dare say you're better schooled than my daughter, and better at keeping your mouth shut than my wife. You'll find tablets on the desk there.'

Amanda sat at the neatly ordered desk, finding a stylus and clean wax tablet. She contained her indignation at being treated in this way by a low-born man who lacked the competence to write a letter himself. He was her uncle, she reminded herself. He deserved respect for that reason alone.

'Take this down,' he began. '"The most perfect Lollius Pertinax, with the magistrates and decurions of Glevum, to Duke Fullobaudes." What is he now, most esteemed duke? Outstanding duke? In my day, emperors knew better than to turn barbarians into senators. Anyway: "We humbly beg your glorious Munificence to heed our entreaty," et cetera. Make up something pretty there. Generals love to be flattered.' He cleared his throat. '"The citizens of the colonia of Glevum have always placed their faith in the empire, though we stand at the very edge of the world. But now the drums of Mars beat loudly outside our gates." Do you have it so far?'

'Just a moment,' said Amanda, scratching hastily in the wax. It was a nervous thought that she was drafting a letter intended for the *dux Britanniarum* himself. She did not know his exact senatorial rank, but she could find out later. 'Ready.'

'That bit about the drums of Mars. Then write: "Your glorious Munificence is no doubt aware of the raids of the Irish along the western shores. The citizens of Glevum greatly fear that the barbarians will strike even into the heart of the province. Our ramparts are sturdy, but our defenders too few. We humbly beg your glorious Munificence not to deprive us of the valiant troops of the Second Legion, or else to send us replacements. We make this humble supplication confident in your wisdom, strength of arms and faithfulness to the divine Emperor Valentinian." Blah, blah. Add some flourishes at the end. Do you have it?'

Amanda finished her notes. 'Yes, uncle.'

'Good girl.' He rose from his chair. Amanda lowered her gaze while the servant pulled Pertinax's tunic over his shoulders and tugged down his undergarments. The smell of naked sweat was becoming quite overpowering. 'Damned flowery nonsense,' he muttered. '"To the duke: Thank you for taking away our garrison as the barbarians are knocking at our gates. Perhaps if we loyal Britons give them the shirts off our backs and prostitute our wives and daughters to some Irish king, we'll buy you enough time to swim back to Treveris with all your Gallic friends."' He raised his arms as his attendant wrapped a long towel around him. 'You can go, niece. Take the tablet and work it over. Then I'll pass it by the council for approval.'

Amanda began to walk to the door, but paused. His words had worried her. Rumours of war beyond the Wall were one thing; the last Pictish war six years ago had not affected her at all, and she had scarcely been aware of it. But the thought of barbarians rowing up the Sabrina, almost to the doorstep of this villa, was chilling. 'Uncle, may I ask – are the Irish really coming?'

'They've been coming for years,' he said. 'They're raiding further up the coast every summer. Of course, as long as they're just burning shacks and killing peasants, why should the empire care? Just wait till they start burning villas and killing decurions, *then* our glorious duke might notice. And that's exactly what will happen – mark my words, young lady – if he strips the city garrisons for this campaign of his.'

As she walked back to the top of the garden, thinking about what her uncle had said, Amanda's anxiety deepened. Before she had been worried about Paul and Julian. Now a shadow was encroaching on everything else she loved. She could almost feel it in the dim sky, in the darkening pall that had by now settled upon the wolds, in the chill of the evening air. She tried to reassure herself that Uncle Pertinax could be wrong. But he was ex-army; surely he knew what he was talking about. He was not the type to sweeten a bitter truth just for the benefit of a sixteen-year-old girl, as her father might have done.

She found her mother and cousin on the upper terrace. Patricia was sitting on the stone bench, and smiled with rare warmth as Amanda reached them. 'You look fretful, cousin. Everything's all right, I hope?'

'Of course,' Amanda said sharply. At once she felt guilty for not responding to Patricia's unusual friendliness in kind, but what else was she to say? *Our brothers are both lost beyond the Wall, perhaps dead. Our homes may be burned to the ground within a year. We might both end up refugees, or worse.* She picked up a small brass bell from the bench and rang it to summon Pinta. 'How's my mother?'

'I think she's asleep.'

Amanda bent to kiss her mother on the forehead. She stirred, opening her eyes, and smiled weakly.

Once the servants had carried Fausta in her chair to the villa and had helped her into her bed, Amanda went to her own bedroom to deposit her book and Julian's letter. On a sideboard she had a small wooden casket in which she kept her most precious objects: silver coins, some favourite pieces of jewellery, personal letters. She paused before opening it. She should read the letter again before dinner, in case she had missed something. Maybe she was overreacting, and Paul and Julian were not in as much danger as she had assumed.

As soon as she put her fingers to the cord binding the letter, she knew something was wrong. She always made the same knot to close her letters, and she was certain that she had made this one especially tight. The cord was too loose, and tied with a different knot. Someone had opened it.

Patricia.

Amanda felt a hot surge of anger. How dare Patricia open her letter? Then came fear: her cousin had read something nobody else was meant to read. She would know about Paul. She might tell anyone. Amanda cursed herself for having left the letter on the stone bench like that. She must not let it out of her sight again. Better yet, she should commit Julian's words to memory, and burn it.

But first she had to deal with her cousin.

Clutching the letter in her hand, fuming, she strode down the corridor to Patricia's room. She flung open the door without knocking. Patricia was sitting at her dressing table, and looked up in surprise as Amanda entered.

Amanda brandished the letter. At once she saw the look of guilt in Patricia's eyes. Struggling to keep her voice steady, Amanda said: 'How dare you read my private correspondence?'

Patricia gasped, affronted. 'What are you talking about? Amanda, I would never—'

'I know it was you, Patricia. I can tell it's been opened. Don't lie to me.'

'Why are you blaming *me*?' she protested.

'You sent me to talk to your father, and when I came back it had been opened.'

'It could have been your mother, couldn't it?'

'Have you so much as looked at my mother for the last month? She can barely raise a spoon to her own mouth!'

'Then one of the servants . . .'

'I know it was you, Patricia! You were the only one with my mother.'

Patricia flushed. 'I didn't stay with your mother,' she said. 'I went back into the house for a while, then came out again. Someone else must have read it while I was gone.' She looked at Amanda pleadingly. 'I'm sorry, cousin. I know you asked me to stay with her. I was only gone a short while, I swear.'

Amanda did not know whether or not to believe her. Either she had read the letter, or she had left Fausta alone in the garden, and Amanda did not know which made her angrier. She had nothing more to say. She returned to her room, needing to think alone.

When Pinta came to call her for dinner, Amanda said she was not hungry and would not be joining them. Let them take offence, she thought. She could not face sitting for an hour listening to her uncle as he tediously recounted his day's work digging ditches. She would not be able to bear the presence of

Aunt Tertia, pious and distant, who sat and stared at her husband and daughter with an air of eternal disapproval. Least of all did Amanda want to spend dinner in the presence of moping, selfish Patricia.

Instead she asked for a bowl of pork broth, which she took and shared with her mother. She missed her father more than ever. If only he were here and not in Londinium. His work there was important, though. He was trying desperately to put together an embassy to the emperor to beg for tax relief on behalf of Corinium, and he had explained to her that this meant winning first the support of the Vicarius of Britannia, who oversaw the governors of the Four Provinces, then the support of the Praetorian Prefect of Gallia, and finally the Master of Offices at the imperial court. All this meant a lot of letters and money and time away from his family. Amanda accepted that. But the more time he spent away, the harder it was for him to protect the family at home. She wished she were older so she could help more in some way, could take on some of the responsibilities so neglected by Lucas. She wished Paul were home.

That evening, after Amanda had finished her prayers, had said good night to her mother and was sitting in front of her mirror preparing for bed, Patricia came into her room. She opened and closed the door so quietly that Amanda hardly heard her enter. She sat on the edge of Amanda's bed, dressed in her nightclothes and shawl. Her hair was loose and unruly about her shoulders, a shimmering mass of fire in the soft light of the oil lamps. Amanda could tell that she had been crying, and did not care.

'What do you want, Patricia?'

'I read the letter from Julian,' she said, forcing the words out quickly, then putting a hand to her lips. She looked ready to break into fresh tears.

Amanda was not surprised at Patricia's guilt. She was surprised at the confession. Whether because she was tired, or because her cousin looked so pathetically unkempt sitting there on the bed with her watery red eyes and carelessly fastened shawl, Amanda felt her anger dissipate. 'Thank you for the truth,' she said.

'I'm so sorry about Paul. I had no idea. I swear I won't tell anyone, Amanda, please believe me.'

Her words sounded genuine. Whether or not she would keep to the promise later, Amanda could not tell. 'Why did you do it?'

Patricia looked away and closed her eyes. When she opened them again, she wiped them with the corner of her shawl. She breathed in slowly several times. She seemed to be gathering herself as though to vault some great hurdle. 'I was looking for something,' she said finally. 'It was a childish thing to do; I hated myself the very moment I opened the letter. Do you remember what I said about Rufus?'

'Yes.' At the mention of his name, Amanda felt her heart thump.

'I know him better than I let you think. We first met in June of last year, at a party in Treveris. It was mostly bureaucrats, a very dull affair. But some cavalry officers were there too, and Rufus was one of them. We ended up talking. Anyway, we met once or twice more that month and it was all very polite. But then in July I came down with a fever and couldn't leave my bed for two weeks. I was staying in Aunt Verica's villa at the time. I hardly remember anything except waking up in my room one day to see Rufus sitting on the couch beside my bed, watching me. So he said he was happy to see me getting better, and we talked, and then he left. My handmaiden told me he'd visited almost every day while I was sick, always stopping in on his way into the city. He gave me a bunch of grapes he'd picked himself from the slopes of the Mosella. He was the only person who came to see me. Nobody else much cared about me there. Treveris is swarming with prettier and richer girls. But he seemed so kind.

'When I recovered we saw each other very often in the city. Somehow we always ended up at the same dinners, or the same parties, or were always sitting near one another at the theatre, and I believe people got used to seeing us together. He was so kind to me. He used to say how much he hated parties, and only went to them when he knew I'd be there. And he used to temper that funny Gallic accent of his, to make himself sound suitably provincial, so I didn't feel like such an odd pudding, I suppose. He said he was in love with me, or at least he let me think so. In August Aunt Verica hosted a party, and there was a storm, so some of the guests had to stay the night. Rufus was one of them. In the middle of the night he came to my room.' Her voice faltered. The pain in her eyes told Amanda all she needed to know.

'I knew I was being stupid,' Patricia continued. 'I knew it. But there it hardly seemed to matter. You get sucked into that world, you see, like into a whirlpool, with the court at the centre and everyone rushing in circles around it. You hold on to whatever you can.

'And then his unit was sent to fight the barbarians, and he left Treveris with the rest of them. By then I'd gone to stay with cousin Hiberia in Lugdunum.'

'Lucas mentioned that. He said you were ill again for months.'

'That was just a story. The real reason was to get me away from Rufus, Treveris, and all the gossip. It was the last I saw or heard of him. I must have written a dozen letters, but he never replied, not to a single one. It was as though I'd never existed. You can't imagine what it feels like, Amanda, to be forgotten like that. To be taken on someone's arm to party after party, until everyone assumes you're as good as married, to spend the night together, and then be cast aside like an old rag.'

For the first time, Amanda felt pity for her cousin. She wished there were something helpful she could say. 'He took advantage of you.'

'That was when I heard about that young widow of his, just before I left Treveris. She was from some old Gallic family. He'd been courting her just like he was courting me at the same time. Everyone else seemed to know about it. There I was, this stupid provincial girl, a nobody, a laughing stock.'

'I remember you mentioned the widow. You said he stole some money from her.'

'Oh, that's what people said. I don't care any more what he did. He got what he deserved in the end, falling from his horse before he even got into battle, so now he can't do anything except limp about.' She shook her head and gave a brief, bitter laugh. 'I wish he'd broken his neck.'

'I'm so sorry, Patricia.'

'Mother heard all about it from Aunt Verica, of course. Father was furious. And I suppose Lucas knows too, like everyone else in Treveris.'

'He's never mentioned it.'

'Mother is punishing me for it now. My parents spent a fortune sending me over the sea, the least I could have done was find a rich husband – me, seventeen years old and still not betrothed! But I had to go and ruin my name, too. I just feel trapped here. The whole summer I've been cooped up at home. Your birthday was just about the only time I was let out, did you know that? Mother hardly even lets me go into Glevum these days, and Corinium may as well be the Moon. You seem so happy all the time, Amanda. You can sit down with a book and be content for hours. I wish I could do that, but I can't. I feel like I'm suffocating.' Her voice broke and she began to cry, her shoulders lurching with every sob.

Amanda rose from her chair and sat beside Patricia on the bed, wrapping an arm around her. 'Oh, cousin! As if *you* want to be more like *me*! I wish I had half your beauty and half your charm.'

Patricia won back some control over her tears. 'A fat lot of good that has done me.'

'It's almost winter, you'll be in Glevum soon, and I'm sure you'll have visitors almost every day.'

'Grouchy army men, gruffish farmers, gnarly old matrons. Nobody comes to Glevum who matters. It's not Corinium. And certainly not Treveris.'

An idea occurred to Amanda that her worse half instantly dismissed. Her better half, emboldened by a suddenly generous and sympathetic heart, pulled it back. 'Well,' she began, 'I can't promise you Treveris, but I could ask Father if you might spend the winter with us in Corinium.'

'Oh, Amanda.' Patricia took hold of Amanda's hand and kissed it. 'I know I can be a complaining pest. I feel so bad about reading the letter, and lying to you.'

'Everyone makes mistakes. Don't think I never get angry, or envious, or do things I regret.'

'But you see, I do want to improve myself. I wish I could be as good a daughter to my mother as you are to yours, and as good a sister to my brother. When I read Julian's letter . . . I realised how much you love your family. I'm such a selfish person. It's terrible how cruel I can be sometimes. I want you to help me, Amanda. I need to forget about Rufus and Treveris, else I'll drive myself mad.'

'I'll help you any way I can, Patricia. I forgive you for reading the letter. You're not to blame for what Rufus did to you.'

'You know,' said Patricia, 'you're the first person to say that to me.'

They spoke a little longer before they said good night, as it was growing very late, and parted as sisters. Amanda extinguished her oil lamps and felt her way into bed, crawling beneath the heavy woollen blankets.

It was a long time before she could sleep. She went over Patricia's words, picturing the scenes she had described in the blackness above her head. Would she have been able to resist the lure of excitement and luxury promised by the court of Treveris, which had already ensnared Patricia and Lucas so completely? Now she understood the caution of her father. A foreign city was no place for a respectable Christian girl.

Yet her relief was tinged with envy and regret. When she thought of Rufus it was not just with simple loathing. She was alarmed by a resurgence of that feeling she had experienced after seeing him the last time: an alien fire that seemed to spark into life in her chest, in her limbs and stomach, and threatened to consume her. This was temptation. She had never before truly felt it, and had not imagined it could invade her with such force. Suddenly her heart pumped blood furiously into every part of her body. Heat rose and flushed through her neck and face. I should pray, she told herself; I should kneel on the cold floor and pray to defeat this feeling. But she could not summon her will against it, and instead she let its strange weight press her into a restless sleep.

XIII

It is well said that a friend is half of one's own soul. For I felt that
his soul and mine were one soul in two bodies; and life became a
torment for me because I could not bear to be only half alive.
Augustine of Hippo, *Confessions*

Paul awoke to the dull smattering of rain on canvas. After the
sound came light. Squinting, he became aware of pain
throughout his body. Every square inch was filled with agony.
He coughed and felt a sharp stab in his lungs.

'Take some water,' came a voice. He felt the cool touch of a
drinking jug on his lips. Water trickled into his mouth. 'Easy,'
continued the voice. 'They beat the hell out of you, and you've
had a fever. You'll be on your feet soon.'

Paul allowed consciousness to return slowly, and waited for
his thoughts to regroup. His head was bandaged, and it was agony
to move his neck. He heard coughs and muttering on either side.
Outside the tent was the noise of a busy camp.

With some effort, he said: 'Where am I?'

'Still in Trimontium. You haven't gone anywhere.'

'How long have I been asleep?'

'Four days. I'm surprised you came around so soon.'

The orderly did not sound like one of the garrison of
Trimontium. Paul tried to reconstruct what had happened to
him, and the effort conjured a series of images, faces devoid of
colour, sounds muffled by the never-ending drone of rain. His
head was still heavy with dreams, indistinguishable from memories. 'Who are you?' he asked.

'I'm a medic with the Pannonian cavalry, from the Wall. A deacon found you in one of the barracks. He hitched a ride up here with us; goes by the name of Felix. He's been helping out with the wounded – not just by praying, I'm happy to say. He's been dragging you all in. He even let loose some of those slaves when the officers legged it. Brave lad, or else a martyr in the making.'

Paul tried to raise himself on his elbows, but a severe pain stopped him.

'Easy there,' the orderly said. 'I've got to see to the others. You need anything, shout.'

Before long Julian came through the tent flap. A smile spread across his weary face when he saw that Paul was awake, but he quickly disguised it when he spotted the orderly tending another casualty at the far end of the tent. 'Praise God, cousin,' he whispered, hurrying to kneel at Paul's side. 'How do you feel?'

'Alive,' was all Paul could think to say. He was not yet certain that this Julian was not a spectre, despite his unwashed, wispy growth of beard, his red-tinted eyes.

'Thanks be to God,' said Julian.

'And to a friend of yours, a little hero called Felix, from what I've been told.'

Julian grimaced guiltily. He glanced at the orderly, who still had his back to them. 'I'm Felix,' he said in a low voice. 'God forgive me the lie, but I don't know which of them I can trust. Close your eyes, pretend I'm praying over you.' Paul obeyed, and listened to Julian as he continued quietly. 'I looked for you in Vercovicium at first, and learned you'd been condemned and sent north. By the grace of God these cavalry were passing through on the way up here, and their centenarius let me tag along.'

'You shouldn't have taken the risk.'

'I couldn't afford to wait. I received a letter from your sister, and learned that I wasn't the only one who knew you were at Vercovicium. Paul, do you remember the day you were drafted? Did you see anyone you recognised?'

Paul tried to anchor his thoughts as the world ebbed vaguely around him. He forced himself to think back to that day. It was like trying to conjure memories from a different life. He recalled emerging from the copse, pushing through the tightly packed branches into the sunlight, and the waiting circle of horsemen. Someone was with him. He could almost picture a face. With effort he fixed on it: an eyeless head, blackened by ash, twisting slowly on the end of a cord above a jumbled pyre . . .

Victor was dead. Paul had the sensation of plunging into an ocean and let out a sudden gasp.

Julian squeezed his shoulder. 'Are you all right, cousin?'

Paul breathed in deeply. He closed his eyes and calmed his thoughts, raised himself above the ocean into the passive air. 'Yes,' he said. There had been someone else outside the copse, too – not a friend, but distant and commanding, disdainful. An officer. 'Agrius Rufus,' he said. 'Agrius Leo's son. He was there. He saw me get drafted. I thought he didn't recognise me.'

'Evidently he did. Back in August he met with your sister at Silvanicum and said as much. He said you didn't end up at Vercovicium by accident – his father made sure you were sent there.'

'Why would his father want me at Vercovicium?'

'That was the part I didn't understand. I still don't. But when I received the letter from your sister, I knew I had to go to Vercovicium to find out what had happened to you. So I got permission from my bishop, and came along the Wall. At first all anyone in the village could say was that you'd been sent north by the new tribune for killing a biarchus.'

'It was an accident.'

'I knew it had to be. But then I spoke to a Christian I knew on the old tribune's office staff, and he showed me this.' Julian reached into his satchel. Slowly he drew out a small bundle of wooden writing tablets, just enough to give Paul a glimpse before slipping it back inside. 'Paul, your old tribune had a special dossier on you. This is a whole file of letters.'

That made no sense. Paul was just an unranked soldier, a pedes. Why would he have his own file in the tribune's records?

'The oldest letter is from Agrius Leo to tribune Bauto, dated four years ago,' Julian continued. 'It backs up everything Rufus said. Agrius Leo did have you sent to Vercovicium after your training. Tribune Bauto was a client of his. Agrius Leo told him to keep an eye on you, to send regular reports, and to keep you safe – until you ever revealed your true identity, or tried to leave.'

Paul felt a sudden urge to get on his feet. He needed to move. Raising his torso up onto his elbows, this time he pushed through the intense stab of pain he felt in his chest, probably from a fractured rib. He twisted his lower body and swung his legs to the side, finally forcing himself into a sitting position. His head swam. As soon as he felt steady, he said, 'What do the rest of the letters say?'

'They just look like receipts – Agrius Leo paid Bauto well for guarding you. Are you sure you're fit to walk?'

'Give me a moment, I'll tell you.' Paul rose stiffly to his feet. He shuffled towards the flap of the medical tent, Julian supporting him, one hand pressed against his chest to lessen the pain of breathing. He tried to think back over his years at Vercovicium. He had always thought that only Victor knew his true identity. He had never even spoken to Bauto until the tribunal when he and Victor were imprisoned for assaulting Braxus. Suddenly that punishment made sense. 'It's true,' he said. 'I was in prison the last time you saw me, but for what I did, I should have been flogged. Bauto knew it was illegal to flog a nobleman. If he flogged me, he could've been put to death himself. So instead he put me in prison to protect his own back in case I ever left the army.'

They bent to pass through the tent flap, into the open air. Remnants of the last storm lay about in puddles, muddily reflecting the flies that swam above them in aimless clouds. They were at the north end of the fort, an area that had been largely left as ruins until now. The light cavalry detachment had set up camp here. Paul and Julian began to wander between rows of tents pitched between the walls of ancient stable blocks.

It was strange to see properly uniformed, clean-shaven soldiers again.

Julian spoke quietly as they walked. 'By the time you got out of prison, there was a new tribune who had no idea who you were, so sent you to Trimontium without a second thought. That's why the cavalry is here. Tribune Bauto wasn't transferred, he was arrested for corruption. It turns out he had a racket going with the prefect here, smuggling weapons into the north. When Bauto confessed, Duke Fullobaudes sent this cavalry unit to arrest the prefect, too. And we found this unholy mess.' He looked around them, grimacing at the sight of the decaying walls, at the shacks that had passed for barrack blocks. 'Nobody was expecting this. No proper rosters, nobody even knows how many enlisted men are supposed to be here. Mules and weapons and rations unaccounted for, slaves and booty lying about the place without owners, because half the garrison fled when we turned up. Everything's pointing towards a new war, Paul. Bishop Ludo's been saying this for months; it's been as clear as day to anyone else who's spent time in the north.'

Paul could not disagree. The Pictish King Keocher had only grown stronger over the summer. His son, Prince Talorg, had led the ambush in which Victor had died. Not just died – been tortured, mutilated, sacrificed to the death-loving war gods of the north. Victor and almost two entire squads butchered. For six years the Picts had not dared provoke Rome in such a way. 'Are we abandoning the north?'

'Hardly. The fleet granaries at Luguvalium are fit to burst. I've never seen so many ships in one place.'

Paul nodded. So much grain being shipped north could only mean one thing. Come the spring, Rome would be on the offensive. 'Who's commanding?'

'Duke Fullobaudes, people say.'

'The duke? That can't be right. He's only in charge of the provincial garrisons; he doesn't have enough men to lead a campaign. Even if he strips the cities and most of the Wall, he won't have enough, not against Keocher's alliance. No, some general must be bringing the field army from over the sea.'

'Perhaps. I don't know. That's just what people say. If God answers our prayers, maybe nothing will happen.'

Paul gave a grim laugh. They had reached the central road of the fort, and had a clear view down it to the old basilica, where the prefect had lived his depraved life until Paul stabbed him in the heart. He remembered the moment vividly, and felt no regret. He would do it again if he could, even knowing that it had not saved Victor. He thought of what the prefect had done here for two years, without the duke, his direct superior, having any idea. Anyone who trusted in Fullobaudes was a fool.

In any case, Paul was done with the army. There was no point waiting to get a discharge, and if he went back to Vercovicium he still risked the death sentence for killing Braxus. Besides, if what Julian said was true, Agrius Leo's men might be on his trail, having lost sight of him for the first time in four years, and Vercovicium would be the first place they would look. For all he knew, one of these cavalry soldiers could be in Agrius Leo's pocket.

He would not let them decide his fate. If he had to go home to answer for the death of Faustus, he would do so on his own terms. He would at least stay a free man until he surrendered himself to his father's judgement. 'I'm going back to my family,' he said.

'As soon as possible, yes. You just need to recover a little.'

'No. Today.'

'You're still too weak, cousin.'

'If you found me,' Paul said, 'Agrius Leo's men can find me. I'm leaving today – alone.'

'Alone? Where do you hope to go?'

'South-west across the hills. I can't go to Vercovicium. I'll stand a better chance of getting past the Wall on the west side.'

'And then?'

'I'll take a boat down the coast.'

'How will you pay for it?'

'I don't know yet. If I get that far I'll think of something.'

Julian shook his head. 'You won't make it in your state, not without money and a guide. The hills are filled with deserters and barbarians. You can't fight, Paul, and you can't run.'

Paul knew what Julian wanted to say – that he intended to come south with him, to bring home the prodigal son he had now found – and did not want to hear it. Paul pitied Julian for his blind faith. He would not be bringing home the prodigal son, but Cain, the first murderer, who had killed his brother Abel and been rightly damned to eternal exile. Condemnation awaited Paul, and he was ready for it. He began walking down the main road to his old barrack block.

'Listen to me,' Julian insisted, sticking close. 'I can get you to Luguvalium. Bishop Ludo will be able to protect you, at least until we can put you on a boat south. I'll have to stay at Luguvalium, but the bishop can give you an episcopal pass in case anyone sees your army tattoo. It would be madness to attempt the journey by yourself. Won't you listen to me?'

Paul stopped. He said nothing, knowing that what Julian said was true. Perhaps he might make it south without help, but in his condition, with no money, with winter approaching, with the mark of a soldier on his wrist that would betray him as a deserter, it would not be easy. Yet he was already indebted to Julian when he did not deserve to be. His cousin should never have taken such risks to find him. He had no idea what kind of man he was trying to help.

But it would be better to arrive home with Julian's help than not to arrive home at all. When they reached Luguvalium, when they parted ways, Paul could tell Julian the truth.

'All right,' Paul said. 'If you want to come with me, I can't stop you.'

'Thank you, cousin,' said Julian. 'Leaving the fort at dusk won't be hard. The guards trust me; I can say we're just looking for a quiet place to pray nearby, as long as we can smuggle out some food, possibly a sword. I saw a stockpile of weapons I can get something from. Can you fight if you have to?'

'Yes. Although I doubt I'd win.'

Paul was surprised to hear Julian laugh. 'I need to return to the medical tent,' he said. 'Let's meet here close to sundown. Until then, it would be better if we avoid one another.'

Julian had begun to walk away when Paul called him back. 'Julian – wait. You said you had a letter from my sister?'

'That's right. She often writes to me.'

'Is she well? I mean, she's not sick?'

'No; at least she said nothing in her last letter. But there is . . .' He hesitated, seeming unsure of what to say.

'What?'

'Your mother, Paul. The lady Fausta. Amanda said she's gravely ill. She was struck down one day, and has been bedridden since with a wasting disease. But your father has brought the finest physicians to see her, and Amanda sounded hopeful. I pray for her daily.'

There may have been hope in Julian's words, but Paul could see little in his eyes. He looked away, over the broken walls and southern ramparts to the windswept peaks beyond. They stared back as always, silent and cruel. 'Thank you, cousin.'

Julian returned to tend the injured. Paul walked through the fort to his old barrack block, empty now. He was the only one of his squad still alive, and anything of value he had owned was gone. Around the back he saw that the door to Caratoc's shed hung open. Paul stepped inside. The bed had been turned over and a chest lay open; scraps of clothing were piled about in careless bundles. Everything else must have been grabbed in the panicked flight of the deserters.

Paul did not know how many times he had been beaten within these four walls. He had stopped counting them as he had stopped counting the days themselves. Now time had begun to flow once again, slowly at first, like a stream trickling from the edge of a swamp, and in the passing moments Paul found an impatient sense of purpose. He did not look forward to returning home, but he knew he had to go. He had to get away from this place.

Outside the shed he stood where Caratoc had thrown him for the last time. This was where the ghosts of Trimontium had tried to make him one of their own, where Amanda, or perhaps an angel assuming her form, had appeared to summon him home. He recalled her words with chilling clarity. She had known what would happen on that patrol and had saved him. And yet Victor had died . . .

It was nonsense. The air around him now was clear. There were no spirits, no angels. He had seen nothing but the invention of a fevered mind, a phantasm, which had spoken a scrap of half-remembered verse. Cowardice alone had stopped him rising to join that patrol; Victor had died, and Paul had not tried to stop it.

The slow hours crept by. At sunset Paul met Julian as planned and accepted a long hooded cloak, tattered but usable, and a sword. He drew the sword quietly from its sheath, checking the blade for imperfections. It was factory forged, not pretty to look at but sturdy enough. He tied the belt around his waist and hid the weapon carefully beneath the cloak.

The sentries at the south gate allowed Julian and Paul to pass without hindrance. They withdrew a safe distance down the main road of the ruined village before they slipped into the surrounding scrub and passed out of sight of the fort. They were still enshrouded by the black bulk of the three mountains, behind which the sky blazed a furious red; but soon they had escaped its shadow and began to pick their way across the open country towards the south.

XIV

What am I to do? Death is at my heels and life is fleeting.
Teach me how to face these fears:
Make me not flee from death,
And make my life not flee from me.
Seneca

'We should have brought a brazier along,' said Patricia, and gave a dramatic shiver.

'Oh, tch, cousin,' grinned Lucas. 'A bit of a bite in the air can only do you good. It's no use spending the whole autumn locked up in a smoky villa. Besides, you've been complaining for the last three days about how much you wanted to get out of the house.'

'Yes, to Glevum or somewhere, not to some soggy field in the middle of the wilderness.'

Lucas laughed and turned his attention back to the river, watching its grey waters. 'It'll be here soon, you'll see.'

Patricia moaned and shivered again. She looked sorrowfully at Amanda. The three of them stood in a meadow on the banks of the river Sabrina, wrapped up in thick layers against the chill of the October morning. Their horses were tethered a short distance away, watched over by a group of servants. Amanda felt for Patricia; it was unpleasant standing for so long in damp grass on so cold a morning, especially after riding for two hours to get here.

'I won't be happy till I'm back home warm with hot food inside me,' said Patricia. 'I thought you said these priests were masters of prophecy.'

'Be patient,' said Lucas. 'All the omens are in place.'

They all watched the calm waters flow downstream and listened carefully to the air. Despite the cold, Amanda was excited to be out here, exposed to the elements, as close to the barbarian west as she had ever been. Amanda could hardly believe that these calm waters might bring a fleet of savages into the heart of the province, but Uncle Pertinax still asserted that the barbarians would be coming in the spring. The city council of Glevum had endorsed his letter to Duke Fullobaudes begging him not to deplete their garrison. Amanda did not want to think what would happen if the duke ignored it.

It had been a relief to Amanda when Lucas had arrived at White Hen House a few days previously and suggested this outing. Neither Amanda nor Patricia had ever seen the fabled chariot of Nodens, a great wave taller than a man, which rushed from the mouth of the river Sabrina up its length, reversing the flow of the waters contrary to nature. Those whom the gods had blessed, Lucas had told them in hushed tones, could see Nodens himself behind the wave, driving his stallions before him; but even ordinary mortal eyes could see the wave plainly enough. 'None can predict precisely when the greatest wave will rise,' Lucas had said, 'except the fabled priests of Nodens, whose temple stands high above the mouth of the river. Only through their sacrifices and mysterious rituals do they discern the intentions of the god.'

Patricia had also been thoroughly excited at first, but her enthusiasm had diminished as steadily as the morning dew had seeped through the seams of her shoes. Amanda was less bothered by the cold and damp than by the prospect of seeing a pagan god for the first time. She knew that her father would have forbidden this excursion had he arrived at White Hen House already.

'I was at the temple earlier this summer, in fact,' Lucas said, waving a finger towards the south. 'That's when I learned the prophecy. They're rebuilding the whole thing; it's quite an impressive sight now. I went with a friend of mine from the city who wanted to go for an eye sickness he had. His left eye was so bloodshot it looked like a plum.'

Patricia grimaced. 'And did they help him?'

'Yes, they did. After a few days he was right as rain. Hasn't had any bother since. His father visits quite frequently for his aching bones when he can't get down to Aquae Sulis, and swears by them.'

None of them spoke for a while. The air was peaceful and quiet, disturbed only by birdsong and the gentle flow of the water. Amanda's thoughts were anything but calm. She was deeply troubled to learn that Lucas had been to the infamous temple of Nodens, which Agrius Leo was paying a fortune to have restored to its former glory. Their father had complained bitterly about the building project, cursing it as a cheap ploy by Agrius Leo to win the support of many influential pagans in the province, those nobles who had not converted to Christianity and still clung to the traditional ways. Aristocrats and commoners alike were already flocking across the river to pay their respects to the ancient god in his new temple. Amanda knew of the pagan priests who worshipped Nodens, god of many faces – hunter, fisherman, healer – and of his mystics who interpreted dreams in return for coin. She had heard of the sacred wolfhounds of the west, which stood guard at the gates and prowled the temple courtyards. But she had never imagined that her own brother might visit such a place, and risk bringing scandal upon their father.

Then Lucas said, 'I'm thinking I might take Mother to the temple.'

His eyes met Amanda's at once. He wanted to see how she would react. But before either of them could speak, Patricia cried out, 'I can hear it!'

They all turned their ears to the wind. Downstream, barely audible at first, Amanda heard a sound like thunder. It rose into a deep, rolling rumble.

'Here he comes!' said Lucas. 'Prepare yourselves!'

Amanda's heart was racing as the rumble approached them. She had not expected it to be so loud. Her body was suddenly rooted to the spot. She wanted to run, but her feet refused to move. Her eyes were fixed on the downstream bend of the river. Why had she agreed to this? She ought to be safely at the villa with her mother, dutifully waiting for her father to arrive. He would be angry with her . . .

By now the noise was filling the air around their heads. 'There!' Lucas shouted. Amanda saw it: a swell stretching the width of the river was gliding towards them against the stream. Where it met the near bank its crest broke apart and foamed and crashed, tumbling in chaos through the branches of overhanging trees and against the grass of the river slope. It was a great mouth tearing towards them, its roar deafening. Amanda felt a shudder down the back of her neck. Her chest was heaving in fright. She forced one foot backwards and planted it solidly on the earth. She forced her other foot backwards. She thought the ground was trembling.

Lucas saw her moving away and rushed to stand behind her, gripping her shoulders. 'No you don't, little sister!' he laughed. Patricia's mouth was wide open in terror and delight. Amanda tried to writhe free, but Lucas was too strong. The wave had almost reached them, and suddenly it had: the bank in front of Amanda erupted with a furious white explosion that flung spray into her face and over her head; she shut her eyes and screamed, but her scream was drowned.

When she opened her eyes the thunder was receding upstream, the great wave speeding on its way to the mountains, the river bulging behind it. She saw no demon riding its crest. Her face was damp, her hands shivering. She realised she was holding her breath behind chattering teeth and released it at once with a laugh of exhilaration. Her limbs, now free, shook with energy.

Lucas was crying manically into the sky. 'Praise be to Nodens! Praise to the old gods!'

Patricia grinned and pulled her headdress back into line. She looked at Amanda with wide eyes. 'Well,' she said in a voice of forced calm, but her mouth clamped shut in a smile and further words failed her. Even Amanda could not restrain herself. They both burst into laughter.

*   *   *

Agnus was pleased to arrive at White Hen House later that afternoon and find his daughter in such good spirits. Amanda did not mention the morning trip to see the chariot of Nodens on the Sabrina, and instead let him suppose that her mood was entirely due to his arrival. She was very happy to see him after all, she thought, as she knelt and kissed his hand. But he had sent her here for two months to suffer the weight of a burden she could reveal to no one else, and she refused to feel guilty that in that one instant she had been able to laugh without restraint, had experienced a precious moment of euphoria in which she forgot all her worries.

Lucas had not mentioned again his idea of taking their mother to the temple of Nodens, and Amanda had decided that he was not serious. He had merely been teasing her in a thoughtless way. She could forgive him that. She felt guilty enough not telling him about Paul, although she knew that her father was right to keep him in the dark. No matter how much Amanda loved Lucas, no matter if he assumed himself to be the family heir, she understood with regret that he could not be relied upon.

Amanda and her father sat for a while with Fausta, one on either side of her bed, Agnus holding her hand. Her eyes were almost closed and it seemed a great effort for her to open them even for a moment. But when she glimpsed her husband, the shadow of a smile came to her lips, and a fragile sigh of greeting. Words were beyond her now. Her breathing was slow and coarse and sounded like torture. There was sorrow in her father's eyes as he watched his wife and realised how much she had worsened since he had last seen her. This time, he and Amanda knew, there was no hope of a recovery.

Her father's presence in the room made everything suddenly real. Amanda felt as though up to this moment she had been half imagining herself in the strange surroundings of White Hen House. It had been a temporary shift, an aberration from the normal world before their move back to Silvanicum or Corinium, before the recovery of her mother and the return of spring. There is my mother, she now thought with fresh clarity; and there is my father. Soon one of them will be gone forever.

'Things back home have been rather fraught the last couple of weeks,' said her father. For a moment Amanda was not sure whether he was addressing her or Fausta, until he looked at her in expectation of a response.

'How so?' she said.

'A number of families came across the river from Caecina's land. They turned up one morning on our doorstep, all but destitute. They said Agrius Leo was breaking their backs. You know this wasn't the best harvest. His agents took so much of their grain that they feared they'd be starving this time next year. So they came to me.'

'They see you as their lord.'

He nodded. 'I wish the law agreed with them.'

'What did you do?'

'What else could I do? I took them in. I settled them upriver, by those fallow fields south of the crossroads. I told Formosus to give them enough grain to sow before winter, and promised them a year to replenish their stocks, and timber to build their houses. Brico will lend the oxen for ploughing.' He looked again at his wife lying on the bed, slipping further away with each breath, and muttered again to himself: 'What else could I do?'

'I haven't heard any more from Julian,' she said, wishing that she had better news to give him, hating to add to his troubles. She had written to tell him about Julian's letter, about how Paul had disappeared, and that Julian was trying to find him. But she had heard nothing from Julian since, and had lived since then in torturous ignorance, one day dreaming of her brother's return, and the next day fearing that he had been lost forever in the barbarian north.

'We must trust in the mercy of God,' her father said, his eyes still on his wife. 'Paul and Julian are in His hands, as are we all.'

'Patricia read Julian's letter, Father. She knows about Paul.'

Her father looked up briefly. 'She's a good girl,' he said. 'You should have someone to share your burden. I hope to keep it from your aunt and uncle for now, though.'

'Don't worry, Father. Patricia won't tell them.'

While Fausta slept that evening, both families gathered for dinner. The mood was light, for Pertinax and Agnus, despite their difference in background and rank, had always shared a rich bond in all things agricultural. Lucas was behaving with rare deference towards his father, and Amanda's envy of Patricia had in the last few weeks given way to real friendship. She found it refreshing to be finally surrounded by easy, good-natured humour in this house, and she was grateful that her visit here should end in such a way. The talk drifted peacefully from farming to weather, from old family stories to plans for the winter. Amanda had already asked her father if Patricia could join them in Corinium, and he had gladly assented. It was fitting, he said, that he should lose a daughter for one season and gain a daughter for the next.

When the tables had been cleared after the last course of meat, during a pause in the conversation, Lucas announced, 'We went for a little jaunt this morning, Father, to see the Chariot of Nodens.'

Amanda tensed at his words. She looked at her father and attempted an innocent smile.

'Indeed,' Agnus said.

'It was very dramatic, uncle,' said Patricia. 'It started with a terrible roar, like thunder, and before we knew it the wave was rushing past us faster than a team of horses. Do you know what it reminded me of, Amanda? I had this image of Britannia as a great living thing, and the western mountains as a gigantic chest; and the wave was like a pulse of blood rushing up the Sabrina. Don't you agree?'

Amanda nodded. 'It was a very curious sight.'

'Well,' said Agnus in a casual tone, 'just so long as you don't go in for all that claptrap about Nodens riding up to the mountains. It's an entirely natural phenomenon, no more mysterious than the tides or the phases of the moon.'

Patricia laughed. 'Oh, Lucas told us about the priests of Nodens, and how they can foretell the biggest and the fastest waves.'

'Did he,' said Agnus flatly.

'And this morning they were proved right,' said Lucas.

A heavy silence followed between father and son, which enveloped the room. None but Amanda recognised it. She hoped that Lucas would not push the subject any further. Now she realised that he had not been restraining himself out of respect for his father. He had merely been biding his time.

'I'd like to take Mother to the temple,' he said. 'I'm sure the healers could help her.'

Amanda could tell from Lucas's tone that this was not the first time he had made the suggestion. Their father's reaction was muted. He dipped his head and cleared his throat with a brief cough.

Pertinax spoke up. 'Didn't someone from your neck of the woods go there a while ago, Agnus? Censorinus, is that right? For a gouty complaint or some such.'

'Censorinus wouldn't set foot in that place,' said Agnus.

'I must be thinking of someone else, then. It's been good for Glevum, though, all that building work. Not to mention the mosaics.'

Agnus ignored him. 'It's out of the question, Lucas. Your mother would never consent to be taken there.'

'She isn't able to consent to do anything at the moment, Father.' Lucas raised his voice and flung his arms wide in a gesture of bewilderment. 'How are we to know either way what she wants?'

Amanda tried desperately to think of some words that might calm Lucas or ensure peace, at least for the remainder of the dinner. Her mind refused to work. She could only watch as father and son turned the dining room into an arena.

'If you paused to consider your mother's feelings,' said Agnus calmly, 'there would be no need for this conversation. Especially not in front of our hosts, who feel for your mother quite as keenly as you or I.' Lucas sank back into his couch. Agnus continued, 'Her piety should be an example to you, as it is to your sister.'

'I don't see her piety, Father. I only see her suffering.'

'They are the same. Striking down the body only allows the soul to shine all the brighter. If you put her in the hands of Nodens, the soul will be extinguished.'

'But she would live, Father!'

'That is by no means certain. It is the hand of God which has struck her down; we may struggle to save her so long as we remain true to his teachings, and to send her to the shrine of Nodens – to have her surrounded by those idiot druids and their superstitious babbling – would be not to struggle, but to surrender.'

'Druids! You know the best physicians are there, Father. Everybody does. Let us take a barge downriver from Glevum. We can let the physicians heal her, and after the winter, when she's recovered, she can return.'

Agnus now spoke with open frustration. 'How many more times must I explain this to you? This isn't a matter of physicians, but faith! If she were to surrender herself to those demon-worshippers – assuming she survived the journey! – what would be the price to her soul? To turn her face from Christ in her final hour – would you have your mother do this? Has your own heart been so corrupted?'

Lucas rose, tossing his napkin to the floor. 'Tell me, Father – is it the demon Nodens you're afraid of, or Agrius Leo and Silvius Fronto and the rest of them? Are you truly afraid of what'll happen to Mother's soul, or of the sneers of pagans in the city when they hear that you sent your own wife to their shrine to be healed?'

'Sit down, Lucas.'

'Pride is a sin, Father! Isn't it? I believe it's pride that's stopping you, not piety. Say it isn't! You could send Mother and she'd be cared for there, but you couldn't bear the humiliation – stamping on one shrine only to send your wife to another!'

Agnus appeared not to react. He stared into space, his jaw fixed, while Lucas glared at him. Finally he turned to Pertinax and Tertia. 'I apologise for the behaviour of my son. I believe he has had too much wine.'

Tertia accepted the apology with a nod. Pertinax was shaking his head in disappointment. Lucas cast a final contemptuous look around the dinner party and walked out.

Amanda watched him leave, seething with feelings – anger at

Lucas and her father, sorrow for her mother, pity for herself; she saw Tertia reach forwards as though nothing had happened, her back perfectly straight, and pluck a piece of bread from a plate with delicate fingers, and she suddenly knew she could not bear the composed air of that room a moment longer. She jumped up and ran after Lucas, ignoring the surprised call of her father.

She searched half the villa before she glimpsed Lucas through a window. He was on the upper garden terrace, a dark shape silhouetted against the stars. She had Pinta fetch her a warm cloak and another for Lucas, and went out to him.

It was long after sunset and the constellations were spread brilliantly across the moonless sky. A gust was rising from the west, bringing with it a dark mass of rain clouds. Lucas saw Amanda approaching across the grass. He accepted the cloak and pulled it around his shivering shoulders. They stood side by side, surrounded by shadows, staring together into the heavens.

'I know you probably agree with Father,' said Lucas.

Amanda did not know what she believed. She only wanted peace in the family, and for her mother to be well. She wanted Paul to come home. She wanted everything to be returned to how it used to be. These desires so crowded her thoughts that there was little room left to ponder theology.

'I'm sorry, Amanda. It must be hard for you, with Mother so ill. It's hard for me, too. And I know it's hard for Father. This is why I turned up here a few days early; we'd already argued about it at home, you see. He won't be moved. Try as I might.'

'Lucas, is it true that the temple doctors could heal her?'

'Perhaps, if she'd gone to them two months ago, when she first got here. But now . . . who knows what the gods have planned for any of us?' He smiled at her sadly. 'Don't be shocked, sister, if I say I turned away from Christ a long time ago. What good has he ever done this family?'

Lucas had pronounced *good* with a small, bitter laugh that said everything. Both of their grandfathers had converted to Christianity, and what had been their fates? Bodenus Faustus had been poisoned for defying a usurper; Cironius Bonus had died an undeserved traitor's death. One uncle had been murdered in the night, another two had been executed. Faustus had been slain by bandits. Their mother now herself lay struck down, beyond all mortal aid.

But most of all, Amanda knew, he was referring to Paul. Lucas must have suffered from his absence in more ways than she had. On one day he had lost both brothers, and suddenly he was the eldest son, with all the pressures and obligations that came with the station. Yet Paul had not been declared dead, and so Lucas was still not the legal heir. He was in limbo, forced to play a role that was not his and might never be. Amanda wished she could tell him about Paul, about the letters between her and Julian, if only to reassure him that all hope was not yet lost, that the hand of God might still be steering their family towards happier times. But she was restrained by the vow to her father, and said nothing.

Eventually the cold proved too much, the threat of rain too close, and she left Lucas alone in the garden. Inside the villa she found Patricia looking for her. 'There you are, cousin,' Patricia called, and rushed to embrace her. 'Please don't worry about all that fuss at dinner, I'm sure it'll be all right. Your father is his old self again already. But you're freezing, have you been outside? Come on, let's get you warmed up in front of a fire.'

'Thank you, Patricia, but I'm simply too tired. I think I'm going to sit with my mother and then go to bed.'

Patricia looked at her with sympathy. 'Well, if you're sure. But remember you need only come and find me.'

Amanda paced quickly and lightly down the corridor and up the staircase to her mother's room. She sat in a chair beside the bed and buried her head in her hands. Before long her fingers were slippery with tears.

She wept for everything she had heard. Her father had always mocked the shrine of Nodens as a circus of superstition and ignorance, but if it was true that her mother could have been healed there, the pain it wrought in Amanda was unbearable. God was forgiving, was he not? It was not too late to try. He would forgive them if, in a time of desperation, they turned to the ancient ways that still had power, keeping Christ's faith in everything else. Amanda thought this, and felt a tempting glimmer of hope within; but in the sudden stab of bitterness towards the hard heart of her father that followed, she recognised a snare of the Devil. No, she told herself: her father was right. The more tempting it was to surrender to pagan superstition, the more fiercely it must be resisted, whatever the cost. She lifted her eyes to her mother, and saw the cost, and once again her mind toppled from certainty into despair.

The barbarians waited beyond the western sea, preparing to strike. Agrius Leo was forcing families off their land. There was no hope in Lucas, little enough in Paul, and her mother was fading. Even the power of prayer abandoned Amanda at this moment, and there was nothing she could do but sit and endure the suffering. She let the sobs rend her throat; she gripped her hair so tightly that strands teased from her scalp; she felt strained breaths force their way through her gritted teeth, while she begged in the gargling voice of an infant: 'Help me, dear Mother!'

A hand touched her head softly, and Amanda looked up. Fausta was awake, and was reaching out to stroke her daughter's hair. Amanda took her hand, kissed it, and held it to her forehead. It was a gesture of submission, a plea for mercy, and her mother seemed to understand, for slowly she took Amanda's right hand and kissed it in turn.

They stayed together, one unable to speak, the other unwilling, taking comfort in the touch of hands while the wind pushed ever more fiercely through the branches of the trees outside, and the first specks of rain darkened the russet roof of the villa.

Fausta died during the storm. Amanda had fallen asleep in the chair by her side. She awoke to find the morning light flooding the room with gold. The air was quiet, broken only by the peaceful song of a blackbird. At first Amanda thought she was holding a piece of marble until she looked down and saw it was a cold hand. Her mother's face was still, her eyes closed and her skin white.

Awareness seeped into Amanda's thoughts. She looked closely at her mother and there was a moment of reflex, a frightened drawing in of breath, a thump of her heart, and then a long, calm breathing out. She felt as though she had finally crossed a bridge that had been drawing closer week after week.

She placed her mother's hand by her side. She rose, closed her eyes, drew in two or three unsteady breaths until she was sure she could keep her composure, and left the room. In the corridor she found one of the house servants. 'Tell your mistress that Lord Cironius's wife has passed on,' she said.

Next she went to her father's quarters. He was freshly risen, and smiled when he saw her. His smile vanished when it was not returned. 'What's wrong, daughter?'

She tried to speak, but her voice caught suddenly in her throat. She could not do it. She did not have the strength.

The hours of that day were the longest Amanda had ever lived. She left her father alone by her mother's side and went to Patricia's room. The two girls sat on the bed, clung to one another and cried and talked until they were exhausted.

Late in the morning Lucas knocked and came in. His eyes were raw and moist. 'I'm leaving now,' he said. 'I'm going to Treveris. There's no point staying here. I need to be somewhere else.'

'But you can't!' Amanda exclaimed with sudden feeling. 'It's almost winter!'

'If I leave now I can take a late boat from Rutupiae. Mother would understand. I'll write to you, Amanda.'

She began to protest, but he had already turned to leave.

XV

Paul dreamed of his mother. He was at home, in the orchard garden of the upper courtyard, following the call of his name. He knew what awaited him, knew, with the helpless fear of the dreamer, that he could not resist going to that dark room where his mother lay, a twitching skeleton from whose bone-dry throat the same rasping syllable emerged again and again. Then he was standing before her, trying to force his eyes away, but no matter where they turned her face would appear. Her voice changed: words appeared between each repetition of his name, too quiet to hear at first, but growing louder and stronger. *I forgive you, Paul.*

She raised her twisted arms towards him and smiled, her lips drawing back to show the toothline of a skull. He fell to his knees on a dirt floor that was as hard as steel, wrapped his arms around his face so that he could see absolutely nothing. The voice only grew louder, filling his head. He felt as though he were collapsing into himself. He would not accept it. The voice became a scream. He tightened his arms until they were almost crushing his head.

*   *   *

He left the dream and sleep in the same instant, his eyes snapping open.

He was lying on forest ground, in a natural enclosure of hawthorn. The thickets surrounded and rose above him on every side. Julian was kneeling close by, rocking gently to and fro, thorns pressing against his head with each backward bend. His eyes were closed and his lips were moving quickly and silently.

For three days they had marched across an unknown landscape, keeping to the high ground where few people came at this time of year. The country seemed never to end; each hill rose and sank beneath them only to be followed by another just as hostile to human feet. Forests sprouted from the earth and loomed before them. Rain fell in brief, light showers, appearing without warning from the grey depths of the sky and disappearing just as suddenly. Paul's chest ached mercilessly, and his stomach was twisted with hunger. Every waking moment he shivered. They should have reached the Wall by now, he was certain. Beneath this roof of cloud, how often had they misjudged their direction and strayed deeper into the wilderness? One more day and they would have no food. When that happened, Paul did not know if he would have the strength to go on.

Yet they kept moving, seeing no living soul. Julian prayed constantly, muttering to himself. He received the blows of nature with what seemed to Paul like perverse relish, keeping his voice steady when he slipped, almost laughing when those hard walls of rain slapped against their lowered faces.

On the fourth evening, as the last trace of daylight was fading from the sky, they came upon the remains of a farmstead close to the edge of a forest. There were two burned huts and what had once been a small granary. Paul and Julian wandered wearily through the ruins, kicking at piles of debris that were slippery and black from the rain, searching for food and finding none. There were no bodies.

'They may have left before it was burned, or been taken prisoner,' Paul said. 'A couple of days ago at the most.'

'Can you say who did it?'

Paul shrugged. 'Picts, Selgovan bandits, deserters. Take your pick.' He kicked a charred wooden beam with the little energy he could summon, snapping it in two. The ash beneath it, kept dry from the rain, erupted in a cloud of black and white that danced on the breeze for a few seconds and came to rest slowly on the jumbled bones of the house.

'Do you think they're still around?'

As Julian asked the question, Paul noticed movement on the ridge of a distant hill. Mounted men appeared on the skyline, half a dozen black shapes against the grey. 'There's your answer,' he said. He looked around desperately. The nearest tree cover was too far away; he ran to Julian, grabbed him, and dragged him down behind the chest-high ruined wall of a hut. 'Don't move. Six riders at least.'

'Romans?'

'No. Picts, probably. Could be the ones who hit this farmstead.' Crouching, he peered around the edge of the debris. The riders seemed to be waiting for something. He gripped the hilt of his sword. When the Picts came he would not have the strength to fight for long. *Kill us or don't,* Paul thought. *Get it over with.*

Julian had started praying, of course, with his eyes closed and lips moving silently. Paul tried to discern the look on his face. He sought the first sign of fear, a hint that his cousin's faith was not without limits, but could see none. When they had been schoolboys in Londinium, Julian had always sought to escape the scrapes and tumbling of rough games either by feigning illness or by slipping away somewhere with a book. The other students had often mocked him for being a girlish coward. It was hard to believe that this Julian, who had followed Paul so deep into the north, was the same person. But he had the same placid, almost expressionless face, the same voice that sometimes shrank to inaudible softness, the same frantic awkwardness in his fingers, which twitched and trembled as though they were the only outlet of physical energy left in his body.

Checking around the wall again, Paul saw that the riders had left the ridge and were riding slowly towards them. This was it. This was as far as fate had chosen to bring him, after all.

Julian finished praying. He opened his eyes, calm and quiet, and looked at Paul as though they were together a pair of suffering saints.

'I'm sorry,' Paul whispered.

'For what, cousin?'

'For bringing you here.'

'God brought us here. He chooses when to call us home.'

Paul truly was sorry. He released the hilt of his sword. Julian had never hurt anyone. He deserved to know the truth. 'I killed Faustus,' Paul said. He was surprised that the words came out so quickly, so easily, as though they had been straining to release themselves all these years.

Julian frowned. 'Paul—'

'Not by accident – not like Braxus, the biarchus. I killed him – murdered him.' He sat with his back against the wall, feeling a strange peace. The riders would soon reach them, and he hardly cared. Telling Julian the whole truth was all that mattered. 'It was the day after my baptism,' he said quickly. 'I was sixteen. I argued with my parents over dinner. Later I came to them and said I renounced my vows. I said I didn't believe. But my father insisted. Everything depended on it, he said – my education, my career, the future of the family. Then it all came out. I told them the only thing I'd learned from school in Londinium was that power attracted the weak. So I'd have nothing to do with politics or law. I'd go to the east instead, to Athens or Alexandria, to study philosophy. He refused, threatened to disown me, so I left that night. I didn't know where I was going. I spent the night at the old barrow, up on the wolds.

'Father sent Faustus after me in the morning, and he found me still at the barrow. I was so tired, I'd slept past dawn. He woke me and told me to come home. He was so angry with me. He was always the better son, and he knew it. I didn't even know what I was doing out there, except the more he screamed at me to go back, the less I wanted to. I never saw him so angry. I pulled out my dagger and told him to let me go. He said I was a coward for not putting the family first. Then, I hardly even know how, we started fighting. He tried to take the dagger from me. I don't remember what happened, but then I was standing, and he was on the ground, and my dagger was in his heart.'

Paul stopped. Over the sound of his breathing, softly at first, rising slowly to an angry pitch, the rain had returned. It pattered insistently on the dead wood and blackened stones, on the saturated soil, steaming where the ground still bore some warmth of the dying sun. Through the haze of rain Paul recalled the image of his brother, seen as though from a great distance, lying in the grass beside the old barrow, the morning sun glinting on the enamelled hilt of his dagger.

At last Julian spoke. 'I wrote a speech for you once. That time Lucas and the others were trying to make me fight them – you remember? In the alley behind the forum in Londinium.'

'Yes.'

'You came and stopped them.'

'I remember.'

'I wrote a speech for you after that. *Laus Cironii*, it was called. A panegyric.'

'I don't remember that.'

'I never showed it to you because I knew you wouldn't like it.'

They sat in silence. Paul let the rain fall heavily on his bare head, soak his hair and clothes, run in cleansing rivers down his face and neck. Slowly he ceased to notice the cold. 'This is why I wanted to go home,' he said. 'To tell the truth.'

'For redemption?'

Paul shook his head.

The rain lightened. Julian rose cautiously and looked over the wall. 'The riders are gone,' he said. He rose and pulled his hood over his head. He nodded to Paul, who understood: they should find shelter and rest. Tomorrow they would continue.

★　★　★

Three days later, Paul and Julian passed through the Wall and approached Luguvalium. As they came to the river below the city they saw why the northern country had looked so empty. A great mass of people was trying to cross the bridge: farmers, hunters, wives and children, wealthy families with their goods on ox-drawn carts, most bearing what they could on their backs, some driving mules or sheep and cattle before them. The land between river and city walls had become an ocean of makeshift camps fed by a steady stream of refugees from the north. Paul stayed close to Julian as they elbowed and pushed their way towards the gates. Military officers were trying their best to organise things, urging newcomers to pitch camp on the low pastures by the river, but few seemed willing to move far from the walls.

The city was just as crowded within. Julian shouted to Paul above the confusion that they would head for the bishop's compound. They passed by a cleric lying on the ground with a bleeding nose being tended by his brothers, while the crowd jostled around him and another man was dragged away by soldiers, screaming curses. A team of boys bustled past, led by a deacon, bearing baskets of bread and fish and buckets of water. Soldiers on horseback were trying to keep order by breaking up crowds of refugees and herding them through the city.

Finally they reached the gate of the compound and Julian hammered on the door. They heard bolts being pulled; the door opened slightly, a cautious pair of eyes peered out, and the door swung back to reveal an elderly priest and a small paved courtyard.

'Christ be praised, my son,' cried the priest as they entered, hurriedly closing and bolting the door behind them. 'We feared the worst after so many weeks!'

'I'm tired, Father Potitus, but well. Where's the bishop?'

'He's arguing with the army procurator, trying to get him to open the granaries for the refugees.'

'How long has this been going on?'

'For a week or so, but in the last two days the numbers have exploded, God preserve us. It feels like all of Caledonia is trying to get inside the walls.'

'We need to see the bishop, Father. This is my cousin, Paul; he's been in the north these past months.'

Potitus studied Paul, looking from his ragged shoes, up his filthy cowl to his unshaved, gaunt face. Paul stiffened at the pity in his eyes. 'You both look like walking corpses. Take a bath and rest, and I'll have food and clothes brought to you. His grace will be delighted to see you in one piece, Julian, but it won't be until this evening.'

Julian objected at first, urging Potitus to take them to Bishop Ludo immediately, but he lacked the energy to argue and eventually relented. The priest led Paul to one of the guest rooms adjoining the church, and called for a servant to bring him hot water, a bathtub, oils and a pair of scissors.

The tub was large and deep enough to sit in, and Paul, now alone, eased his aching muscles into the water. He rubbed oil into his mud-encrusted skin. Every fibre in his body glowed with thanks for his first hot bath in three months. He relaxed his muscles and leaned back on the soft wooden rim, closing his eyes and feeling his pores open with an invigorating tingle. The warmth and relief came over him like a cloud.

He could stay here for a couple of days and recover some strength, but he was already restless to move on. The shadow of Trimontium was at his heels, creeping ever closer, a blackness that was determined to consume him. He needed to keep moving. He had told Julian not to write another letter home in case it was intercepted; and since it would be unwise to use the imperial postal service, he would himself reach the south as quickly as any messenger they sent. Julian had assured Paul that the bishop would give him some money, along with an official travel permit to ensure that anyone who saw the military tattoo on his wrist would not have him arrested as a deserter. A boat would be best from here along the coast to Deva, then the military roads south to Silvanicum. If he could find a boat soon and the weather favoured him, he reckoned the journey would take less than three weeks. He might make it before winter set in.

Home was so close. A vision of the combe formed before his eyes, the long meadow rising from the river up to the front gates, the ash trees in the lower courtyard. One of those trees had looked about to fall when he left. He wondered whether it was still there.

He rinsed himself with a bucket of cold water, dried off and dressed in the fresh clothes that had been left for him. He examined himself in a hand mirror. Even after the refreshing bath, despite the glow it had brought to his face, he appeared to have aged several years since the spring. His eyes were tired and lifeless, his cheeks empty. The beatings from Caratoc had cost him two of his lower teeth, and the bridge of his nose was crooked where it had been broken. He took the scissors and attempted to trim his beard. He could have a groom shave him properly at Silvanicum.

An hour or so later Paul and Julian were summoned by Bishop Ludo. He was waiting for them in his office on the other side of the courtyard, sitting at a reading desk before an open codex. When they entered he rose with a broad smile, kissed Julian on both cheeks and took him in his arms. 'Julian, my boy, returned from the wilderness at last! Rarely have I been so grateful to have my prayers answered. And this is your cousin Paul?'

'Yes, your grace.'

Paul sensed the bishop judging his appearance. He tried to look humble, not because he sought the forgiveness of the church, but because he needed this bishop's help to get home. He had never got on well with bishops. It would be better if Julian did the talking.

'Paul, named for the great wanderer and soldier of Christ,' Ludo said. 'How apt that you have escaped the clutches of death and have arrived on my doorstep! Come, sit, I have heated wine for you.' He ushered them towards a couch beside a brazier, and gave them each a warm mug. He sat on a wicker chair and addressed Julian. 'Tell me of your trials, my son.'

Julian began to recount his experiences to Ludo: discovering Paul at Vercovicium, his disappearance a month later, joining the cavalry when it went north, finding Paul at Trimontium and their escape to the south. Everything he said was true, although he did not explain why Paul, born of a noble family, had been at Vercovicium in the first place, nor that Agrius Leo had sent him there. Paul felt Ludo's eyes shift to him every now and then, each time bearing a silent question.

When Julian had finished, Ludo said, 'You've had a remarkable trial, my sons, and it's to your credit that you have endured it. It is truly inspiring to see those so young undergo such hardships for the sake of each other. You should both eat and rest – but first, Julian, I would like to have a moment with your cousin.'

'Of course, your grace,' said Julian. He rose, kissed Ludo's hand and left Paul and Ludo alone.

At once Ludo reached over to a side table and picked up a letter. 'Two weeks ago a rider brought me this message from a certain Flavius Agrius Rufus. It states that a Dobunnic criminal named Paul, bearing some resemblance to yourself, has deserted from his army service while patrolling in the north. Agrius Rufus, for undeclared reasons, is anxious to capture him. He asks that should this Paul appear in Luguvalium, I detain him and send word immediately. If I do, I will be handsomely rewarded.' He replaced the letter on the table. 'I am sure the senior magistrates and military commanders along the length of the Wall have received similar messages.' Ludo paused. He rose from his chair and stood at the brazier, warming his hands above the glowing coals. 'On the face of things, I have no reason to doubt the word of this pagan Rufus.'

'He and his father are enemies of my family,' said Paul. 'I'm not surprised he's trying to capture me.'

'And you have slipped through his fingers.'

Paul watched Ludo closely. 'Almost.'

'Julian tells me you are not a believer.'

'I am a baptised Christian.'

'That is something quite different.'

'I believe in what can be proved.'

'As did Thomas, until the Lord appeared and showed him the

wounds of crucifixion. We are happier who believe without having seen proof.'

'I won't deny that one can find great happiness in delusion.' The facetious remark came easily, but even as Paul spoke the words he regretted them. This was an old habit of his schooldays in Londinium, during the brief reign of the pagan Emperor Julian, when every classroom was abuzz with argument on the nature of the gods. The world had changed since then. Julian was dead, the march of the Christians continued, and it was foolish to insult the bishop whose protection he needed.

But Ludo was smiling. 'Did you annoy your old tutors like this?'

'All the time.'

'That apostate former emperor of ours, may he burn in Hell, has a lot to answer for.' Ludo picked up the letter from the table and placed it on the brazier. The glowing coals quickly began to singe its corners; moments later it was being consumed by steady yellow flames.

Paul said, 'I am sorry if I offended you.'

'Go, join your cousin and rest. I'll have my secretary write out an episcopal permit for you, and give you some silver – not much, you understand, but enough to get you home safely. If you feel strong enough you can leave in two days, taking our boat along the coast to Deva.'

Paul got to his feet. 'I am eternally thankful, your grace. I swear on the life of my mother that I'll return your gift tenfold to the church in Corinium.'

As Paul was about to leave, Ludo called after him: 'You could return the gift a hundredfold, my son, in the form of your soul.'

Since her audience with Bishop Gregory a month ago, Eachna had been put to work in the kitchen from dawn to dusk. She hated the work, the mockery of the other slaves when she fumbled with a basket or bucket of water, the long absence of Julian. One day the kitchen stewardess, a fat and mean-hearted woman, had told her to empty and clean the latrines. Eachna had refused, making a point of doing so in Latin. She had been surprised by her own defiance, by refusing to do the sort of work she had done many times during her years of slavery; but something had changed in her, and she vowed never to be treated in such a way again. The woman had fetched Ludo, who had commanded that if she would not do what she was told, she would suffer the cane across her hand.

Eachna did not mind the pain, for she had suffered worse. When not in the kitchen she prayed constantly, and in her prayers found dignity, an affirmation that she had done the right thing. She would never again cower before the rod, but would hold up her head and stare her punisher in the eye, just as Christ had never cowered before the lashes of his enemies. She prayed for him to lend her an ounce of his courage. But most of all she had prayed that he watch over Julian.

That prayer had now been answered. She was sitting alone in the slave dormitory that evening, cleaning her bowl with the last chunk of bread, when Julian entered at the far end. There was a man with him, about the same age; he looked weak and emaciated, like a starving rogue or a maltreated slave. His eyes bore a distant look as he glanced about the room, taking in the roughly built bed frames, the plastered walls, the few clothes and possessions scattered about it. His stare passed over Eachna along with the pieces of furniture.

'Good sister,' said Julian as he approached, clasping his hands together and smiling.

Eachna put her bowl to one side and rose happily. 'I prayed for you every day you were gone, brother Julian.'

'And Christ listened. He always hears the prayers of the good-hearted, Eachna, just like I told you. I heard that Bishop Gregory commanded your lessons to stop.'

'Yes. But I don't know why.'

'I'm sure the bishop had his reasons. We cannot in good faith defy his command, even if we do not understand it. But I've spoken with Bishop Ludo, and he has given you another option.' He stepped closer and placed a hand on her shoulder, slowly enough that she could force herself not to flinch from the touch. 'Eachna, I suggested to him that my cousin Paul here buy you from the church. He's agreed to take you south with the next party of clerics to leave, and he'll find you a place in his household until I return in the spring, when I'll take you to my family. You'll be able to continue your lessons there.'

Eachna glanced at the stranger, who was still standing out of earshot at the door, shuffling impatiently. For a moment he returned her glance, not smiling. He had the blank expression of one who was used to dealing with slaves as he might with any tool or workhorse. 'When?' she said.

'The day after tomorrow. Paul doesn't have any time to waste. And the sooner I can get you safely to the south, the happier I'll be. Take a moment to think about it; I want this to be your choice.'

Julian withdrew to Paul at the far end of the room, giving Eachna some space. Before she could muster her thoughts, she overheard Julian's cousin say in Latin, his voice so loud that he evidently assumed she would not understand, 'You never told me she was a cripple.'

Julian looked back quickly at Eachna, smiled an apology, and with his arm brought his cousin into closer, private conference.

Eachna heard no more of what they said, but she read from the urgent tone of their whispers that Julian's cousin was no longer happy with the arrangement. To him, she was clearly a mere piece of property he had grudgingly agreed to buy as a favour, and now found to be damaged. 'I can work,' she announced, enunciating her Latin clearly. They both turned to her, Paul's eyes wide with surprise. 'You needn't worry,' she said. 'You'll get your money's worth.'

Julian raised his hands defensively. 'Eachna, that's not what we mean at all.'

'You never said she spoke such fine Latin, either,' said Paul.

For the first time he was smiling. Even so, his expression reminded Eachna of Bishop Gregory's condescending amusement. 'If all your cousin wants is a one-handed barbarian to amuse his friends at party-feasts,' she said, pointing savagely at Paul, 'I'd just as happily stay here.'

'Eachna, listen,' pleaded Julian. 'Paul has agreed to buy you on my behalf so he can take you south as your legal owner. That's the best way to do it. He'll look after you until I return south, when my father will buy you and grant you manumission. You'll be free. You'll have a document to prove it. You can live at my home and work for my family as a free woman; we'll have you baptised next Easter, and you can read to your heart's content. All we need is your agreement, and I'll ask his grace to have the contract of sale drawn up. Your trials will be over.'

She absorbed his words slowly. He was revealing another path to her. Freedom, dignity, peace. A new life. Was this not what had driven her to strike her old owner with that rock all those months ago, to climb over the bramble thicket of the farmstead to freedom? She was sure that she had been chosen and summoned by Christ ever since that day. At every stage she had been tested, whether in the forests of the north or within the gates of the city. She had prayed for Julian's safety, and now here he was, offering her this chance. Still Christ had not forsaken her.

'I'll go,' she said.

Two days later Paul and Eachna prepared to leave Luguvalium with a party of clerics from the bishop's staff that was sailing south along the coast towards Deva. Paul felt good being on the move again, even if he would not be home for weeks. He collected his few possessions – the new clothes given to him by Bishop Ludo, a letter of episcopal patronage and his contract of purchase for the slave girl, a purse of silver pennies, the sword he had brought from Trimontium – and went to the courtyard, where the rest of the party was gathering to leave.

'Look after Eachna for me, cousin,' Julian said when the party was gathered in the courtyard.

'I will,' said Paul. The slave girl was standing alone by the kitchen door, wearing a warm hooded coat and new boots, with a shoulder bag of spare clothes and food. She kept her face low, occasionally raising her eyes to catch glimpses of the clerics milling in front of her, as though afraid of being noticed. Even wrapped up ready for a journey, Paul thought, she looks a fretful, skinny little creature. He could scarcely believe the stories Julian had told of her, that she had survived her years of slavery among the Picts, and had crossed the northern forests by herself.

Julian handed Paul a small rectangular bundle wrapped in cloth. 'This is your tribune's dossier on you. It includes the letter proving that Agrius Leo had you sent to the Wall. God protect you, Paul.'

The boat party walked down from the city gates to the river docks, the clerics singing psalms to beseech the protection of Christ during their voyage. Besides Paul and Eachna, there would be six members of the bishop's household and four sailors in the open-top ship. The captain announced that the winds looked good for a journey south and the skies promised to stay clear, which raised the spirits of crew and passengers.

Everyone was glad to be leaving Luguvalium. Across the river, below the ramparts of a large cavalry fort, were moored dozens of military warships and transports. Troops, warhorses and supplies were being unloaded on the opposite shore. Paul spotted standards of the Sixth and Twentieth Legions, whose troops were normally garrisoned in cities throughout the Four Provinces. It was grim confirmation of what Julian had said in Trimontium: Duke Fullobaudes was preparing to campaign early in the spring. It looked like he had called on half of the western fleet to ferry troops and supplies from the south – so many of them that Paul wondered if the cities had any defenders left at all.

'There's the *Furor*,' said one sailor, squinting across the estuary at the largest of the triremes. 'Count Nectaridus's flagship.'

'Fullobaudes is mad,' said one of his companions. 'Thinks he can march north and take on Keocher with that lot. A week beyond the Wall, no hot baths, they'll be crying to come home.'

The crew laughed. Paul did not, but he feared that they were right. Even with all the troops at his disposal, with every last frontier soldier, Fullobaudes would not be able to defeat King Keocher in an offensive. The Picts would simply draw them into the mountains and grind them down with ambushes and raids. Paul knew from experience that provincial garrisons were not trained for such a campaign; this was a job for the experienced, better-equipped soldiers of the field army, and they were all committed across the sea, defending the Rhine frontier. Next spring Fullobaudes was sure to march north and crawl back in humiliation. Paul just hoped that he did not get too many soldiers killed in the process.

In any case, he was glad to be leaving the north, finally free of the military. He boarded the boat and a sailor directed him to one of the rowing benches. They cast off from the docks, all except Eachna and the captain at the oars, and set off downriver to the sea.

XVI

We may weep, but we must not wail.
Seneca

Amanda had been standing inside the entrance to the church of Corinium with her father all morning, greeting those who entered, accepting their condolences and thanking them for their prayers. By noon her legs were sore from standing, her hands and lips chilled blue by the draught through the door, her eyes itching from the incense. Father Arcadius, the family chaplain, was in the porch beside her. Noticing her weariness, he leaned over and suggested that she retire for a short while, but she insisted on staying. She listened to the steady murmur of psalms from within the church, a litany to ease the passage of Fausta's soul into the next life, and took strength from it.

She could not recall the last time so many relatives had been brought together. Aunt Tertia, her face solemn, entered with Uncle Pertinax and a weeping Patricia. Aunt Fuscina, the widow of Uncle Viventiolus, had travelled from Aquae Sulis with her daughter Bona, a timid girl about the same age as Amanda. Even Fausta's cousin Senarus, whom Tertia hated and Fausta had barely tolerated, had come from Calleva to pay his respects, along with his second wife and their three young children. Most of the visitors were local landowners and dignitaries, some of whom Amanda knew, most not. She was surprised to see the tall figure of Silvius Fronto, the man who was to have been her father-in-law until the betrothal was cancelled. He entered the porch and nodded to her father, who nodded tersely in return, but they did not shake hands and exchanged no words.

Then Fronto turned to Amanda. Though she had not seen him in four years, he had not changed. He had the same receding dark hair, turning grey at the temples, the same long, dour face. His eyes were grey and sad, heavily bagged. 'My sympathies for your loss,' he said. 'Were my son Bonus not in Gallia, he would be here at my side.' He looked through the arch into the gloomy interior of the church. He was pagan, and knew he was not permitted to enter beyond the porch. His eyes closed for a moment, he hung his head, and a moment later he turned and left.

Some more political foes of her father appeared, their differences with the Cironii forgotten on a day of mourning. Agrius Leo was absent, but nobody had expected him to attend. More important was the absence of his cousin the governor. He was not a private individual like Agrius Leo, but the official representative of the emperor; protocol required him to show his respects to a woman of Fausta's station. And yet he did not come. Amanda knew that such a public snub, on this of all days, had to be causing her father deep anger. For now, he was keeping it hidden.

In the pauses between visitors Amanda's thoughts drifted to that final night with her mother. Only a week had passed since then, but it felt like an eternity, as though time itself had slowed to a respectful crawl. She had cried a great deal each day, especially when waking, but was glad that she had maintained her public composure this morning. With her new responsibilities it would not be proper to display excessive grief. Notes of condolence would arrive over the months to come, each time reviving the pain of her loss, from relatives far afield: Aunt Verica in Lugdunum; her father's sister, Aunt Amanda, who lived in Cantia, and her grown-up daughters in Mogontiacum and Colonia Agrippina . . . the news would not even have reached Gallia yet. No doubt they would hear it from Lucas when he arrived there, if not before.

Her brother had made good his promise to leave. He would be in Rutupiae now, waiting for a ship to take him across the sea. She could not help but feel anger towards him. Had she not lost enough men from her family already? In her short life she had lost her eldest brother and both grandfathers, taken from her by evil men, along with too many uncles – Maximus, Viventiolus, Arigius. Uncle Cretus had drunk himself to death. Uncle Pertinax, rough and hard-minded, offered little comfort. She had never even met Uncle Apollinaris in Lugdunum, or his sons. Of the male cousins she did know, Aunt Fuscina's son Rusticus was a child-man, an idiot, and Julian was now lost – along with Paul. Only Father and Lucas were left. And now, when she needed him most, her sole remaining brother had fled. It was selfish and self-pitying, cowardly, a public insult to their father and to the memory of their mother.

Later, when their mother was buried and the grief had eased, she would pray for the strength to forgive him. But not yet.

Bishop Martin emerged from the nave. 'It's time,' he said.

The procession left the church and made its way through the streets of Corinium, taking the main road by the forum and the market, passing by the basilica and city council chambers towards the southern gate. Four clerics, including Father Arcadius, carried the platform upon which lay the coffin, buried beneath branches of evergreen, and another four carried burning torches, one for each of the Gospels. Agnus and Amanda came after the torch-bearers, with the bishop at their side, followed by other close family. The column of relatives, friends, Christian councillors in their official togas, fellow believers, servants and clients stretched far back into the city; some mourned openly, others sang or stayed silent. On either side of the procession, club-wielding bucellarii kept back the crowds lining the streets and made sure that the urban poor, who had always held the charitable Fausta in great affection, did not come too close to the coffin.

Once through the city gates the procession continued to the Christian cemetery outside the walls. The coffin was brought to an open grave beside the tomb of Faustus and lowered into it, the bishop calling blessings upon Fausta's soul as priests sprinkled the crowd with holy water. When the prayers ended, with the large crowd stretched out expectantly before them, Agnus stepped forward to deliver the funeral oration.

'My wife,' he began, his voice strong and clear in the still air, 'lived and died in fear of Christ, as did her parents. She lived true to the nobility of her lineage – nine generations, from the Conquest, of Atrebatic decurions. She was a proud and virtuous woman. In reputation she was unblemished; in dignity unequalled; in charity unsurpassed.' He paused, letting his words settle in the sympathetic thoughts of the audience.

'I speak to you now,' he continued, 'not only as a grieving husband, but as a grieving Christian. For my wife loved God and the church above all else and never, not even at the doors of death, did she lose that faith. We should strive to follow her example. I am grieved, then, that so few of us are worthy. Many have fled back into the embrace of the old ways. Be warned! Those of you who have entered the abode of Nodens, who have offered libations to Sulis or Silvanus, to Mars or Mercury – turn back from them, I beg you, before you bring disaster upon us! I was in Londinium two months ago; I witnessed the rain of blood myself. Was there ever such a foreboding sign from the heavens?' Some in the crowd were now talking urgently to one another. Amanda could not tell whether most supported her father's words or not.

Agnus raised his voice above their murmurings. 'The pagans defy the edicts of his Excellency Valentinian Augustus; they continue to build temples and offer sacrifices to the gods. Do not join them, my friends. Turn away from the darkness and towards the light of Christ, as did my wife. She asks no great monument of you, no memorial, except your devotion. Turn your lives into her memorial. Live as she died: a noble Roman, in dutiful devotion to the one true God!'

Having finished his oration, Agnus nodded to the bishop and bent down to take a handful of earth from the pile beside the grave. He threw it gently onto the coffin. He reached out to take

Amanda's hand, and she stepped forward to do the same. The priests and deacons had renewed their chanting, their prayers curling into the air with the wisps of incense. By now the crowd was vocal, restless, almost unruly. Amanda saw the bucellarii grasp their weapons and begin ushering the common part of the crowd back to the road. Her father's words had stirred the passions of the city.

Amanda's father had been careful not to mention any names in his oration. Amanda knew that to do so would have been dangerous. Valentinian Augustus was known to be fervently devoted to Christ, but his hold on the western provinces was still not complete: even the praetorian prefect in Treveris, whose authority in Britannia and the Gallic provinces was second only to that of the emperor, was known to be pagan. It had been a clever ploy by Agrius Leo to rebuild the temple of Nodens; it gave the provincial nobles hope that the days of paganism were not numbered, and they had flocked to him like sheep. Through his cousin the governor he arranged tax relief on their lands, and shifted the burden to the smallholders and ordinary peasants. Any brave city councillors who complained were quickly shouted down by his supporters.

Amanda hated Agrius Leo for what he was doing to their province. Even though he was not a native, even though he had no seat on any city council in the province, he seemed to think himself a king in all but name. Only a few nobles, led by Amanda's father, still stood against him. She prayed to God that they would prevail.

Yet God had not saved her mother, and Amanda was losing hope of seeing Paul or Julian ever again. When her father had first told her about the rain of blood in Londinium, she had shuddered with fright; he was not a man who succumbed easily to superstition, but he had seen it with his own eyes. Amanda did not know what they had done to lose the favour of Heaven. She knew they had to fight on, that they could not surrender the faith, but she also wished that her father had not used her mother's funeral to make a stand. He had done something he had always sworn not to: he had opened the doors of their home life and let politics invade.

'It was a brave thing your father did,' said one sympathetic city councillor to her during the feast that evening. 'I just hope he hasn't made more trouble for himself.'

Amanda replied that the peace of his household was always her father's foremost concern, and changed the subject.

She spent the next few days in confined mourning in their townhouse, a suburban villa outside the walls of Corinium, accepting no visitors, bathing at home while Patricia went into the city, and preparing herself for her new role as matron of the house. The steward of the townhouse, an efficient and jovial man named Celerus, began to show her the deference he had always shown her mother, addressing her more formally. Pinta, too, withdrew slightly; not much, but Amanda could sense it. Only her friendship with Patricia did not change. The promise that her cousin should spend the winter in Corinium was kept – indeed, Amanda was thankful to find in her a companion of such openness and affection when she needed one most. She felt that the eyes of the entire household were now trained on her, and she became ever more conscious of her words and movements. When alone she studied herself in the mirror, trying to emulate from memory the bearing and habitual gestures of her mother. Her mourning would last for a full year, during which time she could not marry, even if a suitable husband were found. Until then, at least, this would be her new life.

A week after the funeral she and Patricia were invited to visit the wife of a family friend in her villa on the far side of the city. They stayed for a joyless and awkward lunch, and Amanda was glad when it finished. They said their farewells and climbed back into the covered wagon that would take them back home through the city, escorted by six mounted bucellarii. A number of commoners, clients of the Cironii, had also gathered outside the friend's house, intending to process with them through the city in a public gesture of support.

Amanda and Patricia reclined opposite one another in the cushioned interior of the wagon, hidden from the outside world. Amanda wanted only to spend the rest of the winter in the townhouse, peaceful and secluded, with none of these distractions. An abrupt change in the sound and feel of the wagon told them they had passed through the gates onto the paved streets of the city. Soon they were surrounded by the anonymous bustle of the meat market next to the forum. As they progressed, the noise of the crowd grew gradually louder until it began to have the hectic energy of a great feast day. At that point the wagon trundled to a stop.

'There's no festival today, is there?' asked Amanda, listening to the noise of the crowd. She heard the beginnings of a chant, the sound muffled by the canvas walls around her: *Ju-pi-ter . . . Op-ti-mus . . . Max-i-mus . . .*

'I don't care,' said Patricia wearily, covering her face. 'I just want to go home.'

Amanda opened the flap at the front of the wagon and peered out. An enormous crowd was filling the street, converging on the marketplace. 'What's happening?' she asked the driver.

'The governor's having the old Jupiter column restored, my lady,' he said.

Of course. Amanda had heard something days ago about the governor's plan to restore the old monumental column, surmounted by a bronze statue of Jupiter, which the previous governor had pulled down. It was a petty response to her father's funeral oration, and Agrius Leo was obviously behind it.

'Shall I take the wagon around another way?' the driver asked.

'At once,' she said irritably, pulling the flap closed.

The street was filling up quickly. Within the wagon it sounded as though the crowd were already pressing against them on all sides. She listened impatiently to the yells of the driver and bucellarii as they tried to clear enough room to turn down a side street. The wagon slowly began to move, when suddenly the bustle outside the wagon was pierced by a man's sharp cry of pain.

Patricia jumped in shock. 'What was that? Is someone killed?'

'Stay calm,' said Amanda. She opened the flap just enough to yell out to the driver: 'Move on, now! Use your whip if you must!'

The wagon jolted forwards as it started down the side street, leaving behind what sounded like the beginnings of a riot. Amanda was almost ready to sigh in relief when something solid and heavy struck the outside of the canvas only a foot from Patricia's head. She scrambled in a panic to Amanda's side as several more objects thudded against the roof.

There was a commotion at the back of the wagon, and they saw a hand tear open the rear flap. A young man's head appeared: hairy, sunburned, his eyes full of frenzied hate. He half pulled himself into the wagon, thrashing one arm to find something to grab onto. He grasped Amanda's foot; she shook it free and planted her heel in his face with as much force as she could gather. The man flew from the back of the wagon, stumbling as he hit the ground, both hands on his bleeding nose.

Through the open flap Amanda saw one of their bucellarii expertly use the weight of his mount's hindquarters to push the man roughly aside. The rest of the escort, who had fallen behind as they tried to hold off the main body of the mob, now forced their way up the street to catch up with the wagon, waving their clubs at the attackers and scattering them in the gutters. Amanda had time to note that one of the attackers was wearing the grey livery of Agrius Leo before she pulled the flap shut and fastened it.

They reached the townhouse without further incident and pulled into the courtyard. Amanda climbed from the wagon and told the bucellarii not to go anywhere. As soon as she had taken Patricia, still shaken, to her handmaiden for some honeyed wine, Amanda sought out her father. He was in his audience room with Alypius and a local official. When he saw Amanda at the door he excused himself for the interruption and came to her.

'What is it, daughter?' he asked, seeing the anxiety in her face. 'Are you hurt? What happened?'

'No, we're not hurt. There's a riot in the city. They tried to assault us in the wagon as we passed through.'

Her father's face hardened. 'Tell me exactly what happened.'

Amanda described the attack as best she could. Her father apologised to and dismissed his visitor, then came with Amanda to Patricia, who gave a more emotional account. 'I can only beg your forgiveness, dear niece,' he said, 'that you were abused in this way while under my care. Rest assured I shall catch and punish those who dared do this to you.' He strode from the room, shouting to the servants for his coat, cloak and boots, and for his horse to be made ready. Amanda followed him to the court-yard, where the bucellarii quickly jumped to their feet as their master entered. 'Did you recognise them?' he demanded of the chief.

'Yes, lord.'

'Good. Bring my horse. Summon every man we have and tell them to meet us at the Glevum gate. Quickly, now!'

The stablehands rushed to saddle and bring out his mount while the house servants emerged with his outdoor clothes. As he readied himself, he looked at Amanda. 'Once we've taken them,' he said, 'I may need you and Patricia to stand as witnesses. Will you do that?'

'I think so,' she said. Everything was happening so fast. She had not expected her father to act this quickly. She stood back as he and his retainers, wielding their clubs with fresh purpose, mounted and clattered furiously out of the courtyard towards the city.

Amanda spent the rest of the afternoon in the day room with Patricia. It seemed unnaturally quiet after the chaos of the attack. Her cousin's nerves appeared to have settled, but she was consumed in her embroidery to an unusual degree, her head dipped low to the frame, her eyes and fingers intent on needle and thread, ignoring the cat whenever it came and brushed long-ingly around her ankles. Amanda was troubled by thoughts of her own. She worried about what her father was doing, or trying to do, and what might be happening in the city.

'I hope they kill them,' said Patricia suddenly, not looking up from her work.

Amanda stared at her in surprise. 'Do you?'

'Not in the streets,' added Patricia calmly. 'I don't mean out there now, in some common brawl. I hope they drag them before the court and condemn them. It would be the just thing to do. They should be beheaded in the forum.' She spoke the words lightly, almost absently, as though relating some minor gossip from the town baths.

'If they stand before the bishop, he might be more merciful,' Amanda said. She had not yet considered what punishment their assailants would receive if arrested. It was a serious crime for a commoner to assault a member of the nobility. He would usually pay with his life.

Patricia scoffed. 'I don't think those pagans ought to count much on the *bishop's* sympathy.'

'But they didn't actually hurt us.'

Now Patricia turned to stare at Amanda in horror. 'They grabbed on to your *foot*, Amanda! Imagine what would have happened if our escort hadn't been there!' She shuddered briefly. 'It doesn't bear thinking about; I don't want to think about it. Every last miserable pagan should pay with his life, and that's all there is to it.'

Patricia returned to her embroidery with even greater concentration. She had a point. Amanda had not thought of what could have happened had their escort not returned in time. Had it been a shambolic attempt at kidnapping? Had the riot been planned? The images and noises of the attack played out in her head again and again, but she had seen too little to know what had really happened.

There was no point in dwelling on the event for now. She turned her attention to her own embroidery, and awaited the return of her father.

Agnus entered the day room in the late afternoon. 'We found them,' he announced, waving for the girls to remain seated. 'The rioters scattered when we got there, but we were able to track your attackers down. The two ringleaders were junior bucellarii of Agrius Leo, as we thought. The rest were just some scoundrels they hired from the country. They've admitted that Agrius Leo paid them to provoke a fight with the Christians. It's his bad luck that you happened to be passing.'

Patricia looked aghast. '*His* bad luck, uncle?'

'Of course. Now he has no choice but to surrender his own men for trial. All he wanted was for the peasants to be killing each other. He has no interest in seeing nobility roughed up in the streets, no more than we do. I've even made him agree that Bishop Martin preside over the trial, provided that we don't publicly accuse him of telling his men to attack you.'

'What will happen to them?' Amanda asked.

'The two ringleaders will be beheaded tomorrow in the forum. The rustics could also be executed, but his grace has decided to be merciful. They'll get away with a flogging. I must ask the both of you to identify them for the record, however.'

'Tomorrow?'

'There's no point in dragging this out. The governor has given his support to the bishop, though he's not happy about any of this, and the city council will back us, too. I know it's an unpleasant business, but it's like having a tooth out: the sooner the better. Understand, both of you, that Agrius Leo has disgraced himself with this outrage. It's a real chance for us to put him in his place.'

Amanda and Patricia arose before dawn the next day and awaited the summons to the city basilica. Patricia was in a restless but faintly cheerful mood, and seemed to relish the prospect of a formal public appearance regardless of the circumstances. She drifted about the house from her bedroom to the gardens, to the day room, where Amanda was sitting and trying to read, and back to her bedroom, appearing each time with a new coat or pair of shoes. She questioned Amanda on which headdress better suited her choice of necklace, or whether her fur-lined winter gloves would be warm enough.

A priest and deacon arrived from the city to summon them to the bishop's presence. Amanda and Patricia climbed with Agnus into the carriage that would take them to the city – the same carriage in which they had been attacked, this time with its canvas sides pulled down. They were escorted by twenty bucellarii, in all their finery of cloaks and gleaming belts of brass and leather. As they left the courtyard for the lane that led to the city, Amanda was astonished to see the crowd of clients who had gathered to accompany them. There must have been hundreds lining the lane. They had arranged themselves in order of precedence, the most socially important standing just outside the courtyard gate, and they fell in step behind the wagon as the sombre procession made its way towards Corinium.

The morning sun was invisible, the air deadened by low cloud and a damp morning fog. Amanda watched the tombstones lining the road to the city gates, ranks of them fading into greyness. She studied their peeling paint, their crumbling faces. Cobwebs were strung across them, sagging with dew. Nobody in the carriage spoke, and the only sounds were the trundling of the carriage wheels, the horses' hooves, the tramp of the crowd behind them, and the caws of crows perched somewhere in the mist.

They entered the city, passed through the streets that led to the forum, and came to a stop outside the great east doors of the basilica. This was the centre of law and government for the tribal territory as well as for the entire province. Bishop Martin, dressed in flowing robes and mitre, awaited them at the top of the steps with his clerics.

Agnus climbed out of the carriage and helped Amanda and Patricia to dismount. Holding each of them by the hand, he led them up the steps to the bishop.

'Cironia Amanda; Lollia Patricia; may God bless you,' said the bishop as they took it in turns to kneel and kiss his hand. Amanda felt the same tension she had experienced in his presence at her baptism the previous Easter. Martin seemed too precise in his mannerisms, too cautious in his speech and gestures. Even his smile seemed the result of careful and extended judgement, creasing his young-looking, angular face to a precise degree. He held his chin too high and his back too straight, which gave him the posture of a prim, stiff-necked schoolmaster, and he delivered his foreign vowels slowly and carefully. 'I'm pleased to see you both in such good health after your terrible ordeal. You do your families proud with your courage.' He stepped back and beckoned them towards the open doors. 'Now come; this will not take long.'

Amanda shivered as they entered the icy cavern of the city basilica. She had never been through these doors. It was dark, little of the dull morning light reaching far inside. Grey-faced men moved through the gloom with hurried steps; notaries, staff officers of the garrison, clerks of the tax office, moving between shadows about the business of civic and provincial government. Along the central nave ran two rows of whitewashed columns, between which were placed statues of former emperors and governors. These faces of tradition and authority looked sternly upon Amanda as she walked the length of the nave towards a huge bronze statue of Emperor Valentinian, set in a gigantic apse at the far end.

A number of court officials were already waiting for them, with a notary sitting at a writing desk. The bishop took his place in the high chair on the tribunal below the statue. Amanda was led with Patricia to stand at his side. She looked back down the nave to see that people were still entering through the east doors. All trials were public, and her father had said that this special session would attract a larger audience than most – even rustics who spoke no Latin would want to be there, he had predicted, along with almost every nobleman except Agrius Leo, the governor, and their closest supporters.

She searched for her father among the milling members of the city council, several dozen of whom were assembling at the front of the crowd. These were the local landowners who acted as the leaders of the city territory, and were responsible for its roads and bridges, for the public buildings of Corinium and for the collection of taxes and the organisation of festivals. Next to them was gathering a smaller group of officials from the governor's staff, the representatives of imperial government who administered the province as a whole, which included Corinium, Glevum and many other towns. Amanda could distinguish them by their belts and brooches, the badges of imperial service, which most city councillors lacked. Her father had rare influence in that he was both a city councillor of Corinium and a former imperial official. This, along with his descent from an ancient line of Dobunnic kings and his senatorial rank, meant that he was entitled to stand at the very front of the crowd. When Amanda spotted him take his place, he gave her a reassuring nod.

The bishop waited until the nave was almost full before speaking. 'In the presence of his Divine Excellency Valentinian Augustus, I declare this court in session.' He raised his right arm. 'Bring in the accused!'

A soldier disappeared into the shadows. A minute later he returned, leading five ragged figures who were bound to one another by neck braces and chains. Their hands and feet were manacled. They shuffled across the flagstones barefoot, accompanied by the clinking of iron. The soldier arranged them in a line facing the dais. The crowd watched, only the occasional cough interrupting the silence.

The bishop spoke as the notary scribbled to record the proceedings. 'Cironia Amanda, daughter of the most esteemed senator Gaius Cironius Agnus, and Lollia Patricia, daughter of the most perfect equestrian Marcus Lollius Pertinax, will you swear in the name of his Divine Excellency Valentinian Augustus that you recognise these as the five men who assaulted you on the streets of Corinium on the fourth day before the Nones of November in the third year of the reign of his Divine Excellency Emperor Valentinan, during the consulships of Flavius Gratianus and Dagalaif?'

'I swear,' said Patricia.

Amanda hesitated. She was studying the faces of the five men, though they hung low, their eyes staring vacantly at the floor. The three country peasants were hardly men at all; the youngest looked no older than she. All of them had badly bruised eyes and lips. The skin of their wrists and ankles had been chafed by the manacles to expose pulpy, bleeding flesh.

'Optio, have them show their faces,' said the bishop.

'Raise your chins!' snapped the soldier.

They looked up, their eyes now raised above the dais. Amanda recognised one of them as the bucellarius who had grabbed her foot. The others she did not recognise. Perhaps they were the men who had attacked them, but she could not say.

'Cironia Amanda?' the bishop prompted her.

She pointed towards the man she knew. 'He was one of them,' she said. 'The others I do not know.'

Murmuring began among the councillors and spread through the audience. Amanda could feel her father's eyes on her. Bishop Martin leaned towards her and said quietly, in order that the notary would not hear, 'You need only be *fairly* confident, my daughter. There is no question of their guilt, as they have already confessed. This is merely for the record, at the insistence of your father.'

'I saw only one face clearly during the attack,' she said. 'The others I cannot identify on oath.'

'Lollia Patricia has already sworn,' said the bishop.

'Amanda, of *course* it's them!' hissed Patricia. 'Just say yes!'

A court officer hammered his staff on the floor. 'Quiet in the presence of the emperor!' Silence once more spread the length of the basilica.

Amanda glanced towards her father, trying to read his expression. What did he want her to do? He had arranged this gathering, but would he want her to lie under oath? No, she realised. That would go against everything he had ever taught her about honourable and decent behaviour, and would disgrace the memory of her mother. 'I can swear only to him,' she said, pointing again. 'Him I recognise. The others I do not. I never saw their faces.'

Bishop Martin cleared his throat. The crowd waited in anticipation of his judgement. His voice echoed down the hundreds of feet of the great hall: 'Let it be noted that Cironia Amanda has identified the free man called Formosus, and Lollia Patricia has identified all five men. All of them have confessed to their crime. They acted in consort as free men, without the approval of their lord, the most perfect Agrius Leo. They are hereby condemned as outlaws. We decree that the men called Formosus and Ruricius are to be executed on this same day for the assault of the above-named noblewomen. We have decided, in the light of their youth and foolishness, that the lives of the freeborn brothers Comitinus, Cunedecanes and Cunittus are to be spared. They are sentenced to suffer fifty lashes apiece on this same day. This judgement is given by Bishop Martin of Corinium on the third day before the Nones of November, et cetera, et cetera.'

As soon as the cleric had finished scribbling, the bishop nodded to the guard, who led the prisoners back down the hall into the shadows. The bishop rose. 'In the name of God and the emperor, this court is concluded,' he said. He stepped down from the dais and led a train of priests and deacons towards the side door, which led to the council offices. Some councillors followed him, calling out their petitions and questions; others peeled away and were absorbed into the steady stream of people leaving the basilica by the far entrance. Agnus awaited his daughter and niece at the foot of the dais.

He was not smiling. 'It would have been better had you sworn like your cousin.'

'I was telling the truth, Father!'

'Amanda, I arranged this in order to show – in public – that our family would stand as one before our enemies, unintimidated, unafraid. I don't think Bishop Martin was impressed with your display, and neither was I. Tell me: do you honestly doubt that those were the men who attacked you yesterday?'

'I don't know, Father; yesterday I only heard voices and saw one face. What else could I say when his grace asked me under oath?'

He turned to Patricia. 'Did you see them any more clearly yesterday, niece?'

'Well – no,' she stuttered, adding hastily, 'but you quite positively assured us, uncle, that they were the right men, and they'd all confessed.'

'Exactly.' He looked back at Amanda. 'They *are* the men, and you should have sworn to it. Perhaps you don't realise what is at stake. Your public failure to identify all of them as your attackers will be the only excuse their supporters need to claim their innocence. They'll plead corruption and coercion, and spread the word that not even their alleged victims could agree on whether or not they were guilty. The fact that these are lies makes no difference. People will believe them. Agrius Leo is quiet for now; he'll let the executions go ahead, but when the time comes he can use what happened here to his advantage. *That* is what you have done. I expected better of you, daughter.'

He straightened his shoulders and turned to leave. Amanda burned, but she did not know whether from the humiliation of a public admonishment or from the sense of injustice. 'Father!' she cried. 'Please, I only told the truth! The bishop asked me if I knew their faces, and I knew only one. What else could I have said? Did you want me to lie?'

'Calm yourself, daughter,' he said, coming close. He glanced over his shoulder. 'There are issues at stake of which you are entirely ignorant.'

'Because you've *kept* me ignorant of them. And now I'm just a piece in your political game?'

'Yes,' he snapped. 'That is *precisely* what you are.'

She could tell that he was now having difficulty restraining his anger, and she stepped back in fear. He glowered at her for a moment, then spun with a rush of his cloak and stalked towards the door, followed by Alypius, the bucellarii clearing a path through the remaining crowd. Amanda and Patricia went after him timidly.

By the time they came out into the street, Agnus was already walking away with Peter and the bucellarii. Alypius bowed to Amanda. 'Lady Amanda, your father has requested that I escort you and your cousin home, and that you remain there. He says you are not to attend the executions.'

XVII

Virtue closes the door to no one. It is open to all, admits all,
invites all: freeborn and freedman, slave and king.
Seneca

By the end of the morning the boat had left Luguvalium far
behind and cleared the river estuary. Crew and passengers
rested the oars and raised the sail to catch the northern wind.
Paul accepted some bread and brandy from the clerics, and sat
leaning on the side of the ship as he ate. His arms throbbed with
exhaustion, a good, useful feeling. The breeze chilled the sweat
on his face and chest. He watched the coast slip gently past. The
one-handed slave girl was sitting at the prow of the ship, where
she had been all morning, staring out across the waves.

Shortly before dusk they reached the first coastal fortress. They
beached at the foot of a cliff and the captain directed his crew
and passengers to set up camp in a sheltered spot. Soon the tents
were put up, a fire was roaring and the smell of roasting pork
had mingled with the cold, salty air of the surf. They gathered
around the fire, sailors and clerics together, sharing stories and
gossip. Each spoke as much or as little as he wanted; Paul mostly
when spoken to, Eachna not at all. She sat wrapped in her cloak
and blanket across the fire from Paul, a tight, enclosed bundle
showing half a face and a pair of eyes, which passed intently
from one speaker to the next. Paul could tell that she missed
nothing; it was as though she was there and not there at the same
time, observing everything from beneath a creased, quizzical
brow.

The morning brought another clear sky and a firm northerly wind, strong enough to bring them to the next coastal fort before evening. If the weather stayed favourable, the captain said as they loaded the ship for departure, they might reach Deva itself in just three more days.

Towards noon of the second day, one of the clerics shouted that he had spotted sails behind them. Every person rose and squinted back towards the north. Crew and passengers fell silent. The cleric was right; Paul saw four sails just visible around the last jut of coastline, which they had passed an hour or so before. But it was the colour of the sails that had suddenly silenced his companions: pure black against the blue of the ocean.

'Verturians,' said the captain.

Still nobody moved or spoke, transfixed by the distant sight. Paul had heard tales of the Verturians, savages from the distant northern isles at the edge of the world, a place whose inhabitants were more beasts than men. Their dark sails, dyed with the blood of their sacrificed captives, were said to terrify even the other Pictish tribes. Only the Verturians were wild enough to brave the seas until late in the year, rushing onto shore in the dead of night, their skin painted black. Paul had always thought they were half mythical. He knew they had attacked Luguvalium six years before, but had never heard of them coming further south than that.

'Move yourselves!' yelled the captain, grabbing one of his crew and shoving him down the boat. 'To the oars, all of you!'

Now there was a panicked scramble to the benches as they lifted the oars into place, a hectic chorus of shouts, and a stream of curses and commands from the captain to bring them into a fast, steady rhythm. Paul forced his muscles to heave the oar against the stubborn sea. He could not take his eyes from the sails.

'Faster, come on!' yelled the captain, gripping the steering oar and shifting his stare between the sea in front and the pirates behind. 'Keep it up! We can reach Glanoventa before they reach us!'

Ten men pulled and groaned at their oars, and the ship churned through the water. Eachna passed up and down between the benches, raising a gourd of water to each man's lips. Eventually, after what seemed like an age, Paul felt his back and shoulders buckle. But with a single thought of what they would suffer should the pirates catch them, he pushed himself through the pain with a grimace.

At last the captain yelled for them to ease up. The Verturians were dropping back.

They slowed the pace. Paul felt the relief flood through his body. He squinted at their pursuers. They had fallen back, either outpaced or giving up the chase. There were laughs of relief around him. One of the clerics began to sing and lead his brothers in a prayer of thanks.

'Keep it easy till they're out of sight,' the captain said, grinning. He passed down the aisle, slapping a firm, encouraging hand on the shoulder of each man. 'We'll camp in Glanoventa Bay tonight.'

Once they had lost the black sails, they let the wind take them down the coast for the rest of the afternoon. The sun was hanging low in the west by the time they reached their destination. They returned to the oars and the captain navigated them down a narrow inlet into a wide, calm bay surrounded by forests. Smoke rose from settlements along the shoreline, and beyond the forests climbed the jagged mountains of the lake country. They passed by docks occupied by a pair of military ships, their forbidding prows facing towards the mouth of the bay. Just beyond the docks Paul could see the walls of the fortress.

'That's part of the navy,' the captain explained. 'The rest is up at Luguvalium. Probably explains why the coast isn't being patrolled properly. In the fort there's a full cohort who keep the peace. We'll camp further up the river, the shelter's better there.'

After another mile the estuary turned suddenly and narrowed into a secluded river. They continued to row until the banks were fewer than thirty yards apart, crowded with leafless trees and evergreen thickets, and the captain directed the boat to the edge of a high meadow on one side. It was a quiet spot set above the river, peaceful, with plenty of wood for fuel, and soon they were making camp.

Paul strolled through the grass, kicking apart the remnants of bonfires left by previous campers. The meadowland stretched away to the south, empty but for some farmsteads in the distance. On the north side of the river rose a large hill bristling with trees, and behind it, now hidden from view, lay the fort and harbour. It seemed a safe spot. The sun was dipping into the ocean, bathing the mountains in its dying light. Some stars had appeared in the east.

Unless the weather turned against them, two days from now he would be in Deva. Perhaps ten days later he would be home. After so many months of suffering and waiting, of uncertainty, after more than four long years of being lost, he felt as though he could almost reach out and touch Silvanicum. It would be good to see the old stream again, the path winding up to the villa, its white walls rising from the green of the valley. He prayed that he would not be seduced by nostalgia for the comforts of his old life, that he would still have the courage to stand before his father and reveal the truth of his crime.

He turned around, and was surprised to see Eachna standing a few feet away. 'They're going to cook supper soon,' she said.

Paul saw the bonfire blazing back at the camp. He had not realised how far he had wandered. He noticed for the first time that the slave girl, on the few occasions she had spoken, had not once referred to him as master, as she ought to. Was this some small attempt at rebellion? Even with her back to the setting sun and her face in shadow, her eyes seemed to glitter a light blue. Paul saw their sadness, and their seriousness. He was reminded of the blonde girl in the northern farmstead. It was an uncomfortable memory, and he began speaking to banish it. 'Julian has told me a lot about you,' he said. 'I heard you were caned for refusing to clean out the latrines. You sound like no ordinary slave.'

'I wasn't born a slave,' she said.

'I can see that. One can always tell. There's an old story, you know, about a Spartan boy who was captured and enslaved by his enemies. In olden times the Spartans never stood to be made slaves by anybody. As his first task, the boy's new masters commanded him to clean out the latrines. Rather than suffer the humiliation, he dashed his brains out against a rock.'

'He was a fool.'

'Most would say it was the noble thing to do.'

'It was the easy thing to do. He should have accepted the punishment and stayed alive to fight for his freedom.'

He nodded thoughtfully. 'I see. It seems I've been taking the wrong lesson from the story all these years.'

'Yes.'

Hearing the earnestness of her voice, Paul could not help but laugh. 'You are a serious soul, aren't you? My cousin never said you were a stoic.' She stared at him, saying nothing. 'You don't need to worry,' Paul continued. 'Julian is hoping to come south before Easter. I might not stay home long, but my family will look after you.'

There was still no answer. Paul gave up and was walking past her towards the camp when she said, 'If I hadn't promised him I'd stay with you, I would have run away tonight.'

He stopped, and nodded towards the mountains. 'Over there?'

'Yes.'

'Back to Luguvalium?'

'Yes.'

'You wouldn't last long at this time of year.'

'I'd last as long as Christ watched over me.'

She offered the words with a simple frankness, almost as though she was surprised at having to explain herself. Julian had spoken of Eachna's enthusiastic adoption of Christ as her personal patron and protector, and Paul had scarcely thought about it. But now he found that it irritated him. 'Then run,' he shrugged. 'I won't stop you.'

For a moment it looked as though she might, but before either could move there was a sudden eruption of cries from the camp. From this distance, Paul could see only a rush of formless shadows that came from the blackness and flooded the silhouettes of their companions against the firelight. He glimpsed the flash of blades, and instantly he was running towards the camp, sword drawn.

By the time he reached it, only the captain and two sailors were still alive, backing in his direction, daggers drawn and pointed at the attackers who were now slowly encircling them. They were too many, at least ten, a pack of wolf-like men with snarling teeth. Their skin was painted charcoal black. Paul joined the sailors. He glanced back and did not see Eachna. Hopefully she had already fled.

'Stay together,' said the captain, his voice firm. 'Wait for them.' Paul kept close as ordered. He felt the years of army training spark into life. He could tell that the captain and his men were ex-military.

The Verturians prowled around them. They barked at one another in a tongue Paul could not understand. They were biding their time, sure of victory.

Four of the Verturians began to creep slowly inwards towards their prey. They were armed with daggers and shields. Paul saw that he had the only longsword, though against so many attackers that was not much of an advantage.

One of the barbarians had singled him out. The charcoal paint obscured the features of his face. His exposed teeth, filed to sharp points, gleamed with his eyes in the flickering light.

'Wait!' urged the captain. 'Let them come!'

Paul saw his opponent hang back, wary of the longsword, trying to draw Paul away from the others. He jabbed his dagger first one way, then the other.

When the attack came, it was sudden. The Verturian moved to the right and Paul swept his blade to strike him, but it was a feint; the savage darted back in the blink of an eye, evading Paul's sword and coming at him from the left. Paul, the weight of his swing still carrying his blade in the wrong direction, a dagger lunging towards his throat, dropped and rolled into his enemy's legs. The barbarian tumbled and fell, and was stunned by an inadvertent heel from a sailor to the back of his head. Paul scrabbled on top of him before he could rise and sank the blade deep into his chest. He saw the fury freeze in the Verturian's eyes as he let out a final gasp.

He pulled his sword free and jumped to his feet. The initial attack had lasted moments and left two of the barbarians dead, the other two edging back to their comrades clutching stab wounds and cursing in pain. One sailor had been killed.

The leader of the Verturians was screaming at his men, thrusting his blade at the three surviving defenders. Clearly he had not expected such stiff resistance. Now six fresh Verturians moved towards the centre.

Paul sized up the two men approaching him. They looked small but fast. He would have to take down one as soon as possible. He had been lucky last time, and must not let them trick him again. It was like a double wrestling bout back at Vercovicium, he told himself. He could handle two men, armed or not. He kept his back close to his two comrades, covering their flanks as they covered his, not giving their attackers space to use their numbers.

For a long while they stayed as they were, Paul and his two companions in the centre, double their number surrounding them, hovering just beyond reach. Paul stared at the two pairs of eyes hanging in the blackness before him. He felt completely calm. This was not like the skirmish when they had defended the taxman. Now he felt no apprehension, no fear: not of death, nor of injury. It was as though he were watching himself from far away.

There was an irritated scream from the leader, and all six men, after a final moment of hesitation, attacked at once. This time there was no attempt at a feint, merely a savage, chaotic lunge forwards. Paul, outreaching them easily, instantly stuck his sword into the belly of the man on the left, at the same time stepping towards him to dodge the attack from the right. He yanked the sword from the man's stomach, twisting it as he did so.

His sidestep had taken him away from his comrades. Sensing the opening, another two Verturians leapt into the fray, rushing the captain and the remaining sailor as they warded off their attackers. Neither had a chance; in moments the Verturians had overpowered them and forced them to the ground in a flurry of knife thrusts.

Paul was alone. The Verturians screeched in triumph. He backed away towards the river. Behind him was a steep drop through brambles down into the water. The raiders gave him space, caught their breath and took their time, edged slowly around to his sides. He noticed a strange heaviness in his left leg, and looked down to see a gash in his trousers, and blood seeping through the cloth. He felt the remaining strength fade from his thigh, and in its place came a wave of pain that almost made him stumble. His last dodge had not been quite fast enough. He thought about making a dive for the water, but knew it would do no good. With this leg they would catch him before he swam five yards.

At least they had bought enough time for Eachna to escape. Perhaps she would even make it back to Luguvalium.

The moment he thought this, she appeared at his side. In her right hand she was wielding a branch as a weapon. She snarled at the Verturians in the barbaric tongue of the Picts. They hung back at first, but their surprise quickly turned to amusement, and they began to creep closer.

'Run,' said Paul. 'I'll hold them off.'

'*You* run,' she snapped.

Suddenly another shout came from the trees behind the Verturians; an order to attack in a language Paul knew. A host of figures rushed into the light of the bonfire, charging the barbarians with a roar. They were Roman soldiers. Paul watched as they swept through and cut down the raiders one by one, easily deflecting dagger thrusts with their great oval shields, pushing their spears and swords into the barbarians without mercy, finishing them where they fell.

It was over in moments. The officer, a tribune, picked his way through the bodies to Paul. He was laughing with exhilaration. 'You lucky devil! Who are you, friend?'

'A traveller.' Paul was bent over, his left hand clutched to the wound. He could feel the blood oozing through his fingers.

'Sit,' commanded Eachna, and she helped Paul slowly to the ground.

'Bandage over here!' yelled the tribune. His accent was Frankish. 'Hellish mess,' he said. Paul looked up at him. His face was long and thin, suited to the tallness of his frame, and, like his shoulders and chest, had a look of concentrated strength. Even his eyes were metallic in their sharpness, gleaming in the firelight, peering out beneath a brow that might have been hammered into shape from a lump of iron. But there was an intelligent frankness in his look, and warmth in his smile.

'Are you from the harbour garrison?' Paul asked as a soldier arrived to bind his leg.

The tribune scoffed. 'Lucky for you we're not! Where have you come from?'

'Luguvalium.'

The tribune stared towards the dark line of the northern horizon, biting his lip. 'They should have reached there days ago.'

'Who? What's going on?'

'Mutiny is what's going on.' He nodded across the river. 'Glanoventa, all the forts up the coast, even Galava across the mountains – mutiny. Up at Luguvalium, d'you hear anything about a man called Valentinus? A Pannonian, a military man?'

'No.'

'He was exiled there by the emperor last year, put under the charge of our sorry excuse for a duke. Somehow Valentinus won him over, and the duke – gods spare us! – made him special commander of the mountain garrisons. Now Fullobaudes has gone south to spend the winter feasting and drinking himself sick, leaving Valentinus in charge. The damn fool, giving all those troops to an exile! As soon as the duke's back was turned, Valentinus started buying off his men. Last week he tried to bribe all the tribunes hereabouts to swear loyalty to him personally. They're no fools, they'd follow an ass into battle sooner than Fullobaudes. They said yes.'

'And you?'

'Tried to bribe me too.'

'And what happened?'

He grinned. 'You'll see when we get to Mediobogdum.'

'Why haven't you sent word to Fullobaudes?'

'I tried. But he's somewhere way down south by now, the traitors control every pass through the mountains except ours, and they've got us surrounded. My garrison is depleted enough already. Now we've got barbarians landing on the coast. So it's not safe to go anywhere by boat, as you can see.'

'I need to get to the south.'

'Sorry, friend, you're not going anywhere.'

Paul stared into those hard eyes with steel of his own. 'You mean to keep me by force, tribune?'

The tribune looked amused by his defiance. 'No.' With the toe of his boot he nudged Paul's injured thigh. The pain was sudden and intense; for an instant it flooded Paul's mind, and he gasped with the shock. 'Your *wound* will keep you here, I think. The cut is deep. You need rest and treatment. I'll give you shelter for the winter, at least, and then we'll see.'

'And if your men rebel against you?'

The tribune surveyed his soldiers as they milled about the bonfire and checked the bodies. 'As long as I can keep them frightened enough – and paid – they'll follow me. When the coin runs out, we'll see.' He laughed. 'You don't sound like you're from the ranks, friend, but I can see you are.' He was looking at Paul's wrist, and his military tattoo. 'Deserter?'

'The army decided it didn't want me any more,' Paul said. Between the waves of pain he gathered his thoughts and calmly considered his position. They could not take another boat south, and his leg would need time to heal. It was frustrating, but it seemed that he had no choice but to trust this Frank.

He extended his arm carefully. 'Paul of the Dobunni.'

The tribune reached down to shake his hand. 'Drogo.'

XVIII

Receive this soul, and release me from these cares!
I have lived; I have run the course allotted me by Fate;
And now I will go, a noble spectre, into the depths below.
Virgil, *The Aeneid*

A month passed after the trial, and there were no more inflam-matory public speeches, no more riots, no more abuse in the street. Yet even from the seclusion of the townhouse Amanda sensed that the city was not at peace, merely under truce, as though in hibernation for the winter.

One afternoon her father came to her with news. It was the last thing she had expected to hear.

'Agrius Leo is having a feast, and we are invited.'

Amanda was sitting at her loom. As she realised what her father had said, her fingers fell still. She could not think of how to reply.

'I know, I'm as surprised as you are,' he continued. 'But Agrius Leo is looking for peace, and he wants the world to know it.'

'Must we go?'

'I'm afraid so.'

'But we still don't know what's happened to Paul and Julian. What if his men have found them, Father? And what about them attacking me and Patricia in the street?'

'What happened to Paul is a private matter, and must be dealt with privately. The attack was public, and this feast is a public gesture of reconciliation. You must distinguish between the two.'

Slowly Amanda continued working on her loom. 'So there are

two brands of honour,' she said. 'And we can choose between them as though swapping hats.'

'In so many words,' her father replied. He went to the door, peered into the corridor, and closed the door quietly. He returned to his daughter and sat on a stool beside her. 'Leave your weaving for a moment. Look at me.'

Amanda obeyed. Her father's expression was stern, as it had been in the city basilica a month before, but not unkind. It was the face he wore for the rest of the world.

'Amanda, I'll make Agrius Leo pay for what he's done to Paul. I swear it in the name of Christ, he'll pay for it – in a court of law, when I've gathered enough evidence to accuse him of that and all his other crimes.'

'His other crimes? You mean when he bought the villa Caecina?'

Agnus snorted. 'That was nothing. He did that just to insult me, to show that he could steal from under my nose an estate I'd been hoping to purchase myself. Technically he broke no law. These days, he doesn't *need* to break any laws. He's procurator of the state weaving factories at Venta, and his land holdings almost rival ours. When he turned up in Corinium eight years ago – he was the governor's chief of staff at the time, nothing more – he was already the owner of properties scattered across the province.'

'But he has no family here, has he? How did he come by the land?'

'*That* was precisely the question I asked eight years ago,' Agnus said, smiling at her in approval. 'Amanda, I realise why you acted as you did at the trial. I was still treating you like a girl, but you're becoming a woman, with the wisdom and courage to act according to your own conscience. It was my fault that I did not tell you the whole truth, for then you might have understood what was at stake. So let me ask you now: are you ready to play your part for the good of the family?'

There was a weight to his question that gave Amanda pause. He was offering her another chance. 'Yes, Father.'

'Good. Everything I'm about to tell you must remain a secret

– lives may depend on it. You asked how Agrius Leo came by so much land in our province – a good question. It's taken years for me and Alypius to put the picture together, but it transpired that Agrius Leo had been in Britannia before, during the Winter of Grief. He was one of the secret agents involved in the inquisitions after the revolt of Magnentius was suppressed. He helped draw up the false accusations of treason, paying scoundrels for scurrilous gossip, treating it as evidence, and confiscating the property of innocent men for the imperial fisc. The emperor called a halt to the inquisitions when he heard what was happening, but not before a great many deeds of ownership had also found their way into Agrius Leo's pocket. That's how he amassed his wealth – by arranging the deaths of innocent men, and plundering their estates. He all but murdered them himself.'

Amanda was horrified. She thought of all those falsely accused and executed for treason during the terrible reprisals of the Winter of Grief. She thought of her own family. 'So grandfather Bonus, Uncle Maximus and Uncle Viventiolus . . .'

'That's right. Agrius Leo helped arrange their arrest and trial.'

'But they'd stood *against* Magnentius! How could anyone accuse them of treason?'

'More easily than you might think. During the revolt, Magnentius had forced my father to surrender an estate to him. Someone – an informant with a seat on the city council – dug out the charter from the record office, and showed it to Agrius Leo. On the face of it, it would have looked like our family had willingly supported the revolt, never mind that we'd had no choice, never mind that your grandfather Faustus had already been poisoned for opposing Magnentius. This charter, and the lying tongue of the informant, was all Agrius Leo needed. Were it not for your mother, I would have been arrested as well, and Agrius Leo might now be the owner of Silvanicum.'

Amanda sat speechless, her weaving forgotten. She had known that Agrius Leo was a scheming, greedy bully, and she despised him for keeping Paul from them, but she had never imagined that he had tried to destroy their family all those years ago. Now she well understood the depth of her father's hatred for him.

'Since I've told you this much,' her father continued, 'I may as well tell you the identity of the informant. It was Silvius Bassulus. He betrayed my father and brothers, hoping to get some of our property for himself.'

'Silvius Bassulus!' Amanda gasped. 'I was to marry his grandson . . .'

'Yes. I only learned this part a couple of years ago, by which time Bassulus was long dead. But you see now why I cancelled your betrothal. I don't care if his son and grandson know nothing about what he did. I won't have you marry into that family.'

'If you know all this, Father, why not accuse Agrius Leo publicly? If he enriched himself by falsely accusing people of treason, and taking their property when it should have gone to the emperor . . .'

'He would face the death penalty for that, or at least exile. But knowing it is one thing, proving it in court quite another. I need to find more witnesses who served in the secret service with him or on the governor's staff at the time, who knew what was going on and are willing to accuse him. Such men are hard to find, and many of them are now in Treveris, or retired, or dead. This is why I wanted Lucas in Treveris; but if he can't even finish his schooling without turning into a gambling drunkard, how can I trust him with something like this? If only Faustus were still alive! Or if Paul were to come back . . . I know he hated the idea of politics. That was why he ran away. But if I could tell him what was at stake . . .'

Amanda placed a hand on his shoulder. 'Paul will come home, Father. We mustn't lose faith in God.' She remembered her meeting with Rufus back in August, when Rufus had claimed that her father had known all along where Paul was. Looking at her father now, seeing the pain in his face, how could she believe something so absurd? If Agrius Leo had ever told him that Paul was alive and at Vercovicium, he would have stopped at nothing to bring him home.

Agnus straightened his posture. 'Paul is beyond our help for now,' he said, 'but, as far as we know, he is also beyond Agrius Leo's harm. Agrius lost face after the riot and executions last month, and I've been able to deprive him of some supporters on the council. So he's choosing this moment to make peace. He has no idea how much I know. He thinks he covered his tracks years ago, and that's how we must keep it for now, which means accepting his invitation, going to his party, drinking his wine, and laughing at his jokes.'

'I see,' Amanda said. She stared at the loom before her and imagined the intricate threads of intrigue and self-interest running through the fabric of the province. This was the proper domain of men, one in which women were meant to play their part in obedient silence while keeping their eyes on the family hearth. Something had changed; her father seemed to be inviting her to take on the role of his absent sons. She could not deny its allure.

'At the party, Amanda, we must don our public hats, as will Agrius. He will appear to charm us, and we must appear to be charmed. Then if the opportunity presents itself, I would ask you to converse briefly with his son, Rufus. I'd like you to show him a pleasant and simple temperament. Laugh at his jokes, if he makes them – but not too much.'

'Why?'

'To charm and confound him. And then, when he is vulnerable, I want you to find out how things stand between him and his father. Rufus told you he was trying to find and return Paul without his father's knowledge. My instinct tells me he's lying, but we must be sure. If he is truly working against his father, he could be of great use to us. Can you do this for me?'

Amanda nodded. She would try not to disappoint him again. This was so new to her. She had always been taught that grace and refinement were proper qualities of the Roman matron because they were moral in themselves, not because they could be deployed as weapons. Yet was that potential not the very source of their power? And the thought of using them against Agrius

Rufus had a deep, potent attraction. She did not like the strange, distant power he seemed to have over her. This could be a chance to take control of her feelings, to suppress those base desires that threatened to subvert her will. He did not seem an especially canny sort; more of a dumb, lumbering oaf, ill-suited to this sort of intrigue.

With a flick of her scented hair, Amanda would trip him up. It would be no more than he deserved after his treatment of Patricia.

On the evening of the party, the Cironii wagon drew into the courtyard of Agrius Leo's townhouse within the city, as bright as day amidst dozens of flaming torches. A light flurry of snow was falling through the firelight. Agnus, who had been riding with Alypius ahead of the carriage, helped Amanda and Patricia dismount and led them into the house, one on each arm.

The townhouse was warm and cheerful, its rooms already filling up with guests. Evidence of Agrius Leo's wealth was everywhere. The light of candelabras shimmered on intricate floor mosaics beneath their feet and on the richly painted walls; it flickered across the feast set out on tables in each room, across the sweetbreads and broiled pork, the roasted chestnuts, and the silver tableware on which it was enticingly arranged. Music from somewhere deeper in the house drifted over the heads of the chattering guests. Patricia looked about and clapped her hands happily as a house servant took their winter cloaks. 'It's just like Treveris!'

This was Amanda's first time at a party that was not to celebrate a family birthday or Christian festival, and despite her earlier confidence she felt timid before the milling mass of unfamiliar adult faces. At sixteen she was barely old enough to be attending such an affair. She gripped her father's arm tightly as city councillors and imperial officials jostled to greet him. She smiled at them when introduced, modestly accepting their compliments on her appearance, soberly accepting their sympathy on the loss of her mother. Many she had seen at the funeral, but most not. The

Britons were mostly members of the city council, and those with Gallic or Italian or eastern accents were more likely to be on the staff of the provincial governor, that much she knew; she also knew that there was little love lost between them. Otherwise their long names and faces flowed by with very little to tell them apart.

After several minutes of swift greetings and partings, Agrius Leo emerged from another room. As he approached, faces turned towards him and bodies moved aside as though provoked by some invisible force. Hardly a man or woman he passed did not receive a warm acknowledgement of some kind, whether by word or gesture.

Amanda, seeing him for the first time, studied him carefully. She had always pictured him as a large and bullish figure, a devious-looking villain whose wickedness would be plain to the world, but this was not what she saw. He was not especially tall or broad, solidly built rather than fat. His hair was black and curly above a bearded, dark face. He had the same eyes as his son, strong and stern, but with a liveliness that made him altogether more attractive in appearance.

He saw Amanda and her father, still close to the threshold, and came directly towards them, smiling. 'Most esteemed senator Gaius Cironius Agnus, noble prince of the Dobunni, erstwhile consul-governor of Belgica Secunda, son of Gaius Cironius Bonus Gregorius,' he announced, extending his hands in greeting. 'You are welcome. My only regret in seeing you beneath my roof is that it has taken so long to come about.'

'Most perfect equestrian Flavius Agrius Leo,' replied Agnus. 'I accept your invitation with joy.' He took Agrius Leo's outstretched hands and shook them firmly. Amanda was aware of the many eyes trained on them. 'This is my daughter, Amanda.'

Agrius Leo bowed. 'I count it an honour and privilege finally to meet you, most gracious lady. Allow me to offer my sympathies for the loss of your mother, whose virtue was rightly famed throughout the Four Provinces.'

Amanda smiled demurely, despising him.

'This is my niece Lollia Patricia, daughter of equestrian Lollius Pertinax of Glevum.'

'And along with Lady Amanda, granddaughter of the famous Marcus Bodenus Faustus of the Atrebates, unless I'm mistaken? Such an illustrious lineage can hardly be concealed from those with a nose for it. I can see his ancestral light in your eyes, my dear.'

Patricia blushed and dipped her head.

'Ladies, your presence here is a garland of roses on this humble little gathering. Come, most esteemed senator, since you have graced us with the two most renowned beauties of the province, the least I can do is offer them some wine and cushions.'

He beckoned for them to follow him into a large neighbouring room, where three couches lay vacant amidst the partygoers. Amanda sensed that his hospitality was well practised, the greeting with her father carefully planned. When reciting her grandfather Bonus's name he had included Gregory, a Christian name adopted at baptism, in a gesture of respect that would not have been lost on those around them, and Patricia was still grinning from his flattery of her noble descent. They took their place on the couches, Agnus and Agrius Leo reclining on the first two, Amanda and Patricia sitting side by side on the third. Attendants brought them glasses of wine and set platters of oysters and snails on low tables in front of them.

'A fine house,' said Agnus, looking about approvingly. Amanda marvelled at his affectation of friendship.

'I bought it when I came over from Gallia eight years ago – almost nine years now. I had new mosaics laid, the walls repainted, fixed the roof. All the furniture and statuary I shipped over the sea.'

'What an effort that must have entailed,' said Patricia.

'Luckily I didn't have to carry it all myself,' he laughed. 'I'm glad I won't have to carry it all back myself, either.'

'Carry it back?' asked Agnus.

'Oh yes. Now that my official post as procurator of the weaving factories is coming to an end, I'm returning to Gallia. Not retiring exactly, but I'll have to bid a sad farewell to Britannia.'

Agnus looked genuinely surprised at this news. 'I'd no idea you were planning to leave. What of your properties here?'

'I'm selling most of them, and leaving stewards to look after the rest, along with my boy Rufus. Gallia has been so unsettled these last few years, especially with the Alemanni wiping out those two legions near Treveris last year, I've felt much safer on this island. Shocking business. But Count Jovinus and the field army gave them a proper bloody nose, and things are looking much more peaceful now.'

He was interrupted by the announcement of a new guest whose name Amanda did not catch. Agrius Leo rose from his couch and excused himself, promising to return shortly.

As he walked away, Amanda caught·her father's eyes. He seemed both taken aback and delighted by the news that Agrius Leo was leaving Britannia. This was surely a good thing for the province. Amanda began to feel that she might enjoy this party after all.

Their host returned, bringing with him the new arrival. Agnus, Amanda and Patricia stood as Agrius Leo introduced him. 'Allow me to present the *vir spectabilis* Duke Fullobaudes, commander of all garrison forces in the Four Provinces of Britannia.'

Amanda bowed with the others. As Agrius Leo introduced them in turn, she stared at the remarkable figure of the duke. He was at least a head taller than anyone around him, wide-shouldered, a balding, serious-looking man in his forties. He was wearing the elaborate military uniform of his rank, with a gaudily embroidered cloak and tunic and a heavy golden brooch at his shoulder. With the status of *spectabilis*, "outstanding", the second highest senatorial grade, he outranked everyone else in the building, including her father, and probably everyone else in the province of Britannia Prima. Yet despite his title and his splendid uniform, he could not hide his barbarian origins when he opened his mouth.

'I'm delighted to meet all of you,' he said unsmilingly in a thick Alemannic accent, his words still carrying the rough edges of Latin learned from many years in military service. 'Please, let us sit.'

They all sat. Agrius Leo now joined Agnus on his couch, with Fullobaudes taking a couch to himself. He sat perched on the cushions, his back stiff, looking about the room. He looked ill at ease in the social gathering. When it became clear that he was not about to open a fresh conversation, as was expected of the highest-ranking man in this situation, their host began to speak. 'Outstanding duke, we were in fact just discussing how peaceful the Gallic prefecture is looking at the moment. In the case of Britannia, we have you to thank personally for that, do we not? We've had no barbarians cross the Wall in six years.'

The duke fixed his eyes on Agrius Leo. He seemed never to blink. 'Nor will they cross, as long as I'm in charge.'

Amanda felt strange sitting in the presence of the duke. He had been the recipient of Uncle Pertinax's letter about the garrison of Glevum. She wondered if he had read it. Even if he had, surely he would never guess that she had helped draft it. How could she not take this chance to talk to the man himself, to find out if Uncle Pertinax's fears were justified? 'Outstanding duke,' she began, 'it is such a comfort to know that you are guarding the frontiers on our behalf. I know that the people of Glevum are very worried about barbarians attacking from over the sea. Are they not, Patricia?'

'Most certainly,' Patricia said. 'My father is convinced of it. He talks of little else, except his pigs.'

'Those rumours are unfounded,' the duke said. 'I know more about what's happening beyond the frontiers than anyone. I have many spies moving through the barbarian kingdoms, and there is no cause for alarm.'

'There is talk of a campaign in the spring, outstanding duke,' said Agnus. 'Is it true that the city garrisons will be heading north?'

'Yes,' said Fullobaudes. 'The city garrisons all come from the Sixth and Twentieth Legions, and I need them for the invasion. The king of the Picts has recently committed atrocities against Rome which must be avenged.'

'But at the risk of leaving the cities undefended?' Agnus said.

'This is a military decision. The city militias will be able to keep order until the garrisons return in the autumn.'

Agnus pressed his point. 'And suppose the barbarians raid the south in the meantime?'

'They will not,' the duke said flatly. 'The western coastal forts are to remain fully manned. They will protect your shores, senator.'

Amanda was relieved to hear that. No doubt Uncle Pertinax was right to be upset about the city garrisons being withdrawn, but had he himself not assumed that the barbarians would attack by sea? As long as the coasts were patrolled, surely the province would be safe. She felt one great worry lift from her mind. This thought, and the promised departure of Agrius Leo, helped her spirits slowly rise. Perhaps God was bringing their time of tribulation to an end. Perhaps Paul and Julian were safe, and would soon be home.

While she was thinking, her father had engaged Agrius Leo and the duke in private conversation, leaving Amanda and Patricia to talk to one another.

'That's such good news,' Patricia said. 'Isn't it, Amanda? To think that my father has been crying wolf all this time. Of course the barbarians can't sail up the Sabrina with the fleet guarding it. Sometimes I think he complains just for the sake of something to do . . .' She stopped suddenly. Her eyes were fixed on something behind Amanda. She turned her face sharply to one side as though trying not to be seen. 'He's over by the door.'

Amanda glanced briefly over her shoulder. Agrius Rufus had just entered from the private part of the house, and was standing alone at the threshold. He did not yet seem to have spotted them. He was in formal military dress, a wide leather belt studded with brass fittings, a white tunic, a red cloak fixed at the shoulder with a brooch. He leaned heavily on a walking stick in his left hand and began to hobble towards a table of food.

'Dressing up like a soldier again,' said Patricia bitterly. 'He looks absurd in that costume, as though he did anything more heroic than fall off a horse.'

Amanda's heart was thumping. Fearing that a moment's

hesitation would protract itself until it cost her the chance to speak to Rufus alone, she leaned close to Patricia and said, 'Father asked me to talk with him, and I'd rather get it over with. I won't be long.'

Before Patricia could reply, Amanda rose, smoothed her shawl and straightened her necklace, lifted her chin and walked with an assured, graceful stride towards Rufus. He was standing with his back to her, fingering a plate of oysters.

She kept her voice clear and firm, yet with a friendly note. 'Agrius Rufus.'

He hesitated, and dropped an oyster he had picked up back on the plate. He turned stiffly. He looked so different in his military uniform. The crisp, gold-embroidered tunic was tight across his broad chest and shoulders. He was clean shaven, his hair styled with oil. His was a hard face, rigid in its expressions, the type not naturally suited to smiling; but now he did smile, and the sneering curl to his lips vanished, his eyes softened, and Amanda saw for the first time quite how handsome he was. 'My lady,' he said, bowing. 'I'm very happy to see you here.'

Amanda gathered herself, clearing her throat. 'Since your father was kind enough to invite me and my father to his party, I thought it fitting that we should live in public concord as far as possible.'

'I see.' His smile faded. 'And in private discord?'

'If you wouldn't mind.'

'Well, you have reason enough to hate me. But unfortunately I don't yet have any reason to hate you back, which leaves us somewhat at odds.'

'The very nature of discord, Agrius Rufus. Although, in fact, I believe you *do* have reason to hate me.'

'I do?'

'When we last spoke I called you a liar. I later heard from another source that some of what you said, at least, was true. The rest I'm sure was a lie, but if you wish to hate me for accusing you of total deceit instead of half-deceit, which you more properly deserved, then I won't hold it against you.'

'You're too kind, my lady.'

They were interrupted by an attendant bearing a tray of glasses filled with wine. Rufus took one and offered it to Amanda.

She smiled and took the glass. Rufus took another for himself and the attendant left. They stood together for a short silence, sipping the wine. Amanda felt that so far she was giving a good account of herself. The most important thing, however, was to do what her father had asked of her. 'While we're as alone as I hope we ever find ourselves,' she said, 'would you permit a brief lapse into the matter of our private discord?'

'If it will assist in dispelling it, gladly.'

She dropped her pleasant countenance. 'You told me before that my brother was at a certain fort on the Wall, and from there was sent north. Since then I've received word that he's all but disappeared, and now a friend of mine who had pledged to seek him out has also vanished.'

'I'm sorry, my lady. Who is your friend?'

'That needn't concern you.'

'If it concerns you, it does me.'

'He's protected by the bishop of Luguvalium. I won't tell you any more than that.'

He took the information and considered it. 'A family member, I would presume.' He was staring at her closely. 'Your cousin Julian, am I right?'

She nodded, silently reprimanding herself. She should not have mentioned Julian at all. Now she might have put him in even more danger.

'Don't look alarmed. My father was in the imperial secret service. Did you know that? Intelligence is his business. He knows that your cousin Julian is a deacon at Luguvalium. But there, at least, let me put your mind at rest. The last I heard, which was about a month ago, Julian was safe and sound in Luguvalium.'

Amanda felt a worry lift from her mind. She had received Julian's letter in September, which meant he must have safely returned to the city since. But why had he not written? Perhaps he had returned too late to send another letter before the winter.

'As for your brother, I wish I had such happy news. After I learned he had been sent north, I sent two of my own men to find him. But by the time they finally reached the place – Trimontium – he was nowhere to be found.'

'I see,' said Amanda calmly. 'Please be more specific.'

'There had been a Pictish ambush deep in the forest, and his entire squad had been killed. They say he survived, but soon afterwards he disappeared. A lot of the garrison did.'

'Dear Christ,' she said. It was all she could manage to keep herself calm with other partygoers standing nearby. She continued in a low voice, 'If Paul is dead, my father will not hesitate to burn this house and every other house your family owns to the ground.'

'He probably deserted like the rest. My men visited all the border post commanders, the civil officials, even the bishop in Luguvalium, asking them to detain him if he was discovered while crossing the Wall.'

'And he wasn't seen at Luguvalium?' If Julian had by any chance found Paul, Amanda reasoned, that is where they would have gone. Yet her heart was not hopeful.

Rufus shook his head. 'My lady, you still seem to believe that I'm party to my father's schemes. I tell you now – in confidence – that I'm not. I became a soldier against my father's wishes because I believe in fighting my enemies face to face. If I find Paul, I will not tell my father. I will tell you, and try to bring him home to you. I have no other intentions.'

She stared deep into his eyes, seeking the truth of his words. They were playing a game with one another, she knew. In her heart she wanted to believe him – perhaps too much. She could not trust her instincts with him. She could not even think straight when he looked at her like this. Why had her father given her such an impossible task?

In her frustration she decided he was lying. Everything he said was a lie. He was a mere puppet of his father. 'Please, Agrius Rufus, if you are to lie to me, make the lie a pleasant one. Tell me my brother is awaiting me safe and sound outside in the courtyard, for instance; or tell me that you're planning to join your father when he returns to Gallia.' She set her wine glass on the table. 'If you like, you could embellish your lie by saying that your ship will be loaded down with all these fine statues and trinkets of his, and that it has a leaking hull. Can you still swim with that crippled leg of yours?'

Rufus held her eyes. Now he did not try to hide his anger. 'Perhaps you should remember that your brother's life could still be in my hands.' He turned and began to shuffle slowly back to the door through which he had entered.

Amanda immediately went back to Patricia and sat beside her on the couch. Patricia took her hands, watching Rufus as he left the party. A servant opened the door and closed it behind him. 'What did you say to him?'

'Nothing. He's a pathetic toad.' She noticed that the two other couches were now vacant. 'Where's my father?'

'Agrius Leo spirited him and the duke away somewhere. I'm glad you're back. I was starting to feel neglected, and when that happens I always drink too much wine.'

They stayed at the party for two or three more hours, moving between the other guests, gossiping, joking, discussing politics and literature. Patricia dazzled all to whom she spoke, and this time Amanda was content to stand back, consumed by her own thoughts, and vaguely watch her cousin's natural charm at work. Having spent time in Treveris, Patricia could speak to Gauls as easily as to Britons, and her red hair and willowy figure were enough to seize the immediate fascination of any easterner. As Amanda had expected, her cousin did not want for the attention of young officers and bureaucrats, eligible or not.

Throughout the rest of the evening Amanda found herself glancing through the crowds, looking in vain for Rufus. He did not reappear. Each time she chastised herself: he was nothing to her. What did she care if he was at the party or not? Why did she even want to see him again? Yet each time he had barely left her thoughts before she caught herself seeking him once more.

It was late when they left, stepping quickly to their carriage across cobbles now hidden under snow, Patricia still giddy with wine and conversation, Amanda sullen and depressed. Her father joined them in the carriage for the journey back to the townhouse, saying that he did not trust himself on his horse with such a merry swaying in his head. The three of them bundled themselves into the vehicle, Patricia laughing as they blindly settled on cushions and buried themselves under fur blankets.

'I can't remember the last time I had such fun,' said Patricia.

'I'm very glad to hear it, niece.'

With a jolt the wagon began to trundle away from the orange glow of the courtyard, leaving the sounds of the party behind, and passed through the gate into the darkness of the city streets. The snow had stopped, but gusts of wind buffeted the canvas shell around them.

Amanda could not shake an irrational sense of guilt. It was as though it had sunk its claws into her shawl like a hungry cat, and refused to leave her alone. Of course she had hurt Rufus's feelings – she had meant to! Why then should she feel this sick regret at having angered him? Why was she so upset that he had left the party?

Probably she had drunk too much wine, she decided irritably, and it was provoking irrational thoughts. No doubt she would see things in a better light tomorrow.

Her father's voice came from the blackness. 'I saw you speaking to Agrius Leo's son, Amanda.'

She cleared her throat. 'That's right.'

'How did you find him?'

Amanda was surprised by the question. Surely her father was not referring to her secret task with Patricia present. 'Mopish,' she said. 'We didn't talk long.'

'Good looking, isn't he?'

'I didn't really notice.' Patricia was sitting between them, saying nothing. Her silence was proof enough to Amanda that she found the topic of Rufus uncomfortable. Amanda decided to change the subject, forcing a cheerfulness into her words. 'I did rather like the funny old senator from Massilia, though. He had us in stitches, didn't he, Patricia?'

But her father would not be diverted so easily. 'Since his accident, it seems that Rufus is content to settle here in Britannia, or so his father told me.'

'I didn't know that.'

'Oh, and I have some good news about the Caecina estate. In principle, at least, Agrius Leo is willing to sell the land back to me for a good price. He's also agreed to sell me a number of his other estates, which I'll then be able to donate to the council as civic land. It'll do a great deal to ease the pressure of taxation.'

'That is good news, Father. But can you trust him?'

'Normally I would say no, but he made these assurances with the duke as witness. He genuinely seems to be leaving Britannia, and wants to reduce his assets here. We still need to formalise and negotiate the details, and there are further implications and arrangements involved, of course.' He was quiet for a moment before he added, in a mock conspiratorial tone, 'And you yourself are not entirely divorced from said arrangements, Amanda.'

'How so?'

'Well, nothing's been settled yet, but one of the agreements is that Agrius Leo's son would receive baptism next Easter.'

That was the last thing Amanda had expected to hear. Courting Christian nobles with parties was one thing, but sending his own son to the font – how far was Agrius Leo prepared to go to realise his political ambitions? She would prefer it if his family stayed pagan rather than cheapen the Christian faith with such a fraudulent conversion.

'Rufus, apparently, is quite willing to go through with it. Which brings us to your part in this, Amanda. Provided the sale goes through, once Rufus is converted and resolved to settle locally, and now that you've taken the full measure of him – how would you feel about taking him as your husband?'

Amanda did not know what to say. No thoughts came to her

mind that she could express. After everything her father had said about Agrius Leo, and his schemes against the family, what he had done to them all those years ago – now he was talking about a marriage alliance, as though it were the most natural thing in the world? After he had cancelled her marriage into the family of Silvius Bassulus?

Her father continued. 'Under such an arrangement, after Agrius Leo had sold me Caecina's land, I would give it as your dowry, which would make it your own possession. He'd pay for the rebuilding of the villa, and you'd be living just downstream from Silvanicum. You'd hardly have left home at all. Naturally I wouldn't entertain the notion for a moment unless Rufus were to convert and the Caecina estate to pass into our hands, nor if it were not all but certain that a few years from now Rufus will take on some office that confers senatorial rank. You need only consider the wider implications, Amanda, to see why this alliance would be so beneficial to both parties. It will secure some peace between the factions in the city council. I'm sure you can work out the other advantages for yourself. Perhaps best of all, you'll be able to stay more or less at home and watch over Silvanicum while I'm away.' He stopped, waiting for her response. 'Well? What do you think?'

'It's very unexpected, Father,' she said finally, still uncomfortably aware of Patricia's silence.

'I've no doubt. I won't press you for an answer now. Consider it for a while, let yourself get used to the notion. No marriage could take place until you end your mourning in any case.'

'I will consider it,' she said, and left the matter there. She was tired, and did not wish to discuss it further until she had found time to think. No doubt because of Patricia's presence, her father had said nothing about his plan to prosecute Agrius Leo for his actions during the Winter of Grief. What would this marriage mean as far as that was concerned?

Soon afterwards they were home. The warmth of the carriage had lulled Amanda half to sleep, so that as she was roused by the voices of stablehands outside she was still wondering if she had imagined her father's proposal. But the canvas flap was opened and cold air rushed into the carriage to wake her fully, and she knew she had not. Agnus led her and Patricia into the house, and kissed them each good night.

Amanda took Patricia's arm and they walked slowly down the corridor to their rooms. Neither spoke. Patricia's high spirits seemed to have dissolved to nothing. When they came to her door, Patricia unfurled her arm from Amanda's, muttered a quiet good night and withdrew inside, closing the door softly behind her. Amanda continued to her own room.

As she undressed and prepared for bed, Amanda was less troubled by her own situation than by thoughts of Patricia's unusual quietness. Only once before had she seen her cousin behave in such a way, when she had first confessed of the affair with Rufus. It was clear that Patricia was still in love with him. Amanda did not want to hurt her cousin's feelings, and could not bear to think that Patricia would blame her for taking Rufus away.

Amanda stood next to her bed, hesitating from climbing beneath the blankets. She should go to Patricia and put her mind at rest. She had no intention of marrying Rufus. Nothing had been settled. She had so many unanswered questions for her father.

Taking a warm cloak and an oil lamp, Amanda went to Patricia's room. She knocked softly on the door and waited. There was no answer, and no sound from within. She knocked again. 'Patricia, it's me. Can I come in?'

Still there was no answer. She raised the latch, finding it unlocked, and eased open the door. The room was dark. She raised her lamp in the direction of the bed. 'Cousin, are you awake?'

There was a shape in the bed, but it seemed to be lying on top of the covers. Amanda came closer, and her light fell upon Patricia's still face. Her eyes were closed. She had not undressed or even taken her cloak off, and was lying on her back, her arms by her side. She seemed to be sleeping. Amanda reached out and was about to touch Patricia's arm when she caught the light gleaming on the blankets with a dull red sheen. She looked more closely, her heart frozen, and saw that Patricia's right hand and wrist, and the sheets around them, were soaked in blood.

XIX

For this is the only thing, if there is one, which might
make us fight the tide of death and cling to life:
to be with those whom we understand.
Marcus Aurelius

Drogo had said that these valleys were green and lush in the summer, but Paul could not imagine it now. Even the swampy banks of rivers and streams, busy with scrub and heather, were lifeless beneath the leaden roof of winter. The valley slopes rose steeply, a stubble of tough grass below, naked scree above, and climbed towards mountaintops of crags and passes enveloped in snow.

From this outcrop Paul could look back and see the fort of Mediobogdum a thousand feet below. The tidy rectangle of its walls sat on a spur overlooking the valley floor, guarding the high mountain pass where Paul now stood, thickly wrapped against the wind. A military road approached the pass from the east, winding up to the crest before descending past the ramparts of the fort to the valley floor. From there the road followed the valley west towards the sea, a distant patch of blue in a landscape of grey and white.

There was the road and the fort; everywhere else was wilderness. Across the mountains, ten miles to the east and ten miles to the west, were the rebel forts. The few paths to the north and south, which in any case led nowhere, were made all but impassable by the winter snow.

Above the wind, the sound muffled by his headscarf and the

lining of his hood, Paul heard the voice of the biarchus calling him. He turned to see that the biarchus and his men, a small patrol from the fort, had already begun to move on. He hurried after them despite the stiffness in his leg, knowing that they could not afford to waste time if they were to complete the patrol before nightfall.

It was the twenty-fifth day of December, the feast of Sol Invictus, deep midwinter. This was the first time Paul had felt strong enough to leave the fort since arriving here six weeks before. Back then he had collapsed almost as soon as he entered through its gates, the months of imprisonment, fever, beatings and fatigue finally taking their due. Tended by Eachna, he had not stirred from bed for a long time while his wounded and exhausted body slowly recovered. Even once he had begun to hobble around the fort without a walking stick, it had taken days before Drogo finally gave him permission to join a patrol into the mountains. Any longer and Paul may have had to break out of the fort by stealth, so desperately did he feel the urge to move – to walk, to climb, to do anything but sit inside his room for yet another day and think of how far he was from home.

And then there were the dreams. He felt as though he were being chased by a flood that had begun in Trimontium. He had tried to escape it by fleeing south, but here it had caught up with him and now threatened to submerge him. Almost every night for the last month he had woken in a cold sweat, panting, seized by a feeling of terror that consumed him for long moments until he could place himself in the darkness and remember where he was.

Paul followed the soldiers for the rest of the patrol, climbing over a landscape of boulders and ice, fumbling with his hands for balance while his companions trod nimbly along their accustomed route. Every so often they stopped to survey the horizon, muttering to one another and pointing out things that Paul strained to see, but could not. He did not care that they no doubt thought him a clumsy liability, an aristocratic refugee whose presence they had been commanded to tolerate. The more he could wear himself out, the better his chance of falling into a wonderfully oblivious sleep that night.

They returned to the fort an hour before dusk, having seen nothing unusual in the mountains. Through the winter there had been no movement from the direction of the two nearest rebel forts, no sign that they were planning an imminent assault. Drogo's garrison controlled the only road between them, and he had ordered that no travellers be allowed to pass by in case they were carrying messages for the rebel commanders, or seeking to gather information on Mediobogdum. There was no doubt that an attack would come by the spring, but Drogo insisted that his men, despite being outnumbered and cut off, were in the stronger position. The fort was easily defendable, protected to the east by the steep, narrow pass, and to the west by a sheer cliff face that fell hundreds of feet to the valley floor; they had just enough supplies to see them through the winter; and most of all, he often told Paul with a grin, they had nowhere to run and nothing to lose.

As the patrol approached the gates of the fort, Paul looked up at the half-dozen ten-foot poles erected along the path. Most of the sharpened points were now bare, but one was still capped by a human skull, blown a vivid white by the wind, lodged too firmly on its pole to fall even after its flesh had long decayed and its jawbone disappeared. It was all that remained of the men whom the rebel Valentinus had sent to bribe tribune Drogo two months earlier. Even Drogo seemed unsure of what Valentinus was planning. Whatever it was, it depended on having the loyalty of the mountain forts and the western coastal stations. Perhaps he had bribed even the commanders on the Wall. If he had, Mediobogdum truly did stand alone.

Drogo was waiting at the open gates. He spoke briefly to the patrol leader as they entered, clasping his arm firmly and telling him to get his men some hot soup before coming to report. He then came to Paul. 'I see you didn't run away.'

'There doesn't seem to be anywhere to run to.'

The sentries heaved the gates shut behind them, and Paul

walked with Drogo towards the praetorium, where he and Eachna had been allotted a pair of small rooms. Drills were still underway in front of the headquarters building despite the late hour and the bitter cold. Soldiers tramped and turned to the commands of their drillmaster, gloved hands clutching spear shafts, faces half hidden behind scarves. 'Good work, boys!' shouted Drogo as they passed. Turning to Paul, he said, 'See how I make them drill even on the day of Sol Invictus? It's not because of the mess we're in right now. I've been doing it for years. The difference is, *now* they're starting to see the point of it. I'll give them light duties this evening, though, and they get their bonus and a dose of wine – believe me, wine is the most important thing to keep in good supply this far from civilisation.' He laughed. 'So, did you see anything out there?'

'A lot of rocks.'

'I said you'd be wasting your time. It never changes. I've been here my whole career; not so much as a pebble shifts out there without me or my boys noticing it. Well, I'd better go and hear the report on just how much nothing is happening today. I usually spend this evening up on the ramparts,' he said as he began to walk away. 'Come and find me later if you're bored – with a mug of hot wine if you wouldn't mind.'

Paul entered the praetorium and walked through the internal courtyard, filled with piles of wood and spare building materials, to his room at the rear. It was simply furnished, containing only a bed in which he no longer slept, a small cupboard with a broken door, a desk and two chairs. One of the chairs was occupied by Eachna. She was wrapped in a thick blanket, shivering. She stared angrily at Paul.

He took off his cloak and headscarf and threw them on the bed, at once wondering whether that was a good idea. His room was barely warmer than outside. There was a single lamp burning on the table, of little use against the encroaching dimness. 'Where's the brazier?'

'Someone took it away.'

'You should have got it back.'

'I'm warm enough,' she said. 'You promised you'd be back ages ago.'

'Well, I have no say over how long the patrols take.' He looked in the cupboard and retrieved a bundle of writing tablets and pens, scavenged from the clerk's office, and put them on the table as he sat in the second chair. He did feel some guilt at returning much later than he had promised, but not enough to express it. For the last several weeks he had been giving Eachna daily lessons in Latin, reasoning that she stood a better chance of being accepted by Julian's family if she could improve her mastery of the tongue. But today he was not in the mood, and had been disappointed to see her still waiting when he entered his room. The patrol had not invigorated him as he had hoped. Instead the hours of sweating and freezing over sharp rocks, staring bleakly into grey valleys and barren peaks, cursing the savage, relentless wind, had left him feeling worn and hollow. He had not realised how remote the fortress was, how completely they were trapped. Drogo's confidence had led Paul to believe that there was some unspoken aspect of their situation that would be key to their survival, some secret weapon that would somehow become obvious as soon as he climbed to the top of the pass and saw it for himself, but he had seen nothing. He began to wonder whether the tribune's confidence was simply a manifestation of insanity after so many years here.

At this moment Paul could not see the point of teaching Eachna skills she might never need. But she had already taken a pen and was bent over a wax tablet, holding it fast with the stump of her left hand, waiting for him to begin.

From memory he recited a poem of Catullus, slowly enough for her to transcribe it. He watched as she scratched away with the pen. Her hair was loose, falling to the side and hiding her face, but he knew well enough the look of intense concentration she always had while writing. If she made a mistake she would flip her pen and erase it with a muttered curse, but never give up. She would often continue until darkness had fallen and the glow of the oil lamp was so weak, barely touching the walls of his small room, that he was forced to take the tablet and pen from her lest she ruin her eyes.

They sat beside one another at the table, the fading afternoon light falling through the window, and Paul waited for her to finish transcribing.

'All right,' she said, and put the pen down.

'Now recite.'

She sat up straight, brushing her loose hair back behind her ear, and began. Paul had expanded her knowledge of Latin beyond the Bible, and her pronunciation was improving now that he had begun to tease out some oddities of Gallic dialect that she must have picked up from Ludo. The delicate stresses of poetry were proving more challenging, but he had been impressed by her determination.

'Good,' he said when she finished. 'Now translate.'

'But in return you'll receive pure passion, or whatever is sweeter or finer: for I shall give you grease, which to my girl—'

'No. Not grease, perfume. *Unguentum* is perfume; grease is *unguen*. I doubt Fabullus would be very impressed with a bottle of grease.'

Eachna sighed in frustration, placed a finger on the mistaken word and continued. 'For I shall give perfume, which to my girl Venuses and Cupids gave, and when you smell it you'll beg the gods, O Fabullus, to make you all nose.'

'Better. Now try it again.'

He looked at her left arm, where, in trying to keep the tablet steady, her sleeve had ridden up to reveal the stump of her wrist. She usually tried so hard to keep it hidden that Paul knew how ashamed she must be of it. He had wondered more than once what had happened to her. He knew only what Julian had told him: that she had spent some years in slavery beyond the Wall, had escaped, and had been found and brought to Luguvalium by Ludo. She had not volunteered any more information to Paul, and he had not asked, any more than he had told her about his own past.

This was strange, he thought. She was his property and he

had a right to ask; if they ever made it to the south, Julian's family would expect him to know something about her. Nor could he pretend he was simply uninterested, for if that were the case he would not find himself so often entranced by her quiet fortitude, as he was now.

What, then?

He watched her and listened to the soft lilt of her accent, which lent a strange, haunting music to the stiff Latin lines, and an answer suggested itself. It was not reluctance or lack of interest, but fear. He was afraid because he could sense the pain she kept hidden from the world, just as she kept her mutilation hidden within her sleeve. In her pain he would find an echo of his own.

Eachna had now finished reciting, and she realised that he was looking at her exposed arm. She quickly tugged at her sleeve to cover it. 'Give me another,' she said, holding her pen ready.

Paul did not think of a new poem, but reached out to place his hand on her left arm. He softly pulled up the sleeve, and drew a single finger over the smooth skin of her stump. She froze. He could not see her face, which was again obscured by her hair, but he heard her draw in a sudden breath. They were still for a moment, sitting together as though carved from a single rock.

Suddenly she jumped up, letting blanket and chair fall to the floor, and fled the room, leaving the door open behind her.

Paul sat for a while by himself, his initial surprise giving way to a slow, weary confusion. Eventually, once the last of the daylight had faded from the room, he rose, gathered the tablets and pens and stored them in the cupboard, and lay on his bed. The rest of the building was quiet; he heard nothing through the open door, nor from the ceiling above, nor through the wall that separated Eachna's room from his own.

Paul could not sleep on the mattress. Lately his limbs had found the yielding softness uncomfortable, and seemed to demand that he return to the hard surfaces he had become used to at Trimontium. After rolling to and fro for an hour he lay down, as usual, on the cold flagstone floor, covering himself with his cloak. He ignored the cold and his growing hunger, and did not notice when the oil lamp surrendered a final glow and died.

It snowed again during the night. Paul was awake before dawn and watched the last fat flakes sail down from the lifeless sky, settling on the shack roofs and on the crumbling roofline of the fort, and on the huddled corpses of the prisoners who had frozen to death in the orchard garden with chains on their feet.

Paul stamped his feet and rubbed his rigid hands together. A faint light had appeared in the east. Another day, and he was still alive. He was home, and happy. Nothing could hurt him here. He looked at the men stacked like wood beneath their frozen quilt, and felt no anger towards them, but rather sympathy. He could set a brazier beside them, and thaw them out, and when they were warm enough he could even invite them into the bath house as a gesture of comradeship. As long as they were in his home they were his guests, and he bore them no ill-will.

Victor and Faustus were standing next to the dead men. They were each holding one hand of a slight blonde girl standing between them, whose face Paul could not see. Paul called to them.

Faustus turned and Paul saw the dagger in his heart. Blood trickled from his chest and ran in rivulets down his tunic, staining the ground with a rich bloom that spread across the snow, climbed the white mound of bodies and submerged the blonde girl beside him.

Victor smiled sadly, and held out both hands to Paul. 'You are mad, brother, to indulge your sorrow like this,' he said. 'Such things do not happen except by the will of the gods.'

Grief shook Paul's body with the force of a blow.

He awoke on the floor next to his bed, curled up in a ball with his knees clasped to a chest that heaved and heaved. His cheek and the stone it rested on were slippery with tears. Blackness was all around him, and his ears were filled by the wind howling through the dead crags of the valley. He tried to curl tighter, wrapping his arms around his legs like steel bands, digging his chin into his chest, squeezing himself into nothingness. He felt the empty night outside like the vast belly of a beast that had consumed him, and he hated it. It had taken everything.

It was a long time before he could bring his sobbing under control. When he did, he uncurled himself and sat on his bed, holding his head in his hands.

Through the wind he began to hear the voices of soldiers who were celebrating elsewhere in the fort. Their laughter and music seemed to subvert the raging air, a faint pocket of humanity in the mountainous desert. Drawn by it, Paul got to his feet and tugged the cloak over his shoulders, and left his room.

As he walked from the praetorium along the main path towards the upper barrack blocks, he could make out the instruments more clearly: the vibrant, jumbled beat of palm-drums dancing around the harmony of twin flutes and the solemn drawl of pipes. He found that several bonfires had been lit in the lane between two of the barracks, and almost the entire garrison was now gathered around them, a shifting huddle of figures with backs turned to the darkness and faces blazing with light. Some men were throwing more branches on the fire, laughing each time a burst of sparks flew up towards the stars. Others were carrying around steaming pots of thick chicken broth and plates of bread.

The feast of Sol Invictus was an old imperial holiday that Christians had recently adopted as the birthday of their saviour. The Tungrians had celebrated it, too; it had always been Victor's favourite party of the year, a day when pagans, Mithraists and Christians danced together and drank to the health of the emperor.

As Paul came near he was dragged into the firelight by a man he did not know, who put a cup of wine in his hand and wrapped an arm around his neck. They started to sing to the music, and Paul joined in when he recognised the words of 'The Three Hags':

> 'O take your youth and lover's charms
> And take your fair relief;
> And hold her 'til your loving arms
> Are worn away by grief . . .'

The ballads were old songs from the days of their parents and grandparents, songs that the soldiers had heard as children and which reminded them of those times. Paul sang, drank and watched broad-shouldered Orion march across the night sky. He thought only of the slave girl.

A song ended and a centenarius called the men to calm. He stood between two of the bonfires, bathed in light, his face flushed from the heat. He raised his cup. 'Men,' he announced, his voice rising effortlessly above the crackling of the fire. 'To the emperor; to the tribune; and to us!' Three hundred men roared and cheered with a defiance that for a moment drowned out even the wind.

The cheer for the tribune reminded Paul that Drogo would be up on the ramparts by now. He pushed his way from the bonfire to one of the trestle tables set up outside the barracks, where, amidst the jumble of food and utensils, he found a spare cup and a jug that still contained some wine. Having filled the spare cup and his own, he climbed the nearest steps to the ramparts. One continuous walkway led around the walls, and he took directions from the duty sentries until he found Drogo near the north-west corner tower. He announced himself and offered the cup of wine.

Drogo took it, thanking him. He held it in both hands and sipped it with relish. 'Still warm,' he said happily. He nodded towards the bonfires. 'The boys not keeping you from sleep, I hope?'

'Not at all.'

'Good. They deserve to enjoy themselves.' He turned back to the view beyond the ramparts, the valleys swamped in shadows, the mountains a soft white beneath the moon.

'How long have you been here, tribune?' Paul asked.

'Twenty-three years,' Drogo said. 'I came as a fresh recruit right after the war of Constans. This place was empty then, but they decided to bring it back into service. Those barrack blocks down there I helped build with my own hands. I was made biarchus, centenarius, primicerius, finally tribune. There wasn't much competition for the posts.'

'You never wanted to leave?'

'At first, yes. But this country . . .' He shook his head. 'When I started I always heard nothing but stories of battles and glory, of how Constans rounded up the Picts not twenty miles north of here and routed them to a man. All those veterans are long gone now. I'm the last of the old garrison. I have just one year of service left. All those years we waited for the barbarians to come back, watching the mountains. I was afraid they never would.'

'And now they have.'

'In a manner of speaking.'

'Tribune, the rebels must have ten times our number. When they come – do we stand a chance?'

Drogo laughed. 'Honestly, that's not something I think much about.'

Paul left him and walked back along the battlements. The tribune had as much as admitted that their position was hopeless. The rebels might tolerate Drogo's defiance through the winter, when he could make no move against them, but once the snows melted it would be a simple matter to plug the valley and the pass and either starve him out or storm the fort. Paul considered that he might try to escape across the mountains, but the attempt would almost certainly fail. Drogo would be unlikely to give up any of his already precious supplies; even worse, the country was savage and unfamiliar, the high ground impassable, the valleys lawless at the best of times and now swarming with raiders.

Paul reached a staircase, but paused before he descended. Instead he went to the edge of the rampart and looked over the battlements. This side of the fort was directly above a cliff, and the ground beneath the ramparts seemed to drop into a bottom-less void. The dark gulf of the valley stretched towards the west. It would be so simple, he thought, to climb onto the battlements and throw himself into the emptiness. It would be quick. He would not even see the rocks before he hit them. Perhaps it would not even hurt. Why should he torture himself by waiting for some unknown end, when he could bring one upon himself now? What made him think he deserved to live?

His hands were on the icy stone of the ramparts. It would take only a moment to climb over them.

He could not do it. Even as he pictured himself falling into the blackness, he knew he could not. It was not that he was afraid, nor that he thought himself worthy of life. There was a new force upon him that had grown over the past few weeks, ever since Eachna had begun to nurse him back to health. The force bore her name, but its essence still escaped him. It was not so much an answer, as the promise of one, which pulled him towards her. She was a mystery; confounding, fascinating, a distortion in the world he thought he knew. The fact that she had fled from his touch, the fact that she was a slave, the fact that he feared her pain as much as he feared his own – these drew him away from the wall.

She did not want him to come into her room, but he pushed in anyway. She tried to leave, but he gripped her shoulders and held her firmly. She squirmed but could not get free. Yet she did not cry out or try to hurt him. He looked at her and commanded, begged her to tell him.

In the end the tension seemed to diffuse from her body, and her face broke into tears. Paul held her and she sobbed onto him violently, as though a reservoir of sorrow had been pierced. The flood shook her limbs. She wound her arms around him, anchoring herself to him. Paul was shocked by the agony he had released.

She cried on, and sometimes tried to speak, but her throat lurched with every word. Her eyes swam with tears as she looked into his, and the tears washed down her rough, reddened cheeks and bled into his clothes. He cupped her head between his hands, felt the mess of tangled hair and the shape of her skull beneath. They stood together for a long while until their bodies were exhausted and shaken to the core, until they shared the same vast, floating feeling that followed. Eachna staggered and Paul held her, taking her over to the bed.

That night, long after the soldiers' revelries had ended, they lay together awake and silent, looking through the window at the midnight clouds sailing past in a blue-black sky. Eachna gripped Paul's right hand in her own. It was only when the last cloud had passed overhead, and the window was filled with cold, distant stars, that she began to speak.

She began in her usual quiet, earnest voice. Sometimes she had to stop, and wait for her voice to steady itself. Paul said nothing, but listened, and every word she spoke was left in his memory.

She had been born in Hibernia, which in her native tongue was called Ériu, and at the age of thirteen had been taken by pirates. They had sailed across the sea and far to the north, beyond the lands where the Romans lived, up the ragged coast until they came to a deep, rocky harbour, where she was unloaded and exchanged for two cows. She was taken by a Pictish man and his boy through a land of foothills and forests to a tiny settlement high on a slope and far from any other place. It was a group of huts encircled by a single bramble hedge, containing fewer than twenty people. She was taken by the head male, who said he wanted her for menial labour. His wife had died during the frost, he said, and she was a replacement.

He raped Eachna on the very first night, only hours after she arrived. There were no threats, no tentative advances. He simply climbed onto her suddenly and took her. The next morning he did the same, and the following night, and frequently thereafter. She sobbed without pause for days, eventually driving the man to such anger that once he almost cracked her head open with a log.

At this point she brushed back some hair and showed Paul a scar on her temple. It was the first scar of many, she said.

The weeks passed and Eachna never spoke to any of the community. She was for the most part ignored, and ordered to stay in her master's hut. She considered running away, but was too afraid. If she was caught the punishment would be savage; if not, she would almost certainly die in that strange and remote country. She grew used to the pangs of hunger and to the cold, and to the miserable hardship of the most arduous labour. She learned not to speak, scarcely to think.

Then, after a year had passed, things became worse. The man came in one night and did not lie grunting on top of her as he usually did, but struck her without warning. When she tried to rise he struck her again. He shouted that she was barren and a witch. By the time he was finished, Eachna's face was a bleeding mass of torn skin; her nose was broken, and a shoulder bone was snapped. She lay alone for hours, and nobody came to help her. She could not move for the agony; she felt the blood congeal and plaster her skin and hair. She fainted, and awoke, fainted, and awoke. Then finally she passed into a deep oblivion.

She came to her senses back on her bed, her wounds having been grudgingly treated.

The man had wanted her to give him another child, but she had proven infertile. For a while he left her alone, and she began to hope that he had lost interest in her. Then Eachna noticed a certain darkness in his looks, which she tried her best to ignore, for fear of what it meant. Until, after a few more weeks, when her wounds had almost healed, he came in one day and beat her as harshly as before. Finally, in a moment of delirious hatred, Eachna slapped him across the face. He stared at her, speechless, and then left the hut.

Shortly after he returned with a meat cleaver and, forcing Eachna to the floor and holding her there, clumsily hacked off her left hand.

Eachna narrated this calmly to Paul, but then her eyes suddenly screwed up in anguish at the memory. He reached out and took her handless left arm, and pressed the smooth skin of the stump to his lips. He kissed her forehead and asked her to stop, told her that she need not say anything more. She had said enough.

Over the nights to come she would tell the rest, and Paul would speak of his own pain. He would talk of Trimontium and Victor. He would tell her about his childhood, and why he had fled his home and family. He spoke of his horror that he would never see his mother again. Finally, when he had reached the last, darkest corner of his fear, he told her about Faustus.

XX

You are difficult and easy, bitter and sweet just the same.
I cannot live with you, nor without you.
Martial

It was a relief to enter the warm air of the inn after a long morning on the road. Pinta had cautioned Amanda against it, reminding her, by the tone of her voice rather than a direct assertion, that inns were not the sort of place a high-born lady ought to enter. Amanda had simply replied that the two mules drawing the coach looked tired, and that she desired the stop for their sake as much as for hers. While the animals were taken by the driver to be fed and watered in the stables, Amanda, along with Pinta and their two accompanying bucellarii, were led into the dining hall by the landlord. His wife and daughter were finishing a hasty clean of the tables, and they stopped and bowed to Amanda as she entered.

'Would my lady desire some refreshment?' the landlord asked in awkward Latin.

'Just mugs of warm wine,' replied Amanda, speaking in British to put him at ease. The landlord smiled obligingly, beckoned Amanda and Pinta to the table nearest the fire and fussed his wife and daughter into the kitchen. The bucellarii sat at a table across the room. The hall was otherwise empty, there being few travellers at this time of year. Amanda had hoped as much. She had wanted to stop less because she was tired than because she needed some quiet time to gather her thoughts before continuing the journey. The inn was perched on the very edge of the wolds, just over halfway between Corinium and Glevum, where Patricia was awaiting her arrival.

The landlord brought Amanda and Pinta their wine and went to see to the bucellarii. Amanda wrapped her hands around her mug and waited for the heat to seep through her gloves and into her palms. It was quiet apart from the fire and the occasional subdued clatter from the kitchen. After the continuous creaking and jolting of the carriage, she appreciated the stillness.

It had been more than two months since Agrius Leo's party and the night when Amanda had discovered Patricia unconscious on her bed, her wrist cut. She remembered vividly trying to revive her cousin, getting no response, and rushing for her father and Celerus, who had come and tended Patricia calmly while Amanda could barely control her own hysterics. It was lucky, they said, that Patricia had apparently fainted as she cut her first wrist, for had she cut both she would likely have died.

After a few days of recuperation, during which Patricia had refused to be seen by anyone except Agnus and the doctor, she had asked to be sent back to her parents at Glevum. Amanda had seen her only briefly as she departed, when they shared a light kiss and no words. Weeks passed, Christmas came and went, and Amanda heard nothing. Eventually she wrote to Patricia on the pretext that they might sit together for a joint portrait. She had brought Patricia's reply with her from Corinium, and now opened it to read one more time.

> *To my beloved friend and sister Amanda, Patricia Tecla sends greetings.*
>
> *Come, sister. I shall expect you as soon as you are able to make the journey. Please greet your father for me.*
>
> *Farewell in Christ.*

It was not the brevity of the letter that troubled Amanda, for she had been prepared for an even curter reply, or for no reply at all. Rather, it was the name Tecla. This was not one of Patricia's birth names, but the name of a Christian saint. Why would Patricia have adopted it? The unexpected invocation of Christ at the end of the letter only deepened her worry. Patricia was baptised but had never shown any religious sensibility before, and Amanda did not know what to make of it. She feared it might be insincere, an affectation that sprang from the same resentment and envy which had driven Patricia to take a blade to herself. Perhaps by a show of piety she was now hoping to make Amanda feel so guilty that she would refuse to marry Rufus.

Amanda knew she ought not to suspect her cousin of such a thing, but the alternative worried her even more. For what if Patricia had indeed discovered Christ, and had taken on Saint Tecla as her particular guardian? Of course Amanda would love her cousin to learn some temperance and modesty; had she not always tried to steer her in just that direction? But for it to happen now, like this, in a moment of grief and loneliness that Amanda had helped cause, or at least failed to avert – no, she did not want Patricia to be so transformed because of her. She wanted her old cousin back, the vain, impious, girlish Patricia, whose warmth was all the more real for her faults.

Thus what Amanda had intended as a journey of reunion and reconciliation now filled her with anxiety. It would be so simple to reject Rufus, and everything would be back to normal. Yet the world had changed and she knew she must change with it. She could not defy her father. She could not refuse to marry when so much depended on it. She had always known that the day of her marriage would come, and that she would be fortunate beyond expectation if it was to a man of her choosing.

From the inn, the carriage followed the winding road down the scarp of the hills and towards the western vale. February mists hung low over the fields and farms, a ghostly ocean that stretched as far as sight, broken by islands of black forest. To the left, tucked in its valley, its tiled roof rising above the mist, was White Hen House. The household had withdrawn to Glevum for the winter, although Amanda knew that her Uncle Pertinax spent much of the season at the villa. She was thankful for that. It would make her stay in Glevum a little easier if he was not there.

Another two hours brought the carriage to the city. It was

smaller than Corinium, a colony of sea traders and retired soldiers, ramshackle and rough, unimpressed with its own imperial origins. As they passed the forum, Amanda noticed that it was suffering from neglect, which had left its paving slabs ruptured by plants. Even on the main street some of the buildings were abandoned.

The carriage drew into the enclosed yard of the townhouse and was met by Tertia, who was wearing a thick embroidered cloak, her head covered by a shawl. Amanda climbed down from the carriage and bowed. She had expected Patricia to greet her, not her aunt.

'Did you have a pleasant journey?' asked Tertia.

'Quite pleasant, aunt, thank you.'

'Patricia is inside; her girl will take you to her, and bring you something to eat. I'll see to your things.'

Amanda followed the handmaiden to a heated reception room, where she found Patricia sitting on a couch with a book. Patricia, hearing her enter, rose and crossed the room to her, smiling warmly and taking Amanda in her arms. 'It's been so long, sister,' she said as they embraced. 'It's wonderful to be together again.'

'I know,' was all Amanda could say. She was at once relieved by Patricia's affection and unsettled by her appearance. For this was not the Patricia she knew. She was wearing plain wooden sandals and a common dress of unbleached wool; her hair was unset, bound only with a piece of string and not even washed; there was no trace of make-up or jewellery, no familiar scent of perfume. She looked gaunt, her cheeks colourless, and Amanda could feel her bones through the cloth as they hugged. Had they passed on the street, Amanda would not have recognised her.

'You'll find me changed, I'm afraid,' said Patricia, leading Amanda to sit beside her on the couch. She picked up the book and placed it on the low table in front of them. 'You see how I'm trying to improve myself with reading, but I don't have much stomach for it. All the other nonsense, though – the frills and trinkets and perfumes – I can get rid of *them*, at least. And it's done me a world of good.' Patricia was smiling, but scarcely tried to conceal the sadness in her eyes. She dropped her gaze to the floor and creased her brow. 'Don't be angry I didn't write to you. I wanted to, but I've never been a great letter-writer, and I'm quite beyond redemption in that regard.'

'I'm not annoyed, Patricia. I was only worried about you, after everything that happened. I didn't know whether I should write or not. Remember, at Corinium you didn't want to see me.'

'I am sorry about that, too. I wasn't myself for a few days. I didn't know *who* I was. That's why she came to me – blessed Tecla. She came to help me clear my mind of all those cobwebs that fill the world, all that noise, rushing about me until I didn't know myself any more. She said to me what Saint Paul once said to her: "Fear only the one God, and live a chaste life." It sounds so simple, doesn't it? She came to me once before, too, when I was sick in Gallia, but I wasn't ready to listen then. I was never ready to listen, until that night, when I tried to cross the chasm unbidden, and she reached out to stop me. I could feel her grip around my wrist. She called me sister, and said she had always been with me, from the moment of my birth, my nurse and protector.'

Patricia fell silent, looking into space. Before Amanda could reply, the maid returned with a plate of bread, cheese and meat, which she set on the table. Once she had gone, Amanda said, 'You don't look well, Patricia.'

'I *feel* well. Isn't that the important thing? I'm no philosopher, but I understand what Tecla says about getting rid of all that worldly detritus to become one with God. When I was in Lugdunum, cousin Hiberia told me about these women in Rome who live in their houses without any frippery, without seeing any men except priests and their family, who simply pray and devote themselves to a pure and simple life. It's quite a liberating thought, Amanda, that one need not marry after all.'

'But what about your father?'

'There are some girls in Rome who live like this regardless of what their fathers say. There was even a scandal a year or two back where one girl was beaten to death by her father because she wouldn't marry.'

'Oh, Patricia . . .'

'If I had my way, I'd run off by myself into the west and live in a cave somewhere,' Patricia said. Then she added, with a quiet laugh: 'But at least Glevum in wintertime isn't all that different from a wilderness, is it?'

Amanda gave a hollow echo of the laugh. She felt little humour at the change in her cousin. The depth of her transformation was worrying, and Amanda did not know how to react. It was too drastic, too sudden; she felt that Patricia was not running towards liberation, but fleeing from pain. It was clear that she had been virtually starving herself for weeks. She had not even glanced at the plate of food before them. Amanda remembered that the purpose of her visit had been to sit for a joint portrait. There seemed little point in reminding Patricia of that now.

'You're very quiet, sister,' said Patricia, touching Amanda's arm. 'I hope I haven't shocked you.'

Perhaps Tecla truly was guiding Patricia, perhaps not, but Amanda knew the root cause of this change. Since she was now here, she had nothing to lose by addressing it. 'Is this because of my engagement to Rufus?'

Patricia withdrew her hand and smiled, her posture stiffening slightly. She had obviously been prepared for such a question. 'There's no point denying it, I suppose. But I'd hate for you to feel you were to blame for this, Amanda. Rufus rejected me a long time ago, there's no doubt about that. I have thought about it a great deal. I felt rather like a bee that has lost its sting – it has only one, you know, a part of itself, and once it loses it . . . And yes, I kept a childish hope alive in my heart, regardless. I admit I was envious and bitter that he was suddenly your neigh-bour, and I was afraid . . . oh, I don't know – none of that matters now. I was saved, and I have a new path.'

'But to go to such extremes, Patricia – it isn't healthy. You look so weak, and you know you're prone to sickness. You need to eat.'

'A plunge bath for the soul,' said Patricia. 'That's how I like to think of it. I do eat, just not often, and only bread and porridge, sometimes a bit of fruit and honey. The rest of the time I sit and think, and pray, and she prays with me. Besides, I'm no harder on myself than Julian.'

'That's different.'

'How, except that he's a man? Can't women devote themselves to God just as completely?'

'He doesn't starve himself.'

'Oh, Amanda, don't be melodramatic! I'm hardly starving to death. I'm shedding what I don't need, getting rid of flesh just like I got rid of my wardrobe and everything else.'

'And does your mother approve?'

'Oh, tsh! Before I was too frivolous to be respectable, now I'm too frigid to be eligible. I don't think it's possible to please her either way. At least it will save my parents the trouble of finding a husband for an old maid like me.'

Shortly afterwards a servant appeared to announce that the bath house was now ready, should they like to refresh themselves. Amanda obliged, but Patricia declined, saying that she had taken to bathing only once every two days, and was hoping to reduce it to once a week as she eased herself out of former comforts. And so Amanda took a long and lonely bath, worried for her friend and troubled that it was her fault.

Amanda had not seen Rufus since the party, and would not until their betrothal was formalised at a ceremony in the spring. She had accepted the promise of engagement with, she hoped, the quiet obedience that her father expected of her, but however much she presented a stoical facade to the world she could not deny that the union appealed to her on a base level she did not fully comprehend, except that it was somehow shameful and overwhelming. Whenever she thought of Rufus, even with thoughts of hatred and anger, she was clutched by desire. It was so different to the clean ecstasy of the soul she sometimes felt in prayer: it was raw, brutal, a force of the flesh that she feared she could not resist – or, even worse, did not want to resist.

Amanda stayed at Glevum for just three days, when she had planned to stay for a week. Her love for Patricia had not diminished; on the contrary, she felt so deeply for her cousin's disappointment and misery, and was so sensible of her own part in it, that she could not bear to stay. It would have been easier were she truly opposed to the union with Rufus, as she pretended to her cousin. But she had never had a gift for deceit, and she found it torturous to maintain the fiction. Another time she reminded Patricia that she and Rufus were not yet betrothed, much less married; they were, if anything, engaged to be engaged, with a great many questions hanging over the future. But this reassurance, too, was only half felt.

As Amanda was readying to leave, Patricia came and hugged her. 'I wish I were a tablet I could just wipe clean,' she whispered. 'But Tecla will show me the way now. Trust me, sister.'

With a mixture of relief and regret Amanda bade farewell to Patricia and her family and spent a long day travelling back to Corinium. She prayed that her cousin would soon recover from what Tertia had called her 'silly monkish play-acting'. As Patricia herself had said, it was the fashion in Rome for young women to renounce marriage in the name of Christ and hide away like hermits, and Patricia was nothing if not devoted to fashion. Perhaps this phase would quickly pass, or Julian would return home and convince her to abandon it, or she would meet a suitor who would help her forget Rufus and all the pain he had caused her.

Amanda's father had travelled to Londinium on business two weeks earlier, but had returned by the time she reached the townhouse outside Corinium shortly before dusk. Alypius greeted her in the courtyard, and said that she should await her father in his study. 'He's brought you a rather nice surprise, too,' he added with an enigmatic smile.

The study was empty, warm from the heated floor. Her father's desk was covered in heaps of scrolls and writing tablets. A high, curtained window overlooked the pasture behind the townhouse, with another in the opposite wall facing the corridor, but otherwise Amanda was surrounded by cupboards and shelves that reached up to the ceiling, full of tidily arranged scrolls and books transferred from Silvanicum for the winter. In the centre of one wall was a shelf upon which stood a bronze bust of Valentinian Augustus, flanked by the pair of water clocks that her father had built years ago. She went to the shelf, drawn by the offbeat drips that counted delicate time in the stillness of the room, each pair like a heartbeat of the unblinking emperor between them. His eyes, stern beneath arched eyebrows, glared across the room. Amanda hated the bust. She read its harsh expression as the contempt of a soldier for the world of learning, and did not like lingering in the room because of it; nor did she hope ever to meet the emperor himself, if he had an ounce of the cruelty suggested by his sculptor.

She heard footsteps in the corridor, and a moment later her father entered the study. 'There you are!' he announced. 'Returned early, I see! How's your cousin? And your aunt and uncle?'

'They're well,' she said. Now was not the time to discuss her worries about Patricia.

'Glad to hear it. It's almost suppertime, but first I have a gift for you, and also some news. Gift first, I think.' He lifted a saddlebag that lay on the floor and placed it on his desk. There was something large inside it. He reached inside and brought out a leather-bound codex. 'Here,' he said, and offered it to her with a warm smile. 'A gift from Bishop Gregory of Londinium.'

'The *bishop*?' She took the codex carefully in both hands and examined it in wonder. The value of such a codex was far beyond her estimation. Its leather binding was decorated with brass and silver fittings, and the parchment was at least as fine as any on the shelves around her. She was humbled, and at a loss to understand how she had earned such a gift. 'From the bishop?'

'Himself,' said Agnus. 'I happened to mention that I was hoping to purchase a copy of Saint Paul's epistles while I was in Londinium – it being so difficult to get anything written up in Corinium these days – and before I knew it he'd pulled one out as though by magic. He bought it in Ariminium a few years ago: that's genuine Italian parchment there, my dear. And of course when I mentioned a certain avid student and daughter, whose fame, I admit, has won admirers even in the basilicas of Londinium, he had it put in a fresh binding and refused to take a penny for it – and so here it is, with his blessings.'

'May God bless the bishop,' said Amanda, pleasantly surprised. The thought of her name being discussed in the capital of the Four Provinces made her nervous. But with such a gift in her hands, she could do nothing but smile.

'Amen,' said Agnus. He rose from the couch and replaced the saddlebag on the floor. Then he stood behind the desk, shuffling the mess of paperwork into some order. 'Now I'm afraid I must give you my news, which is altogether more disappointing – to me, at any rate. It concerns the suggestion, you remember, that you marry Agrius Rufus for the good of the family.'

'Yes,' she said. Her throat went suddenly dry. She sensed what he was about to say.

'It's come as something of a humiliating shock to me that Agrius Leo has now withdrawn from our agreement.' As he spoke, Agnus continued tidying away scrolls and tablets, checking their contents, stacking them neatly into groups on the desk or slipping them onto the shelves behind him. 'We met in Londinium and he told me. You can well imagine how I reacted; suffice to say, I later did penance for my outburst. My only consolation is that, according to rumours at least, it was Rufus's decision, not his father's. It seems that the boy has changed his mind and is refusing to go through with it. This means, of course, that Agrius Leo's humili- ation is even greater than mine, and it's fuelled gossip of a rift between the two of them, which is obviously to our benefit. I know that you must share in my frustration, having set your mind on a course of sacrifice that is no longer necessary. But at least it means that you won't have to marry the wretch after all, eh? I'll find you a good Christian husband in Gallia instead, see if I don't.'

He looked at her, smiling. She remained seated in the chair, holding the book tightly. 'May I go and read this in my room?'

'Of course,' he said. 'It's yours now, you can take it wherever you like. I don't expect you to leave it in the study.'

'Thank you,' she said, rising. She bowed and left the study for her bedroom. Once there, she closed the door behind her and stood facing her bed.

So that was it. Casually arranged, casually dismissed, her second engagement cancelled like an unwanted order with a baker. And not for political reasons, which she could have perhaps accepted, but because Rufus was *refusing* to go through with it. He did not want her. He had rejected her just as he had rejected Patricia.

Of course he had, she thought bitterly. If he did not want Patricia, with all her beauty and grace, why in the name of Christ would he settle for a short, dark girl like her, a second-rate provincial who had never even been to Treveris? She obviously shrank to insignificance in his ambitions, and he was unwilling to tie himself to her when another two or three years might open a world of fresh opportunities. He would probably choose some Gallic bride from a distinguished senatorial family, pretty and cultured and wealthy. He would forget all about the pompous little British girl who had once offended him at a winter party.

She was by now holding the book so firmly that her fingers had turned white. Her chest was shuddering. The deep injustice of it swamped her. When her engagement to Silvius Bonus had been cancelled three years ago, she had felt only relief. This was different. She might have been able to cope with it were her mother here, ready to sit with her and teach her what to do, but without her there was no centre to the world, no rope to reach for. Her mother had been taken, cruelly, unfairly, leaving her alone and adrift.

In an instant of fury she flung the book into the wall. She went to her dresser, crowded with boxes of make-up, bottles of perfume, jewellery, a collection of childish bronze figures, and swept her arms across it, sending a storm of objects clattering. She snatched a silver vase from the nearest shelf and threw it at a brazier, knocking it over with a clatter; she grabbed her favourite red-gloss pot, a gift for her birthday, and smashed it at her feet. She tugged the blankets from her bed and dragged them across the floor. She pulled open her drawers and tore out handfuls of clothes and threw them over her shoulders, and when the drawers were empty she turned and picked up her wicker chair, closed her eyes and with a tearful heave threw it into the furthest corner of the room.

Panting, sobbing, Amanda looked around at the chaos she had created. Her anger dissolved, leaving only shame at its violence. Again she had failed, this time worse than ever before. How could she possibly imagine herself ready to be a wife, ready to be anything?

The door opened behind her. There was a flash of grey: the cat, which had been skulking under the bed, darted out into the corridor, brushing past the feet of her father. Pinta was peering nervously into the room over his shoulder. He came in, dismissing Pinta, and closed the door. He regarded the destruction calmly. 'This is disappointing, Amanda.'

'I'm sorry, Father,' she wept, 'I'm sorry! But I'm lost. I'm trying, but I miss her so much . . .'

'I wish I could be with you more often, but you must know that's not possible. You're a lady now and you must control yourself like one. I know you miss your mother. Think of her example. Console yourself with the lessons you've been taught.'

'I know everything the lessons say, Father!' Amanda cried. 'Shall I recite for you? Seneca says, "You've buried someone you loved, now look for someone else to love." Plutarch says we should never let our sorrow become even greater than the memory of our joy. And Cicero says it's foolish to mourn what happens to all of us. And I know everything holy Cyprian says. I know it all, Father, I've read it all! Tell me something new; not some old piece of philosophy or some rot about Heaven. I know all that. It doesn't help; it doesn't put her back in my arms, or put her smiling in her chair, or put new words on her lips. Please, Father, say something; I can't bear the pain. I don't want to live. I've prayed and prayed, but in God's name I don't want to live!'

'Amanda,' he whispered softly, feeling her despair. But he could say nothing more of use.

XXI

That which cannot be sunk rises again only stronger,
And springs forth higher from the lowest depths.
Rutilius Claudius Namatianus, *On His Voyage Home*

It was raining, as always. The solid cold of winter had given way to a lighter chill that was carried on the breeze; the snows had thawed on the bare mountaintops, and the streams, fat and noisy with meltwater, fed the marshes in the valley floors. Occasional floods of sunlight broke through the clouds, glittering on the wet rocks and scrub, and on the droplets, which seemed to dance in the air.

It was the first time Paul had not felt cold while away from the fort. He crouched in the open above the track that ran through this low pass, the main route from the rebel fort of Galava through the mountains to the north. A few yards behind him, on the lower slopes of the valley, was a small, dense forest, which concealed forty soldiers. Beyond the road, in another forest on the far side of the valley, was hidden a wing of thirty cavalry. The pass narrowed at this point to only a few hundred feet: a boggy, treacherous stretch, hemmed in on either side, offering no chance of escape to anyone caught on the road. A perfect place for an ambush.

The primicerius, Kunaric, emerged from the cover of the trees and crept to Paul's side. 'The scouts have seen them entering the valley two miles to the south. They're on their way.'

'How many?'

'Perhaps five squads.'

Paul considered the news quickly. Up to forty men, a sizeable detachment. If the rebels decided to hold their ground it would be a tough fight, even with the advantage of numbers and surprise.

'What shall we do, senator?' Kunaric asked.

'We follow the plan.' They hurried back to the trees. Kunaric, a wide-jawed Brigantian in his late twenties, was a career soldier whose ambitions were set on a high command in the field army. Years ago he had even hired a tutor who had taught him how to talk like an officer from the educated classes. In Paul he obviously saw another opportunity to better himself; at first Paul had found his continual questions and half-correct classical allusions irritating, but slowly he had come to admire the man, and almost consider him a friend. Kunaric was a good soldier, smart and dependable. If anyone deserved advancement, he did.

The rest of the soldiers were waiting in the shadows, tense and silent. Paul felt their doubtful eyes on him. He had spent enough time in the ranks to understand how they must feel, asked to follow someone who had arrived in the fort at the start of winter and spent two months sick in bed, who had finally emerged and was suddenly revealed by the commander to be a secret envoy from Duke Fullobaudes charged with assessing and securing their tactical situation. Drogo had proposed the idea when Paul demanded to be given some active role in the garrison. Not having the authority to commission a new officer, he suggested that Paul's aristocratic bearing and military knowledge could still be of some use to morale, and so a secret agent of the duke was born. It was a convenient, absurd fiction, but one that had so far worked, and it was no more false than the life Paul had led for the last few years. The men and the officers accepted the story without question. After all, how else could an aristocrat know so much about army life?

Earning their trust in his abilities, however, was something else. For three months now Paul had accompanied units on patrols through the mountains, acquiring a keen sense of the garrison's resources, its men, the surrounding terrain. Nothing he had seen changed his earlier opinion that their position was all but hopeless. They were too few, too isolated. No news had come from outside the mountains; Duke Fullobaudes was likely still in the south, completely unaware that Valentinus, his right-hand man, had spent the winter plotting against him. Paul and Drogo still had no clear idea of what Valentinus intended to do. Their evening talks always ended the same way: Drogo would raise his hands, laugh, and say that he did not care if they won or not. It mattered only that he preserved his oath to the emperor.

Perhaps the tribune truly did not care. After so many years in the mountains he was unable to see beyond them, and had accepted that they would be his tomb. Perhaps he even savoured the prospect of a terrible and glorious defeat.

Paul cleared his thoughts and focused on the valley below. Now he needed to concentrate. The only advantage Drogo seemed to have was an informant in Galava, the eastern rebel fort. The informant claimed that some of the biarchi and enlisted men were bitterly unhappy with their tribune for swearing loyalty to Valentinus. The informant had revealed that a detachment from Galava containing the disgruntled biarchi would be marching through this pass on this day, and Paul had convinced Drogo to let him spring a trap. His desperate hope was that the biarchi would agree to defect, and that their men would follow. He knew it was a gamble. If it worked, there may yet be hope. If not, Mediobogdum would soon fall.

Down in the valley two lightly armoured men on horseback came along the road, scouts from Galava. It would not be long now. Paul waited until they had passed out of sight and turned to Kunaric. 'Make ready,' he said.

Kunaric relayed the order to the biarchi, and there was a brief rush of noise as soldiers tugged leather covers from shields, tightened straps and armour, tested weapons and were brought into order. One soldier waved a signal across the valley to the cavalry.

Soon the head of the rebel column came into view. As they slowly approached along the road, Paul counted their numbers. The scout had been right: forty men in double marching order, two officers on horseback at the front, apparently not expecting any trouble. Paul had already established exactly how long it would take for his men to run from the trees to the road, and each squad knew precisely what role they had to play. If they could surround the rebels quickly enough they might shock them into surrendering without a fight. Everything depended on how the rebel biarchi reacted.

His men waited around him, crouched, eager, poised to unleash hours of pent-up energy at a single command.

He nodded to Kunaric. 'Now.'

Kunaric jumped to his feet and thrust his sword towards the road. 'For the emperor!'

They burst from the cover of the trees with a roar, plunging down the grassy slope to the flank of the rebel column. Paul saw the confusion in the faces of the troops below, the jostle of uncertainty as their formation fragmented and the biarchi tried to bring their squads into battle order; the seeds of panic as they looked around and saw a second wave of attackers, a full wing of cavalry, charging from the opposite side of the valley and encircling their rear. Realising they were surrounded, the rebels hurriedly doubled their battle line, two ranks facing in opposite directions, the pair of officers dismounted between them.

Paul was almost at the road, a hundred feet from the solid shield wall of the rebels, when he yelled for his men to hold. With an efficiency that impressed him they halted the charge and formed a single line facing the rebels, where they held position, spears forward, panting from their lightning sprint. On the opposite slope beyond the rebels waited the cavalry, also drawn up in formation, javelins at the ready. Each soldier was frozen, waiting for orders. Paul could hear the two rebel officers, both of junior rank, conferring urgently, no doubt confused by the sudden halt in the attack and unsure of what to do.

Making the most of their bewilderment, Paul strode forwards until he was standing halfway between the lines, on the bank of a narrow brook that ran alongside the road. He was not in uniform, wearing a plain tunic, cloak and trousers, with no armour except a simple helmet, and no shield. He left his sword in its sheath. 'I am a special agent of Duke Fullobaudes, duly appointed commander of the British garrison under his majesty Valentinian Augustus. You men are following the rebel Valentinus, who will soon pay for his treachery. If you remember your sacred oath to the emperor now, you will be welcomed back into the ranks of your brothers in arms and rewarded for your loyalty. If you do not, you will die. Rome offers forgiveness only once. Choose.'

One of the officers called out from behind his men. 'We follow the orders of our lord Valentinus.'

'The duke is rallying his forces as we speak,' Paul said. 'Your plot has failed.'

'That's a lie!' called the officer. 'The duke is a fool! Let me give *you* a choice: join us, and perhaps our lord Valentinus won't slit your throat!'

Paul had feared that the officers would be loyal to Valentinus. They were probably exiles themselves, brought over by Valentinus from Pannonia to judge from the man's thick accent, and had nothing to lose. If they surrendered they would eventually be executed anyway. But they were clearly rattled and insecure, their men undoubtedly more so. 'Then I address the men of Galava,' said Paul, switching from Latin to British. 'These strangers have been placed over you as officers, but they have no authority and no honour. They are exiles, outlaws, enemies of the empire. Are these the sort of men you will pledge to follow? Have you forgotten your sacred oaths to the divine Augustus?'

The two foreign officers, unable to understand Paul's words, were trying to harass the biarchi into launching an attack, yelling mutiny and damning them to death if they disobeyed orders. This man was an imposter and a liar, they screamed, sent to sow discord. They promised wealth and glory to any who remained loyal. None but a madman would move against Valentinus.

The biarchi wavered. Their nervous squads held the defensive lines. Paul had meant to sow discord, as the officer said, but now it was beyond his control whether or not the seeds grew into mutiny. He withdrew to his own men and prepared to order an attack if things did not go his way.

Moments later the senior rebel biarchus, an enormous, red-bearded veteran, walked up to the officer, grabbed his tunic and plunged a dagger into his neck. The officer collapsed to his knees, gargling his last curses, as his comrade was likewise taken and stabbed to death by a pair of soldiers.

The red-haired biarchus came through the ranks and stood on the opposite bank of the brook, his bloodied dagger still in his hand. 'Beliato, senior biarchus of the first century of the garrison of Galava,' he said.

Paul came down to meet him at the stream. He felt like grinning with relief, but kept his face solemn. 'Your loyalty to the emperor is appreciated, biarchus Beliato.'

The victory was celebrated later at Mediobogdum as the defectors were welcomed into the ranks of Drogo's garrison. Paul considered the success in a more sober frame of mind. On the journey back to the fort Beliato had told him that he despised their tribune for his lack of honour, and resented the foreign officers whom Valentinus had sent to the fort. Nonetheless, they had brought a great deal of silver with them, and silver mattered more to most soldiers than honour. Most other biarchi at Galava would have stood and fought, he said.

This news made another such move too risky to contemplate. Drogo had only three hundred battle-ready men at his disposal, plus the forty new arrivals, which also made a direct assault on the rebel forts out of the question. Supplies were running low, and foraging in the surrounding valleys would be difficult. Their best hope was that the rebels would be panicked into attacking very soon, without taking time to properly prepare and while morale at Mediobogdum was still high.

That evening Drogo mounted the battlements above his celebrating men and gave a speech to stoke their fighting spirit. Paul stood below and watched in calm detachment. He was not in the mood for drinking. In their desperate situation he found a sense of purpose, even peace. More than that, he sometimes saw the faces of his old comrades in the soldiers around him, and by hearing the same jokes, the same songs, listening to the same complaints about drills and fatigues and rations, garrison life had wrapped itself around him like the arms of an old lover. Every day he thought of Vercovicium and Victor, and often spoke to Eachna about them. Military life and the bonds it forged between men were strange to her, but she understood the pain of his loss.

He returned to his room, where she was already asleep. Paul changed into his nightclothes and climbed into bed next to her. She lay on her side facing him. He watched her small, spare limbs, her bony shoulders, as they rose and fell with each breath. A tangled mass of blonde hair lay spread over the pillow. On one side it was turned a soft silver by the grey moonlight, on the other a deep orange by the glowing embers in the brazier. Her sleeping sighs were slow and quiet.

Although she was asleep, her face spoke to Paul. It reassured him; he saw the intelligence in her creased brow, which taught him caution and consideration. The quick humour in her tight, thin lips told him to laugh at the foolishness of the world and smile at its foibles. You confuse me, Paul, it said, but I will not let you defeat me. For all your mournful moods and love of solitude, I know you better than you realise.

It was strange how natural it felt to lie here and watch this girl, his slave, and feel this way. From his past life he recalled a fellow schoolboy whose father was known to sleep with his slaves. The father had become a figure of mockery, an indulgent and weak-minded clown for succumbing to such a dull and common temptation. It was the sort of thing a pretentious city tradesman would do, or a country farmer who knew no better.

Those old feelings meant little. She was here next to him, and it did not seem to matter who she was, or where she had come from, so long as she did not go. In her Paul had found living redemption. He could never wash away the guilt of killing Faustus. He realised that now. He could not simply go home and expect to be cleansed through confession and condemnation. Every day of his life he would have to atone for his crime, seeking justice not in exile or his own death, but in sacrifice and courage of spirit, in striving selflessly to protect the family he had betrayed.

For this, Eachna was his guide, his inspiration. He knew that if he could one day match even a fragment of her nobility, no matter what the world said of him, there would be hope.

When the rebels attacked two weeks later, Mediobogdum was ready for them. Drogo had spent the days after the ambush conferring with Paul, Kunaric and the other centenarii and had decided on a strategy for defence. They could expect to see three hundred men approaching from Galava, with four or five hundred from Glanoventa in the west. The enemy plan would be to pinch Mediobogdum between these two forces, leaving no escape route; they could then besiege the fort or assault it as they saw fit.

Such a plan, however, would depend on the two forces reaching Mediobogdum at the same time. What if, Drogo suggested, one force could be delayed? The rebel leaders would no doubt advance up the valley slowly and warily, especially after the ambush. A light skirmishing force could easily delay the troops approaching from the coast. This would leave only the smaller force from Galava to begin with, and with luck they would not have much stomach for a fight.

There had followed hours of debating in Drogo's office over the particulars of the plan – how best to prepare the fort defences, how to dispose of their own meagre resources, how far down the valley the skirmishers should attempt to harass the force from Glanoventa. The more they had argued, the more the officers had run around the same fears and uncertainties again and again, until Paul had wanted to crack their heads against the wall. What if the enemy did not behave as Drogo expected? What if the troops from Galava put up a tough fight? What would they do when the much larger Glanoventa force arrived?

Drogo had finally confronted their doubts with a blunt truth. He had sat on the chair behind his desk, looked each of his officers in the eye, and said, 'We need not win for the fight to be worth it.' Kunaric and the officers absorbed those words in silence. Paul knew each of them by now, and knew them to be tough, experienced and reliable. Drogo encouraged debate among his command staff, but his orders, once given, were always obeyed. No one had raised the possibility of negotiating a surrender.

Paul had barely awoken one morning and was watching the dawn sunlight creep along the rafters of the ceiling when the horn sounded – not the usual reveille, but a battle horn. It jolted him to a sitting position. Eachna stirred beside him, squinting and wiping her eyes. 'They're coming,' she said.

The moment the garrison had awaited since autumn had finally arrived. Paul did not feel relief, as he had thought he would, despite the many days of restless anticipation. Nor did he quite feel fear, either, but rather a low, yawning dread that seized him as he climbed from the bed and found his tunic, breeches, shoes, belt. Eachna watched him as he dressed.

They both knew that these could be their final moments together. The last four months had been the happiest and most peaceful of Paul's life, a strange sort of peace that he had never imagined existed: peace from his nightmares, from the troubles that had followed him for so long, a sanctuary that had seemed to exist outside time and space. It was more than he deserved, far more, and a week ago, had he been told that it would be followed by the peace of the dead, he would not have called it unjust. But at this moment he felt that he would do almost anything to escape it.

When Paul was dressed, Eachna rose from bed, kissed him and took him in a long embrace. They stood pressed together while shouts and commands, the quick tramping of hobnailed boots and the noises of a garrison preparing for battle surrounded them, rising and rushing past the window and echoing down the corridor outside. There was no hammering at the door, no voice summoning them to rise. Maybe, Paul dreamed, they could stand here and be forgotten, ignored as the battle was fought around them and won or lost, ignored as the victors cleared away the dead, forgotten in this room until life had fallen back into mundane routines like dust settling on the arena floor.

'I have a knife,' Eachna said. 'In case.'

He looked into her eyes. 'Don't use it. If they get inside, go to the north gate and head into the mountains. Make for Luguvalium. Bishop Ludo will protect you.'

'If they get inside, that means you're dead.'

'I want you to get away.'

She smiled. 'I don't care what you want.'

He was helpless against that smile: kind, knowing, amused because he still thought he could command her like a slave. There was no point arguing with her. Of course they could escape together, somehow sneak out of the fort during the battle, but that would be a betrayal not just of Drogo, but of their love. Paul loved her because she would never let such a cowardly thought cross her mind, and he would not be deserving of her love were it to cross his. So, bound by honour not to flee, they waited amidst the rising dread until the last possible instant, when Paul finally unwrapped himself from her arms.

While Eachna prepared to help the medics in the fort hospital, Paul went to find Drogo and his command staff in the head-quarters. Forces from Galava and Glanoventa had been spotted by scouts at first light. Just as Drogo had predicted, it was a coordinated attack intended to trap them in the pass. A troop of archers and light cavalry had already been despatched west to delay the larger enemy force an hour or two down the valley. The eastern force numbered only two hundred and fifty – deser-tions had taken their toll, Drogo grinned. The plan would proceed.

It was a calm morning, clear-skied and almost without wind. Paul waited on the eastern ramparts, his eyes fixed on the crest of the pass half a mile distant. The line of the road appeared in a cleft between two vast shoulders of granite, and fell steeply over undulating ground towards the fort. The scouts had already reported that the enemy was climbing the opposite side of the pass. As he watched, Paul noticed dark specks appear in the cleft, silhouetted against the morning light. Moments later a battle horn sounded from a corner tower. Paul twisted to look down the western valley: still nothing from that direction. So far Drogo's plan seemed to be working.

'To arms!' Drogo roared from further along the ramparts. 'Squads, stand to! Make ready!'

Paul climbed down from the ramparts. Two wings of cavalry had already left the fort, taking a little-used goat trail to the south in order to encircle the approaching enemy and strike them from the rear. As soon as they did, Kunaric and Paul were to lead an infantry sally and deliver the killing blow. Kunaric was waiting with their men, one hundred and fifty of the toughest troops in the garrison, ready to charge through the east gate. He nodded as Paul approached. 'Ready?'

'Ready,' said Paul. He had been given the armour of one of the rebel officers slain at the ambush. The helmet had needed extra padding, but otherwise the uniform fitted him perfectly. It felt at once strange and natural to be wearing it.

'At Thermopylae,' said Kunaric, 'the Greeks built the statue of a lion to honour the men who died defending the pass. Think we'll get one of them?'

'Only if some of us live to tell the tale,' said Paul.

'Ah, never mind, then.'

They waited restlessly. They had gone over the plan a dozen times. In order to conserve ammunition, Drogo had ordered the ballistas to hold until the rebels were within six hundred feet, the archers until they were within four hundred. The cavalry would then charge their rear, hopefully hitting them before they reached the walls of the fort. At that moment, Paul and Kunaric would lead their charge.

At the first horn signal and a bark from their commanders, the ballista crews on the corner towers began to work their machines. Soon the second horn sounded, and the archers released the first flight of arrows over the ramparts. Then came the third horn, distant and faint, not from the fort but from the pass itself. The cavalry had begun their attack.

'Stand ready!' yelled Kunaric. 'Form up!' The sally force

hurried into tight formation at the east gate, where two soldiers stood ready to open the doors. 'Remember, quick and smooth into the wedge, and stay tight!'

Minutes passed in the cool shade of the gatehouse. Above them archers and biarchi yelled and swore, urging one another on against fear and exhaustion. An enemy arrow found its mark, thudding into the shoulder of a man on the battlements. Paul watched him totter and stagger backwards before a neighbour caught him and lowered him slowly into a sitting position against the stone. He was clutching the base of the shaft, his face screwed up in pain.

A final horn sounded from the corner tower. The cavalry had hit the rebels. Kunaric unsheathed his sword. 'Open the gates!' The pair of soldiers jumped to obey, lifting the great wooden crosspiece and throwing it to one side, taking hold of the handles and pulling the doors open. 'With me!' cried Kunaric.

They advanced as they had practised dozens of times, the first squads sprinting out of the fort, making ground, then slowing to allow those behind them to catch up and fan out either side into a wedge formation, the biarchi shouting in turn above the thunder of feet that their squads were in position: and at that moment Kunaric and Paul, weapons bare, set into the charge with a roar. The rebels were still one hundred yards up the mossy incline of the pass, a mass of troops thrown into disarray by the lost momentum of the aborted assault, by the cavalry grinding into them from behind, by the constant peppering of missiles. Some turned to see the sally force racing towards them and tried to form a coherent line, but they were too slow.

Paul chose his first target, a biarchus in the front rank struggling to tug his men into position. He plunged towards the man, knocked him to the ground with a powerful lunge of his shield, and in a swift, pure motion thrust his sword into his throat before he could rise. The point sank through flesh, severing an artery with a gush of blood, before it met something hard; with another push it snapped through the spine and the man lay lifeless.

Kunaric was already in front of Paul at the tip of the wedge, pushing the rebels back with his shield firm against his shoulder, thrusting and hacking with his longsword. On either side their men kept the formation tight, shields interlocked, spear points jabbing high and low into the enemy ranks as they forced their way step by step up the slope, pressing the rebels into the cavalry. Paul squeezed back into the front rank next to Kunaric. Rebels who were struck down, or who tripped on rocks, or whose feet sank into the boggy ground, were trampled where they fell, and any survivors were finished off without mercy by the second and third ranks of the wedge.

'Keep on!' Kunaric screamed, his voice bursting next to Paul's ear. 'Push them back! Kill them!'

Paul felt like he had when fighting the Verturians: detached, calm despite the blood thumping through his veins and the haze of blood and sweat around him, as though this were a problem of grammar that could only be solved with clear thoughts and a level head. The soldier facing him punched forwards with his shield; Paul braced his back leg and took the blow against his shield boss. The soldier thrust his spear at Paul's face; Paul ducked, letting the point miss him by a finger's width. For a moment the rebel was overstretched and off balance; it was the moment to strike. Paul lifted his shield and plunged his sword into the man's knee, splitting it open. He collapsed screaming. Paul readied himself for another to take the man's place. It was so simple, he thought, realising that he was good, very good, at killing.

On they fought, butchering for every inch of ground until they could not advance without trampling over the squirming bodies of the fallen. There was nothing to do except hack and stab every inch of enemy flesh they could see. Another man fell to Paul's blade, and he caught another in the back of the neck as he turned to flee; and then, so suddenly that they might have been lifted into the air, the enemy line was broken. Rebels began fleeing up towards the crest of the pass, desperately, hopelessly trying to escape the cavalry who were running them down. Some made for the rocky crags on either side where horses could not follow.

The wedge dispersed and Kunaric and Paul stood side by side, panting, their swords bright with blood. Kunaric had a bad cut across his cheek, which he seemed not to notice. He shouted for some squads to chase after the fleeing rebels, commanding the rest to check the fallen for survivors. Officers and biarchi were to be taken prisoner, pedites were to be cleanly executed where they lay. Paul looked back to the fort across a stretch of ground littered with the dead and wounded. It looked like they had pushed the rebels a hundred yards up the valley before they had broken. Now the frenzy of battle had been succeeded by an anguished stillness. The air was laced with moans, cries, the shrill whinnies of injured horses. Soldiers ambled between the fallen, looking for dead or wounded friends, despatching enemies who still lived.

'It could've been much worse,' Kunaric said to Paul an hour later, when they were back on the ramparts. The rebels from Galava had been demolished. More than a hundred now lay scattered among the rocks and turf of the pass, the rest, including their tribune, having fled into the mountains. Drogo had lost forty men, including those too badly wounded to fight on. They had cleared the bodies of their own from the battlefield, but did not have time to collect up those of the enemy, and crows were already gathering and settling on the dead.

From across the fort came a scream. Nobody paid any attention to it. Drogo was interrogating the only rebel officer to have been caught alive, and there had been many of his screams over the last half hour. Kunaric took a bite from a chicken leg, and offered the rest to Paul, who shook his head. He was not hungry. He felt drained. Kunaric was right; it could have been much worse. These rebels had been demoralised, diminished, poorly led. They had almost been ready to flee before battle was even joined. The troops from Glanoventa would be different.

Soon afterwards scouts reported that the second enemy force was rapidly approaching from the west, having shrugged off their harassers. The soldier who brought the news to the battlements addressed Paul. 'The tribune wants to see you in the head-quarters, sir. Your girl, too.'

Paul went to find Eachna in the hospital, a large timber building next to the headquarters. He nodded to the soldiers sitting on the ground outside, the lightly wounded who would be expected to fight again before the day was out. The main sick bay was at the rear of the building. It contained twenty beds, almost all of them now occupied. Orderlies moved between the injured men, checking bandages, giving them water. The medicus acknowledged Paul as he entered. 'No amputations yet, thank God. These boys will be all right. We lost a couple already though. You looking for your girl? She's there at the far bed.'

Paul saw Eachna kneeling next to a man who had a red-stained dressing across one eye. At first he thought she was praying, but he came closer and saw that she was speaking to the man, and he was listening calmly. His uncovered eye was closed, but he was smiling.

Eachna noticed Paul and got to her feet. They embraced, holding one another tight. 'I'm telling him about Hibernia,' she said. 'He says he used to know someone from there.'

They found Drogo in his office, alone. Before him on the desk were spread what looked like every scouting report from the last few months, every strength report, every scrap of intelligence he had been able to find. 'Come in!' he called when he heard them at the door. He laughed and stabbed his finger at Paul. 'I knew I was right to put you out there! You and the boys made a real mess of them. Another few sallies like that and we'll send the lot of them running back to the coast!'

'It didn't take much to break them, tribune,' said Paul. 'What about the cohort from Glanoventa?'

Drogo appeared not to hear the question. 'I thank you for what you did, Cironius. You of all people have no need to be here. I was half expecting to turn around and find the pair of you gone this morning. After all, who'd choose to die in a place like this?'

'We chose to fight here, not die,' said Eachna.

'Well, you've done that, all right. Now you can leave.'

Paul looked at him in surprise. 'You want us to go?'

'I'm *ordering* you to go. We can hold off the Glanoventa lot. My scouts say half of them have given up already and turned back.'

'Then we should stay until you fight them off.'

'Oh, no. You're going *now*. And you're taking this with you.' He beckoned them to approach the desk, and picked up a tablet. The pale wood was smeared with the blood on his fingers. 'I've written down here everything I could get out of the optio we captured. He was one of Valentinus's henchmen. This is far bigger than we thought. All of the Four Provinces are in danger. You need to get this to the south.'

'What did he say?'

'Bribing the northern garrisons and the coastal forts is only part of Valentinus's plan. He's also made a pact with the barbarians. When the duke marches north he'll be heading into a trap, whether he's killed or captured by the Picts, Valentinus doesn't care. Once the duke is out of the way, Valentinus will be supreme commander. He'll send orders to the coastal fleets to stay in dock, and let the Picts and the Irish strike deep into the southern provinces, wherever they like, spreading terror. When his barbarian friends have got enough silver and slaves, Valentinus will march south like a saviour and pretend to fight them off. The city councils will worship him, the provincial governors will be too scared to do a thing, and Valentinus will have himself declared emperor.'

'That's insane,' said Paul. 'He has no claim to the throne.'

'Neither did Valentinian before he was elected,' Drogo said. 'Nor did Magnentius when he rebelled seventeen years ago. And remember that Constantine himself began as a usurper in Britannia. Don't you know your history? Any man can call himself emperor if he has enough troops at his back!'

'That's just it –Valentinus doesn't. The entire British garrison wouldn't stand a chance against the emperor's field army.'

'You're forgetting that Valentinus has barbarian allies, and plenty of them. A lot of Britons will back him. He still has old friends in Pannonia, where soldiers grow like wheat, and even in the imperial court. His brother-in-law Maximinus is Prefect of Rome. If Valentinus manages to take over Britannia, between them the emperor will be trapped with nowhere to move. Rather like we are now, in fact.'

Paul felt a creeping dread, as though a dark shadow were about to fall across the island. 'And the duke has left the cities undefended.'

'Yes he has. He's been getting false information from his spies. He has no idea what's waiting for him in the north, or what will happen as soon as he launches his campaign. The cursed fool's played right into Valentinus's hands. He should never have been made duke.'

'Where is he now?'

'You know as well as I do. He spent the winter in the south, but he could already be heading back to the Wall.'

'We need to find him.'

'It may already be too late. You should head south, warn the cities. They'll listen to you – you're a senator, a nobleman. Tell them everything. Try to get word across the sea. But watch who you talk to. The optio said that Valentinus has civilian supporters in the south. He didn't know all of them, but some are written down here.'

Paul took the tablet and opened it. It was a letter from Drogo, addressed to all loyal servants of the emperor, summarising everything he had just said. At the bottom were written half a dozen names. Paul recognised only one of them. 'Agrius Leo,' he muttered.

'You know that man?'

'I know him.' Paul closed the letter. This was it. Whatever petty reasons Agrius Leo may have had for keeping him at Vercovicium, this letter implicated him in treason against the empire. It would be his death warrant. 'All right,' Paul said. 'We'll leave straight after the battle.'

'No, you'll go now or I'll have you thrown out. This is too important. I've already asked for provisions to be made ready. Don't tell anyone in the fort, just leave. Don't worry about us.

You've more than repaid your debt. It was providence that brought you here, Cironius, so you could take this news to the people who need to hear it. I fear it's already too late for the duke, but there's still time to protect the cities – if you move now.'

Paul knew Drogo was right. There was little doubt that Fullobaudes was doomed. And if Valentinus had made a deal with Keocher, leaving the provinces open to every savage this side of world's end, there was no telling how many more would die.

He held out his hand to Drogo. 'I'll report faithfully everything you've done here, tribune.'

Drogo took his hand and shook it. 'Senator, it has been an honour to uphold my oath.'

Their final view of Mediobogdum was from the south side of the pass, just before they followed the goat trail around the high ground that would take them out of sight. They paused, buffeted by the wind that swept between the walls of rock and the wide-open air of the mountains, and looked back. The rebel force from Glanoventa had appeared, creeping up the western valley like a great dark caterpillar.

Drogo had lied. They were not the withered remainder of the coastal garrison. Paul judged that close to a thousand troops were converging on the fort. The fight up the narrow climb to the gates would be tough, but even from this distance it was clear that their numbers would prevail. Mediobogdum would fall.

'Drogo doesn't stand a chance,' he said.

Eachna was looking down into the valley as though at a funeral procession. 'He must have known.'

Paul pulled the hood over his head against the raging wind. 'Come on,' he said. 'Before they see us.'

XXII

Nunc canto tibi siluestris Siluanici, Amanda;
ludes responsum calamo tenuique agresti
dum frigidae fluitantibus tendunt umbrae aruis.
Hesperius's song for Amanda

May had come to Silvanicum, Amanda's favourite month, bringing with it the full colour and warmth of spring. The orchard apple trees were in glorious pink bloom, rising from a sea of bluebells whose scent drifted down the ivy-wrapped colonnades. Amanda had taken special care supervising the garden this year, and had instructed the chief groundsman to lay fresh gravel on the central path and to plant ornamental box hedges on either side. It was not to her taste, but her father had requested it to impress their new guest. 'Decimius Hilarianus Hesperius will be used to such refinements,' he had said.

Three months had passed since Agrius Rufus had rejected her, and the pain was at last beginning to fade. Now she thought only of their coming visitor: Hesperius, son of the leading professor of the imperial court. It was hard to believe that in less than an hour someone of such grand connections would come walking into this very garden. His family might not be of the best origins, but twenty-five years ago his uncle had served in Londinium as consul-governor of Maxima Caesariensis, and even the noblest senators could not afford to ignore someone whose father had become so close to the divine emperor. Amanda had been looking forward to his arrival for weeks, ever since Lucas had written to announce that he would be returning in the first week of May, promising to bring Hesperius with him. He was eighteen years old, attractive, rich and popular, her father told her – and, he added with a wink, still not betrothed. Amanda was no less excited by the thought that, with a renowned professor for a father, he would also surely be cultured and well read, someone close to her own age with whom she might talk as an intellectual equal. God knew she longed for that.

Amanda was in her room when Pinta came to tell her that her father had returned from the city with Lucas and his Gallic friend. She paused only to check her reflection before she went out into the courtyard garden and waited at the head of the gravel path. She heard voices from near the stables, laughter both familiar and unfamiliar, as the party dismounted and entered the villa.

Her father was the first to come into the garden, followed closely by Lucas and another young man who had to be Hesperius. They were all talking merrily with one another, and her father even had his arm around Lucas's shoulder. Amanda could not help but smile to see them on such good terms.

Lucas was the first to spot Amanda. 'Hello, sister!' he said, coming forward to hug her. 'I'm sorry I stayed away so long.'

'I'm just happy you're back, Lucas.'

'You will be when you see who I've brought with me. Amanda, this is Hesperius.' He beckoned for his friend to come forward. 'Now, I only ask that you forget everything bad I might've said about him. He's all right, really.'

Hesperius smiled and bowed. He did have an attractive face, Amanda thought. It was soft-featured but earnest, with inviting blue eyes; his hair was light brown, almost blond, and carelessly tousled in the manner of a poet or philosopher. Before she could utter a greeting, he raised his hand to stop her, then placed it over his heart. 'Forgive me, my lady, if I forego the pleasantries of refined society for just a moment. As we reached the villa I composed a little ditty in your honour, and I am suddenly quite unable to restrain myself. May I?'

Amanda glanced at her father, who nodded indulgently. She smiled at Hesperius. 'Very well, honoured guest.'

Hesperius took a slow breath and began to recite in a smooth, measured voice, slowly and with feeling:

'Now I sing to you, Amanda, of wooded Silvanicum;
    You'll play the response on a slender, rustic reed-pipe
Until the cool shadows stretch across the flowing fields . . .'

Agnus clapped. 'Bravo! A pretty little verse.'

'It sprung from my head more or less fully formed, like the fabled goddess of wisdom,' said Hesperius. 'I love the air here; it's as though I'm breathing pure inspiration! I must admit I find this country almost as beautiful as my hostess.'

'I'm afraid I'll be a disappointment to you,' said Amanda. 'I don't play reed-pipes.'

'Well, no matter. Your voice, my lady, is sweet enough music for me.'

There was something disarming about his manner, his disregard for the convention that by now they should each have reeled off a tedious list of one another's titles and parents. It was his freedom from the burden of a true aristocratic heritage, perhaps, that let him turn around and admire the garden with such frankness, marvelling at the richness of the apple blossom. While her father went to manage some business in his library, Amanda wandered with Hesperius and Lucas through the upper courtyard, from one plant to the next, aimlessly and delightfully, talking and laughing without pause. An hour passed, and she scarcely noticed.

After the evening meal, a simple and merry supper of boiled pork and vegetables and wine – for the true feast, Hesperius asserted, lay not in the extravagance of the food, but in the warmth of the company – Amanda lay in bed unable to sleep. She was still giddy from the alcohol, but also from Hesperius, who had somehow raised the mood of the entire villa, even the servants, into the clouds. She had not realised how sombre Silvanicum had become without her mother or Lucas. Hesperius had entertained them through dinner with stories about his ancestors and relatives, a wonderfully mixed bag of impoverished nobles, freedman doctors and eccentric academics, even a vagabond great uncle who had amassed a fortune in trade before he was stabbed to death by a jealous husband in Londinium. Amanda had never seen Lucas get on so well with their father, with none of the sulks or sarcasm of the past. She ran through the whole evening in her head, half searching, through habit, for a hint of discord or insincerity, but could find none. Even Lucas and Father Arcadius had shared one or two jokes. It had been a perfect dinner. This, she thought as she pulled the blanket tight up to her chin, was all she wanted from life. 'I think I adore him,' she whispered, grinning in the darkness.

Days of sun and leisure came and went. Hesperius, like Lucas, liked to rise late, and the pair of them spent much of each morning hunting with dogs. They returned to the villa around noon for lunch, and whiled away the next few hours in the garden, the baths or wandering in the woods. Hesperius took a tablet with him at all times, on which he jotted down pieces of verse as they occurred to him, sometimes even when Amanda or someone else was in the middle of a sentence. 'Forgive me,' he would mutter, interrupting them, 'but the muse has taken me.' He would scribble down a line or two, apologise again, slip his tablet back into its pouch, and beg for the talker to continue. She asked him to recite some of his own compositions, and he obliged. He was very good; by far the most talented poet Amanda had ever met, and she told him so. 'It's all down to my father,' he said, shaking his head modestly.

During the second week of his stay, Hesperius began sending Amanda bunches of flowers he had gathered while hunting. He would tie together a small bundle of bluebells, hawthorn blooms and cherry blossom, write a witty epigram to go with it, and give it to Pinta, who would bring it to Amanda. 'I'm not to say who it's from,' Pinta would declare with a conspiratorial smile.

Amanda looked forward to these daily gifts. She was relieved that her attraction to Hesperius – for she could not deny that she was attracted to him – was not the base, irrational desire she had felt for Rufus. Hesperius made her laugh, stimulated her, charmed her. She secretly pondered the suitability of a match between them, as she was sure her father already had done. Hesperius was a young man of the highest prospects, son of a rising family, heir to what would be a fortune enriched beyond imagination by the favour of the emperor. He was witty and talented. True, he seemed to share Lucas's poetic sensibilities and his Christianity was probably not much more than skin deep, but Amanda could overlook these faults, which would surely fade with maturity.

The third week brought heavy rain, confining Hesperius and Lucas to the villa. There were no more floral gifts. Amanda was content enough using the time to manage some neglected aspects of the household with Ecdicius, and her father spent most of his time in the library. Lucas and Hesperius lounged about the villa eating, drinking, sleeping and playing with dice. At one point they declared themselves so bored that they went out hunting anyway, but returned half an hour later smeared in mud and soaked to the skin. 'Well, that was fun,' laughed Hesperius as he entered the villa and happened upon Amanda in the corridor. He stood before her, his hair plastered over his scalp, a steadily expanding puddle of rainwater at his feet.

One afternoon Amanda was sitting on a cushioned ledge of the colonnade, a copy of Catullus on her lap, listening idly to the symphony of rain in the orchard garden: a thick pattering on the leaves of the apples trees, a dull blanket of noise on the lawns, louder and harsher on the gravel path and the tiled roof above. The villa was quiet, even the kitchens, as though its occupants had been driven into hibernation by the downpour. Amanda loved the sweet, sleepy melancholy of heavy rain, loved the way it subdued all urgency, loved the freshness it gave the air and how she could reach out from the dry shelter of the house and watch the drops stream over her hand.

'Uncle Sanctus always said it rained a lot here,' came a voice. Amanda looked up to see Hesperius ambling slowly along the colonnade towards her, brushing his fingers against the curling ivy. 'Now I see he wasn't lying.'

'It's good for the garden,' said Amanda.

The rain had subdued Hesperius, too, it seemed. He reached Amanda and perched himself on the same ledge, resting his back against the opposite column and looking out into the orchard. He shifted one foot on the ledge so that his toes were almost touching hers. When he spoke he sounded weary. 'One can have too much of a good thing. I was born in Burdigala. I need the sun like . . . well, like you probably need the rain.' He nodded at the book on her lap. 'What are you reading?'

'Catullus.'

'My old friend Catullus. Do you have a favourite?'

'I like his poem to Calvus on the death of his wife.'

'I know it. The yearning to revive old loves, weeping for friend-ships lost . . . not one of his happier ones. Fine choice, though.'

'Do you have a favourite?'

'I do.'

'May I know which?'

He smiled mysteriously. He turned back to the rain, staring vaguely through the orchard. Amanda glanced at him, trying to read his expression in this rare moment of silence. He looked every inch the poet, she had to admit: wistful, distant, longing for heartache worthy of the world's attention. She wondered if there was another woman in his thoughts.

'I was hoping to see your cousin Patricia while I was here,' he said suddenly. 'Her family lives not far away, am I right?'

'That's right, twelve miles to the west.' *Please*, she thought, *not Patricia* . . .

'I know her from Treveris, though not terribly well. Such a sweet girl. Everyone was shocked when she took off to Lugdunum like that. I heard a strange rumour that she's recently sworn off men.'

'She's devoted herself to Christ, yes.'

'So it's true.' He rested the back of his head on the column and gazed into the sky. 'Pity.' His eyes shifted to hers. He nudged the side of her foot playfully with his toe. 'You don't have any intentions in that direction, do you?'

'Not yet, no.'

'Glad to hear it. All things in moderation, as they say; like anything else, piety, if pursued to excess, becomes a vice. Life is too short to spend the whole time fretting over what comes after it. Don't you think?'

'I suppose so.'

'Especially when one is young. We'll have time to worry about the future when it arrives.' He started to recite:

> 'Suns can set and rise once more;
> But for us, once our brief light fades,
> Comes a night of eternal sleep.'

It was a poem of Catullus. Amanda could not help herself from adding the next lines – ones she knew well.

> 'Give me a thousand kisses, then a hundred,
> Then another thousand, and a second hundred,
> And still another thousand, and another hundred . . .'

Their stares locked, and they laughed together. 'That's your favourite poem of his?' she asked.

'Are you surprised?'

She shook her head. 'No.'

'Would you like me to recite for you?'

'Please.'

'All right.' He shifted forwards until he was sitting near enough for them to touch. He placed one hand on the ledge beside her, leaning forwards, and with his other hand he took light hold of hers.

She had never had a young man outside the family so close before. She instinctively pressed her back against the column, but felt no desire to escape. He was close enough that she could smell the oil on his skin, the perfume in his hair. Her heart was beating urgently. It was not proper behaviour. They were so exposed. What if a servant saw them? What if her father passed by?

As though in answer to her thoughts, he began to whisper.

'Let us live, my Lesbia, and let us love,
And let us judge the gossip of old men
As worth not even a penny . . .'

With each line he moved closer and spoke more softly, until the words had faded and the space between their lips was almost nothing; and then he moved forward and pressed his mouth against hers.

She wrapped her arms around his neck, and she felt his hand shift to her ankle, and the press of his fingers through her dress as he traced the shape of her leg, slipping up to her knee, to her thigh, coming to rest on the curve of her waist.

He drew back slightly and ended the kiss. The cool air brushed between their lips. Amanda opened her eyes to see him looking into hers. He said, 'I think I was in love with you before we even met.'

He kissed her again, harder and more passionately, pressing his body still closer against her. He moved a practised hand up her arm and past her shoulder, briefly held the back of her neck and traced his thumb along the line of her jaw, then ran his fingers gently over her collarbone, over the stones of her necklace to her breast, which he gripped with a satisfied moan. Startled, she broke the kiss.

'What's wrong?' he asked.

'Nothing,' she said, and tried to push him away. 'Someone will come.'

He removed his hand, but was still fixed to the ledge like iron, his face close. 'Let them.'

'If my father hears—'

Hesperius chuckled. 'Oh, what can *he* do to me?'

With that one sentence he became a different person. He had not even tried to hide the arrogance in his voice. A moment ago Amanda had been enthralled, seduced. She suddenly felt all her warm feelings dissipate. She wanted to be away from him. 'Let me go,' she said.

'You are a silly girl,' he said, leaning in for another kiss.

She turned her face away from his. 'I said, let me go.'

He stopped, shook his head with a bemused laugh, and sat back. 'Amanda,' he said, 'your father would be delighted if I were to seduce you. It would be the best stroke of luck any Briton's had in years. After all, you could hardly embarrass yourself worse than your cousin Patricia did in Treveris.'

'Stay away from me,' she muttered, and rose from the ledge. She wrapped her shawl around her shoulders, left the book of Catullus where it lay, and walked with dignified steps along the deserted corridors to her room.

She spent a long time thinking over the encounter. She had been wholly under his spell, and willingly so, until he spoke those words: *Oh, what can* he *do to me?* Such dismissiveness, such contempt for her father's authority in his own house – that would have been enough. But it was not just that. It was his heartless mockery of Patricia. It was the disrespect, as though he assumed that she would jump and obey at a snap of his fingers, like everyone else in his world. It was the arrogant assumption that he, being who he was, could do what he liked with no regard for decency and no thought for other people. No doubt he had already seduced many girls this way. Amanda was not about to be his next conquest.

Amanda did not tell her father about Hesperius's attempt to seduce her, for it would only force him into an impossible decision between defending her honour and offending the best contact to the court he was ever likely to host. Instead she kept to herself, saying little at mealtimes and ignoring Hesperius as far as was possible without arousing suspicion in Lucas or her father.

When the sun returned the hunting trips resumed, but Amanda was glad that the flowers and epigrams did not. Pinta, who had taken to waiting for Hesperius in the upper courtyard to receive his presents for Amanda, was disappointed to be left empty-handed. 'I'm sorry, mistress,' she said. 'I'm sure he'll remember tomorrow.'

'I think we've both grown tired of that little game,' was all Amanda said.

Another week passed, and the day of Hesperius's departure grew nearer. He and Lucas would travel to White Hen House to visit Patricia before turning south and heading back to Treveris for the summer. Agnus asked his daughter to arrange a large feast on the eve of their departure as a memorable farewell. She dutifully set about the task, discussing the menu with the head cook and writing to a long list of grandees, including Bishop Martin and a host of others who had begged, petitioned or bought invitations from her father. Amanda noticed that governor Lucius Septimius, Agrius Leo's cousin, was not on the list. This was a deliberate snub, retaliation for his failure to attend the funeral last year. Less surprising was the absence of Agrius Leo himself, since relations had again soured after the cancellation of her betrothal to Rufus. Amanda cared little about this. As promised, Agrius Leo was preparing to leave Britannia, and he would soon be out of their world – at least until her father had gathered enough witnesses to have him dragged before an imperial tribunal. She would have nothing more to do with him or his son.

In any case, acting as host to Hesperius had certainly won Agnus new friends in Corinium. The large summer dining room of Silvanicum was filled to capacity; new couches and tables had even been built to accommodate the number of guests, and more servants hired to help in the kitchens. Amanda had expressed her worries to her father over the steadily bloating cost of the feast, but he had dismissed them. 'One cannot pay too much for this type of investment,' he had said. She had also tried to set out the seating arrangements well in advance, placing the three dozen guests according to rank as she thought best, until her father had asked Alypius to cast his eye over her plan. 'Good heavens, girl,' Alypius had gasped when he saw it, 'you can't put the supreme provincial judge next to the chief agent from the Bureau of Letters – that is, unless you *want* the feast to end in a bloody brawl.' After that, she had left it to him.

Amanda spent the feast reclining next to Lucas, with Hesperius and her father on the neighbouring couch. Alypius seemed to have done his job with typical efficiency, for the mood was merry and the conversation, as far as she could overhear from the men and women talking around her, was pleasant. On the dais where she was sitting, Hesperius was, naturally enough, the focus of all attention. Close by perched Bishop Martin, as well as several other imperial and civic officials whom Amanda scarcely noticed, and who were too busy ingratiating themselves with the chief guest to notice her.

The dessert had been eaten, and the tables were filled with platters of fruit and cheese, when the conversation turned to poetry. 'I've heard you're quite a poet yourself, Hesperius,' the supreme provincial judge, a Syrian, was saying.

'In my idle moments I like to pick up a pen, it's true,' Hesperius replied.

'Will you indulge us?'

'Oh, I don't think my scribblings will be of any interest to this industrious company. My uncle Sanctus once visited this villa when he was governor, and here I am, a poet – the most useless of all creatures, the peacocks of the human race.'

'Tch, civil servants need poetry in their lives more than anyone. Is that not true, friends? Shall we have young Hesperius give us a song?'

Cheers of encouragement came from the men and women along the length of the hall. After a moment of feigned reluctance, Hesperius tossed his napkin on the table, rose from his couch and stepped down to the lower floor. 'Very well – as it happens I do have a piece I've been working on. It's a little rough around the edges, however, so I must beg your indulgence.' He turned to face the dais and bowed to Agnus. He began to recite.

It was a lengthy panegyric, witty and passionately delivered, in honour of his host and of Silvanicum. He expressed his joy at receiving the invitation to visit far-flung Britannia, the drama of the sea-crossing and the exhaustion of the journey over land, his rapture at the idyllic beauty of the countryside, the fortitude and industry of its people, the many happy weeks he had spent here.

His audience was spellbound. Amanda wished every line were the last. She was glad when he finally came to the closing verses.

'For if the Fates would deign to have me free,
And have me rule my life by my decree,
My soul by sweet caress would then impel,
Within this noble Troy henceforth to dwell;
But now Apollo by his heartless will
Commands that I his prophecy fulfil.
On the rising sun to me he came;
Charged by Jove, to me he called by name.
Do not kindle sorrow in my heart, or grieve;
I could this country never freely leave.
Yet dear Silvanicum I must forsake,
And from this sweetest dream awake.
Beloved one, I feel the shadows high above;
Hesperius flees: away, my life, my soul, my love!'

The audience applauded and called out their admiration. Hesperius bowed and smiled graciously. Amanda was the quietest, offering polite applause and trying not to appear as troubled by the song as she was. Hesperius bowed again, and as he rose his eyes caught hers for an instant. She looked down immediately and blushed, and prayed that he did not mistake her shyness for encouragement. The judge began to praise the poet's wit, his fine delivery, his clever command of the fineries of Virgil, and the exquisite play in the final line. Hesperius accepted the praise happily and modestly, quite properly attributing any skill of his to the hard work of his father and former tutors, and the party had soon embarked on a discussion of the merits of a strict education.

Amanda kept silent, not so much because she thought that Hesperius's poem had been execrably dull and insincere – and no doubt recited in some form or other in many dining rooms before this one – but because she could not forget the final two lines, which he had delivered with his eyes firmly on hers. 'Beloved one', *amanda*, he had said. It was so carefully ambiguous; he could have been referring to the 'sweetest dream' instead of to her name. But his final words, a plea to a lover to join him in his unwilling flight – was she mistaken in thinking herself addressed? It was vanity, she told herself, to think so. But she could not forget the taunting intensity of his eyes, and she felt a fear rise in her chest.

The next day, from dawn well into the afternoon, was busy with risings and breakfasts and baths, walks and meetings between the guests of the night before, the dismantling of the tents in the lower courtyard, the packing of wagons and saddling of horses, and finally a long train of departures. Hesperius and Lucas were the last to leave, heading for White Hen House. Amanda kissed her brother farewell and asked him to deliver a letter she had written to Patricia. She bowed to Hesperius, wishing him a safe journey and saying nothing more. It was not difficult to smile as he mounted his horse and rode out of the villa.

Silvanicum was quieter without Hesperius, but Amanda was not sorry for that. She found she had missed the tranquility of a guestless house. It was most of all a relief that he had not tried to seduce her again before he left. With the chaos of so many visitors, it had been simple enough to avoid him for the last two days. The allusion to her name at the end of his poem had been nothing more than a final, pathetic gesture – as though it would have swayed her! She was glad to be rid of him. First Agrius Rufus, now this. Amanda was starting to wonder if Patricia did not have the right idea.

Late that evening, however, her father called her to the library. He was standing with a book in one hand, a glass of wine in the other. When she entered he replaced the book on its shelf and picked up another glass of wine from the desk, offering it to her. 'Thank you for all your efforts, Amanda,' he said. 'Bishop Martin was very appreciative.'

'It was an honour, Father.'

'Hesperius was very appreciative, too. I'm glad the two of you got on so well. He expressed to me his sadness that he was forced to leave when he did. Now, I know it's not considered proper for a young man and woman who are unrelated to communicate with one another . . .'

'You want me to write to him?' she asked, surprised.

'Well, not quite. He's made a special request, in fact, that you go to Treveris for an extended period.'

'To stay with *him*?'

'No, with Aunt Verica and Uncle Apollinaris, of course, though no doubt you'd see a lot of Hesperius, too. He seems to have taken a very special interest in you. I told him that of course I'd have to ask you first. And I stipulated that you would have to travel there with him and your brother – I'm not having you sent by yourself. I'll be going down to Londinium in a few days, so Hesperius will meet me there, and you can join us ten days from now and I'll see you off on the boat. What do you say?'

'It is very flattering of him, Father, but I'd rather stay here. Ecdicius relies on me to help with the household. And then there's Patricia – I wouldn't want to leave her.'

'I know it's a bit sudden, not to mention a big change. But opportunities such as this come by rarely, if ever. You should think about it. Hesperius is extremely fond of you – at the moment. To put it politely, he is not the sort of man who lacks other options.'

'Did he mention marriage, Father?'

'He made several allusions in that direction, yes. Of course nothing is official yet, but he is quite enamoured. He came to me and declared his feelings quite properly. And from my point of view, even before anything is settled it would be very beneficial to have my most sensible child in Treveris. You find him pleasant enough company, don't you?'

She did not quite know how to express her objection without mentioning the encounter in the colonnade. Hesperius had worthy qualities enough – his cleverness, his learning and wealth, certainly, and his outward modesty – but there was nothing in their sum without that nobility of spirit that could bring them to flourish. He had betrayed a weakness of character that had wholly soured her opinion of him, and that was not going to change. She knew he wanted her in Treveris only to complete his conquest of her – and if he had been this bold here, in her home, what might he do in his own? Would she end up like Patricia, humiliated, gossiped about – or worse?

Her father was growing impatient. 'When I was a young man I knew his uncle as governor – as honest and upright as they come. Furthermore, Hesperius, as well as being a man of considerable wealth and potential himself, is also third cousin once removed to the Vicarius of Britannia.'

'Yes, Father.'

'And his father, Decimius Magnus Ausonius – well, I hardly need remind you of the fact that he was recently appointed tutor to the emperor's son.'

'I understand, Father. But unless there is a prior agreement of matrimony, I don't see—'

Agnus raised his hand and she fell silent. 'Heaven knows I have not lately sought to patronise you when it comes to politics. Have I?'

'No, Father.'

'Then consider our position. Agrius Leo is about to leave Britannia, possibly for good. He's allowing me to purchase some of his property. But this all seems too easy, and I still don't fully understand his intentions. Men like him do not simply pack up and leave. It may be that in Treveris, close to the imperial court, he'll be able to do us even more harm than he could here. I need someone there I can depend on. Perhaps one day Lucas will be granted a post in the imperial service, but do you think he'll achieve this on his own merits? Hardly. He must find a patron, like everyone else.

'And now consider further the state of Britannia. It's been years since British feet trod far into the court of the emperor. Scarcely a man presiding even in the basilicas of Londinium is British. The Britons are rebels and savages, the emperor is told; at best, troublemakers unfit to govern even themselves.'

'You know that's untrue, Father.'

'Truth has nothing to do with it. The world is changing; the days of Constantine and all his dynasty are finished. It takes an act of divine aid for a Briton to win the emperor's ear even for a moment, and only after years of bribes and favours. Think of this: in the Four Provinces of Britannia there are perhaps a dozen men who could gain a private audience with the emperor. There are several score more who would be allowed to meet these men, and beneath them, yet more. We are senatorial, but of the lowest rank, and I am perhaps three audiences removed from ever speaking privately to the emperor – an impossible number.

'Hesperius, now, is only one. His circle *is* the imperial court. A word to his father could be passed on to the divine emperor directly. Given a few more years, should God bless Gratian with the throne, Ausonius and all those connected to him will rise as though into the heavens. Hesperius will be promoted to an even higher senatorial rank. Then he will have the ear of the emperor personally. And who will have *his* ear before all others? A woman.'

Amanda listened to his reasoning and her heart sank. She found no words to answer her father. To resist would make her a thankless, selfish daughter, while to agree would condemn her to follow yapping after a man she could not possibly admire, much less love, and did not trust.

'Amanda,' said her father, softening, and put his hands on her shoulders. 'I know you'll be happy, once you reconcile yourself to it. Scarcely a woman in Britannia wouldn't envy you this opportunity. I'm sure it's only a matter of time before the two of you are formally betrothed. And think of the good you could do, for the family, for Lucas!'

Amanda started and stopped several times before she was able to speak. When she did, her voice was hesitant and careful. 'If I could be his wife,' she said, 'I would gladly agree, and rejoice in it. It would break my heart to leave Silvanicum, but I'd do it.'

'I know you would.'

'But – I don't believe I *could* be his wife.'

'Do you doubt his intentions?'

'Yes, Father. Suppose I do go with him to Treveris, and then he ignores me? He's sure to choose some Gallic bride instead.

Everyone would know me as that silly British girl who followed him across the sea like a yapping lapdog.'

'His word is enough for me.'

She could not blame her father for trusting Hesperius, who charmed everyone he met. She had not wanted to tell him. Now she had no choice. 'He tried to seduce me, Father. Here, in the villa. Even after I asked him to stop, all he did was mock you. I don't trust him. Whatever he may have said to you about love and marriage, I don't trust him.'

Agnus turned away, his fingers scratching his beard. He released a long breath while he studied the regular, precise patterns of the floor mosaic. Finally he looked up at Amanda. 'Then you understand what kind of man he is. Perhaps it's better that you find out now, so that you suffer no illusions. Amanda, one need not be married to a man to have influence over him. Think of the power Helen had over Paris, or Cleopatra had over Mark Antony. They were vain and greedy, true, as you've always known. But imagine if Cleopatra had had a heart as good and pure as yours! Think what history she could have made! Hesperius has his faults; he is young. But if they are to be cured, he needs you, Amanda. Given time, he would realise that he could not live without you – that if he let go of you, his life would not be worth a breath. He will come to love you, even if he doesn't already. Go with him, Amanda, and whatever happens you will always have my blessing.'

Amanda did not know how to answer. She could scarcely believe the words she was hearing. A concubine. It was unheard of for a girl from a senatorial family to fill such a role. Her father was not only prepared to abandon her to that fate, but was pushing her towards it. She could not account for it. She would be polluted, regardless of whether or not Hesperius eventually married her. And without dignity, what was the purpose of living?

'I don't need your answer now,' continued her father. 'You can sleep on it. He won't be sailing for over a week.'

The prospect of thinking further about it horrified Amanda almost as much as the proposition itself. She feared that if she dwelled on it, restlessly and miserably, as she knew she would, she would lose her grip on what she now felt to be so utterly right. She had to make a decision now, although it filled her with terror. She could only pray that her father would understand – or if not understand, at least accept.

'I won't go with him,' she said. She found herself unable to look up.

'You've scarcely given it a thought.'

'I have – I've thought about it a great deal, Father, during the past several weeks. But he was so contemptuous of you . . .' She hardly knew what to say. It seemed so clear in her mind, but in the awful presence of her father, bearing down on her now with such a weight of disappointment and incredulity, she could hardly form her thoughts into words.

'His opinion of me is not your concern. You will go with him.'

She took a slow breath and steadied her voice. 'I will not.'

'No,' said Agnus firmly. 'No, this will not do. This stubbornness cannot come from a daughter of mine. This selfishness – this disobedience!' He came closer. 'You *will* consider it further. You will think about everything I've said. And since self-interest seems to be the highest cause you deign to follow, you will consider what sort of a future a daughter may have who has crushed the last, desperate hopes her father once had in his own offspring; who has betrayed all the duties of a child, despite an upbringing of the finest education and purest Christian guidance in the virtue of obedience; who, in spite of this, has succumbed to the unholy rebelliousness which seems to infect these times like the plague. Consider these things, and *then* I will hear your answer.'

He seized her wrist. She started at his sudden grip, so uncompromising, so unlike him, and in her shock she let out a short scream. This only served to anger him further, and he dragged her roughly from the room. Fear rushed through her body, and she struggled in vain to break his grip. All decorum, all dignity abandoned her. She held herself back no longer, but screamed and cried, and swore that she would never betray him or leave his side, and begged him not to harm her, to show her mercy.

He released her. He turned away and rested his palms on a window ledge, looking into the blackness of the garden, and waited to catch his breath. 'I will be driven mad like this,' he said. 'I will not have a treacherous daughter make me a raving Euclio. Nor have this house turned into a theatre by her ranting.' He closed his eyes for a moment, while Amanda waited. Then he turned to her, and said in a quiet voice: 'You will go to your room and remain there until tomorrow. You will pray to God that he turns your heart away from this shameful display of disobedience. And ten days from now you will join me in Londinium and I will put you on a boat to Treveris.'

These words, laid out before her with such calmness, grieved her more than any violence could have. A blow struck in anger could be regretted and forgiven, the fury that drove it could evaporate. But there was cold reason behind his words, a course of action decided on long ago, and a firmness that Amanda did not believe would weaken. She fought to understand, but failed; and it was this failure, even more than her father's anger, that tortured her as he walked away.

XXIII

And we were baptised, and all the worries of our past life
fled from us.
St Augustine of Hippo

'Do you renounce Satan and all his works?'
'I do.'

'Do you believe in God the Father, the Son and the Holy Spirit?'
'I do.'

'Then I baptise you, sister, in the name of the Father, the Son and the Holy Spirit. Go in peace to love and serve the Lord.'

Eachna stepped out of the baptismal tank onto the wet flagstones of the church. The sacred water ran in refreshing streams from her head down her face and neck, seeping through the white gown to touch her skin, cold and pure, cleansing in its sharpness. The next baptismal candidate had already stepped into the tank, and the bishop's voice was repeating once again the spiritual interrogation as Eachna left the church and came into the clear light of day.

At once she was met by an old woman who took one of a bundle of evergreen wreaths from her arm and placed it around Eachna's neck with a whispered blessing. Eachna thanked her, and the woman smiled and moved aside to await the next convert to emerge from the church.

Eachna heard someone call her name. Paul was standing half hidden in the crowd, waving to her; she went to him, eager for him to touch her for the first time as a Christian, because, though he did not believe, he had waited for her all morning and now shared in her joy, and the liberation of rebirth had only magnified her love for him. As they embraced, it seemed to Eachna that the sun was blazing with unusual warmth for late spring. She still could not quite believe that they were here, in this strange city, when a week earlier they had been ready to die in the mountains. But God had guided her and Paul to safety, to the steps of this church, and had inspired the heart of the Bishop of Viroconium to add her to the list of catechumens even though he did not know who she was or where she had come from. There were so many desiring salvation in these parts, the bishop had said, hundreds of families from the imperial estates around the city, that he had been forced to spread the baptisms across the Sundays following Easter. Eachna had been welcomed, accepted and reborn.

The very next day, while they were still at lodgings in the city, Paul suggested that they marry. It would be a good idea, she agreed. They stood before the bishop and the Christian community in the church, where Paul publicly declared that he was freeing her from slavery. Then they recited vows of marriage and received the blessing of the bishop, and after mass they left the building as man and wife, surrounded and heartened by the goodwill of strangers.

There was no time to wait, Eachna knew. They had already spent three days in the city. Paul had spoken to the two magistrates of the city council, warning them of the barbarian raids on the coast and urging them to raise whatever militia they could to man the timber palisades of their city. He had not told them of the conspiracy. That news he dared reveal only to the provincial governor himself in Corinium, still several days away.

The next morning they were walking away from Viriconium, along the road to the south, when Paul stopped suddenly. He was looking across a meadow towards a distant wood.

'What's wrong?' Eachna asked.

He pointed to a copse in the distance. 'That's where they

arrested us.' He stared at it for a long time, as though expecting to see his younger self somewhere through the branches.

From that moment he was quieter than usual. As they continued over the following days Eachna noticed him staring at seemingly innocuous landmarks with strange intensity: a small shack at a crossroads, a broken millstone left lying in a drainage ditch, a ridge of blue hills to the west. She realised that they were now retracing the path he had taken when he fled his home, and he was silently recalling the sights and memories of five years before. At night, when they stopped at village inns or roadside lodges and were lying together in bed, he would tell her about the memories he had rediscovered that day, and let the memories lead him back home to stories of his family and childhood. He spoke most often of his brother Faustus and his sister Amanda, who he said was just a little younger than Eachna. He wondered aloud how she would have changed over the years, and said how happy he had been to learn from Julian that she was not yet married. She and Eachna would get on very well, he predicted, or not at all. They were both as stubborn as mules.

The first sign of the saltworks was a feathery wisp of steam drifting up from the horizon. As the hours passed, the wisp grew into a thick white column rising from the crown of the forest. Within a mile of the works Eachna thought she could smell the salt in the air. The road was becoming busier, too. They walked past a convoy heading in the opposite direction, a heavy wagon carrying salt north with a mounted military escort.

'When we reach the saltworks we'll be in Dobunni territory,' said Paul. 'It's only another two days from there.' They would reach Silvanicum first, but the most important thing, Paul said, would be to continue to the city of Corinium and deliver the news of the conspiracy to the provincial governor.

The road emerged from the forest into the open valley of a small river, which it crossed at a bridge ahead before continuing into a busy-looking town. Along the river to the right were the saltworks, a row of pans producing thick clouds of steam that almost obscured the cranes and wooden walkways and the scores of slaves teeming around them. On a spur overlooking the crossing point was a fortress. Here, at least, there were still plenty of soldiers: watching the slaves, protecting the wagons and salt stacks, standing guard at the bridge. As they reached the river, one soldier ordered Paul and Eachna to halt. 'Travel pass,' he shouted over the bustle of the saltworks.

Paul gave him the episcopal pass of Bishop Ludo. The soldier cast his eyes over it, unimpressed. 'Bishop of Luguvalium?'

'That's right.'

The soldier shook his head. 'Doesn't mean anything to me. A bishop's pass is no good here.' He gave the tablet back to Paul.

'It was good enough for the Bishop of Viriconium.'

'Well, I'm not the Bishop of Viriconium. I can't let you cross without an authorised pass. Move aside, now.' He beckoned for another trader with a wagon to approach, checked his documents and waved him across the bridge.

Eachna could see the frustration building up in Paul. 'Perhaps he just wants a bribe,' she said.

'Of course he does, but I'm not bribing my way into my own fucking country. My father owns half of these saltworks.' He went back to the soldier. 'Biarchus, this pass has got us through every town and fort we've stopped at for ten days. Feel free to play your games with anyone else, but not us.'

'Can't be helped, citizen. You need a pass from military or civil government, not the church.'

'Let me see your commanding officer.'

Neither Paul nor the soldier seemed willing to give way. Eventually a middle-aged man approached them from the salt-works. He was expensively dressed in a light linen tunic and embroidered cloak, but his boots looked old and sturdy, and Eachna noticed that his hands were rough from years of work. 'Biarchus, return to your duties. I'll deal with this matter myself.'

The soldier saluted while the man gestured for Paul and Eachna to follow him. 'We'll go to my house,' he said.

He did not say another word as he led them along a track beside the river, passing the rows of brine tanks, yards piled high with fuel, stabled oxen, trundling carts of salt and tools. Slaves who came near bowed to him, soldiers saluted. Even supervisors standing many yards away, looking tough with their rods and salt-stained torsos, saw him through the drifting curtains of steam and nodded.

His house turned out to be a villa screened from the saltworks by a dense line of trees. Eachna and Paul followed him through the front courtyard, where the remains of old paths and flowerbeds were indiscriminately covered by crates of ceramics or coiled heaps of rope, into a porch half filled with chopped wood, and down a corridor to a domestic room at the back of the villa. The wall paintings were faded and peeling, the mosaic floor chipped, but the couches and cushions around the room looked comfortable.

Eachna was inspecting the worn furnishings as the man closed the door, giving the three of them privacy. She was surprised to see him then drop to one knee in front of Paul.

'Get up, Finán,' said Paul.

The man got to his feet. He seemed almost ready to cry. 'My lord, I never expected to see you again.'

'I could say the same to you.'

'Sit down, please sit! Have you been walking? Where did you come from? No – don't tell me anything unless I need to hear it. Here, sit, and I'll pour you some water.'

They sat together on one of the couches while Finán went to a side table and rummaged around for a pair of mugs. He poured the water and handed the mugs to Paul and Eachna before settling himself on a couch facing them. He watched Paul drink, smiling and waiting for him to finish before he spoke. 'Five years,' he said simply.

'Five years,' said Paul.

There was a heavy silence. Eachna could see that Finán was eager to hear more, but too nervous to ask. She too wanted to know what was going on, who this man with the Irish name was, and how he knew Paul. 'Thank you for the water,' she said.

'You're welcome,' he smiled, looking at her for the first time.

'I'm surprised you recognised me, Finán,' Paul said. 'I didn't have a beard last time we met.'

'I recognised the nose. You Cironii have a very distinctive profile, you know. The beard'll have to go when you get home, though. It'll frighten your sister.'

'I trust you won't tell anyone about this.'

'No,' said Finán, his eyes widening. 'Of course not!' He chuckled and glanced at Eachna. His eyes flicked between her and Paul. Now he was clearly wondering what her status was.

'I'd be grateful if you could host me and my wife tonight, Finán,' said Paul, 'if you have a spare bed.'

That seemed to answer his unspoken question. 'Of course!' he exclaimed. 'I don't exactly have many visitors here. This place is far too grand for me, anyway. But I have a few spare bedrooms, and I'll have the finest one in the house spruced up for you. If I may ask – will you be heading home tomorrow?'

'That's the plan.'

'Well!' Finán clapped his hands together, delighted. 'The heir of the Cironii returning to Silvanicum – what a day that will be! Five years away, and home you come.' He wiped his eyes, which were beginning to water, with the gold-fringed hem of his cloak. 'Don't worry, not a soul will hear anything from me. Your father – now, the last I heard, he's visiting some of his eastern estates on the way down to Londinium. He's been entertaining a guest at Silvanicum for the past month, some bigwig from Gallia. Your sister will be at home, though. Still not married. We all thought her father had plans for her and this Gallic fellow, but nothing's come of it, at least not yet.'

'And my mother?'

Finán's smile vanished. His face seemed frozen, staring into space, lost. At last he let out a long breath and shook his head sadly. 'I'm sorry, my lord,' he said.

Paul cleared his throat. 'When?'

'In the autumn, last October. She was at your aunt's house outside Glevum. It was peaceful, I heard. Dignified. Hundreds came to the funeral. I grieved with your family then, and I grieve with you now.'

'Your sympathy is appreciated. I heard before winter that she was ill. I tried to come home, but . . .' He paused, and took a moment to steady his voice. 'But it proved difficult.'

'Your return will be a long overdue blessing for your family, my lord.'

Paul rose from the couch, and Eachna rose with him. 'We'll take a bath in an hour or so – just a tub, no need to fire up the bath house. And then I'd thank you to have some food brought to us. Nothing fancy – I doubt my stomach could take it these days.'

Finán got to his feet and laughed. 'Now, do I look like the sort of man who keeps stuffed larks in his kitchen?' He showed Eachna and Paul to a spare room in a secluded wing of the villa. He offered to have it cleaned up, but Paul declined, and he left them in peace.

Paul dropped his satchel in the middle of the floor, undid his cloak and let it fall to his feet. He stood limp-shouldered, gazing down into nothing. Eachna sat on the edge of the bed and held out her hand. Slowly, vacantly, he came forwards and took it, and sat down next to her. He buried his face in her shoulder and they wrapped their arms around each other.

'Cry,' she whispered into his ear. 'I want you to cry.'

'I don't care what you want,' he said, his voice muffled in her clothing. He would have laughed had his voice not broken at that moment into sobs.

XXIV

Those whom true love has seized, it does not release.
Seneca

'Don't tell me he's still there,' Amanda said.

Pinta shrugged. 'He's still there.'

'For heaven's sake. Does he not need to eat?'

'We could leave by the side door and have servants bring the mares around to us.'

'What, skulk out like an errant kitchen boy and sneak through the vegetable patch? Not likely. He'll get fed up soon enough, you'll see.'

Amanda dismissed Pinta and paced in frustration around her room. Since dawn she had been looking forward to taking a ride across the estate, and now she was all but trapped in the villa. Her father had left three days earlier to supervise some of their properties to the east, and in their sober parting, the first time they had spoken since the argument, he had simply said, 'I will see you very soon.' He was expecting her to join him in Londinium within a week. He had already given instructions for the journey to Ecdicius, to the chief groom Brico, to Peter, to the stablehands, to the kitchen staff and the bucellarii. The wagon already sat in the lower courtyard, its panels scrubbed clean and wheels oiled. Everyone was prepared except Amanda. Would she truly go to Londinium, and then go with Hesperius to Treveris? She could no longer see any escape. These might be the last days she spent in Silvanicum for years. Who knew when she would see these walls again? And when she did, would she be married or not, old or young? Would she become another Patricia, returning in disgrace to a life of humbled seclusion?

She stopped pacing, put her head in her hands, and tried to calm her thoughts. She was driving herself mad with the anxiety. This is why she had wanted to go for a ride, just her and Pinta, while the weather was fine and she had space and time to calm her thoughts.

Perhaps he had gone now. There was no reason not to find out for herself. She left her room and walked around the garden colonnade to the south wing, which was little used except when the villa was full of guests. She walked down its long, empty corridor to a sparsely furnished guest room at the far end of the wing. She entered quietly, closing the door behind her. A small window gave a view out in front of the villa, overlooking the pasture as it sloped down to the river. She crept to the window, and by pressing her face against the upper corner could just about peer down and see the tree outside the front gate.

He was still there.

'Damn Rufus,' she muttered. He was sitting in the shade of the oak, resting his back against the trunk. She could see no walking stick, no mount or litter, and no servants. She knew from the servants that he was still in residence at the villa Caecina and he must have walked all the way here by himself. Pinta had not mentioned that. She had simply reported that Agrius Rufus had appeared at the front gate shortly after dawn, requesting an audience. He had been turned away by the doorman, naturally enough, but had refused to leave. He had simply said that he would wait until she was willing to meet with him.

It was now late afternoon and he was still there. Unless they crept out of the side entrance into the woods as Pinta had suggested, Amanda would not be able to leave the villa without him pestering her, and since he was high born it would be illegal and scandalous to remove him by force. Yet by waiting outside the villa like some common petitioner he was harming no one more than himself. He would lose the respect of any servants or peasants who saw or heard about it. Amanda's main concern was that they might gossip about how Rufus was some kind of lovesick boy with whom she had been conducting a clandestine affair.

She returned to her room and read and played with the cat until the last of the afternoon light failed. Pinta brought her some food for supper. 'Still there,' she said. 'Mistress, the doorman asked if he might allow Agrius Rufus in, just so he can sleep inside the gatehouse. It's too late for him to go back now, and it'll be a cold night.'

'No,' Amanda said firmly, stabbing her knife into a lump of cheese. 'He wanted to wait outside, so let him. He can walk home in the dark well enough.'

Dawn came, and Pinta roused Amanda with the news that Agrius Rufus was still outside. He had spent the night under the tree.

'Has he asked for anything?'

'No, mistress.'

'Has he still not said what he wants to talk to me about?'

'No, mistress.'

Amanda sat up in bed and blinked the sleep from her eyes. So Rufus had spent a cold, damp night on her doorstep when he could have wandered home. If nothing else, he was persistent. 'Have the doorman take him some breakfast. Just bread and cheese from the kitchen, something like that. I'd rather not let him starve to death on our doorstep. It would look bad.'

As soon as Amanda had dressed, she hurried discreetly to the room at the far end of the south wing. From the window she saw Rufus under the tree, precisely where he had been the previous day. Dew glistened on the grass around him and mist was snaking its way up from the river. As she watched, he got stiffly to his feet and a figure emerged into view from the front gate. It was the doorman, bringing him a platter laden with food and a mug of water. They exchanged some brief words, Rufus took the platter and the doorman went back inside. Rufus returned to his place beneath the tree and began to eat. He looked content, almost happy.

She did not know if it was the refreshing air of the dawn, or perhaps the quiet gratitude with which she saw Rufus accept the food, but Amanda no longer felt angry, as she had the day before. Maybe she should have let him sleep in the gatehouse last night. It had been rather cruel of her to leave him outside when it was clear that he intended to stay. She leaned on the windowsill, her eyes fixed on him, and wondered why he wanted to see her. Was this his way of apologising for having cancelled their betrothal? If so, it was a strange, penitential way of going about it – but he was only a soldier, after all. One could hardly expect a soldier to know how to behave towards a lady.

The only other possibility was news of Paul. Perhaps he had not wanted to write a letter for fear of it being intercepted, and was unwilling to entrust the news to anyone but her. But what news? She had already written to Julian again, but had so far not received a reply. It had been months since Paul's disappearance into the barbarian north. Winter and spring had come and gone, and new information may have emerged as the snows thawed from the mountains.

Amanda smiled coldly as she remembered how Rufus had put her in a similar situation almost a year ago. Then he had not dared venture beyond the edge of their estate; now he was besieging her in her own home. And so much had changed in that time. Her mother was gone. She had found an unexpected friend in her cousin. She herself had grown and matured.

And her father had hardened. The innocent days of her childhood were done with, slowly giving way to the duty, sacrifice and disappointment of adulthood. In a few days she would embark on a journey that would decide the course of her life, a life in which that young man now sitting beneath the tree would have no part. She was surprised to feel regret at that thought. It was strange that the son of Agrius Leo had somehow become a part of Silvanicum, that she should suddenly feel herself tied to him almost as if he belonged here, as if he had always been here, even though she had met him only three times in her life, and each time had parted from him in anger.

Well, she had nothing to lose. She would let him see her, she would hear what he had to say, and people could think what they liked. Her father was expecting her to prostitute herself at the imperial court anyway. Let us judge the gossip of old men, she thought absently, as worth not even a penny . . .

Pinta was surprised when Amanda announced that Rufus was to be admitted, but did not object. Amanda waited for him on a stone bench in the orchard garden, where they could have a private conversation yet stay in clear view of the rest of the villa. It was not long before Pinta returned with Rufus. As soon as she saw him, shabby and unkempt as he was, his hair in disarray and his chin dark with stubble, Amanda was gripped by the old feeling that had ruled her for so many nights. Why, oh God, did she have to feel this way about him, of all people?

Pinta bowed and left them alone. Rufus stood before Amanda, relaxed, his arms at his sides. He was actually smiling, and seemed entirely unaware of the spectacle he presented in the midst of the finely sculpted flowerbeds.

'I hope the night wasn't too uncomfortable,' she said.

'I used to sleep under trees all the time. I've rather missed it.'

'Will you tell me what this is about?'

'You.'

If only he would take his eyes from her and stop smiling for a moment, Amanda would be able to collect her thoughts. She tried to summon her old resentment against him, perhaps a trace of the anger that had torn her apart when he had rejected her, but it was like trying to pick up a shadow. She could be angry with him, but not hate him. She had never hated him; she had only pretended to. Even now she felt a strange, calming pleasure in his company.

'I can leave if you like,' he said, his voice open and apologetic.

'After waiting outside all night to see me?'

'Now I have seen you.'

'What about your message?'

'I don't have a message.'

'Agrius Rufus, it's too early in the day to be making no sense.'
She gestured to a vacant bench opposite hers. 'Please sit.'

He bowed and sat on the bench, keeping his back straight. For
the first time he looked at the garden around him, studying the
clumps of delicate rosemary between the hedges, the beds of
roses and lilies, the spikes of purple foxglove rising in the shade
of the apple trees. He breathed the scented air deeply.

'I see you're not using your stick,' observed Amanda.

'I'm feeling much better these days. Tell me, did you design
the garden?'

'Partly. We had some of it relaid this spring for a visitor from
Gallia. My own taste is somewhat different.'

'How so?'

'Less orderly.'

He nodded, and reached out to trace a fingertip around the
lip of a sagging foxglove bloom. They sat in silence for a while.
Amanda was almost afraid to move a muscle. She wished her
heart would calm itself. By rights she should have thrown him
out when it became clear that he had no message to give her,
and yet she had not. Instead, by some terrible, wonderful compul-
sion, she had asked him to sit in her garden, in the place she
loved the most, surrounded by its cooling shade and busy colour,
and she did not even feel that it was wrong.

He spoke without looking at her. 'I imagine you'll miss this
place when you go to Treveris.'

'You know about that?'

'Of course. We share cousins among our house slaves, you
know.'

'And what have they been saying?'

'That you'll be leaving very soon. And that you'll soon be
betrothed to Hesperius. A good man. A little spoiled, perhaps.
But cultured and rich.' He smiled. 'A better catch than me,
anyway.'

Amanda did not return his smile. If it was a joke, it was in
poor taste. 'Nothing has been decided upon yet, Agrius Rufus.
I'm going to Treveris to stay with my relatives, not to take a

husband. If people must spread rumours, I'd prefer them to be true.'

'So you won't be married to Hesperius?'

'I don't know. It's not in my hands. Maybe, maybe not.'

'How long will you be gone? Are you staying through the winter?'

'I don't know,' she said with a touch of annoyance. 'Forgive me, Agrius Rufus, but I'm a little surprised at your sudden interest. Not very long ago, if you recall, we were about to be betrothed. I can't pretend I was happy with the arrangement, but I was reconciled to it. And then you rejected me, did you not?'

'I'm sorry if I hurt your feelings.'

'You *rejected* me. Don't worry, I'd already gathered from my cousin that you weren't the type to honour any kind of agreement where women were concerned, so I can't pretend I was surprised.'

His expression grew cold. He leaned forwards, staring at her from beneath a dark brow. Even as Amanda saw the tension in his body and heard the anger in his voice, she was fascinated by how suddenly the warmth could drain from his lips. 'Whatever your cousin has told you about me is poison. Yes, she and I were close in Treveris. I felt sorry for her. She was lonely and upset. But I never promised to marry her. She was hysterical. When it became clear that she was letting fantasies compound in her mind, I stopped seeing her. It seemed the least cruel thing to do.'

'And the widow whose money you took?'

'There was never any money. That woman was a snake, a harpy. She *offered* me money to prance around on her arm like some kind of doll, and I refused. Such people cultivate scandal like they would a herb garden, and you can see how its seeds get carried everywhere on the wind, even to this corner of the world! That was when I left Treveris. I never could stand the place. You can't breathe without sucking in lies.'

'Or in your case, breathing them out again. Don't think I've forgotten that you lied to me almost the first time we spoke.'

'When?'

'At the crossroads. You told me about Paul, and you claimed

that my father already knew where he was. Perhaps you don't recall?'

He shook his head fiercely. 'No, I never said that.' He glanced over his shoulder before he continued, keeping his voice an insistent hiss. 'All I said was that your father knew Paul was still alive, which was true. But he never knew *where*, because my father kept that a secret. I saw Paul after he ran from home; he was caught near Vercovicium looking like a common vagrant. I was there. They confiscated his ring, which bore the seal of the Cironii. He pretended he'd stolen it and the press gang believed him. They gave Paul the choice of enlisting or losing a hand. Afterwards I took the ring and sent it to my father, who showed it to your father as proof that he knew where Paul was. Then he arranged for Paul to be stationed somewhere safe on the Wall.'

'As a hostage.'

'More or less. My father has been trying to make use of your brother for years. He promised several times to bring Paul home if your father would pledge to support him.'

'And?'

'Your father refused. All he had to do was agree once, and Paul would've been sent back home.'

Amanda shook her head. It could not be true. She remembered her father's words: *In God's name, I would give my right arm to have Paul back home . . .*

'Then Paul disappeared from the Wall,' Rufus said. 'My father gave me the task of tracking him down. That's when I decided to bring him back to you. I'd learned what my father did to your family in the Winter of Grief. It made me sick to be a part of that. And that's why I've refused to go with my father back to Treveris. He can disown me, I don't care. I want nothing more to do with him – nothing.'

Amanda felt torn. Either her father had lied before, or Rufus was lying now. She could not bear to imagine either. Yet it had begun, at least, with Rufus: the blame traced back to him. 'If you saw Paul get arrested, you could have said who he was. You could have exposed his true identity there and then, and he would have been sent home that day.'

His shoulders dropped. 'I know.'

'Instead, you doomed him to years of exile. I still don't know if he's alive or dead. Has anyone heard from him since he vanished, any of your spies or friends? Do you have any idea where he is?'

'No. I've tried, my lady, believe me. Had I known what my father would do, I would never have sent him the ring in the first place. I've regretted that choice ever since. But he was so disappointed in me. He never wanted me to join the army, all I wanted was to win back his favour. At the time it seemed like such a small thing, just a face I recognised one afternoon, a boy who'd run away from home.'

'A small thing!' Amanda cried bitterly. 'Have you any idea how deeply we've suffered for it? I lost two brothers that day. And to you Paul was just a face . . .'

'I *am* sorry; I hate myself for what I did. But it was his choice, Amanda. *He* chose not to come home. And since he disappeared I've done everything in my power, spared no expense, to bring him back to you. I've sent men to the edge of the world trying to find him. I want to see him back here where he belongs, with you and your father. I never wanted to injure him. And the thought of the pain I've caused you, too, and now that you're leaving . . .'

'Oh, I see – you came to clear your conscience!'

'No.' He rose from the bench. 'I say again: I've never lied to you, and I never will. But I know you have every right to despise me for what I did, and I won't stoop to ask for your forgiveness. You should go to Treveris hating me, as you always have done. But even so, knowing that it might be for the last time, I needed to see you again.' His voice was awkward, uncertain. 'Now I have seen you,' he said, 'I wish you a safe journey, my lady, and a joyful life.' He began to walk away.

'Wait,' she called, rising from her seat.

He stopped and turned. She saw despair in his expression for the first time. For an instant he met her eyes, but looked away quickly, as though the sight of her were too painful to endure.

'We could have been married,' she said weakly.

'I want you, Amanda,' he said, his eyes on the ground. 'I've been driven half mad for your sake. The torture of knowing what I did to you – what my father did to your family all those years ago – and then a promise of matrimony! But how could I accept you if you were forced into my arms by someone else? I'd sooner see you go to Gallia and choose Hesperius or any other clown than have you allotted to me by my father, by political treaty, like a piece of cattle.'

'I thought you hated me.'

He looked at her finally, with effort. 'How could anyone ever hate you?'

She did not speak. They were by now standing some yards apart, with only grass between them. The chains of decorum and decency that had always restrained her were suddenly no more substantial than the sun-filled air. The force that had for so long pulled her towards Rufus was doubled in its reflection. No passing servants, no thoughts of her father or her precious reputation, would hold her back.

'Your father isn't here, my lord!'

'I know,' snapped Paul, tugging off his cloak and throwing it into the doorman's arms. 'Where is he?'

'Who?' asked the doorman.

'Agrius Rufus, in the name of Christ! You just said you let him in!'

'Only at your sister's request, my lord!' The doorman tried desperately to wrap the cloak into a bundle as Paul walked through the gatehouse into the lower courtyard.

'And where is he now?'

'In the orchard garden, my lord, with the lady Amanda.'

Paul stopped and steeled himself. He had been preparing to see Amanda again, not the son of Agrius Leo. In his mind Rufus had not changed since the last time they had met, on the day Paul was drafted. Paul could see him still: an aristocratic officer sitting on his warhorse, pompous and distant. It was Rufus who had given Paul's ring to Agrius Leo. It was Rufus who had later sent men to hunt Paul down. Were it not for Bishop Ludo's honesty, Paul might now be in Rufus's hands, or dead.

Most of all, his father was a traitor to the emperor. It was almost a divine gift that he was here at Silvanicum on the very day of Paul's return, as disgusting a thought as it was, without friends or protection. Nothing could better describe Rufus's cowardly arrogance than that he had sauntered into Silvanicum as soon as the master of the house had turned his back, when the only person left to defend it was an innocent girl.

He saw a group of bucellarii standing outside the stables, and waved them over. They ran to him at once, astonished but eager. 'I want you men to stay down here. If he runs, don't let him out.' He pointed at Eachna, who was still waiting in the gatehouse, fear obvious in her face. 'Look after her.'

'What are you going to do?' Eachna said.

Paul started towards the upper courtyard, one hand on the hilt of his sword.

Of the flood of feelings that rushed through Amanda, the most awful was the sense of injustice: that she should be standing here, with her mouth against his, with his hands running the length of her back and hers grasping his neck as though hanging on for her life, knowing that soon they would part and never again be together. In his every caress was the urgency of a half-starved man taking the last meal of his life. She thought only vaguely, if at all, of the world beyond their bodies, and nothing of what the future would bring apart from the horror of his absence. She was insensible to the warm sun on her skin, to the sudden flutter of starlings from their treetop nests as the gate from the lower courtyard crashed open, to Pinta's cry when, watching from the colonnade, she saw a ragged figure march into the garden.

The first thing Amanda noticed was that Rufus had been wrenched away from her, leaving her arms empty. She saw him pulled backwards and twisted around, thrown violently to his knees, picked up, gripped, hurled against the trunk of a tree, where he struck his head and staggered in a daze. His attacker, silent and methodical, took a handful of Rufus's hair, raised him up straight, forced him back against the tree, and with his free hand he reached down and pulled a sword from its sheath. Rufus was dazed, gasping, his head pinned against the trunk, his confused eyes seeking out Amanda.

'*Stop!*' she screamed.

The attacker paused, about to bring his blade up to Rufus's throat, and turned to look at her. He was young but had the face of a weary, beaten old man: ruddy, bearded and broken-toothed. It was a long moment before she recognised him.

XXV

*If there is any good in philosophy, it is this – that it never looks
into pedigrees. All men, if traced back to their original source,
spring from the gods.*

Seneca

There was a scream from the upper courtyard, a girl's cry.
Eachna jumped; the doorman, already struggling to contain
himself, threw Paul's cloak to the floor and began to run up the
path from the gatehouse to the upper courtyard, with the bucellarii close behind.

Eachna ran after them, rushing through the flickering shade
of the trees, the wings of the villa rising like cliffs on either side.
They passed through a second, smaller gatehouse into a burst
of colour surrounded by columns and windows and sloping
rooflines. She saw Paul with one hand holding a terrified young
man against a tree, his other hand holding a sword loosely by
his side. Near him stood a dark-haired girl in a white dress whose
face was a tearful mess of shock and entreaty. She was still
screaming at Paul to let the man go, but Paul did not move. She
gave a final cry – 'Brother, if you love me, let him go!' – and
Paul released his captive and dropped his sword carelessly on
the grass.

The young man staggered a few steps away from the tree but
stayed on his feet. 'Paul,' he gasped.

'Go,' replied Paul. 'Come near my family again and I'll kill
you.'

Reluctantly, wordlessly, the man went across the grass to the lower gate, where the doorman was beckoning for him to hurry. As he left he did not notice Eachna or the bucellarii. He was looking not at Paul, but at Amanda. She seemed to return the pain in his stare, Eachna thought, until he had passed through the gate and it was closed behind him.

Paul looked at Amanda. 'Where's his father?'

'I don't know,' she said. The pain and confusion had not left her eyes. 'What happened to you, Paul? Where have you been?'

He did not reply, but let out a short gasp, as though he had suddenly burst to the surface of the sea. He twisted and cast his eyes around the garden, taking in every detail with the cautious hope of a man who needs first to convince himself that he is not in a dream. His mouth eased into a grin. 'Nothing's changed,' he said, and looked down at himself, and laughed.

Other figures had now appeared on the shadowy fringes of the garden, faces peering between the columns: serving staff, cleaners, stablehands, kitchen workers, a woodcutter with his axe. Each stared at Paul in silence. Amanda turned and addressed them. 'This is my brother, Paul. Back to your duties, all of you.' They began to leave. She beckoned to a middle-aged man. 'Ecdicius, please arrange for his room to be made ready.'

'Don't worry about that,' said Paul. 'I need to continue to Corinium at once to deliver an important message to the governor. Eachna here will be staying, though – you can sort out a room for her.'

Amanda's gaze fell on Eachna for the first time. Eachna had the sensation of being looked upon from a great height. Amanda said, '*Eachna?* What is that, Pictish?'

Had there been a trace less resentment in Amanda's voice, had the pretty crease of her eyebrows been less expressive of instant distaste, perhaps Eachna would not have felt such irritation. This Roman girl had no idea of the torments she and Paul had suffered to set foot in this garden. Eachna said: 'My name is Irish. It means "steed".' To Paul she said, 'I'm coming to the city with you, like we said.'

Paul came close to her and spoke in a low voice. 'No, you'll wait here. I need to travel fast. It'll be easier if you stay here where I know you'll be safe. Please.'

'She can stay,' said Amanda. 'Ecdicius, have an extra bed put in the servants' dormitory.'

'No,' Paul said to Ecdicius, 'she'll have one of the guest rooms. Make sure she's comfortable. Until I return she's to be treated like any other visitor.'

'As you wish, lord,' said Ecdicius. He bowed to Paul and Amanda, and hastened from the garden.

Amanda was looking between Eachna and Paul with open-mouthed incredulity. 'Brother, who is this barbarian, and why can't she bunk with the rest of the slaves?'

'She's my wife,' he said simply. 'I'll be back as soon as I can; until then, you'll find that Eachna can give a perfectly coherent account of herself.'

'Why must you leave at once? What's so important in the city that it can't wait another day after five years?'

'I have no choice, Amanda. I'll explain everything when I return.'

'You burst in here, try to commit a murder before my eyes, dump this girl on me and tell me she's your wife – do you know I'm supposed to be on the way to Treveris a week from now?'

'No. But you can cancel, can't you? Have a messenger ride to Father. And write to other people, too – family, friends, everyone.' The doorman had run to fetch Paul's cloak, and he emerged back into the garden bearing it, panting heavily. Paul took the cloak and fastened it around his neck before bending down to retrieve his sword from the grass. 'I can reach the city by noon if I set off now. I wish I could stay.'

Paul came to Eachna, held her shoulders and kissed her briefly, and before she could speak he was gone. Amanda hurried after him through the gatehouse to the lower courtyard, followed by the doorman and the bucellarii, and Eachna was left alone.

Her solitude had barely begun before the strangeness of her surroundings encroached upon it. She was standing on a straight gravel path bordered by knee-high hedges that had been clipped into perfect lines and right angles, something she had never before seen. It was as though here nature itself had been compelled to obey the rigid orderliness of the Roman world. She looked about and observed how the flowerbeds, trees and bushes were groomed into an unnatural tidiness that seemed to stifle them; even the ivy wove itself up the columns of the colonnade in a doomed attempt to escape, its trimmed fingers touching the eaves of the roof as a prisoner might forlornly touch the top of his cage.

The weaker part of her, roused by fear, wanted to chase after Paul and insist that he take her to the city, to beg and scream until he agreed. But she suppressed the fear. Paul has abandoned me here, she thought angrily, but I will not go running after him like a mewling pet: I will not degrade myself.

Soon Amanda returned, alone and scowling, and she turned her frustration on Eachna. 'Girl, my brother demands that you are shown a degree of respect fully inappropriate to your origins. I will accept you as a guest for his sake. Until he returns do not presume to command any of our slaves, least of all the house staff, as though you are their superior. You are not. Remember that your presence here is suffered, not welcomed. Now follow.' With that she started along the path to the far side of the garden, and Eachna came after her in silence.

The room to which Amanda led her was through the colonnade and down a long corridor. It was bare except for a bed, small table and chair, clearly not the room that was already being prepared, for Amanda called for a servant to transfer the new bedding to it and to have a wardrobe and brazier brought in. It was obvious to Eachna that she was being shunted to the most remote corner of the villa, but she did not care. There was a glazed window overlooking the pasture below the villa, and from the corridor outside she would be able to look down into the courtyards. At least here she could observe the business of the place, even if she was left to herself.

'Food and clothing will be brought shortly,' said Amanda. 'If you require anything else, you may find a servant and ask them to ask me.'

'A pen and tablet,' Eachna said at once. 'If you wouldn't mind.' Amanda looked at her coldly. 'Very well.'

For the rest of the day Eachna was left alone except when a servant brought her food: bread, cheese and fruit in the afternoon, boiled ham and vegetables in the evening. She left the room only once, when she ventured down the silent length of the south wing and found the communal lavatory near the kitchen, only to be told to use the labourers' outhouse behind the vegetable garden. In her room she tried to pray, but somehow could not find the voice to address divinity, so instead sat at a desk in front of the window overlooking the river and scrawled and erased line after line on her tablet. She wrote down what she would say to Paul when he returned, and what she would like to say to Amanda now, and she found that by turning her feelings into scratches on wax they obtained a kind of solidity and clarity in her mind.

She could not sleep during the night, but lay awake in bed and listened to the unfamiliar sounds of the valley. The slow hours of darkness drew by, and when it became clear that she would find no sleep before dawn, she rose from the bed and moved the chair to the window. Cocooning herself in a blanket, for she had been left no fuel for the brazier, she sat and looked through the warped glazing into the hollow blackness of the night.

This was the worst and longest hour, the hated stretch before the first promise of dawn, when it seemed forever uncertain that the sun would rise again. The invisible business of the night was done with, the owls and yelping foxes withdrawn back into the silence of their nests and dens, and the whole cavernous world was suspended and still, as though hovering on the edge of death.

Eachna had looked many times before into this eternal void, and this time, as always, her mind turned finally and quietly to God. A lifetime ago, when she was a slave in the Pictish country and had sat through this hour on the bare earth, she had prayed to the sun, and it had never failed her. Now she prayed to Christ, but the prayer was the same. Eventually it was answered, not with a single glorious revelation, but with a faint grey light in the east, an uncertain glow hovering on the horizon, that sprouted and only slowly began to rise and unfurl itself across the sky.

The light brought life to the valley below, to the combe and to the villa within it. Eachna returned wearily to the bed. Paul would now be rising in Corinium, she thought. He would surely find himself surrounded by friends, enemies, inferiors, all clamouring after him, demanding answers and begging favours. Old men would talk of the law, imperial agents would talk of politics, priests and bishops would talk of divine deliverance, and Paul would be drowned in all their talk and have little time to think of her.

The door opened and a servant entered without knocking. 'The mistress wants you to join her in the baths,' she announced, and left.

Eachna rose from bed and began to dress, and realised that she did not know where the baths were. She barely remembered how to find her own way back to the orchard garden, so confusing were the corridors, steps, doors and turns of this palace. Nor had she ever been to any Roman bath house. There had been public baths in Luguvalium, but she had never been allowed inside, and the custom had struck her as altogether foreign and unnecessary: why all that fuss with great vaulted roofs and furnaces that consumed whole cartloads of timber, when a river or a simple tub of water would do?

Eachna was still trying to collect enough courage to leave the room when the door opened again, more softly. It was Amanda. She stood in the doorway wearing a fine green dress and woollen shawl, her uncombed hair resting in heaps on her shoulders. Eachna was surprised enough to see her at all, and even more surprised to see that she was smiling. 'Did you sleep well?' Amanda asked.

'Yes,' said Eachna.

'I sent a message for you to come to the bath house, but then I remembered that we have two, and you might not know how to find either, so I thought I'd come and fetch you myself. If you're ready, I'd very much like for you to join me, and we can talk a little.'

Eachna nodded, uncertain how to take this sudden change in attitude. She understood hostility. It was rarely anything but what it seemed, and she had learned to trust unkindness as a measure of humanity, the natural condition of most people she met. Thus where Amanda's coldness yesterday had caused Eachna no great anxiety, at least next to Paul's absence, now her warmth caused instant suspicion; and Eachna hesitated before she followed Amanda's beckoning hand into the corridor. They walked back to the main body of the villa, the wing at the top end of the combe, past a series of steps and heavy oak doors, past the kitchen and along the gleaming floor of a colonnade. A few leaves had drifted in from the garden and had not yet been swept away, but otherwise everything was fresh and clean. The white paint of the columns shone in the sunlight, the polished brass door handles glowed and the air was touched by the smell of mint and parsley.

Further down the colonnade they reached a side door, which Amanda entered. Eachna followed cautiously, came down a passage through another door and found herself in a large, decorated room, softly lit through high windows that gave the air a strange green tint. On either side of a set of shelves waited two house slaves, one of whom approached Amanda, bowed, and began to help her undress. The second slave came to Eachna and gave the briefest of curtsies before kneeling to remove Eachna's slippers. Eachna tensed, uncomfortable with the touch of a stranger, let alone with another slave treating her like nobility, but she obeyed the slave's gestures and turned stiffly and raised her arms, letting the slave gradually disrobe her until she and Amanda were standing naked in the centre of the room. Eachna folded her arms over her chest and let her hair fall over her back, in her shame trying to conceal the worst of her scars. Nobody, not even Paul, had ever seen her like this, wholly exposed in cruel, clear light. She felt skinny and withered, her ugliness only deepened by glimpses of the unblemished skin of her hostess. She could sense Amanda and the slaves appraising her and trying hard to contain their revulsion.

'Shall we?' Amanda asked. She led Eachna back through the passage to a room where the air was even warmer, almost stifling. Steam rose from a large bath at the far end of the room. Eachna felt her skin tingle in the heat. She followed Amanda to the bath, entering the water by a set of steps, and sat facing her.

'That's better,' sighed Amanda. 'I'm sorry if I seemed rude by leaving you alone yesterday. My brother chose a complicated time to return home. I had to write letters and decide about a hundred things.'

'Are you pleased to have him back?'

'Of course!' said Amanda, giving, Eachna thought, a strikingly pretty smile. 'You mustn't take my behaviour yesterday as representative. Now, Eachna – I hope I'm pronouncing your name right – my brother didn't tell me much about you before he disappeared, except that you formerly belonged to the Bishop of Luguvalium. Is that so?'

'Yes.'

'And so can I ask if you know the monk Julian?'

'I know him.'

'He's my cousin, though I'm sure you already know that. Do you know him well? Did he ever talk about me?'

'No,' said Eachna. In fact Julian had once told her about Amanda, and had praised her piety. But Eachna chose to ignore this now. She did not want this girl to trespass on the memory of her teacher, friend and protector.

'Well, I don't suppose he would talk about his family with slaves. Did he teach you to speak Latin?'

'Paul taught me too. I've been speaking it for over a year now.'

'So you were at Luguvalium with Julian and Bishop Ludo, and then Paul came along – when was that?'

'Just before winter.'

Amanda nodded thoughtfully. 'I see. And he'd left Vercovicium in the summer, so he must have been in the north for some months. Where did he go? What was he doing?'

'Julian found him.'

'But where?'

'Another fort.'

'And brought him back to the city, where he met you.'

'Yes.'

'And he stopped there for the winter, before bringing you south?'

'No.'

'Oh. Then what did happen?'

'We took a ship south three days after Paul arrived. We were attacked by pirates so we stopped for the winter at another fort, and then we continued after spring came.'

'Wait – pirates? You talk like that's the most natural thing in the world. Go on, tell me more – I still know nothing about the past five years of his life. I'm quite glad he left you here, really, so I can ask you instead. Please, go on.'

It was becoming clear to Eachna that Amanda was only tolerating her because she was a source of information about Paul. She had asked no questions about Eachna's past, and appeared to have no interest in her beyond her relationship with Paul and Julian. Eachna wanted to return to her room in the far corner of the house and be left alone until Paul came back. She shifted position in the water awkwardly. How long were these Roman baths supposed to last?

'Don't be afraid,' said Amanda. 'You can speak openly here, of all places.'

'I'm not afraid.'

'For instance, what did he do when he was on the Wall? Was he an officer? Did he fight in any battles?'

'I don't know.'

'But he said you were married. I'd expect his wife to be in his confidence about such things.'

'You should ask him,' Eachna said. 'I'd like to return to my room.'

'Oh, really – I'm his sister! I have more of a right to know than you do! If what you say is true, and he hasn't confided in you, then one can only conclude that his decision to marry you was either insincere or insane, which I must admit was my first thought anyway.'

'You don't know anything.'

'I know that the Cironii are of princely stock,' said Amanda. 'I can well appreciate that my brother has feelings of pity for you. But for him to take you as a wife is utterly impossible – out on the frontier, maybe, but not here. Under Roman law a senator's son can't marry a freedwoman. When our father gets home we'll see what *he* has to say about it.'

Eachna stared at her. She could sit and listen to Cironia Amanda for hours and answer her questions, but she knew that at the end of it there would be no understanding, no closeness. There was a chasm between them that did not seem worth the effort of crossing. Paul was rooted in Eachna's world now. Whatever of his foundations had once rested here in Silvanicum had long since been washed away. He belonged to Eachna.

Eachna rose from the bath. Ignoring the servants, she walked back to the changing room, leaving a trail of water behind her. She took her tunic from the shelf and pulled it over her damp skin, recovered her slippers, and returned to her room.

It would have been demeaning to call after the barbarian as she scurried away across the wet floor, so Amanda remained in the bath and let her go.

She stretched her limbs lazily through the water. She knew she had done wrong yesterday by ignoring Eachna, whom she had instantly looked on and dismissed as a symbol of Paul's contempt for Silvanicum, like the mud he had traipsed through the gatehouse. But last night had she not prayed for forgiveness, and this morning had she not resolved to treat the girl with proper Christian compassion, accepting her as a guest and friend? And this was the result!

Well, she reminded herself, one could not expect a savage to have any concept of civility or gratitude. Eachna was no doubt frightened and confused, and it was the way of frightened and confused animals to distrust all attempts at kindness.

More than anything else Amanda needed someone to talk to, and, despite herself, she thought again of Rufus. There was nothing she felt she would not tell him, nothing she did not want to tell him, if only he were here. But of course, she reminded herself each time, it was impossible. He would not come back after Paul's parting threat, nor would she want him to. If only Paul had not left again so quickly, she would have tried to explain that Rufus was not the same as his father, that Paul knew nothing about him.

She could not help but feel anger towards her brother for having stormed back into her life in this degraded, savage fashion, for assaulting without cause the man she loved, for having left her with this girl who he somehow imagined could be a decent, respectable wife. What was he thinking? She had always imagined Paul's return as a scene of joy, but instead he had rushed through the villa like a whirlwind, leaving behind a trail of unfamiliar sights and feelings that had made Amanda feel so sick she had retreated to her bedroom and not emerged for hours. It had been plain enough from his brutish bearing and his scruffy appearance, from the rustic edge to his voice, that all those years in the army had undone the brother she had known. He had not even explained why he needed to ride so urgently to see the governor.

There was only one other person she wanted to see. After returning to her room she wrote a letter to Patricia, telling her of Paul's return and asking her to come as soon as possible, and sent it by courier to White Hen House.

Patricia arrived shortly before noon the following day. Amanda was sitting in the library, composing yet another note to distant relatives, when her cousin appeared at the door. Amanda dropped her pen and came to greet her. 'I'm so glad you came, Patricia – I wasn't expecting to see you so soon! Here, you haven't even taken your coat off. Let me call a servant for you.'

'Of course I came, after I received your note. Mother and Father are beside themselves with the news.'

Amanda summoned a servant to take Patricia's riding coat, then led her to a shaded bench in the garden where they could sit in the warm June air and talk in private. Patricia had changed little since the winter, except that she had regained some weight, or was perhaps simply being a little less extreme in her self-denial. She still wore no make-up, no necklace, no bracelets or earrings, only a plain brooch to fasten the shawl she wore over her tunic. Amanda was disappointed to see that her cousin had proved so steadfast in her reformed life, but she could not deny that there was a new radiance to Patricia's beauty. Her voice, too, had changed; she now spoke as one used to long silences, carefully and quietly, and though her smiles were less frequent and more restrained than before, they were all the more elegant for it.

They sat together for a while, Patricia listening as Amanda described the events of Paul's return. Amanda included as little as possible about Rufus, except that he had happened to call at the villa just before Paul arrived. She did not mention the kiss. She described how Paul had almost killed Rufus but had let him go, and how Paul had told her, as he was readying to leave at the front gate, that Julian was safe and well in Luguvalium. He had said little else before disappearing again.

At that point Patricia spoke. 'You never said why Rufus came to the villa in the first place.'

'I can't really say,' Amanda replied. 'He was hardly here before Paul arrived.' She could not meet her cousin's searching stare.

Never had Patricia so much resembled her brother; her silvery green eyes, free from liner and shadow, appeared to see effortlessly through Amanda's attempt at deceit. Patricia smiled gently. She reached out and touched Amanda's hand. 'I've come to a conclusion these past months. I've realised that my feelings for Agrius Rufus were inspired by a devil. It's the only way to make sense of it. When a devil takes hold of you, its sole purpose is to destroy you from the inside any way it can, with hatred or greed or envy – and that's what happened to me. It almost succeeded, too. If Tecla hadn't saved me, if she hadn't inspired you to come to my room, it would all have been over. But now, with her help, I've defeated the devil, or almost defeated it. I don't hate Rufus like I used to. He isn't to blame for anything that happened: it was all me, my own weakness. If I have any anger towards him now, it's because of how he treated you – I mean, cancelling your engagement the way he did.'

'That was no great sorrow for me,' muttered Amanda.

'One drawback of accepting me as a sister, Amanda, is that I can tell when you're lying. Of course you're in love with Rufus. You can't hide a thing like that. I sensed it a long time ago.'

'Patricia . . .'

'When I saw you speak together at the party last winter, I knew for certain. I saw then that he was in love with you, too.'

'All we did at that party was argue.'

'No one argues quite like two people in love. I'm sorry I tried to turn you against Rufus. It was cowardly and cruel of me. I can't begrudge you your happiness. There's nobody in the world I love more than you, Amanda.'

Amanda finally raised her eyes. She could see no trace of artifice in Patricia's smile. She felt ashamed that she had tried to conceal for so long something that was so obvious. She took Patricia's hand and kissed it gratefully. 'I don't think I deserve such a sister.'

'That's something else we have in common. So tell me what happened, then, from one undeserving sister to another.'

'You're right. He said he cancelled the engagement only because he thought I despised him. And he said – well, he said all sorts of things. Not that any of it matters now.'

'So he came to see you.'

'He wanted to before I left for Treveris.'

'*Treveris?*'

'My father wants to send me there – perhaps he won't now, I don't know; I've written to tell him about Paul.'

'But why? To keep an eye on Lucas? My mother wasn't terribly impressed with his behaviour when he and Hesperius came to visit. Lucas was drunk on the very first evening, and ended up putting one foot in the fishpond.'

'To be with Lucas, and Hesperius. My father thought I might ingratiate myself at court for the good of the nation.'

'Oh.' Patricia shuddered. 'Then thank God that Paul came

home when he did. More than enough girls are already sent by
their parents from across the empire to *ingratiate* themselves at
the imperial court. I always thought your father had more sense
than that.'

'Hosting the great and famous Hesperius turned his head, I
think. Especially after Hesperius asked him to send me back to
Treveris on a boat, like some piece of furniture he'd taken a fancy
to. I truly didn't know what to do.'

Patricia looked at her closely, and suddenly threw her head
back and laughed. For a moment Amanda was offended, but
Patricia regained control of herself as she tried to explain. 'I'm
sorry, I'm just imagining that sot Hesperius trying his tricks on
you! Oh, Amanda, no wonder he was so grumpy when they
turned up at White Hen House!'

Amanda could not resist smiling. 'Well, he did try his best.'

'Tell!'

'Right over there, on the colonnade. He practically pounced
on me. *Let us live, my Lesbia, and let us love . . .*'

'Oh God, not Catullus! Oh my goodness, really, what a narrow
escape you've had . . .' She calmed herself, and wiped her eyes
with the corner of her shawl. 'Well, I thought Hesperius stank
back in Treveris, and I'm not very surprised to find that, like bad
wine, he only gets worse with travel. Pity the poor girl he eventually marries, that's all I can say.'

'Oh, yes – speaking of poor girls, it seems that Paul has found
one for himself.'

'What, he's married?'

'No. Well, he thinks so, but nothing will come of it. He brought
back a former slave girl, Irish, I think she said. He calls her his
wife, and she believes him, which is the truly sad thing about it.'

'Where did he find her?'

'At Luguvalium. He got her from your brother. She belonged
to the bishop, and apparently Julian was her teacher. It seems
they teach barbarians Latin on the frontier these days. Anyway,
for some reason Julian asked Paul to bring her south, and then,
well, somewhere between Luguvalium and here he lost his mind.'

She shrugged. 'I can hardly recognise him as my brother now. He's turned half barbarian himself.'

'What's her name?'

'Eachna. It means "steed", apparently. She's a cripple, too – missing a hand.'

'And she's in Corinium with Paul now?'

'No, she's here, in the villa.'

'Really? Where?'

'In her room, I suppose. I tried talking to her yesterday, but she practically refused to say a word, then she went off in a sulk. It's a strange thing not being able to punish a barbarian in your own house, I can tell you. So in the end I just let her go.'

They sat in silence. Patricia seemed lost in thought. Eventually she said, 'Can I see her?'

'She wants to be left alone.'

'I won't bother her, I just want to say hello. She does know my brother, after all.'

Reluctantly Amanda took Patricia through the villa to Eachna's room. The door was closed. Amanda opened it and entered to see Eachna sitting on a chair at the window, watching the path down to the river. She had a writing tablet on her lap, a pen in her hand. When she saw Amanda she rose quickly, and the tablet fell to the floor.

Amanda took her cousin's hand and led her into the room. 'Eachna,' she said, 'this is Lollia Patricia, daughter of equestrian Marcus Lollius Pertinax.'

Eachna and Patricia stood apart and studied one another cautiously. Amanda noted that the girl did not bow as she should have, or even say anything in greeting. She would really have to be taught some etiquette, at least to the level of the domestic servants, if she was to remain in the villa. On the one hand she was too crude and clumsy in her movements to be taken as well bred, and on the other she had a hostile air of defiance about her that was a bad trait in any kind of commoner, especially a crippled one. Perhaps Amanda could arrange for some lessons while Paul was away.

Patricia stepped forwards and picked up the fallen tablet. She held it out to Eachna. 'I'm Julian's sister,' she said.

At first Eachna gave Patricia the same sidelong, wary look she had been giving everyone else, but then Amanda noticed a slow softening of her features. As she continued to stare at Patricia, ignoring the tablet, Eachna's brow furrowed and her lips tightened, as though she were fighting the urge to cry. Patricia noticed it too, and held out her arms, and to Amanda's astonishment Eachna fell into them.

The two young women embraced one another, their eyes closed, while Amanda stood by. Neither Eachna nor Patricia spoke, and there was a quiet peace about them that kept Amanda from saying anything further, despite a pang of irritation that Patricia's offer of kindness should be instantly accepted where hers had not been.

In the end, having never felt more alone in her life, Amanda quietly left them and returned to the library.

XXVI

The good and wise man – the sort whom Apollo
Could hardly find among all the thousands of mankind –
Is his own judge, and searches out his whole self down to the
last nail.

Ausonius, *Eclogues*

Three days of waiting in Corinium. Paul paced back and forth in the audience antechamber, his boots scuffing on the faded mosaic floor. In his right hand he held the tablet entrusted to him by Drogo, who was probably now dead along with Kunaric and the rest of his men. Paul had not been able to get any other news about the situation in the north. Upon his arrival in the city three days earlier, after washing, shaving and changing clothes at his family's townhouse, he had marched with a handful of bucellarii to the imperial offices in the forum and demanded an audience with the governor on a matter of provincial security.

'I will submit your *request* for an audience with the governor through the proper channels,' the clerk had said.

The days had passed, and Paul's repeated enquiries had been ignored. No imperial official had been willing even to speak to him, as though there were a general admonition against it. Each dawn he rode with some men to the cemetery, leaving them at the entrance and walking to the graves of his mother and brother, where he stayed an hour or more, lost in his thoughts. After that there was nothing to do but return to the house and wait for a summons. The sudden return of the eldest son of Cironius Agnus had already caused a stir in the city, bringing flocks of petitioners and messengers to the townhouse. He had refused to see any of them. He wanted to speak first to the governor, and then to his father. Anyone else could wait.

He thought every other moment of Eachna, happy that she was safe at the villa. This was how he reassured himself at night when he reached across the bed out of habit, seeking the warmth of her body, and found that she was not there, as she had been every night for the last half-year. Were she with him now, she would listen to his complaints and cock her head sideways in her attentive way, and remind him with a wry frown that all men who were drawn to power were idiots in their own way.

Finally, around noon on the third day, a messenger had appeared at the house and announced that Lucius Septimius, most perfect equestrian and governor of Britannia Prima by imperial decree, would grant him an audience at the fifth hour after sunrise.

The fifth hour had now come and gone, and still they kept him waiting. Paul paused at the open door, which looked out onto the courtyard of the governor's compound. His retinue, half a dozen bucellarii, were idling about the gates. They were unarmed, it being illegal for retainers to bear weapons within the precinct of the imperial government.

Now he wished he had paid more attention to politics when growing up. Faustus, four years his senior, had always been the one to involve himself in their father's grown-up conversations. Paul understood the difference between the city council, formed of local landowners who represented the tribe, and the foreign officials of imperial government. In Corinium these two authorities faced each other coldly across the forum: on the south side stood the basilica and the city council offices, and on the north, separated by a wall, was the compound of the provincial governor, Lucius Septimius. Paul could only vaguely remember their father's accounts of rivalry and mutual suspicion between the city councillors and imperial officials, the never-ending feuds that always seemed to come down to power and money. Unlike Faustus, Paul had soon wearied of hearing about them.

But Faustus would have known which councillors and imperial officials to approach, and which to avoid; he would have known how to negotiate the different factions and interests and alliances. Even the governor was different from five years ago. Governors held office for only one or two years, and Paul had no idea who this Lucius Septimius was.

Still, it did not matter. When Paul returned to Silvanicum he would await his father. He hoped he would find the courage to tell him about Faustus, and accept his judgement. If he was banished and stripped of his birthright, he would never see Corinium again. For the moment the only important thing was to warn the governor of the approaching danger, so he could begin to root out Agrius Leo and the rest of the conspirators, and organise the provincial defences before it was too late.

The doors to the audience chamber opened, pulled inwards by a pair of slaves. His three days of waiting were over. Paul peered into the shadowy interior and saw three figures sitting behind a table at the far end of the room, framed by drapes and candles. A bust of the emperor stood on a plinth behind them. The man in the middle, with a gem-encrusted brooch fastening his cloak, had to be the governor, Lucius Septimius. The man on the governor's left was dressed in the uniform of a tribune, and looked like the commander of the governor's personal garrison. The official on his right was probably his chief of staff.

Paul walked into the audience room, stopped in front of the table and bowed to the governor, remembering the protocol he had learned years before. 'Most perfect equestrian Lucius Septimius, governor of Britannia Prima, I thank you for granting me an audience.'

The governor nodded. He was fat, grey-haired. His eyes had a sleepy, vacant look about them. 'Most esteemed senator Gaius Cironius Agnus Paulus, son of senator Gaius Cironius Agnus, this imperial audience is granted to you by the munificence of his Divine Excellency Valentinian Augustus. In lieu of his physical presence I am permitted by imperial decree to speak with his voice. You may address me.'

'Most perfect governor, I returned from the north a few days ago, bringing you an urgent dispatch.' Paul offered Drogo's tablet to the governor. 'This is a confidential message from tribune Drogo, commander of the cohort at Mediobogdum in the country of the Carvetii. It contains information vital to provincial security.'

The governor took the tablet and passed it to the tribune at his left, who opened it. He cleared his throat and began to read. '"Tribune Drogo of the Fourth Dalmatian Cohort sends greetings to all loyal subjects of his divine majesty Valentinian Augustus. Let it be known that I am a loyal soldier of Rome and have always tried to fulfil my sacred duty, never thinking of my own safety or asking for reward beyond the love of his imperial majesty," et cetera, et cetera . . .' His eyes skipped some lines. 'He writes that several cohorts in Carvetii country have murdered their commanders and joined a general insurrection against the divinely appointed imperial government. He claims that the rebellion is being led by a certain Pannonian exile by the name of Valentinus, who has allied himself with the barbarians with the intention of leading Duke Fullobaudes into a trap, seizing control of that province for himself, and declaring himself emperor. At the bottom is a list of names of supposed conspirators.' Seeming unimpressed, he passed the tablet back to Lucius Septimius.

The governor quickly scanned the letter. 'When did he write this?'

'A fortnight ago,' said Paul. 'I spent the winter at Mediobogdum and can vouch for everything he says. His fort was about to fall to the rebels as I left.'

'And where did he get his information?'

'He captured one of Valentinus's men.'

'A man will say anything under torture,' said the governor hurriedly. He looked to the tribune, who shrugged.

'That's true,' the tribune said. He looked up at Paul. 'Cironius Agnus Paulus, this so-called rebellion isn't news to us. We know about Valentinus and his stirrings on the frontier. We know he's temporarily managed to buy off some isolated garrisons, but it's no cause for alarm. He and all his allies will soon be brought to justice by Duke Fullobaudes.'

'But the duke is heading into a trap,' said Paul. 'It's right there in the report.'

'How could a single tribune of a small mountain cohort have any kind of idea what's happening outside his own valley? I've no doubt that his report is honest, but I seriously doubt its accuracy.'

'Quite right,' said the chief of staff. 'There's no reason to imagine that Valentinus has the means or desire to form an alliance with the barbarians. As for this list of names . . .'

'I was in the north for months,' insisted Paul, stepping closer. 'King Keocher was preparing for war a full year ago. He's formed a federation of tribes from the Wall to the northern isles, and with the help of Valentinus he's planning to ambush Fullobaudes and the Sixth and Twentieth Legions. Then he'll let the barbarians run riot over the southern provinces – including this one.'

The tribune shook his head. 'If any barbarians were seriously planning to invade, the duke would know it from his spies.'

'His spies work for Valentinus.'

'In any case,' said the chief of staff, 'the provincial defences are quite sufficient.'

Paul stared at them in disbelief. How could they be so deluded? 'This city is garrisoned by a cohort from the Twentieth, or at least it was until the duke took it for his campaign! I presume the imperial cohort will leave with you, esteemed governor, at the first sign of trouble. Then who'll be left to defend us? The militia? They could hardly protect the walls of the city itself, never mind the countryside!'

The chief of staff picked up the tablet and waved it loosely in the air. 'This Drogo clearly has delusions of grandeur, setting himself up as the great saviour of the provinces. The idea that Valentinus would declare himself emperor is preposterous!'

Paul argued, but it soon became clear that it was useless. Eventually he asked permission to leave the divine imperial presence and walked out of the audience chamber into the sunlight of the courtyard. He had to return home immediately. If the governor refused to listen to Paul, surely he would listen to Paul's father.

Some hours later, as he rode with his bucellarii from the forest onto the river path that led downstream to Silvanicum, it felt to Paul as though this, not his brief stop three days before, was his true homecoming. Immediately after his audience with the governor, he had come back to the townhouse to find a message that his father had cancelled his journey to Londinium, and had returned to Silvanicum to await his son.

Paul knew that he would have to submit to a public display of joy at being reunited with his father. He did not look forward to it. He would confess to his father later, in private, and accept whatever punishment he was given. If he was disowned and cast out, he would not argue, and would leave quietly, never to return. If his father demanded that he stand trial for fratricide, he would hold out his arms to be put in chains. His only request would be that Eachna be treated with respect.

He saw the crowds as soon as he turned the last bend in the river path and the villa came into view. It looked like they had been gathering for days. There were tents and campfires, around which groups of peasants, including some women and children but mostly men, were cooking their evening meals. Paul and his bucellarii were noticed almost at once: as the call went up through the camp like a ripple, the people left their steaming pots and rushed to line the path that led to the front gate. They cheered Paul as he approached them as though in triumph; some hailed his return and the restored glory of the Cironii, some praised the name of Christ in garbled Latin; many young men waved clubs, axes, even branches above their heads. Paul forced himself to smile and wave to the faces below him, gently urging his mount through the crowd.

The front gate of the villa opened before Paul reached it. The crowd parted to make room, and Paul's father emerged. Paul dismounted as the cheers died down around him like a suddenly calmed storm. He made the final few paces up the path until he was facing his father. They stood alone in the centre of a circle.

For a long moment, neither of them spoke. At last Paul came to his father and knelt before him on the hard mud of the path. He hung his head low and closed his eyes. 'Father,' he said, 'I have returned.'

He felt a palm rest on the top of his head. The storm of cheers rose once more, and they embraced, then Agnus addressed the people and told them of his joy, promising a feast that same evening in honour of his heir's return. Then, with his arm around Paul, he took him through the gate into the villa. 'We can talk in the library,' he said, and kept hold of his son as they walked along the path to the upper courtyard, watched and trailed by house servants.

'Where's Lucas?' asked Paul.

'Londinium,' said Agnus. 'On his way to Treveris to dice and drink.' When they reached the library, he held the door open and beckoned to Paul to enter.

Paul stepped meekly into the room. This was where he had argued with his parents for the very last time. He remembered clearly the anger in their faces when he had renounced his baptismal vows and said he was going to study philosophy in the distant eastern empire. It seemed so ridiculous now, the childish fantasy of a spoiled boy who knew nothing of the world. He remembered how he had cursed them. Even now he felt the shelves of philosophy and ancient wisdom glare upon him in silent condemnation. In his mind this room had become a temple he had desecrated.

But to Agnus, it was just his study. He went to his desk and began stacking and tidying away the loose parchment, scrolls and books strewn across it. 'Your sister,' he said, 'has still not learned to tidy up after herself. I don't trust the servants to put things away properly, so I ask her to do it. Then I come back after only a week away, and it's always the same.' When the desk was clear he sat behind it, and gestured for Paul to take the wicker chair facing him.

Agnus drew himself up straight in his chair as though preparing to say something, but he only stared at Paul in silence. He is doing the same as me, Paul thought: studying, exploring, waiting for the other to give something away. Their most recent common ground was this room and what had happened within it. The five years since then felt like a lifetime.

Agnus leaned back and tapped his finger on the smooth wood of the table. 'Tell me everything that happened, son. Running away, how the brigands murdered your brother, everything.'

'All right.' Paul's eyes drifted across the room and met the hard stare of Valentinian Augustus, whose bust glowed a dull red in the sunlight. That was new. The last time Paul was in here he had been under the gaze of a different emperor. He reached into his belt pouch and took out a wooden tablet, a copy of Drogo's letter, and placed it on the desk. 'Don't read this yet,' he said. 'Not until I've said what I have to. But keep it safe. It's more important than anything else.'

'Very well.'

Paul's mouth felt suddenly dry, his hands cold and damp. He was about to ask for some water, but stopped himself. There was no point trying to put it off any longer. 'I fled north from the villa,' he said. He spoke slowly, thinking through his words. 'It was already dark. I took the road over the hills, until I came to the old barrow. I slept there for the night. I don't know what I was planning to do. Maybe I would have returned home in the morning. But I was woken by Faustus.'

He took a moment to gather himself. The memories now rose painfully before his eyes. He began to tell his father about the argument with Faustus, how they had raged against one another. Paul had always envied his older brother; he had not needed to dig deep within himself to find such anger. He told his father about the knife, and how Faustus struggled to take it from him. He told of how they had fought, falling to the ground, wrestling with more fury than he could describe, as though they had been possessed by a pair of demons.

At that point his voice wavered and failed, and he began to

weep. He bent forward, clutching his head in his hands. He shook with sobs. He had told Julian and Eachna, but he could not tell his father. It would kill him even to speak the words.

Slowly Paul steadied himself. He sniffed deeply, coughing up phlegm, wiping his eyes with his sleeve. He had to continue.

His father spoke first. 'You killed your brother.'

Paul raised his face. He blinked through bleary eyes at his father. He nodded.

'The morning after you left, Faustus insisted he go after you alone,' continued Agnus. 'He swore he could bring you back. When neither of you returned, I went myself with Peter and two men. We found Faustus at the barrow. Peter swore at once that bandits had done it, but he knew better. It was clear enough what had happened. We found your dagger. Faustus's ring was still on his finger, his purse still full.

'There at the barrow I swore them to secrecy. They were to say that bandits had murdered and robbed Faustus, and that you had vanished without a trace. I never spoke of it again, not even to your mother. We took Faustus to the city and buried him.'

The room passed into a heavy silence. The distant sound of music and singing came from outside the villa gates, a celebration of Paul's return.

'A month later,' Agnus continued, 'I was in Corinium. As far as I was concerned, you would have been better off never coming back. In God's name, I wished you dead for what you'd done. That was when Agrius Leo came to me. He said you'd been pressed into the army. He claimed he knew where you were, showing me your ring as proof. He promised me that he would have you discharged and returned safely to me – if only I pledged to support him on the council. He wanted me to back him in Londinium, not to block his purchases of land, not to veto the use of civic funds to build pagan temples. Each time he told me: Give way, and your son will be brought back to you.

'But I refused. I knew I was condemning you to exile, maybe even death. The more I had to watch your mother mourn the loss of you and Faustus, the more I wanted you to suffer. Even as the years passed, and my desire for vengeance passed with them, still I refused to give way. I left you in his hands.' He paused, his jaw tight. 'I chose to sacrifice you, Paul, for the good of the province.'

When he had finished speaking, Paul sat up straight in his chair. His father had known the truth of his crime all along. It was difficult, but Paul looked him in the eye. 'I murdered Faustus,' he said. 'I've come home to face your judgement, Father.'

'Do you expect to be forgiven?'

'No.'

Agnus watched his son for a long moment. He got up from his chair, went to one of his shelves and drew out a thin codex. He turned to a certain page and began to read aloud.

'And the Lord said to Cain, "Where is Abel, your brother?"

"I do not know," he replied. "Am I my brother's keeper?"

"What have you done?" the Lord said. "Your brother's blood cries out to me from the earth. Know, therefore, that you are now cursed upon the earth which opened its mouth and received your brother's blood from your hand. When you work the land, it will give you no fruit. You will be a wanderer and exile upon the earth."'

Agnus closed the codex and replaced it on the shelf. 'Even when confronted by God, Cain denied his crime. When he was condemned, he begged for mercy.' He returned to his seat. 'But you've come home and confessed. You've freely surrendered the truth when you could have lied. Understand, Paul, that I never will forgive you for what you did. I wish I were a better Christian. On the other hand I could punish you. I could disown you and cast you out into exile. But answer me this: would any punishment I gave you make you suffer more than you already have?'

Paul thought of all he had endured in the last year. He thought of Trimontium and everything that had happened there, of the loss of Victor, of the journey with Julian, of the Verturian attack and the long winter in the mountains. He thought of how he had found Eachna and come to nurture the hope that he might one day be worthy of her. Redemption was not to be found in self-loathing, nor in a sprinkle of holy water, nor even in the forgiveness of his father. It would lie in his actions, from now until the day he died.

'I want to serve,' he said. 'As Faustus would have.'

'I never loved you any less than him, Paul. You were still young.'

Paul picked up the tablet from the desk and offered it to his father. 'Let me serve the family. Please.'

Agnus took the tablet and opened it. As he read, his eyes narrowed. 'Where did you get this?'

'I was there through the winter. At Mediobogdum. Tribune Drogo saved my life.'

'Christ protect us,' whispered Agnus as he continued reading. Finally he reached the list of conspirators at the bottom. The colour drained from his face. 'Who else has seen this?'

'Only the governor in Corinium, earlier today. I thought it best to show him as soon as possible. He still has the original; this is a copy. He wouldn't listen though, Father. Perhaps if you were to speak to him . . .'

Agnus slammed the tablet on the desk. He sprang abruptly from his seat and began to pace around the room with the desperate, directionless energy of a caged animal. The look on his face was almost one of panic.

Paul had never seen him like this. 'Father?'

Agnus stood still. 'Governor Lucius Septimius,' he said, 'is Agrius Leo's cousin.'

Paul had not known that. He sat in silent horror as the implications became clear. He had walked into the governor's office brandishing evidence of a conspiracy in which the governor himself might well be involved. No doubt Septimius had already rushed to send word to his cousin that they were exposed. 'Father, I'm sorry . . .'

'Do you remember the Winter of Grief?'

'Of course.'

'Agrius Leo was part of the inquisition. It was he who had your grandfather and uncles executed, and almost killed me, too. He's been trying to destroy our family ever since. I knew it.' Agnus seemed ready to grab the nearest shelf and hurl it to the floor in anger. 'I *knew* it, God damn me for a fool! Him, the governor, and those others . . . This is why he's leaving the province. He knows what's coming. No doubt he's going to turn up at Treveris acting the refugee, and be Valentinus's eyes and ears at the imperial court. He's kept me busy with taxes and peasants and talk of weddings; he let me think he was giving up, and all along he was planning *this* . . .'

Paul got to his feet. 'This is my fault.'

'There's no time for that now, boy! It makes little difference; we'd never have time to get word to the imperial court anyway. I have to think. Duke Fullobaudes was due to start his campaign over a week ago. If that letter is right, he's probably already dead.'

'We could send a message to the vicarius in Londinium.'

Agnus shook his head. 'A lecher and a drunk. I'd say he's involved in the conspiracy himself, if he weren't so useless. Our only hope is to get word across the sea with someone we can trust.'

'What about the bishops?'

'The bishops! Good. We must get word to Bishop Gregory in Londinium. He's pigheaded, but incorruptible. His couriers can send word to the imperial court without risk of interception.' He went to the desk and picked up the wooden tablet, calling loudly for Alypius, who was waiting in the anteroom outside.

The door opened and the dutiful secretary appeared. 'My lord?'

Agnus handed him the tablet. 'Make a copy of this by your own hand. No one else is to know the contents. When you've done it, come back to me. And have our two best couriers prepare to ride to Londinium, leaving within the hour.'

'Yes, my lord.' Alypius bowed and left, closing the door behind him.

'In the meantime we'll move the household to Corinium,' said

Agnus. 'If the barbarians are coming, we need to be in the city. We must keep the truth quiet for now; there's no need to cause panic.'

'But won't Agrius Leo and his cousin be in the city? Will they move against us?'

'Perhaps. But if we go in force, with as many bucellarii as we can muster, they'll think twice before causing any trouble. We'd be in more danger here, that's for sure. In any case, I believe their plan must be to leave the province as soon as possible, especially now that their part in the conspiracy is exposed.'

'When shall we leave?'

'Tomorrow morning, after the feast. We need time to gather the bucellarii and get supplies.' Agnus returned to his seat with a satisfied grunt, and placed both palms flat on the desk. He had regained his normal composure. Once more he was senator Cironius Agnus, lord and prince of the Dobunni. The crisis seemed to have given him renewed focus and energy, as though he relished the uncertainty of what the coming days would bring. 'Sit,' he said.

Paul did as he was told. 'Tell me how I can help, Father.'

'You can help by being what the people out there believe you to be: the lawful heir of the Cironii, and a prince of the Dobunni tribe. You can devote every ounce of strength to protecting those you love, and defending your people. And listen to me.' Agnus leaned forward on his elbows. 'You must never tell anyone else what happened at the old barrow. Not even your sister, and certainly not Lucas.'

'I don't want to lie to them.'

'I'm commanding you, Paul. Telling them won't change what you did. God knows, and that is enough. If you want to do penance, or to make peace with whatever gods you choose to follow, do so in secret. But it must never become known, or the name of the family will be ruined. Do you understand?'

'Yes, Father.'

'Good. Now tell me everything you know about this conspiracy.'

★ ★ ★

As soon as he had finished speaking with his father, Paul went to find Eachna. He entered the corridor of the north wing to find the villa bustling. Both kitchens had been fired up in preparation for the evening feast, and servants were frantically bringing food out of the stores and carrying trestle tables down to the lower courtyard. As soon as Father announced that the household was leaving for Corinium in the morning, it would become even more hectic. Paul wanted to escape the noise and commotion, and to find a brief respite from the thoughts racing through his head. So much was happening all around him, as though the world had been picked up and shaken.

When he asked the first house servant he saw where he might find his wife, he was surprised to be directed to the end of the south wing. Surely one of the better suites had been available. He walked along the corridor that divided the two courtyards and connected the north to the south wing, bounded up a wooden staircase to the upper floor, and almost ran down to the far end of the wing. He entered the room without knocking, and saw Eachna sitting at a desk with what looked like a book of scripture, tracing her finger across the page and reading softly to herself. She had not noticed him enter. He watched her for a while, not moving or speaking, until she gradually became aware of the draught and turned and saw him. She sprang from her chair and he took her in his arms.

He was surprised by the rush of happiness he felt at seeing her after only three days apart. He pressed her tightly into himself, loosening his embrace only to kiss her lips, and kicked the bedroom door closed as she began to pull him towards the bed. He let her guide him onto the mattress, let her unfasten his new leather belt, his gilded brooch and embroidered cloak, and toss them to one side. She ran her hand over his linen tunic and slipped her cold fingers beneath it to his chest, and he helped her lift it over his head. Only then, with these things discarded on the floor, did she again wrap her arms around his bare flesh and run her lips over his collarbone, his neck, to his mouth, while he undressed her in turn.

She lay back, bringing him down on top of her, and he rested his elbows on the mattress and cradled her head in his hands, their faces so close that the tips of their noses touched and the blue of her eyes was all he could see.

'A party?' She raised her head from his chest.

'In celebration of the family's reunion,' said Paul. He traced an idle finger down the length of her arm. 'That's what all the commotion outside is.'

Even with the door to Eachna's room closed, they could hear the noises of the feast being prepared. Eachna turned her head to listen more closely. Those slaves are doing the sort of work that she will never again have to do, Paul thought. He reached up and drew his fingers through her hair. 'I wish we could go for a ride on the estate, but we'd be mobbed. Have you been out yet?'

'I've hardly been outside this room.'

'Didn't my sister invite you out with her? She used to go riding every day.'

She did not answer, but instead looked away, and after a moment rested her head back on his chest.

'Eachna?'

'I don't mind staying in here,' she muttered.

Now it became clear to Paul why she had been put in this room instead of one of the better suites. Amanda was treating her with scorn. Could his sister be so callous? Had she lost all sense of compassion? He remembered seeing her in the garden in the arms of Agrius Rufus. What if he had already managed to twist Amanda against her own family?

He eased himself up into a sitting position. 'I'm going to have a word with her,' he said.

'Paul, no. There's no need. Now you're back, it doesn't matter.'

'You're my wife!' he said, more sharply than he intended. 'You're my wife.' He had not yet spoken to his father about Eachna, and was in no hurry to do so. He knew well enough that, legally speaking, the son of a senator could not marry a former slave, and that in the eyes of society she would never be more than his concubine. He did not care. Legal or not, she was his wife, and in his home he would have her treated as such.

He reached down from the bed to grab his clothes, complaining as he dressed himself that he would have expected such behaviour from certain snobbish relatives, but not from his own sister, kind, pious Amanda. He ignored Eachna's protests, laced his boots, and left the room, telling her to stay, not bothering to argue when she refused and followed him.

He went first to Amanda's suite and burst in to find her sitting with somebody. He did not look closely at the second girl, only noting that she was wearing the plain gown and headdress of the religious before dismissing her as irrelevant. 'Sister,' he snapped, 'why do you treat my wife with contempt?'

Amanda looked at him, open-mouthed. 'Your wife . . . !'

'As sworn in front of a bishop and a Christian congregation. Is that not enough for you?'

'But Paul,' she began, and seemed lost for words. She looked towards the door, to where Eachna had now entered, and pointed at her. 'But she's a *savage!*'

It was hard for Paul to control himself against that: he did not want to hit his sister, never that, but he did want to grab something, anything, and smash it, simply to release his anger; yet he did control himself. He clenched his fists and held his tongue until he could breathe out slowly and speak in level tones. Then he said, 'You must never call her that again.'

Amanda closed her mouth and sat still, watching him as she might a stranger.

'I intend to occupy my old quarters upstairs,' he said. 'Eachna will stay with me there.'

She glanced up to the timber rafters of her ceiling, only for an instant, but long enough for Paul to detect the revulsion she was half trying to hide. *He*, she was thinking, her brother, would be right above her with *that* creature, sharing a room, sharing a bed, while she, Amanda, would be lying here below, with ears that could not be closed, and an imagination that would paint what her eyes could not see . . .

'If my choice of wife offends you so much,' said Paul, 'perhaps you should think again about your own choice of lover. Or do you not know that he's been trying to have me killed for the last year?'

Amanda rose sharply from her chair and walked out of the room.

Neither Paul nor Eachna stood in her way, and the other girl did not move from where she sat. Paul looked at her again, and for the first time recognised her.

'Patricia?' he asked, not quite ready to believe it could be his cousin. In his memory Patricia was still a spoiled young girl given to tantrums, whose head had been filled with dreams of the city. Now that head, free of all ornaments, was half hidden beneath a religious veil.

'Don't be angry with her, Paul,' Patricia said quietly. 'Things have been difficult for her, especially after losing your mother.'

Paul stared at Patricia, looked to the door through which Amanda had left, turned back to Patricia. In her eyes he saw a calm wisdom he had never expected to see, and he saw the pain that had borne it. Five years was a long time when one was so young. Long enough to make a new person, as it had made him.

Patricia stood up. 'Go and talk to Amanda,' she said. She reached out a hand to Eachna, and Eachna took it. 'I'll keep your wife company for now.'

Amanda had not gone far, only into the garden. She was sitting on the bench beneath the apple tree. The place was busy with servants taking things down to the lower courtyard for the party.

Paul came and sat beside Amanda on the bench. Neither spoke for a while. Then she said, 'I've no doubt that she is very noble and brave and admirable. But she cannot be your wife.'

'She already is.'

'Paul, you can't just turn up after all these years with some barbarian girl, call her your wife and expect everyone to play along. You know it's not even legal.'

'I don't see why it should involve anyone except me and her.'

Amanda almost laughed: a quick, sarcastic exhalation. 'If only we could all just run off and marry whomever we liked.'

Her words unsettled him, and he did not reply at once. It did not feel right to be sitting here and talking to his sister like this. Perhaps he should not have expected her to accept his sudden return so easily. No, of course he should not have; if Amanda spoke now with the dignity and moral certitude of their mother, it was because she had matured into it, as she was meant to. She was no longer an eleven-year-old girl with a teasing disregard for the conventions of grown-ups; the girl who had once helped Paul smuggle sweet almonds from the dinner table in her napkin so they could enjoy them together in secret. She was an adult who had already taken on more grief and responsibility than was her due. He looked sidelong at his sister, whose eyes were downcast, and saw her for the first time as a woman.

'I will accept her,' Amanda said, slowly, 'if you promise not to harm Rufus.' Before Paul could think of what to say, she went on, 'You've misunderstood him, Paul. I did, too. I think everyone does. But Rufus is different. He sent men to save you, to find you for my sake, not kill you. He wants nothing to do with his father. And still people judge him, as though he chose to be born the son of that man.'

'True,' said Paul. 'Anyone might be born the son of a Gallic tyrant.' He waited for Amanda to nod in agreement before he added: 'Anyone might be born the daughter of an Irish barbarian.'

She glanced up and caught his eyes. Her mouth fell open, hung silent, and closed again. She looked across into the foliage of the orchard, to where a blackbird was perched warily on a branch. She breathed out deeply. 'What a disappointing clutch of children we must be,' she said.

The garden was for the moment quiet and empty. From the lower courtyard came the clatter of tables being erected and the shouts of staff making arrangements for the party. Perhaps a feast was just what they all needed, Paul thought; a grand ritual as for a wedding or birthday, with the bonfire blazing and purifying the air, the declaration of a new start for the family. They could not return to how things had been five years before, nor could they simply continue where they had left off, as though Paul had never fled home, Faustus had not been killed, their mother had not died.

Alypius emerged from the west wing and started down the gravel path of the garden, heading for the lower courtyard with a leather courier's satchel. As he passed, he paused briefly to bow and smile at Paul and Amanda, before continuing on his way with calm, dignified steps.

Paul watched Alypius leave the garden. One would never guess that the secretary was carrying letters crucial to the safety of the Four Provinces, letters that some men would kill to keep from reaching Londinium. Paul hoped the couriers made it. Tomorrow morning the Cironii would be leaving for their city, and he feared what the coming days would bring.

XXVII

Do you seek the road to freedom? You shall find it in every vein
of your body.
Seneca

Corinium rarely saw a procession of such splendour. The household approached the grand Glevum gate from the north road, a great train of noise and colour that drew hundreds to the streets and windows of the city. The heralds came first: Peter and a squad of mounted, green-cloaked bucellarii. Agnus followed after them, splendid in his full senatorial uniform and belt and brooch of office, riding a majestic white horse. On his left rode Alypius, and on his right Paul, who was wearing a green cloak and a red tunic that had once belonged to Faustus, the borders and sleeves bearing the purple and yellow embroidery that indicated his senatorial rank. After them came Amanda in an open carriage, accompanied by Patricia, Eachna, and some elderly servants. Three more wagons carried furniture and food-stuff, clothes, and the iron-banded chests that contained a fortune in gold and silver. The treasury wagon was guarded by the rest of the mounted bucellarii – some fifty of them, each with a longsword hanging from his hip – and last of all came two dozen household servants on foot.

Even though the townhouse stood outside the Glevum gate, Agnus had decided to lead the procession directly through the heart of the city. They rode down the main street, the heralds blasting on their horns, the cheering crowd swarming the porti-coes on either side. As they approached the forum, Paul saw that a host of imperial officials and city councillors had gathered to watch them pass. Among their astonished faces he spotted the governor with his chief of staff, along with Rufus. Beside them was a black-haired, bearded middle-aged man who stared at Paul and his father with undisguised contempt. It was a face Paul had not seen for many years, but with a shudder he recognised him as Agrius Leo.

They rode past the forum and basilica and public buildings, past the market where the governor had restored the column to Jupiter, until they went through the Calleva gate at the south end of the city. There they turned right to follow the long road around the outside of the city walls, passing the amphitheatre and a number of surburban villas until they finally reached their own.

Paul rode into the courtyard with his father and Alypius. The open carriage trundled in behind them. Paul's body ached from the journey, especially from the stiff posture he had maintained for the three miles of the procession. He knew it was important, though. Now every tongue in the city would be speaking of his return and the restored fortunes of the Cironii. Soon the townhouse would be besieged by even more petitioners than usual, all those hoping to win the favour of legal support or sponsorship for some official post on the council. Paul hardly felt himself ready to enter that world, but he would have his father as a guide.

Besides, though the city did not know it yet, there were more important things to worry about. As he dismounted, Paul observed the high spirits of the bucellarii, and almost envied them their ignorance. Earlier that morning, amidst the preparations to leave Silvanicum, Paul had told Amanda about the conspiracy. Otherwise only his father, Eachna and Alypius knew. The rest of the household was oblivious to the threat gathering beyond the western horizon, and they assumed that the reason for this unseasonal move to the city was to celebrate Paul's return. The bucellarii seemed especially puffed up from wearing their swords, which they were rarely allowed to do in public. They had no idea that they might have need of them sooner than they thought.

It was already June. If the Irish barbarians were to invade

according to plan, it would be in a matter of days; weeks at the most. When they came, the safest place in the province would be behind the towering walls and bastions of Corinium.

Paul went to the carriage and helped the women dismount in turn by the steps. Amanda wore expensive fur-lined shoes and a mantle of yellow and red, while both Patricia and Eachna wore only simple brown cloaks that left them indistinguishable from the servants. Paul had suggested to Eachna that she try some finer clothes, but she had declined. She seemed quiet and distant, reluctant to meet his eye. During the morning's long ride he had frequently glanced back at her in the carriage, but he had not once seen her talking to Amanda, nor had she returned his smiles. She had refused even to attend the feast yesterday evening, remaining in his bedroom. 'I don't belong here,' she had told him, speaking British instead of Latin, and he had found it difficult to get another word out of her. In the end he had gone to the feast himself, and by the time he had come to their bed she was asleep, or pretending to be.

There would follow the usual hour of chaos as Celerus, steward of the house, attempted to direct the unloading of the wagons. As well as the servants, he had to find space for the huge number of bucellarii and their horses, which meant clearing out the agricultural barn attached to the courtyard. Paul took Eachna into the house, to what would be their bedroom. She had brought only one bag, including some simple clothes and several books that Paul had borrowed from his father's library. She put the bag on the bed, and looked around the room. It was small but elegantly furnished, with a pair of wicker chairs and footstools, and a cushioned couch and wardrobe. It had a heated mosaic floor and walls painted with golden panels on red. Eachna looked as though she had been happier with the bare plaster walls and flagstone floor of their room at Mediobogdum.

'I need to go to my father,' he said, and left her alone. Soon he would stop trying to hide his irritation. Perhaps Amanda was not trying hard enough to be friendly, but he could hardly blame her if Eachna seemed so determined to sulk. Had she imagined it would be easy to find her place in his family? Or did she fear that he was going to cast her aside?

Agnus was awaiting him in his study, sitting at his desk. 'Your sister is upset with you,' he said as Paul entered. 'She says you're claiming that barbarian girl of yours as your wife.'

'She is my wife, Father. We were married at Viriconium.'

'She's a barbarian, and a freedwoman. Two reasons she cannot be your wife.'

'My sister has no—'

'In the name of Christ,' Agnus said, his annoyance clear. 'You could at least humour your sister. That girl is not your wife, and there's an end to it. Have a concubine if you must, but don't pretend she's more than that. If you want to serve the family, that's where you can start.'

Paul let out a frustrated breath. 'Father. If you spoke to her, you'd understand. She's like no other person I've ever known.'

His father shook his head indulgently. 'Every young man always fancies himself the first ever to fall in love. No, son, I think it better if I don't speak to her. She may not join us at meals, nor at public gatherings, nor may she stand with us at church. Apart from that, you can treat her as you like.'

Before Paul had a chance to reply, Alypius entered the study carrying a pile of tablets. 'These are the accounts you asked for, my lord.'

'Good. Place them on the table there.' He gestured for Paul to take a seat. 'You're about to have an education in the cost of popularity. We're going to plan the biggest festival this city's ever seen.'

Paul remained standing. 'Father, how can you even be thinking of wasting money on a festival? What about the invasion?'

'I said we're *planning* a festival. We're not necessarily going to give it. It will give us a good excuse to stockpile food and gather our supporters in the city without causing panic. When the invasion comes – *if* it comes – we'll be well prepared. Always remember, son, that what you do is sometimes less important than what people think you're doing. That's a lesson Agrius Leo could teach you, too. Now, sit.'

Paul sat down. 'What about soldiers?'

'That's the tricky part. The city garrison went north weeks ago. All we have is the militia, and whatever bucellarii our noble peers may be willing to give to the city.'

'The bucellarii aren't trained to fight like an army.'

'Then they'll have to learn quickly. We can start gathering supplies straight away, but building an army will take time, and must be done with discretion. I can't simply stand before the council and accuse the governor himself of treason – he'd arrest me on the spot. I can talk to our clients easily enough, at least the more reliable ones, behind closed doors. Then I can try some of the councillors with lands to the south of the city, the ones who'll suffer most from an invasion.'

'Lossio and Artorius,' offered Alypius. 'And Silvius Fronto?'

'It may come to that,' Agnus said. 'Without the western fleet protecting the coast, it's clear enough that any invasion will come from the south, up the Sabrina estuary. The territory of Aquae Sulis would be hit first, and Glevum. Luckily we don't have much property in those parts. Our biggest problem is that we still don't know *when* the invasion is coming, or even if it will. Agrius Leo and the governor still haven't left the province. If we start building a private army and nothing happens, we risk being accused of treason ourselves.'

'The invasion is coming,' said Paul. 'I'm sure of it.'

'Then if you're right, I can only pray to God that we still have time.'

They did not have time. Next morning Paul was awoken at dawn by an insistent knocking on his bedroom door, and a voice through the wood. 'Master?'

He climbed wearily from bed and went to the door, opening it slightly. It was Celerus. 'What is it?'

'Master, there are visitors.'

'This early?'

'The lady Fuscina and her children.'

Paul wiped his eyes and tried to focus on him. 'All of them? Were they expected?' Celerus shook his head, and Paul saw the effort with which he was maintaining his usual self-control. Something was not right. 'I'll be there in a moment.' He shut the door and went to find his clothes.

Eachna stirred. 'What's wrong?'

'My aunt Fuscina is here,' he said, tugging a tunic over his head and fastening the belt. 'God knows what she's doing arriving at this time. She lives a full day's journey to the south.' He sat on the bed and began lacing his boots. 'It's starting,' he said. It was not possible. They had not had time to prepare. Agrius Leo and his cousin were still in the city. Had the barbarians attacked earlier than they had expected?

Eachna had climbed out of bed, and was busily dressing herself with an air of purpose and determination Paul had not seen in her since their arrival at Silvanicum. For a moment they were back at Mediobogdum, rising to the horn of battle.

When they were dressed, Paul and Eachna came out into the courtyard, in time to see Fuscina hobbling through the gates, leaning on a staff. She was wearing a travelling coat, but on her feet she wore house slippers, which were torn into little more than rags. Her feet were black with dirt and blood. She was not yet forty, but her grey-streaked hair and the weariness of her expression made her look like an old woman.

She came to Paul and collapsed against him, weeping. Behind her came her two children, Paul's cousins. Bona, who Paul reckoned must be sixteen years old now, had always been a frail girl, pallid-skinned and nervous like her mother; but she was calm, leading her older brother Rusticus by the hand. He was whimpering to himself through trembling lips. His small, simple eyes darted over his surroundings, resting only briefly on Paul. They were followed by a small wagon drawn by oxen and driven by a servant, and loaded with sacks and bundles of clothes, hastily piled. More servants came after the wagon. All were in a sorry state: exhausted, footsore, fearful.

'Celerus, have them seen to!' Paul shouted, and the steward hurried to obey. 'Fetch a physician from town, and put more men on the gates. Come on, aunt, let's get you off your feet.'

Paul and Eachna helped Fuscina into the dining room, where they settled her on a couch. Bona entered, leading Rusticus to another couch. She wrapped her arms around her brother as he hung and shook his head, still whining. Fuscina looked up at Paul clearly for the first time, held out her arms, and when Paul sat beside her she took him in an embrace. 'God save you, Paul, God save you!'

'Aunt, what's happened?'

'The house, Paul, it's gone; everything . . .' She closed her mouth tight, and shut her red, tear-filled eyes. 'Savages,' she whispered. 'Yesterday evening. They came from the river at dusk. We'd just finished dinner.' She nodded towards her children. 'It was the little one's birthday.' She had always called Rusticus her "little one". He was her first-born son. When he had been born simple, Uncle Viventiolus had wanted him exposed, but Fuscina had refused. Nor had she allowed him to be hidden away like a shameful secret, instead celebrating his birthday every year with great festivity. 'We'd finished dinner, and there was a cry from the yard, and the next thing we knew they were everywhere. Savages. We had no time. We ran to the stables, took what we could. My poor boy, he doesn't understand.'

'This was yesterday? You travelled through the night?'

'We didn't stop until we got here.'

'That's more than twenty miles.'

Fuscina did not seem to hear. 'We heard you'd come back, Paul. Thank God you did – thank God, thank God!'

Patricia entered, leading some servants bearing food and bowls of water. 'Your wife and I will look after them, Paul,' she said.

Paul left them and went to the courtyard, where his aunt's house staff were being seen to. Men and women wept, servants shouted and bustled. He saw Alypius approach, a single point of calm in the surrounding chaos. 'Master Paul, I sent a boy to the city to find out what was happening. He says more have arrived from the south.'

'More?'

'Hundreds of refugees are pouring through the city gates. They say the Attacotti have come up the Abona and are burning everything in sight.'

Paul helped calm and organise the mass of newcomers in the courtyard, sending some to the barn, and others inside the house. So many would not be able to stay here for long; some would have to move inside the city. It had begun, far sooner than he had imagined. He saw Peter drag his bucellarii from their barracks in the barn and bring them to order. Paul watched them groan and complain and form into shambolic ranks. They made fine bodyguards, he thought, and they loved a good procession, but they were no soldiers.

'Paul, come with me.' It was his father emerging from the house with energetic strides, his cloak sweeping behind him. Paul hurried to his side, and stayed with him as he moved about the property. There was much to do. Agnus had just been with Fuscina and her children; now he needed to check the servants in the courtyard, then the bucellarii in their barracks, where he supervised the distribution of weapons and the deployment of a small guard outside the front gate. He made sure the food stocks were safe, ordered a full inventory to be taken, and checked that the animals were securely penned and fit to be driven into the city at a moment's notice. He had the house servants gather all the most valuable goods and books and load them in advance onto the large hay wagon. When the wagon was full, he ordered Celerus to have three trustworthy servants collect the heavy chapel plate in leather satchels and take it into the woods for secret burial.

Paul studied everything his father did. He watched how he brought calm wherever he went, and even in the midst of such confusion somehow found time to compliment and encourage his servants.

More news gradually arrived from the city. It seemed that the previous afternoon a huge Attacotti warband had been seen sailing up the mouth of the Sabrina estuary, and had split into raiding parties to ravage the undefended farms and country houses around Aquae Sulis. Dozens of farms had been attacked; villas had been plundered and torched; those people too feeble or too slow to escape had been butchered or taken prisoner. Paul's aunt and cousins had been lucky.

Paul had heard of the Attacotti, vassal tribes of the Irish from across the western ocean, and he knew how such pirates operated. They would be on foot, for their light boats were unsuitable for bringing warhorses across the sea. Normally they would not stray far from the rivers that allowed them to attack suddenly and silently, nor venture too far inland where they would be lumbered with captives and booty and could easily be hunted down.

But he also knew that this was no ordinary raid. Not in his lifetime had the western pirates been so bold as to strike the heart of the province. It could only mean that the conspiracy was succeeding, and that the western fleet had allowed the barbarian ships to sail up the coast. No wonder Agrius Leo had long planned to sell his estates and flee the island, knowing what was to come.

Late in the afternoon, as Paul was with his father in the study, poring over a map of the Four Provinces, there came the noise of scuffling and yells on the street outside. They both rushed into the courtyard to investigate.

Three bucellarii were standing in front of the gates, one of them holding a horse's reins. Agrius Rufus was on his knees before them, a hand touching his lips. He had just been punched. The street was otherwise empty, the usual gaggle of clients and petitioners having retreated within the safety of the city walls. It was strange that Rufus had come to the townhouse unescorted.

Rufus rose slowly. He wiped a trickle of blood from his chin and looked at Agnus. 'Your men are excessively loyal, senator Cironius.'

'State your purpose,' snapped Agnus.

'I've come to warn you,' he said. 'My father and the governor are on their way. They're going to arrest you.'

'On what charge?'

'Treason.'

Paul lurched forward and grabbed the front of Rufus's tunic. 'You fucking rat. You're the only traitor here.'

'I'm no traitor,' snarled Rufus, struggling to free himself from Paul's grip. At a sign from Agnus, the bucellarii pulled the two of them apart. 'My father only just told me about his plans,' said Rufus, straightening his cloak. 'I knew nothing about this invasion until it happened. Think what you like, but I'm no traitor. I took a sacred oath to serve the emperor. I won't break it even for my father.'

'You said he's on his way,' said Agnus. 'With how many men?'

'I don't know. A detachment from the governor's bodyguard; some of our own men. He'll bring an order from the governor for your arrest, and take you from the city at once, by force if he has to.'

'He's leaving the province?'

'Yes. He wanted me to go with him, but I refused. He doesn't know I'm here.' He looked urgently down the road towards the city. 'I'm ready to serve you, senator Cironius, if you'll take me.'

'I certainly will,' said Agnus. He nodded to the bucellarii. 'Seize him.' Rufus cried out, but before he could move, two of the bucellarii took hold of his arms and began to drag him into the courtyard, the third following with his horse. 'Bind his arms and feet, and tie him up in the barn with his beast.'

A crowd of other bucellarii had gathered in the courtyard, and they laughed as Rufus was taken roughly towards the barn. 'You can't do this!' he protested. 'I'm telling you, my father is coming!' He received no reply except mockery, and then he was taken inside the barn and out of sight.

'What shall we do with him?' Paul asked his father.

'Keep him safe until we know he's telling the truth about wanting to serve me.'

'You don't mean you believe him?'

'Not yet. But people say that things have been cold between him and his father these last few months.' He saw the captain of the bucellarii enter the courtyard. 'Peter! Make sure Agrius Rufus is not harmed, and prepare your men. Put more men outside the front gates and post archers at the high windows. I want this villa turned into a fortress. Agrius Leo is on his way. Move, quickly!'

'Agrius Leo has no evidence against you, Father. He'd have to bring you before an imperial court. He can't do that without any proof.'

'He knows the conspiracy well enough to convincingly manufacture my involvement in it. As for proof, the imperial court is all too ready to believe a Briton guilty of treason these days. No, this is a very clever move he's making. If he brings me as a traitor to the emperor, they'll trust him all the more.'

'Father!' Paul and Agnus turned to see Amanda emerge from the house. She was fresh out of bed, still in her nightclothes, with a shawl pulled around her shoulders. She stood beneath the portico at the edge of the courtyard. 'The servants are saying you've taken Rufus prisoner!'

'Get back inside, girl.'

'But he's innocent, Father. He's done nothing wrong!'

Agnus went to her, took hold of her shoulders, and guided her gently back into the house. 'That may be the case, but I can't take the risk. For the moment I need to keep him safe. He won't be harmed, I promise. Now go, dress yourself properly. You must appear calm for the servants.' Once Amanda was inside, he turned to Paul. 'Now we have even less time than we thought. Come.'

Paul followed his father back to the study. Agnus loomed over the parchment map on the desk. It showed the Four Provinces, the ragged outlines of barbarian country, and the most important cities and roads. With one hand he pointed at Londinium, and with the other at Aquae Sulis. He sighed in frustration. 'It's a hundred miles to Londinium; our couriers will take at least two days to get there. We can't expect any kind of help from Londinium for a week, and probably no kind of help at all.

Meanwhile the barbarians are burning villas only twenty miles to the south.'

'And Agrius Leo is coming to our gates as we speak. We need to get you away from here.'

'I'm not running,' Agnus said calmly. 'The point is, whatever Agrius does, he'll have to leave in a couple of days. But we need to think in terms of weeks.'

'You're so sure Agrius Leo won't be able to take you?'

Agnus did not answer. Instead he took up the map with a flourish, rolled it and placed it aside, and handed Paul a wax tablet and pen. 'Listen carefully, and take notes,' he said.

Agnus began to list names of city councillors. He told Paul the status and wealth of each, their characters and reliability, who belonged to which faction, and who might be most easily swayed. The two elected magistrates for this year, Attius and Porcius, were Agrius Leo's men, but they were not the wealthiest of their class, nor the most influential; their hold over the council was still uncertain, and would only weaken further once Agrius Leo and the governor fled. The Christian Artorius was one of the most influential landowners to the south, and he could be swayed, along with Matugens, Tocius and others. More important, Agnus said, were the Gallic families: Mamilianus, Pomponius, Thallus, all of them clients of Silvius Fronto, the wealthiest man in the province after Agnus and Agrius Leo. 'It pains me even to consider it,' Agnus said, 'but we will need his support.'

The web of names and alliances and rivalries spinned and thickened around Paul until he began to feel smothered. They were too many, it was too complicated, and he did not understand why he needed to know all this when his father and Alypius could deal with it, when the more pressing threat was a barbarian invasion a day's walk to the south, when their first priority should be to get his father as far from here as possible. Eventually, having confused the factions and names of two councillors for what felt like the hundredth time, Paul rose from the desk in frustration, said he needed some air, and went to the courtyard. Finding little peace among the bustling chaos of servants, refugees and retainers, he left the house by the back door.

There was a meadow behind the house, common grazing land that stretched several hundred yards to the stone ramparts of the city. Between two copses Paul could glimpse the north gate. Now that news of the attacks had spread far into the countryside, wagons, horses and pedestrians were entering Corinium at a steady trickle. Some farmers had driven their herds to the city. The south gates, Paul knew, would be even busier. Soon the city would be fit to burst, its population doubled within a day.

He heard the back door open and close, and his father appeared at his side. The two of them stood together, leaning on the fence that divided their property from the common land.

'Look at the city, Paul,' said Agnus. 'The garrison from the Twentieth is long gone, and won't be coming back. When the governor leaves, all his staff and the hundred men of the imperial cohort will go with him. Then who'll be left to maintain order?'

'The city council and whatever militia they can raise.'

'Exactly. The same council that Agrius Leo has spent the last few years turning inside out for his own profit. He's bankrupted the city, divided it against itself, bled it dry; he's conspired against both the emperor and the people, and now he plans to leave us to the mercy of barbarians. If the city is to survive, the council must be united. It needs a strong figurehead, one who represents both tribal tradition and loyalty to the empire.'

'Meaning you.'

'No,' Agnus said. 'Meaning *you*.'

Paul shook his head in disbelief. 'I only came back a few days ago. The council is a mystery to me.'

'Perhaps that's for the best. Not understanding all the petty squabbles will make it easier for you to rise above them.'

'But *you're* here; they don't need me.'

'I won't be here forever.'

'I won't let Agrius Leo take you, Father.'

Agnus looked at his son with patience and compassion, as

he had not done since Paul was a boy, and smiled. He said, 'I know.'

The dull brown train of people, vehicles and animals continued to move into Corinium. From the ramparts came the occasional flash of a helmet or spear. Fresh smoke columns rose from the city, from cooking fires lit by the new arrivals in the open spaces within the walls. When the governor's personal troops left, Paul knew, the only defence would be the city militia, who were under the command of the council. And if the council was paralysed, there would be no chance of meeting the invaders in the field. The best they could do would be to hide behind the city walls and watch their country burn.

'We were princes long before the Romans came,' said Agnus. 'Our ancestors founded this city. Cironii paved its streets, built its walls, its temples. We bear its name, and it bears ours. For the sake of our people, and for the honour of our ancestors, we cannot let it fall.'

When he was growing up Paul had often heard his father speak like this about Corinium: the foolish old story of how their royal ancestor, King Corio of the Dobunni, had supposedly founded the city after driving away a monster that had been terrorising the tribe; Corio's building of the forum and market; the rebuilding of the amphitheatre and defences by his descendants in the time of Marcus Aurelius; the countless achievements of the Cironii, which were inscribed on their monuments within the city and on their tombs outside it . . . Throughout his childhood Paul had been half buried by this weighty and tedious heritage, until one day he had come across the work of the ancient philosopher Lucretius. Some men, Lucretius wrote, drive themselves to ruin for a scrap of statue and a name. Those words had stayed with Paul, and from that moment on he had felt little more than contempt for the glory of his forebears. Everything had followed from that: his desire to study philosophy in the east instead of rhetoric in Treveris, his renunciation of his baptismal vows, the argument with his parents, and then Faustus . . .

Yet now, as his father spoke the same words Paul had heard

so often before, he listened as though for the first time. He felt the dark threat gathering about the city, and understood. Corinium was the family, and the family was Corinium. Regardless of the empty pomp of statues and inscriptions, he could not deny it.

'If a man is made to run the course,' his father said, 'it's better that he is trained to it while his flesh is young and his bones strong. If an old man is left untrained and then put to the test, he will be found wanting, and is left no choice but to bow and take his leave with whatever dignity he still has. I was tested too late, Paul. I was never meant to lead this family. My brothers, may Christ watch over them, were the better men, stronger and wiser. I only pray that I'm worthy to rejoin them in the next life.'

Paul glanced at his father, who was again staring across the meadow to the north gate. He wanted to ask his meaning, but at that moment the voice of Celerus came from the doorway behind them. 'My lord,' he said, his voice trembling, 'Agrius Leo is approaching from the city.'

Agnus breathed in deeply. 'Celerus, fetch my cloak and belt.' The steward bowed and departed. 'Paul, let us prepare to greet our guest.'

'Father, you can't. He'll seize you.'

Agnus shook his head calmly. 'No, he won't.'

'Stay in the courtyard. Let me go.'

'Fourteen years ago he sent men to take me, and I didn't have the courage to show my face. In memory of your mother, this time I do.'

'Then let me stand at your side.'

Before Agnus could answer, another voice came from behind them. 'Let me, too.' It was Amanda. She was still wearing her house slippers, but had pulled on a travelling cloak. 'In memory of Mother.' She stared at him, fearless and resolute, with a quick upwards tilt of her chin that reminded Paul suddenly of their mother. The resemblance was heartbreaking.

As Agnus saw his daughter, the hard crease of his brow relaxed.

He smiled at her sadly. 'I have treated you so cruelly.' His voice was thick with regret.

'We must stand together,' she said.

Paul went with his father and Amanda to the courtyard. Celerus brought a heavy green cloak and golden brooch, and a wide belt of leather and gleaming brass. Agnus took the cloak and secured the brooch on his right shoulder while Celerus fastened the belt around his waist, completing his senatorial uniform. 'Peter!' Agnus called.

The captain ran to him and bowed. 'My lord?'

'Unbind Agrius Rufus. Keep him here in the courtyard until I say so.'

While Peter went with two of his men to the barn, Agnus ordered another pair of bucellarii to open the gates. He walked out, Paul at his left side, Amanda at his right.

A screen of their bucellarii stood in front of the house facing the lane. They watched Agrius Leo as he came up the road to the townhouse. He was mounted alongside two imperial officers, and followed by a dozen of his own bucellarii and about thirty of the governor's troops on foot.

He pulled up on the lane directly in front of the house, some twenty yards distant. He was unarmed, but the two riders beside him, wearing the uniform of junior officers of the governor's cohort, had thrown their cloaks over their shoulders to reveal sheathed swords. Agrius Leo's bucellarii and the imperial troops, in battle dress, assembled themselves in a single line behind them. There were no soldiers from the city militia, Paul noticed. Had the council forbidden him from taking any?

Agrius Leo saw Agnus and addressed him directly. 'Gaius Cironius Agnus, we are here to arrest you in the name of the divine Valentinian Augustus.'

'On what charge?' Agnus replied.

Agrius Leo reached into a saddle pouch and drew out a scroll. It was rolled and sealed with a heavy wax stamp. 'Treason. We have a warrant signed and sealed by the governor.'

'The province is under attack, senator. Have you not noticed?'

'At times of crisis we must be especially vigilant. If you come peacefully, I promise that no harm will come to your family or your people.'

'And if I refuse?'

'All who attempt to protect you will be complicit in your treason, and will receive no mercy.'

'You're getting ahead of yourself, Agrius. Here I stand behind twenty armed men – with your son.' He snapped his fingers. Peter led the unbound Rufus out into the lane.

Agrius Leo glared at Agnus, the frustration clear in his face. His sharp stare shifted suddenly to Rufus. 'This is your last chance, boy. By defending a traitor you become a partner in his crime.'

Rufus neither replied nor moved an inch.

Agrius Leo watched them intently for a long moment. His eyes met each of them in turn: Paul, Amanda, Rufus, Peter, all of the bucellarii, as though memorising each face. 'Very well,' he said finally. 'You are all condemned.'

The siege of the Cironii residence began. Peter withdrew the bucellarii inside the front gate, and with his booming voice and a few sweeps of his massive arms commanded them to reinforce it with planks of wood hammered into place. Armed men and servants hurried to and fro, carrying more wood to board up vulnerable doors and windows. Archers used a ladder to climb onto the roof of the main building, which gave them a clear view over the lane and the surrounding meadows. The townhouse was busy with shouts and the frantic noise of hammers on nails.

'You see?' said Rufus as he followed them back into the court-yard. 'My father has disowned me. Let me stand by your side, senator. If I'm to die, let it be with a sword in my hand.'

'Trust him, Father,' pleaded Amanda.

Agnus examined him carefully. 'If he wants to serve me,' he said to Amanda, 'he can. Both of you go to Celerus and find something useful to do. But he shall not have a weapon.'

As Amanda led Rufus across the courtyard, Paul went with

his father to an upper-floor window that overlooked the lane. They saw that Agrius Leo had left his men in front of the house and had ridden back towards the city, no doubt to beg for more troops from the city council. With luck they would refuse him. For the time being Agrius Leo had not nearly enough men to storm the house, or even to fight them should he try to burn them out. This was good. They had enough provisions to last several days, the courtyard well was deep and full, and time was on their side: Agrius Leo, after all, was the one desperate to flee the province.

Paul shared these thoughts with his father as they walked back down to his study. Agnus listened carefully before shaking his head. 'You're right that he can't afford to besiege us for long. But if he needs more men, he'll get them. Threats, bribes – that man has a way of getting what he wants.'

'Then I could go to the city council and talk to them myself,' said Paul. 'After sunset I could leave across the meadow.'

'And how would you even get into the city? Curfew will be sounded at dusk. The militia will be everywhere. You'd be just as likely to be arrested on the spot and imprisoned yourself. No, he has us trapped.'

Deflated, Paul collapsed in a chair before his father's desk. 'Then what should we do? If he brings more men, I don't see how we can defend the house. He'll just burn us out like rats, and wait for us outside.'

'He probably will. Though not straight away; it would be imprudent to do so until the last possible moment. It would create a bad mood in the city.'

Paul was astonished by his father's casual tone. They were imprisoned in their own house, hemmed in by tired and frightened refugees; they were now all implicated in treason against the empire; the country to the south was being ravaged by barbarians; Agrius Leo might return at any moment with another fifty men, and they had no hope of relief. And his father sat behind his desk and mused about their fate as though considering the next move in a game of soldier's bluff.

'If we fight,' pondered Agnus, 'we will lose, and you and I will both end up on the scaffold. What happens to me isn't important. *I've lingered for years, despised by the gods, and useless.*' He paused, and looked at Paul expectantly.

'Virgil,' Paul said, almost by instinct. He was surprised how easily the recollection came to him. For a moment he was back in his old classroom in Londinium, reciting the scene from the sack of Troy: Aeneas begging his father to flee the Greek fury; his father refusing, stubborn, ready to die in the ashes of his doomed city . . .

Agnus smiled. 'I'm glad all that money I spent on your schooling wasn't completely wasted. Try not to worry, son, we still have time; he won't try to storm us yet. You can sleep easy tonight.'

'What's your plan?'

'You'll see tomorrow.' He rose from his desk, took a burning candle from the shelf, and used it to light a large oil lamp by the window. He returned to his chair. 'Now, it's getting dark, and you should get as much sleep as you can, but before you go, I wanted to talk about your wife.'

'Eachna?'

'I spoke with her this morning, when I went to see to your aunt Fuscina.' There was a knowing note to his voice, in which Paul read his approval of Eachna. Whatever they had talked about, she had clearly won him over. 'She reminds me of a girl I once knew in Treveris, when I was young, before I married your mother. Your uncles knew about her, but nobody else. God, they teased me for it! But she was the daughter of a lowly treasury clerk, a commoner. Nothing would ever have come of it, so in the end I let her go.' He paused, a faint, sad smile on his lips, and stared into nothing. 'Now, son, I loved your mother with all my heart.' He leaned back in his chair. The sky had already darkened in the east, and despite the light of the lamp he was slipping ever further into the gloom. 'But that first love,' he continued, 'is never to be equalled, nor forgotten. You have my blessing, Paul – and my envy. She is wise and worthy. Be prepared for scandal and mockery, and be prepared to ignore it.'

'Thank you, Father,' said Paul.

'Good.' Agnus rose. 'Now embrace me, wish me a restful sleep, and fetch your sister. I'd like to talk to her, too.'

Paul embraced his father, who held him for a long time. 'Sleep well.'

XXVIII

And behold joy and gladness, slaying oxen, and killing sheep,
eating flesh, and drinking wine: let us eat and drink;
for tomorrow we die.

Isaiah 22:13

In ancient times, when Socrates had been tried and condemned by the Athenians, even given the chance to escape his cell, he had taken his own life. In the time of Caesar, Cicero had bowed his neck to his executioners when they caught him in his litter. Mark Antony in turn, deserted and betrayed in Alexandria, had fallen on his sword. And Seneca, the philosopher who had failed to teach a tyrant wisdom, had cut his own veins when falsely accused of treason.

It was strange, Paul thought, that these were the first things that came to mind when he was brought to see his father's body the next morning. Not grief, nor even shock, but the memory of schoolroom exemplars.

His father lay on the bed, dressed in a clean tunic, on white sheets, at peace. There was no blood; Alypius, with whom Agnus had shared his plans for suicide, had tended to his corpse and laid him out with dignity in his senatorial uniform, and had kept vigil by his side through the night. When dawn came, obeying his lord's final wishes, he had summoned Paul.

Paul stood and looked at his father in silence. But of course he had thought straight away of Socrates and Seneca and the rest. He had been supposed to.

Now he understood his father's plan.

* * *

Eachna waited with Patricia in the courtyard as the funeral cortège assembled. She had never spoken to Paul's father before yesterday, when she had been helping Patricia comfort the refugees. Ignoring her at first, he had then begun to ask her about herself: simple questions, with no hint of disapproval, and she had answered them honestly. He had seemed so calm, at peace with himself and his world even as it was falling apart around him. He had said nothing about what he was planning. Eachna did not understand why he had done it.

Once everyone was ready they opened the front gates. Paul and Amanda were the first to leave the courtyard, walking on foot in plain clothes, with four servants carrying Agnus on a makeshift bier behind them. He was surrounded by flowers picked from the house garden. After the bier came Eachna, Patricia and Rufus, followed by Fuscina and her children, and finally Alypius, Celerus and the rest of the servants.

It was shortly before noon. Paul had commanded the bucellarii to remain behind, and had insisted that no one in the procession was to carry a weapon.

Agrius Leo was with his men on the lane outside. He watched as the cortège left the house and continued in solemn indifference past him and the soldiers, heading towards the main road and the north gates of the city. He said nothing, did nothing, but Eachna could see the frustration in his dark eyes.

Traffic stopped and moved aside as they approached the gates. When the militia guards realised whose body lay on the bier, they hastily cleared a path along the road ahead of them. Eachna saw Paul take Amanda's hand as they passed through the city gates. They walked slowly, giving time for the news to spread, and by the time they reached the basilica many hundreds of people were lining the streets, mourning, praying, crying out the name of the Cironii.

They paused outside the open basilica doors before Paul and Amanda entered, and the rest followed. Eachna's heart began to thump as they went deeper into the great space. Steep shafts of sunlight plunged through the grey, smoky air. The noise from the street outside was muffled, but voices and footsteps within the hall echoed frighteningly. Eachna was glad to be between Rufus and Patricia, and she kept her face low in case she should be spotted and ejected as a barbarian by one of the many long-gowned men emerging like spectres from the shadows around them.

At the far end of the basilica, in front of a great apse, Paul instructed the servants to lay down the bier with the feet pointing towards the door, as was tradition. On a plinth at the back of the apse was a bronze statue of the emperor, wielding a globe in one hand, a sceptre in the other, his eyes raised heavenward. Eachna was gazing at the statue when she heard rapid, noisy footsteps. A man was approaching from the aisle, waving his arms. 'No, no, no! This is a basilica, not a charnel house! Remove the corpse at once!'

Paul looked the man up and down, his eyes lingering on the embroidered tunic, the cloak fastened by an enormous round brooch. It was clear to Eachna that this was a man of substance and power, though she had no idea who he was. When Paul replied, he addressed the funeral cortège and the clerks and officials who had gathered around them; everyone in the basilica except the man who had spoken. 'I know I've been away for some time,' he said, 'but have the council's powers of judgement become so impoverished that they now elect magistrates who do not know how to use proper address before a lady in mourning?'

The man was dumbstruck for a moment. He glanced nervously at Amanda. 'Lady Amanda,' he said, and bowed to her, and then to Paul. 'Most esteemed senator. You have my sympathies on the loss of your father. He was a most honoured man, a most—'

'Magistrate Porcius, forgive the irregularity, but we hoped to let our father lie in state while I make a public address to those who choose to pay their respects.'

'Senator, I understand your grief, but with the city in such a condition, surely the bishop's church would be more . . .'

'The church won't be large enough,' Paul said simply.

The bier remained where it was. Porcius retreated. Paul and Amanda stood at the head of the body, while Eachna and the other mourners assembled behind them in the apse. A great many clerks had already come from the offices adjoining the basilica and gathered in the aisles, and were peering between the columns into the nave. Now members of the city council began to appear, some from the aisles, some hurrying from outside. They came and gathered around Porcius, forming a small crowd in front of the bier. The ordinary citizens were then admitted and flooded in from the far doors. There was some jostling and impatience at the entrance, but as they neared the apse their pace slowed and conversations stopped. Eachna stared out at the gathering ocean of people, more than she had ever seen in her life: rich and poor, merchants, labourers, artisans, slaves, women, children, stretching the length of the nave.

When the hall was almost full, Paul stepped forward to the head of his father. A hush spread through the crowd.

'Councillors,' he announced, speaking in British, 'citizens of Rome, tribesmen of the Dobunni – I thank you for the respect you show by your presence. It is a bitter thing to lose a father. It is a worse thing to lose a father by his own hand – and worst of all when he took his life not because of disgrace, nor fear, but because of honour. Because, falsely accused of treason, his love for the emperor was such that he could not bear the shame of being brought before the divine presence even to deny it.' He half turned, raising one arm to indicate the statue of the emperor at the rear of the apse. 'Instead he now lies in the divine presence, in death as in life, a loyal servant.'

Paul began to walk around the bier, closer to the audience. 'And he died not only for love of the emperor. He was a Cironius, a prince of the Dobunni. He sought to preserve not just his own honour, but the honour of his people – *your* honour. He would not have the lies against him sully your name. The blood of the fatherland flowed through his veins. Ambushed, betrayed, defenceless, when he could no longer protect you by living, he chose to defend you by dying.

'And I ask you – where now are his persecutors? Where is Agrius Leo? Where is the governor? I do not see them among us. I can tell you where they are: at this moment, as the barbarians are burning our homes and massing before our gates, they are preparing to flee. They will load their wagons and mules with coin, they and their men will take to the road, and then they will take to boats, and they will not look back until they are safe and sound back in Gallia.

'And why should we expect anything different? This is not their land. It is *ours*! My father has shown us the way! Now is not the time to weep, but to fight – to give our lives if we must. For what man is not ready to die for his home and loved ones? I tell you, there is not even a slave here who does not shudder at the thought of these walls crashing down, who does not desire to see our tribe stand proud and free, who is not ready to rush to its defence against the barbarians of the west. How much more readily should you free men, you proud men of the Dobunni, muster in the name of freedom?'

The crowd was beginning to cheer; Paul raised his arms, and it quietened. 'I have returned to take my rightful place among you. I speak now as the heir of my father, as a senator of Rome, and as your prince. Councillors, I urge you to remember the dignity of your office. In this moment of crisis, forget your petty differences and serve the people with courage and wisdom. And you free men of the tribe, take heart! Let us not cower behind these walls. To arms! Let us take the fight to the enemy, and drive them from our land! I tell you: no barbarian who preys on the weak, who strikes from the shadows only where he fears no danger, can stand against a nation of brave men defending their homes.'

If Paul had planned to say more, the crowd did not let him. Somewhere in their midst a man cried out his name, others followed, and the chant quickly rose and spread throughout the hall until the air itself was alive with the passion of a thousand voices. The councillors, too, applauded; Eachna saw that magistrate Porcius was now standing with both hands clasped to his heart, tears pouring down his cheeks. It was a release, an entire city sharing a moment of revelation.

Even Paul seemed surprised by what he had unleashed. He glanced back at Eachna as though hoping for her approval, and for an instant she saw the smile on his face, and felt such love that he should at that moment look to her, ignoring the crowd that was chanting his name, that it was all she could do not to run over to him.

Paul went to the councillors and was immediately surrounded. Some took his hands and pledged allegiance to him and to the memory of his father. They ushered him through the crowd and into the aisle, out of sight, Alypius following close behind.

'Where are they taking him?' Eachna asked Rufus.

'To the council chambers. Now the hard part begins.'

Slowly the crowd began to leave the basilica, but those who left were replaced by newcomers desiring to see the body of Agnus, to kneel and pray in front of it, and to express their sympathy and loyalty to Amanda, who did not move from his side. Eachna saw how she received the peasants with as much dignity and respect as she did the nobles. She was strong of heart, Eachna could not deny that.

Away from the bier, the basilica was busy with frantic huddles of men and clerks racing from one office to another. One figure in particular caught Eachna's eye, approaching from the far doors with a long, awkward stride, wearing a hooded cloak. He was halfway down the nave when suddenly she recognised him, at almost precisely the same moment as Patricia, and they cried together: 'Julian!'

He smiled when he saw them, but first paused at the foot of the bier to kneel and whisper a brief prayer. He then took Amanda in his arms, and beckoned for Patricia and Eachna to come to him. He kissed them each in turn. 'Gracious sisters, in blood and in Christ, I'm glad to find you safe!'

'Where have you come from, cousin?' asked Amanda.

'From home, and before that from the north.'

'And your parents?'

'They're in Glevum, safe for now, but I'm worried.' He leaned in closer. 'I bring word that the barbarians are moving up the Sabrina.'

'To Glevum,' said Patricia, the horror plain in her face. 'They would never dare attack a city – would they?'

'Not attack, no. I learned this from my father this morning; it isn't common knowledge yet, so you must tell no one. The council of Glevum has invited them. Raiders are said to be approaching from the north, too, and the council is hoping to hire one batch of savages to defend them against the rest.'

'Inviting wolves into the house to defend against bears in the garden? Surely Father would never allow it!'

'He's just one voice in fifty. The duke's been captured north of the Wall, and most of the Sixth and the Twentieth have been wiped out. Count Nectaridus is dead, the western fleet has been virtually destroyed, the Wall's been overrun, and the northern provinces are in chaos. An exile called Valentinus had the magistrates of Luguvalium murdered and signed a pact with the barbarians. Bishop Ludo spoke out against him and was arrested. The last thing he did was make sure I and some other brothers got out of the city. Has none of this news reached you yet?'

'No.'

'Where's Bishop Martin?'

'He's still in Londinium,' Amanda said.

'Then where's Paul? I need to tell him at once.'

'In the council chamber. Go, Julian – but tell him discreetly.'

'I understand.' With that he hurried into the aisle.

Amanda turned to the servants still standing close to the bier. 'We'll take my father to the church,' she declared. 'He can be watched over there by the clergy.'

The servants lifted the bier carefully and left the basilica, followed by Amanda, Patricia and Rufus, and last of all Eachna. The refugees were still filling the streets, the forum, the market-places and the temple courtyards. They numbered in the thousands. Some noticed the bier with interest, some followed it, but most were too tired, or too distracted. It was like Luguvalium all over again, Eachna thought. The city had the same fearful desperation in the air.

When they reached the church, Rufus, being pagan, did not enter, but waited outside with a young deacon while the others entered. This was larger than the church of Luguvalium, and more finely decorated with paintings and red drapes. Eachna stood apart as Amanda instructed the servants to rest the bier before the altar and asked a sweating, worried-looking priest to watch over her father. He clasped his hands together and rolled his eyes heavenward, and swore that his lips would not cease from prayer until God had delivered them from his fury. Halfway through this declaration he lowered his eyes, and they froze on the door of the church. 'Equestrian,' he said suddenly.

Everyone turned to the door. Eachna saw a tall, thin man standing there. Over his shoulders hung a brown cloak, beneath which he wore a knee-length tunic with a thin red border. His leggings and leather boots were stained with mud from the road. He was old, in his sixties, but began to walk towards them with strong, dignified steps, his shoulders square. A few yards short of the bier he stopped and bowed to Amanda. 'My lady,' he said.

'Most perfect Silvius Fronto,' Amanda replied, dipping her veiled head.

Before Silvius Fronto could speak, the priest came forward, bent low, his hands still clutched to his chest. 'I beg the equestrian's forgiveness, but in the absence of his grace Bishop Martin, I feel obliged to remind him that pagans are not permitted to enter the sacred house of Our Lord.'

Silvius Fronto turned slowly to look at the priest. Eachna had never seen such mournful eyes. '*Pagans?*' he muttered. His ancient voice was low, trembling with anger. *Paganus* meant rustic, a country bumpkin. Eachna had heard many Christians apply it insultingly to those not of the faith, even to noblemen – but never to their faces. 'I was governor of Lugdunensis Tertia,' Silvius Fronto continued. He stepped closer to the priest. 'My son Bonus is a deputy judge at the imperial court. My grandfather was among the foremost nobles of Gallia and stood at the right hand of Gallienus Augustus.' He towered over the priest. 'Tell me again, holy father, that I am a *pagan*.'

'Most perfect equestrian,' the priest said, retreating with short backward steps, 'I meant no disrespect to your noble lineage. My choice of words was regrettable. It is simply the fact that a profane presence . . .'

Silvius Fronto tensed, about to speak, before Amanda stepped in. 'Who is more pleasing in the sight of God, Father Antoninus – the Pharisee who clings to earthly custom, or the man who desires to honour a good Christian soul?'

The priest considered her words for a moment. He smiled painfully, bowed again, and shuffled to the edge of the nave. He waited in silence while Silvius Fronto stood at the foot of the bier.

Eachna could see no obvious sign of grief on the equestrian's face. He did not sob, or dab his eyes, as so many mourners had done in the basilica. No tears glistened in the candlelight. There was stone discipline in his expression, the same dignity Eachna had seen and admired in Amanda. 'Your father and I shared many unkind words,' he said. He glanced at Amanda. 'And an even unkinder silence these last few years. But there was no man I respected more.'

'Your sons are well, I hope?' Amanda asked.

He nodded. 'They thrive.' He stood for a moment longer in silence, watching the face of the corpse, before he turned to leave. He paused before Amanda, and placed a light hand on her shoulder. 'I already spoke to your brother in the council chambers, my lady. Whatever help I can give – it is his.' With a final bow he left the church.

Amanda called to the priest, who scurried over to her. She began speaking to him in a respectful whisper. Eachna could not hear her words, but she saw the priest's head dip and bob nervously as he listened.

She felt a hand touch her arm. 'That was Silvius Fronto,' Patricia said. 'Once upon a time Amanda was meant to marry his son.'

By the time they re-emerged from the church, Rufus and the young deacon were on the street debating what was to be done about the refugees. 'The church is trying to gather food and building materials,' Rufus told Amanda as he saw her. 'The council is allowing a refugee camp to be set up within the walls, in the open public ground at the south end of the city. But the church is short-handed with the bishop away, the militia is busy manning the walls, and the governor is still cowering in the imperial precinct with my father, loading his wagons.'

While Amanda, Rufus and the deacon discussed what should be done, Eachna noticed a family of newcomers passing by in the street. There was a country farmer with a heavy sack slung and fastened over his shoulder, one hand gripping a staff and the other the hand of a young boy. His wife was behind him, carrying a wailing infant in her arms. They were lost and tired and close to despair.

Eachna at once felt their pain, and it pulled her towards them. She crossed the street, came to the woman and offered to take the infant from her. The woman began to weep, but smiled through her tears and thanked Eachna, and handed her the child. Eachna said that she would take them to the south end of the city, where they would be safe and cared for. The father, too, thanked her and blessed her name, and said they would follow her.

At that moment she realised she had lost her sense of direction, and did not know which way was south, let alone how to get to the public land Rufus had mentioned. But Patricia appeared beside her, took the young boy's other hand with a cheerful greeting, and said she would lead the way. Together they set off down the street, Eachna cradling the infant closely to her chest. She looked back at the church, where Amanda was still standing beside Rufus, watching them go.

After talking briefly to the deacon, Amanda returned with Rufus to the basilica. They did not speak. She was thinking irritably of how Eachna had simply walked over to help the peasant family, and then Patricia had followed her, and the pair had disappeared without asking her permission.

That had given her a pang of annoyance. Now that her father was gone, was she not the second most senior figure in the family? Her father's sacrifice and Paul's speech had won over the council and the people, even Silvius Fronto. Once she had feared passing through the streets of this city. Now when the throngs of people watched her pass by, she felt imperious, invincible. It was the aura of her noble blood, the same shield that had defended her mother against the soldiers all those years ago: no more the shy country girl of a year earlier, she was now a woman, and a princess of the Cironii. Yet how was she meant to lead if she was treated as irrelevant by her best friend and her brother's supposed wife?

Rufus stopped when they reached the door of the basilica. He took hold of her hands. 'I'm going to ride to Glevum to see what's happening. You'll be safe here with your brother.'

It dawned on Amanda that Rufus thought he had been valiantly escorting her through the streets of a hostile city. Was he, too, trying to make her seem useless? 'I am the daughter of Cironius Agnus,' she said. 'No one in this city would hurt me.'

He smiled indulgently, infuriatingly. 'I admire your courage, Amanda, but you need to be sensible. My father is still in the city, along with his supporters.'

'They wouldn't dare lay a finger on me,' she said, believing it absolutely. 'Go to Glevum, Agrius Rufus. I'll tell my brother where you've gone.'

She tried to pull her hands from his, but he held her fast. 'Amanda,' he said, a hurt and pleading look in his eyes.

She knew instinctively what he wanted to tell her, but could not: that he was about to ride into danger, that the risk was great, and that she ought to beg for him to stay. But she did not want to play such games. There was too much happening. The door of the basilica awaited her, and within it was Paul, and they needed to decide what to do, for they were the last of the Cironii and no sacrifice would be too great. With a strong tug she freed her hands from Rufus. 'Ride safely.'

He gave a sharp nod. 'I'll be back as soon as I can,' he said, and left her alone on the basilica steps.

He had barely gone five paces before Amanda felt a lurching sickness in her stomach. Even so, she did not call after him and he did not look back. She simply stood and watched until he was lost in the crowd. Then she turned and entered the basilica, and as she walked down the nave she told herself that she was being a fool. He was an experienced soldier and would surely return.

She found Paul and Julian at the far end of the nave. 'Sister,' Paul called when he saw her, and beckoned her over. 'Julian has told me the news about Glevum.'

'Rufus is riding to investigate,' she said.

'By himself? Maybe he's not such a coward after all. I haven't told the council about it yet, though I'll have to soon, before they find out from somewhere else. The last thing we need is some craven saying we should hire the bastards instead of fighting them.'

'So will they fight?'

'I think so. Magistrates Attius and Porcius are with us, at least as long as Silvius Fronto is. The council has lost all faith in the governor and Agrius Leo – they can leave now, it doesn't matter. The path is clear. I'm trying to convince the councillors to muster a full cohort of militia. They knew I was serious when I pledged a thousand acres of land to the city as a sign of our resolve.' He grinned, evidently pleased with his success.

A new sense of united purpose had gripped the city by the middle of the afternoon. Agrius Leo had returned to the governor, and both had remained hidden behind the bolted gates of the imperial precinct all day, along with most of the governor's cohort. Paul had commanded Peter to keep the forum empty of civilians. It would not help, he explained to Amanda, if a mob were allowed to gather. Any physical harm that befell imperial agents, justified or not, would revisit the city a hundredfold when the emperor heard of it. The governor and Agrius Leo must be allowed to leave in peace.

So, when the gates of the precinct finally opened, Agrius Leo and the governor faced no mob, merely Paul, Amanda, and a handful of councillors.

Agrius Leo emerged first, on horseback. Behind him came more mounted men, including the governor, the tribune of the garrison and some senior officials, all thickly wrapped for a long journey. Still within the precinct Amanda could glimpse a host of infantry and lesser clerks on foot, and some mule-drawn carts, all readying impatiently to leave.

Agrius Leo told his companions to hold back while he rode alone to face Paul in the centre of the forum. The sun was by now sinking low in the west, throwing a splash of red across the flagstones, and onto the face of Agrius Leo. Amanda could hardly believe that this was the same man who had welcomed her so charmingly at a party all those months ago. Now there was no charm, no warmth in his features, only hardness. She had wished to see some hint of fear in his eyes, but could not.

'Cironius,' he said as he reined his horse to a stop, looking down at Paul. His voice was flat, emotionless. 'The governor demands passage from the city for himself and for all imperial officials and their families.'

Paul waited for a moment before answering, as though considering it. 'Granted.'

'You do not *grant*,' said Agrius Leo. 'You *obey*. Anyone who attempts to obstruct us will pay with their lives.'

'Why should we wish to obstruct you?'

'Your father may have escaped justice, Cironius, but the emperor will not forget your attempt to harbour him. When we return, you will answer for that crime.'

Paul nodded. Amanda thought she saw him smile. 'It's a long road to Treveris. The barbarians are coming.'

They exchanged no more words. With a turn of his head and a sharp hiss, Agrius Leo summoned the others to follow him. Amanda and Paul stood and watched as he rode towards the forum gates. After him came the governor, then the rest of the mounted men, and the clerks and the imperial garrison on foot. Last of all came Agrius Leo's wife and household, his movable wealth loaded on wagons whose wheels yawned and complained as they trundled through the forum gates. Paul had arranged for some militia to wait outside on the street and escort the column safely out of the city.

Soon afterwards news came that Agrius Leo's deserted town-house had been invaded and ransacked by a mob. The report disturbed Amanda, but Paul refused to condemn it. Agrius Leo's house, he said, was now the property of the citizens, and they could do with it as they liked. Besides, he was occupied once more with the council. Eachna and Patricia were busy assisting the clergy, Rufus had departed for Glevum, her father's body was being tended to in the church, and Amanda was left in the centre of a whirlwind of activity with nothing to do. When she asked Paul if she could help him win more support among the city elite, he laughed. 'It's hard enough getting them to listen to me, never mind a sixteen-year-old girl. Why don't you help Eachna and Patricia with the refugees?'

Nothing appealed to Amanda less. She was not a barbarian or a handmaid of Christ. Such work was beneath her. It would be better if she returned to the townhouse, she said, and Paul did not object, provided she take an escort.

Soon Peter arrived with a carriage and a troop of bucellarii and took her back to the house. After the commotion of the last two days, the place was hauntingly quiet. Fuscina had decided to take her children and household to a friend's house in the city, feeling safer behind its walls. Rufus was long gone. Lucas was still in Londinium, or maybe already sailing to Treveris. Once Peter had returned to Corinium, the building was empty except for Pinta, Celerus and those other servants who had stayed behind, and six guards, the rest of whom had been ordered into the city by Paul to assist the militia.

Pinta brought Amanda some food, which she tried to eat, but she found she had no appetite. She wanted to dictate a letter but did not know who would be able to deliver it, nor even to whom she should send it. She thought of a dozen things that might help keep her mind busy and distracted from the worries that loomed over her. Prayer, reading, weaving, going over the household accounts: none helped for long. She felt like a ship adrift in a storm without rudder or anchor. Several times she imagined going to her father to ask for help, until at one point she even opened the door to his library and had to remind herself that he would not be waiting inside; at that moment her grief, too long suppressed, finally seized her. She quickly entered the dark room, closed the door behind her, sat down with her arms folded on the desk and her head resting on her arms, and did not move from the spot until her tears were exhausted.

Evening was well advanced when there was a knock on the door. Amanda sat up straight, wiped her eyes and smoothed her hair, and said, 'Come in.'

It was Julian, silhouetted against the lamplight of the corridor. 'It's dark in here, cousin. Are you all right?'

'I was just praying,' she said.

He came into the room, closing the door. 'I thought I'd come and find you. We didn't get to talk properly earlier.' He went to the shelf where her father had kept the fuel for his fire, took some kindling and piled it in the standing brazier. He lit it with a fire-steel. The sparks flashed like lightning in the darkness until the kindling caught and a soft, warm glow spread through the room. He carefully added a few lumps of coal and blew until the fire was strong.

Amanda watched him standing at the brazier, holding his hands to the warmth. He was smiling from the pleasant feeling. But Amanda sensed that there was something deeper to his smile: satisfaction of purpose, the pleasure of having direction and conviction at the worst of times. She envied him.

He was still staring at the flames when he spoke. 'It's strange, isn't it, how our paths appear before us? I remember how, a year ago, we were all scattered from one another, distant in space and in spirit. And now here we all are, surrounded by danger, but together.'

'Except my parents,' she said.

'In spirit, they are with us too.'

·

'I wish I could feel their presence as you do.'

'You don't just feel their presence, cousin. You live it. Their spirit is recalled through your words and deeds. If you let them direct your hand now, as they did during life, they will never truly leave the world.'

Amanda did not feel the presence of her father here in his library, where she had so often sat and talked and laughed with him, but his absence. 'I don't know what to do with myself,' she said.

'Come with me back to the city. There are people there who need help.'

'Are Patricia and Eachna still helping?'

'Tirelessly. My sister has changed almost beyond recognition. It's a true wonder to see them bring hope to those who have none – you should see it, Amanda, and you'll see how you can honour your parents better than by sitting alone in a dark room.'

Amanda returned with Julian to the city, entering it on horseback under the first folds of night. Helping refugees was a noble idea, but her trepidation only grew as they neared the southern end of the city and caught the first sights and sounds of the refugee camp. She heard music and singing, saw the flare of campfires in the velvet sky, smelled the smell of cooked meat.

They had barely reached the edge of the camp when they were recognised and a throng quickly gathered around them. One rough-looking peasant took the reins from Amanda with a toothless grin and gave them to his young daughter, who proudly led her mount between the rows of canvas tents and luggage, towards a clearing on the banks of a stream. There was a great bonfire and a crowd of people sitting and standing in groups around it, churchmen carrying steaming bowls of stew and jugs of ale, a group of musicians bringing together their pipes and drums, preparing to play. Amanda saw bearded peasants next to long-cloaked city councillors, laughing and drinking with them like brothers. From the mass of figures emerged Paul, hand in hand with Eachna, with Patricia not far behind.

Paul helped her dismount. 'There you are, sister! We've missed you – here, come and join us; I'll get you some wine. The dancing is about to start.' He took her hand and led her through the crowd. 'Make way there for the daughter of Gaius Cironius Agnus! Make way, make way!' The crowd parted, cheering, as Paul brought her to a log covered by a rug near the bonfire, and beckoned for her to sit. 'You have pride of place, dear Amanda – at least for now, until you are obliged to dance in honour of Father.'

Amanda stiffened. Dancing in the home was one thing, but in public, in front of all these commoners, to their peasant music . . . 'I can't – not here.'

'Of course you can,' said Patricia, putting her arm around Amanda. 'It's the tradition at peasant funeral feasts. I've promised to dance later, and one can't go around breaking promises, so you may as well dance with me.'

Julian, a cup of wine already in his hand, laughed. 'My sister's right, you know. As scripture tells us: *You have turned my mourning into dancing; you took away my sackcloth and clothed me with joy!*'

'Amen,' grinned Paul. 'Sit, Amanda, get yourself warm. The music's about to start. This one's called "the Song of the Owl" – a victory dance!' He took Eachna's hand and led her to the space in front of the fire where dancers were beginning to assemble.

The song started with drums: half a dozen players on drums of different sizes, some strapped over the chest, some set on the ground. From silence sprang a powerful rhythm that Amanda felt through her feet to her chest, that shook the log on which she sat, that awoke a sudden vitality in the air around her. The dancers began to stamp and turn in time to the drums, whooping. The force and volume of the fast, thumping beat was like nothing Amanda had experienced before. Patricia, sitting beside her, laughed with delight.

At that moment a woman's voice broke through the drums with a sharp, high, twisting lament whose words Amanda could barely make out. Her voice was joined by another, then another, until all three voices were dancing through the percussion, feeding from its energy and rising through the flame-licked air into the emerging stars.

The people sang and danced long into the night. Eventually the drummers took a break and a piper played a slower song, which Amanda, emboldened by several cups of wine, judged would offer a good opportunity to dance while allowing her to maintain some dignity. Patricia joined her in the circle, and it was not long before Amanda was enjoying herself. She did not dance again that night, but was happy to sit with Patricia in the warmth of the fire and listen to the music.

Later an elderly woman was brought out from the crowd and urged to tell a story. Amanda did not recognise her, but the people seemed to know who she was. She wore a huge, thick coat that hung about her so fully that Amanda could not tell whether or not she was a hunchback. Her hair was covered by a white headscarf, framing a round, wrinkled and kindly face. She took her place before the fire and when the audience was silent she began her story.

'The Great Mother,' she began slowly, 'possessed a cauldron in which she hoped to create a perfect race of creatures. Every day she would pour a little of her life and wisdom in the cauldron with a silver ladle and stir it. Her consort, Mercury, who was envious of her power, desired to know her secrets and wanted to taste her brew, but she would not let him.

'One night, while the Great Mother was asleep, Mercury sneaked into the kitchen where the cauldron simmered. He took the silver ladle and was about to taste the broth when the Great Mother awoke and realised what he was doing. In her fury she snatched the ladle from him and threw it to the floor, and kicked the cauldron with such anger that it flew from the house and fell from the heavens to earth.

'It landed not far from here, in the place that is still called the Vale of the Vessel; indeed, the great cauldron itself can still be seen, upside down where it fell, as a great mountain. And the Great Mother's potion spilled from the cauldron and flooded the vale, and from its imperfect brew sprung the imperfect race of men. We were born in a moment of greed, envy and anger, and we have carried these flaws with us to every corner of the world.'

When the story was finished and everyone had applauded, Amanda asked Patricia, 'That's the vale of Glevum, isn't it?'

'I believe so. Do you remember the big hill you can see from the top of our garden? People call it the Cauldron. I always wondered why.'

Amanda pictured the view from Patricia's garden across the vale, in the middle of which rose the great wooded hill, rounded and bowl-like. Her next thought was that Rufus would have seen that hill when he approached Glevum. She prayed that he had been careful and had found safe lodgings in the city.

As she was distracted by these troubling thoughts, her gaze fell absently on Paul and Eachna, who were standing together a short distance away, just outside the circle of firelight. Patricia leaned close and said, 'Your new sister-in-law is a strange and noble girl, did you know that?'

Amanda, who had not realised she had been staring, quickly looked away from the couple. 'I'm sure she is,' she said.

'I asked her if she was of noble birth, but she swears her parents were just ordinary fisherfolk. She was taken from them when she was just a little girl. It's such an awful thought. Can you imagine? She's suffered so much. I could tell she didn't want to talk about it, but you can see it in her eyes.'

'Why did you think she was noble?'

'Can't you see it? It's just in the way she looks at you.'

'With contempt, in my case.'

'Oh, really, cousin!' Patricia said, nudging Amanda in the side. 'She's intimidated by you, that's all. Try to think how strange all this is to her. Paul is all she has, and they've hardly had a moment together since they came back. Ignore my opinion if you like, but you should trust his.'

Amanda looked back at Paul and Eachna. They were standing closer to the fire now, Eachna in front, Paul behind, with his arms wrapped tightly around her and his cheek resting on her hair. They looked into the flames, the same quiet, content expression on their faces, oblivious to the music and laughter around them. In that moment of peace Amanda could see what they had found in each other. She would give anything to have Rufus here, holding her as Paul was holding Eachna.

After a short while she saw magistrate Porcius approach Paul and apologetically draw him away, leaving Eachna standing alone. A nearby deacon was refilling cups from a jug, so Amanda took her mug and Patricia's, let the deacon pour honeyed wine into them, and went to Eachna. She offered her one of the mugs, and Eachna smiled shyly and accepted it.

'I hoped tomorrow I might help you and Patricia,' Amanda said. 'With the refugees.'

Rufus returned from Glevum the following day, having ridden since dawn. Late in the morning Paul met him in the study of the townhouse. Rufus confirmed the earlier report: the council of Glevum had made a deal with the Attacotti, offering them money, land and horses if they did not ravage their personal estates. They were expected to arrive and make camp south of the city within three days.

'I have an idea,' Rufus said. 'There should still be a heavy cavalry training unit based near Viriconium. I trained as an officer with them myself.'

That had been when he witnessed Paul get drafted. 'What of them?'

'The duke might not have called them for the campaign. If I take the military road north, I can be there in three days. I know the training commander. I can try to bring him south.'

'How many soldiers?'

'That depends on the training rotation, but normally a full squadron, thirty men. I know it's not many, but they're ironclads. They'd make a difference.'

Paul did not need long to think it over. He told Rufus to do what he could, and return south as quickly as possible. Time was running out. The longer the Attacotti had to settle outside Glevum, the harder they would be to remove. Rufus had told him that they were from two Irish tribes, the Déisi and the Uí Liatháin, and numbered at least fifteen hundred men in fifty boats: not raiders, but an invading army. To make matters worse, they had been joined by King Keocher's feared son Talorg and his Pictish warband. Paul had received that news in grim silence. Prince Talorg had been responsible for the ambush in which Victor had died.

After talking the news over with Alypius, Paul took it to the tribune of the militia and the city magistrates, tactfully reducing the number of invaders to one thousand and not mentioning Prince Talorg.

They reacted as Alypius had predicted. Glevum was an old military colony, and many of its councillors were veterans: if they had given the barbarians safe haven, Porcius and Attius lamented, what chance did Corinium have? The city council, drafting every last veteran and reserve militiaman they could find, had raised only four hundred men, and they might add to that a few score bucellarii, plus whatever volunteers they could gather from the refugees, mostly hunters with their bows or slings. The men of the Twentieth who were normally billeted in the southern cities were lying dead in some Pictish valley; the governor had taken what remained of the imperial garrison when he left; and the small towns of the province would be in just as poor a state and would not send aid. They could perhaps protect Corinium if they stayed within its walls, or tried to pay the barbarians off – but there was no question of meeting Attacotti warriors in the field.

Paul waited until they fell silent. 'Gentlemen,' he said, 'that isn't good enough. If we coop ourselves up in the city we'd be giving the barbarians licence to roam at will. I doubt you want to see your estates in flames any more than I do mine.' He glanced at Alypius, standing at the side of the room, who gave him an approving nod.

The tribune in command of the militia, a stout, square-faced veteran named Belator, scoffed. 'Then what do you suggest? Are you going to conjure up another cohort with a fine speech?'

'I can do better than that. As we speak, Agrius Rufus is riding north to locate a cavalry detachment near Viriconium. He's going to bring them south to liberate Glevum.'

'How many?'

'A half-wing of ironclads.'

The effect of this news was immediate on the councillors. Magistrate Porcius spoke up. 'When will they arrive?'

'A week from now,' said Paul. 'We'll meet him in the Vale of the Vessel, combine our forces, and drive the savages back into the sea.'

By the time the meeting was over, Paul had just about managed to keep their support, and they had agreed to appoint him prae-positus, the acting commander of the city militia and whatever other forces he could gather. He left the basilica with Alypius and they stood for a while on the street outside, watching the morning bustle of the city. People were heading to or from the markets, which were open and even busier than usual. Yesterday the council had issued a price edict to prevent extortion by unscrupulous traders, and it seemed to have worked. The butchers in the slaughteryards had their hands full; many herds of sheep, goats and cattle had been brought into the city, too many for the amount of grazing available, and there were many mouths to feed. Paul himself had bought fifteen head of cattle from a refugee farmer and donated them to the church as food for the needy. Fewer animals would be good, he thought, as he looked down the street and saw how much manure they had left while being brought through the town.

Alypius wrinkled his nose at the stench. 'The sanitation officer and the treasury clerks spent half an hour yesterday arguing over who should pay for all this to be cleaned up.'

'Did they reach a decision?'

'They had to end the meeting. The smell from outside was too bad.'

Paul laughed, but he could believe it. If these councillors could not organise themselves to shovel up shit from their own doorstep, they would not stay united for long. Paul had said they would meet the savages in battle in a week because he did not believe he could hold their support much longer than that. In truth, his confidence had been nothing but bluster. In the general chaos Rufus would be lucky to find any ironclads near Viriconium, and luckier still if they agreed to come to the aid of Corinium. Furthermore, he had mentioned only a single squadron – thirty men, not the two hundred and fifty of a half-wing. In the meeting Paul had not thought, merely asserted what he wanted to believe, and only now did the realisation of what he had done begin to dawn on him.

One week from now they would meet the barbarians in battle, and Paul had no idea how they would win.

XXIX

Look, an army is coming from the land of the north; a great
nation is being stirred up from the ends of the earth. They are
armed with bow and spear; they are cruel and show no mercy.
Jeremiah 6:22–23

The following week brought heavy rain, but still no Rufus,
and no reinforcements. The council had agreed to send out
riders, as many men and horses as could be spared, in every
direction, bearing documents sealed by the magistrates that
commanded all military forces to gather at Corinium. It was a
desperate move, and a hopeless one, since so few regulars were
left in the cities and small towns of the province; any regular
troops that remained would be found at the imperial tax depot
of Cunetio to the south or the saltworks of Salinae to the north,
but they would never leave their posts at the command of civil
magistrates who had no authority over them. Any local militias,
meanwhile, would not want to leave their own homes and
families.

Paul knew all this, and had admitted it to the council, but he
nonetheless argued that it would do no harm to try. Magistrates
Attius and Porcius reluctantly set their seal to the letters not
because Paul had convinced them that the situation was desperate,
but because he had convinced them it was not. Agrius Rufus
would bring enough troops to ensure victory, Paul had said, and
Alypius had instructed him carefully how he should say it. The
word of Silvius Fronto had also counted for much. Paul liked
the honourable old equestrian, despite the evils his father Bassalus

had committed against the Cironii fourteen years ago. Fronto had not been involved in that conspiracy, it was clear; he had not even known of it until Paul's father had confronted him with the proof. Such was his old-fashioned sense of patrician honour that Fronto had accepted the shame as though it were his own. Towards Paul he now behaved with respect, quietly offering his aid, supporting him before the council.

When not pestering the council for more money or rations, Paul spent every waking moment of that week working with Belator, the tribune of the militia, to drill and equip the few fighting men they had. They had managed to gather the four hundred militia from the city, along with some two hundred bucellarii, more than Paul had hoped for, recruited from Silvius Fronto and the other noble families. The refugees had supplied a couple of hundred more men, mostly archers and slingers, and they had some light horses for scouting, though none trained for war. It was a ragtag force, but morale was high; each man had taken an oath to Paul as the appointed general of the city. They believed in him, and he believed they would stand their ground.

At noon on the seventh day after his father's funeral Paul was standing on the bare-turf crest of a hill overlooking the Vale of the Vessel. Off to his right lay the city of Glevum; to the left, the wide, silvery sheen of the Sabrina estuary as it stretched towards the sea; and directly ahead, some two miles distant, was a low rise that steamed with the smoke of a hundred cooking fires. Behind the rise, along a stretch of the river, Paul could just make out a forest of boat masts. The barbarians had arrived.

Tribune Belator was standing beside him, surveying the tactical situation with the sharp eye of an experienced soldier. A week ago Belator, who had a wife and a brood of children in Corinium, had seemed at home among the tidy, clean-faced figures of the city council. At first he had sided with them against Paul, grumbling when they grumbled, withdrawing with them to whisper in the shadowy corners of the basilica. But days of drilling the militia in the fields outside the city had awoken something in him; he had shrugged off the complacent habits of his retirement post like a man climbing from the cosy blankets of his bed. He seemed, slowly, to be recognising some value in Paul as a soldier. Paul in turn was glad to have found another precious ally in the city.

'We can't win,' said Belator. 'Unless Agrius Leo's boy turns up with those ironclads, we haven't got a chance. They're clean over a thousand, judging from the size of that camp; nearer fifteen hundred, I'd say. And the Attacotti are born warriors.'

'So we're fewer,' said Paul. 'Numbers alone don't win battles. We know the country, they don't.' He pointed at Glevum. 'And right over there is another city militia, if we can get it to come out.'

'We already sent a messenger. They wouldn't even open the gates for him.'

'Maybe not, but my uncle's one of the councillors, and never in a thousand years would he back down without a fight.'

Belator snorted. He and Paul had already discussed the decision of the Glevum council to negotiate with the invaders, and Belator had made no secret of his contempt. Glevum prided itself on its military origins; once a year the city councillors paraded through the streets bearing the original foundation charter, and in its presence renewed their oaths to the emperor. Belator seemed to find it perversely delightful that the tough-talking council of the old colonia had baulked at the first chance in years for a real fight.

'This is the plan,' said Paul. 'See the hill the Attacotti are camped on – you see the bottom of the slope? The ground there always floods after heavy rain. But in the centre there's a ridge of higher ground, a causeway a couple of hundred yards wide – you see? On either side it'll be an ankle-deep bog; a man can't fight in that. If we can draw them down this side of the hill and meet them on the causeway, their line will be squeezed onto the dry ground, and they'll have to face us on a narrow front. They won't be able to flank us.'

'Assuming they don't decide to just wait on the hill,' said Belator. He did not sound convinced. 'So we approach this end of the causeway, form our line, and they come down, outnumbering us two to one. Then what?'

'We kill them.'

Belator laughed. He looked across at Paul, grinning. 'The best plans are the simplest ones, eh?'

'It might be months before the emperor can send help. We have to face the barbarians now, before any more arrive. For all we know there could be another twenty ships coming up the river. If they get that kind of foothold at Glevum we'll never be rid of them. Put up enough of a fight now, they'll think twice about landing here again.'

'If you say so.'

Belator walked back to the camp on the other side of the hill. Paul stood alone for a while, his eyes fixed on the enemy. It would be a savage fight, whoever won. He was no longer worried about the tribune's loyalty or courage. He recognised Belator's fatalism for what it was: the grim acceptance of a soldier who was ready to die for his cause. The feeling took him back to Mediobogdum, to a silent moment in Drogo's briefing the day before the final battle, when his officers, without a single word or gesture, had made a shared pledge to defend the fort to the death.

Paul and Eachna had been spared that fate. Eachna was now safe in Corinium with Amanda and Patricia, but for Paul there would be no escape – unless Rufus had found more troops than even Paul hoped for.

Rufus finally arrived late in the afternoon. Paul was in his tent with Julian, whom he had appointed his secretary, and Alypius, whose contacts and organisational skills now served him well as marshal. Unsurprisingly, Silvius Fronto and the other tribal nobles who had given Paul detachments of bucellarii had chosen to remain safely behind the walls of Corinium. Paul was going through the rosters when he heard the deep blast of a horn, and he quickly left the tent, followed by Julian and Alypius. In the centre of the camp they saw Rufus appear at the head of a column of ironclads. The cavalry came at a thunderous trot into the open area in the centre of the camp, the terrible bulk of the broad-chested chargers filling the space. They were in full battle dress; their great iron-tipped lances, twice as tall as a man, fastened to rider and mount by heavy clinking chains. Men from the militia gathered around them as the riders pulled into disciplined ranks.

Rufus jumped from his saddle and came over. Paul grasped his arm in greeting. 'By God, I'm glad to see you.' At that moment, carried on a swell of relief, he felt his last doubts about Rufus dissolve. 'Where did you find them?'

'North of the saltworks,' said Rufus, still out of breath. 'Two squadrons from my very first unit; rookies, but ready to fight. Rode like bastards to get here. We armoured up and had to leave everything else behind.'

'What about the troops at the saltworks?'

'Deserted. No trace of them.'

The dark-skinned junior officer of the cavalry unit had dismounted and was approaching them. He saluted Paul. 'Most esteemed senator, Centenarius Xobas reports that the third and fourth squadrons of Morbian cataphracts are fit and ready for duty.'

'Who's your commander, Xobas?'

The officer looked almost surprised at the question. 'You are, senator. The last orders we had were ten days ago, to wait for the fleet to take us north from Deva. But then the duke was killed and we heard the fleet was burned at Luguvalium, so I decided to bring my men back to the training camp to regroup.'

'There's no chain of command at all?'

'It's chaos. Half the frontier garrisons have deserted. The care-taker garrison at Deva was about to mutiny before we left. I'm only glad you managed to find us.'

After instructing Julian and Alypius to help Xobas make camp on the east slope of the hill, Paul took Rufus to the crest to discuss strategy. Rufus listened, nodded, and when Paul had finished he stared sceptically at the enemy camp. 'Even two squadrons of ironclads won't do much against so many.'

'They'll make a difference. They're exactly what the men needed to see, and the last thing the barbarians expect. When we advance I want you to bring them around the right flank, right under the walls of Glevum. Let the city get a good look at you. It might just convince them to stick their necks out. Then you continue around and hit the barbarians in the rear.'

'If the Attacotti see us coming, they'll stay on their hill.'

'So stick close to the treeline, and don't start to flank until we've already drawn them down to the causeway. We'll keep them busy until you've managed to get into position. Believe me, when the ironclads slam into the back of them, they won't have time to count how many you are. We need the shock to break them, like a hammer.'

Rufus ran his eyes over the terrain. 'These horses aren't bred for speed. We'd need half an hour at least. Can you hold the line that long?'

Paul saw the battle play out before his eyes. He could almost hear the faraway riot of the battle on the causeway, see the wide sweep of the cavalry as they flanked by the city, crossed the hill and struck the Attacotti in the rear. The plan depended on drawing every last barbarian down to the low ground. They would be tough, savage, ready for a fight. If the Britons were to hold the line long enough, it would have to be through sheer courage and discipline, not strength. 'We can hold it.'

Paul and Rufus had barely returned to camp when Julian announced the approach of a rider from the enemy camp. 'Go and make sure the ironclads are well hidden by the trees,' Paul told Rufus. 'We don't want any of their scouts spotting them.'

Paul rode with Julian and two bucellarii down the slope to intercept the approaching figure at the base of the hill. They stopped as soon as they were close enough to talk. 'Announce yourself!' Paul called.

The visitor was wearing a long cloak of animal hide. On his bare arms he had a number of tightly wound golden torcs, which betrayed him as a man of substance. His hair was long and flowing in the Irish style, and his beard knotted. His mount snorted and stamped unhappily as he tried to hold it steady; it was clearly unfamiliar with him – stolen, no doubt, from one of the villa estates nearby. 'I bring a message from my lord King Ailill Tassach of the Uí Liatháin, vassal of King Crimmthan Már mac Fidaig, and from Prince Talorg mac Keocher of the Picts. To whom do I speak?'

The messenger had spoken in Latin, and Paul replied in the same tongue. 'My name is Cironius Agnus Paulus, prince of the Dobunni, senator of Rome, son of Cironius Agnus and acting commander of the garrison of Corinium. Stranger, you and your lords are unwelcome here.'

Even from this distance Paul could make out the rider's amused grin. 'The lords of Glevum have made us feel very welcome so far! My king has no desire to shed your blood, Cironius Agnus Paulus of the Dobunni. Fifty pounds of gold and fifty good steeds will buy our friendship.'

'I think you value your friendship too highly, barbarian.'

'That is my king's offer,' said the rider. 'My lords are generous. They reward their friends well. You should think of your own future, and consider that.'

'You can take this message back to your lords: if they want to buy this land fairly, they can.'

'Very well. Your price?'

'One hundred Attacotti heads for every inch of ground.'

The messenger's smile had faded. 'Take counsel with older and wiser men, Cironius Agnus Paulus, and send my king an envoy tomorrow morning. He will not be harmed.' With that, he tugged on his reins, spun his horse about and cantered briskly across the scrub fields to his own camp.

'We're lucky the magistrates aren't here,' said Julian as he and Paul rode together back up the hill. 'If they knew how many barbarians we were facing, they'd sell their own daughters for peace.'

'We have to make a stand,' Paul said. Speaking to the messenger had only increased his resolution. 'If we give them gold and horses now, they'll just want more. Soon we'd be their slaves.'

Rufus was waiting for them at the camp. 'What news?'

'Tomorrow morning we fight.' They walked together to Paul's

tent, where Paul sat on the tree stump that was serving as his chair. He pulled off one leather boot. Somehow a pebble had worked its way inside and was irritating him immensely.

Rufus stood in the eaves of the entrance. 'Did they offer terms?'

'Yes,' said Julian. 'Slavery versus death. Paul chose for all of us.'

'Good,' said Rufus quietly.

Paul tugged his boot back on and looked at his cousin. 'Julian, tomorrow I want you and Alypius to stay up here and watch the battle. The moment it looks like things are going against us, ride back to Corinium. Take Amanda and Eachna to my cousins in Calleva with as much gold and silver as you can carry.'

'I will. But if Corinium surrenders, you know Calleva will be next.'

'Then take them to my aunt in Durovernum, and then to Gallia if you have to. Somewhere will always be safe.'

Julian and Rufus stood in silence for a while, and Paul remained seated. Each was lost in his own thoughts. When Rufus next looked at Paul, he said, 'You've been in battles before?'

'Aside from that one in Londinium market, when I broke your nose?'

Paul did not know why he said that. He wanted to see how Rufus reacted, perhaps. He was pleased that Rufus smiled, if awkwardly. 'I mean proper battles.'

'Yes. You?'

'No. I joined the cavalry a couple of years after the last Pictish war ended. Eventually I requested a transfer to Gallia to see some action.' He rubbed his leg. 'I was mobilised against the Alemanni last year, but my horse slipped crossing a stream.'

'Are you sure you're strong enough to ride?'

Rufus was squinting against the deepening red glare of the sun, and did not hear the question, or at least did not answer.

Paul rose. 'Let's gather the men.'

Giving the speech was the easy part. Paul had spent enough time in the ranks to know what manner of words stirred the hearts of soldiers. The army had assembled on the peak of the hawthorn-crested hill, pressed shoulder to shoulder, and by the time they had been stilled by the drone of the general's salute played on the long, curving horn known as the buccina, the horizon was a black ridge before the furnace of the heavens. Before this fire stood Paul, whose shadow played across their faces as they watched him pace the knoll. Down in the vale they saw the muted lump of the hill where the invaders waited, lost in the cool grey blur of twilight, and could count the flickering pin-pricks of their campfires, like a reflection of the emerging stars, and know that each fire might warm a dozen men. When he had completed his speech the men clashed swords on shields, lifted their standards, which were topped with the open-mouthed heads of dragons, and cried his name – not the name of the city, as he had expected, or the name of the emperor, but the name of the Cironii.

Paul had known good leadership and bad. He had thought that somehow the feeling of a great commander would come over him with the cheers of his men, blooming and spreading its branches like a well-fed plant. But he walked the camp that evening with Rufus and Belator and felt like an imposter, in a way that he had not when giving the speech. Most of the men in the militia were far older than him. Wary of appearing presumptuous, beneath his armour he had chosen to wear the uniform of his senatorial rank, the red tunic with embroidered borders and roundels, rather than full military uniform. They greeted him as their general, yet sometimes when he was speaking to them moments came, brief and intense, when he felt as though he were standing outside himself, drawn out by some greater power, and made to stand and look at the scene like a stranger. And even as he felt his mouth move and heard words come out, and saw the listeners smile or nod or laugh, he wondered how it had happened that he was to lead an army into battle with the next sunrise.

They walked the camp, visiting the militia, the archers, and the bucellarii of the rival noble houses who had found their own way to come together against the greater foe and now sat side by side around the same cooking fires, and the cavalry in the field below. Paul had deliberately invoked no god in his speech, leaving it to each man to call upon divine aid in whichever way he saw fit. He saw Julian leading a group of Christian soldiers in prayer, and other huddles of men offering sacrifices to Mars, Nodens or the Great Mother in whose vale they would fight, and heard the arcane mutterings of Mithraists. He asked Belator if he intended to pray. The old tribune said he preferred not to attract the attention of the gods before a battle, just in case they were unhappy with him. Rufus, Paul was pleased to learn, followed no religion but the old-fashioned cult of the emperor. 'I'm here when the gods want me,' he said. 'They've ignored me so far, so I ignore them.'

After Belator had gone to his tent to sleep, Paul and Rufus continued the circuit of the sentries and watch commanders. They took a torch with them since it was now past sunset, and they spoke loudly to one another so the nervous guards should not be surprised by their approach. Paul had the strange light-headed feeling of being drunk, though he had not taken any alcohol.

By the time they had finished their rounds the camp was quiet and still. Julian and Alypius had already retired. Most of the men had gone to their beds either to sleep or to spend the night staring into the black void of a canvas roof. Those who remained sitting around the campfires were older – some of the city militia Paul knew to be retired regulars who had been unable or unwilling to live on the meagre scraps of land they had been awarded at discharge. Several, Belator included, were old enough to have fought during the great Winter War of Emperor Constans more than twenty-five years ago. Paul was depending on them, and they knew it. Perhaps they were not as strong or as fast as they once had been, but they were the clamps that would hold together the front line, the ones who would keep men fighting who would otherwise flee.

Paul and Rufus returned to the centre of the camp. 'Do you have a place to sleep?' Paul asked.

'With the ironclads,' Rufus said, nodding to the lower field.

Paul was about to say good night, but there was something

else he needed to say that he had put off for as long as he could. 'I don't want you to lead the charge tomorrow.'

'But the men—'

'Lead them into position at the enemy's rear. If all goes to plan, hold back with a small guard when they charge.'

'Why? I can't afford to hold back. We're few enough as it is.'

'If the attack fails you're to ride to Corinium with Julian and Alypius.'

Rufus was staring at him, baffled and angry. 'Cironius, do you doubt I can fight?'

'First, I don't know if you're strong enough yet. Second, at least one of us needs to survive. If I fall and Belator falls, you need to take command of the remaining garrison and protect the city.' Rufus said nothing. Paul could see the frustration in his eyes. After days on the road seeking allies, every waking moment obsessed with defending the city, after finding the cavalry like a gift from the gods and racing to lead them to battle just in time, of course it was difficult to let go. 'This isn't about glory and heroism,' Paul said. 'It's about strategy. You've proven you can be trusted. Isn't that what you wanted? I need someone of your status in the city. Alypius can help with the council, but he can't command soldiers, and nor can Julian. Lucas must have sailed for Gallia, or he'd have returned to us by now.'

'The captain of your bucellarii, Peter – he's a good leader.'

'A freedman, like Alypius.'

'But I'm not even from your tribe. You think they'll trust me after what my father did?'

'You've already shown you're not your father. Silvius Fronto will vouch for you. And if the council doesn't listen – *especially* if they don't listen – I still need someone who can protect my family with the sword.'

Paul could see his words beginning to take effect. What he said was true, but what he had not said was also true: should Rufus avoid the battle and return to Corinium, he would be reunited with Amanda. Paul understood what Rufus must be feeling at this moment, for he was feeling the same. He would have given almost anything to escape death and return to Eachna, but honour forbade him. For a commander it was not a possibility, but for Rufus it was. The least Paul could do, after so many years away, was try to preserve the happiness of his sister. 'If it makes it easier,' he said, 'I could demand that you swear an oath not to join the charge tomorrow.'

Rufus nodded. Paul held out his hand. On one finger he wore the seal ring of the Cironii. Rufus knelt before him, took his hand, and kissed the ring. 'I swear,' he said. Then he rose, bowed briefly, and left.

Paul dreamed that night of battle and defeat. He awoke in his tent, covered in a skin blanket on the ground, glad to find himself shivering and alive, with the pale grey of morning hurting his eyes. The dream lingered like a sour taste. He did not believe that dreams foretold the future, and he let the vague memories of sleep dissipate like threads of gossamer. The day was solid and real, and lay before him; nothing was decided. A dream meant nothing.

He rose from the ground and stretched his stiff limbs. He had slept wearing his boots and mail shirt, with his sword at his side in case the enemy tried a night attack, and so he needed only pull on his cloak and helmet before he left his tent to test the morning air.

He walked to the crest of the hill, nodding to the sentry, and relieved himself in the brambles. The first rays of sun were peering over the shoulder of the hills behind him, touching the silvery mist of the vale with gold. The conditions were good. The low-lying mist would help cloak the deployment of the cavalry and muffle the sound of their approach. The grass shimmered with dew, but the earth beneath was firm and dry, good for holding ground against a charge. And when the mist cleared they would be fighting with the sun low behind them, which meant it would be in the enemy's eyes. All of this was good, but none of it would win the battle.

The rest of the camp was soon awake, roused by the biarchi. Paul had given the order that each squad should light not one but two cooking fires at breakfast, and should use damp leaves that would smoke well. With luck these fires would be counted by the enemy, who would thus overestimate their numbers and bring every man they had to the fight. Any men left in the enemy camp would be a stumbling block for Rufus and the cavalry.

'Good morning, senator,' Belator said, ambling towards Paul with a smoked fish in his hand. He tore the fish in two and gave one half to Paul.

'Morning, tribune. Any trouble during the night?'

'None reported.'

'Good. If they didn't try to infiltrate us, they must be sure of themselves.'

'Or maybe they did, and we just didn't spot them.'

'Ever the optimist,' said Paul with a wry grin. Belator laughed.

The moments of that morning seemed to carry Paul along with a life of their own: a tapestry of sights, smells and noises, energetic and vivid, as he oversaw the assembly of the cobbled-together centuries, inspected the leather straps of their helmets, the edge of their blades and the fighting spirit in their voices. He convened a war council with Rufus, Julian, Alypius, Belator and the centenarii, and was surprised to see his own confidence reflected in their eyes. Whatever fears had surfaced in his sleep were long buried. He had not felt like this since charging from the gates of Mediobogdum, when he had been seized by such exhilaration, such singularity of purpose, that thoughts of surrender or retreat had faded into another universe.

An hour later, with Paul leading on foot, eight hundred men sank into the mist of the vale. As the fog swirled thicker around them Paul realised how easy it would have been to lose orientation had he not sent ahead scouts, hunters who knew this corner of the country well, to plot out the mile-long march to the causeway and guide them in. When the sun rose higher the mist would quickly burn off, but for now it was good; it cloaked their advance and obscured their numbers.

Eventually the final scout emerged from the mist ahead, running hunched along the front of the marching line, looking for Paul. 'Senator, this is the start of the causeway. Some of our best slingers are hidden in the marshes, as you ordered.'

'Good. You've done well. Now go up the causeway and keep watch for the enemy.' The hunter nodded and disappeared into the mist. Paul raised his right arm and called for the advance to halt. His command was echoed down the line in either direction. He nodded for Belator to call the archers forward, and they quickly settled into a skirmishing formation in front of the battle line. He had instructed them to harass the enemy as they approached, aided by the slinger marksmen who were now perched in the branches of trees in the waterlogged fields on either side of the causeway.

'Awaiting the senator's order,' said Belator. The cornicen stood next to them with his brass buccina. A single horn blast would signal for Rufus to begin his flanking manoeuvre. Then it would be a matter of holding the causeway until the cavalry were in position.

The triple battle line was an army of ghostly statues, its far flanks still invisible to Paul. The dragon-head standard of the city militia, its tail hanging limp, stared into the mist with a silent, frozen snarl, beads of condensation on its snout. Paul peered into the grey soup before them. It had begun to lighten, but it was still too thick. They needed visibility of two hundred yards to make full use of the frontal archers, and to allow the slingers hidden in the marshes to cover the width of the causeway. But he knew they could not afford to linger for long. Somewhere out there waited the savages. They would have seen Paul leading his army down into the vale, and were surely also making ready for battle, expecting him to come to them. He had no intention of doing that. Any chance of victory, slight though it was, depended on luring the Attacotti down to the causeway.

Paul sensed the impatience for action behind him. His men were ready to fight. Soon the damp chill would set in and sap their energy.

He closed his eyes and breathed in slowly. *Let us fight well*, he prayed, even though he knew his prayer went unheard.

The scout reappeared from the mist. 'Senator, they're coming!'

Paul felt relief and fear at once. He unsheathed his sword and held it high. Moments later the buccina sounded behind him. In the stillness of the air it seemed even louder than normal. The long, low blast carried deep into the fog. Paul's eardrums throbbed as it resonated in his helmet, and his heart, woken into new life, began to thump. He stepped back into the front rank beside Belator while the cornicen and standard-bearer retreated to the rear. Centenarii and biarchi yelled orders down the line; archers notched their arrows; shields were locked, swords readied in the front rank and spears in the second.

They waited. Slowly the mist continued to clear, but still not enough. Patches of blue sky appeared overhead, and grass was beginning to shimmer in the dull light of the sun.

A man in the front rank coughed and Belator hissed for silence. He turned his head. 'I hear something.'

Paul strained to listen. At first it was difficult to hear through the padding of his helmet, which half muffled his ears. But then he caught it: a distant cry of alarm, coming faintly through the fog. Then he heard another. The barbarians were advancing and the hidden marksmen were picking away at their flanks. They could not be very accurate in these conditions, but with the enemy bunched up on the dry causeway they did not have to be.

A faint shadow emerged in the distance. As it approached it took on the form of a shuffling, bristling mass of half-naked savages. 'Ready!' Paul shouted. 'Archers, three volleys! Front rank, ready darts!'

The archers quickly loosed their arrows and the enemy began to charge. The mass became sharper, more solid, each man more distinct; their battle cry, an indistinct roar in a savage tongue, rolled before them across the open grass of the causeway. After three hurried volleys the archers hastened through the battle lines to the rear, and the lead-weighted darts of the front rank, flung underarm, rained down on the attackers with deadly effect. Barbarians were struck and tumbled to the ground, but the charge did not slow. The first rank reformed its shield wall. Moments later the charge struck home.

This was the first test. The shield wall must not break. Here in the centre of the line Paul was surrounded by Belator and the most experienced men of the militia. They knew how to take a charge, how to absorb the impact with their shoulders and legs, how to crouch and angle the shield so it deflected the force upwards and exposed the attacker to a sudden spear thrust from the second rank; but all this had to be done with precise timing by each man, and even as Paul felt the trained, deadly reflex of Belator and the veterans, and heard the anguished cries of the first barbarians to strike them, he feared that the rest of the line would not be able to hold. But he shut out that thought. From the moment weapons clashed the outcome of the fight was beyond his control.

They lost no ground to the first, disorganised charge. Those attackers who had fallen had already been replaced, and continued to press on the front rank in a chaotic storm of blades and bodies. Paul could hear nothing except the din of metal and wood and indiscernible cries. He did not have time to look far beyond the rim of his shield or the point of his sword, no chance to judge the size of the enemy attack except to feel that an endless horde was forming from the mist and trying to trample him into the earth. But these Attacotti had little experience fighting against a Roman shield wall, and were slow to learn that the first two ranks fought together. Valiant as they were, time after time the attackers were caught by an unexpected spear thrust from above, or by the savage sweep of a sword from below, which sliced into their unprotected legs and brought them writhing and helpless to the ground. The earth soon steamed with their blood. Paul lost all sense of time.

Suddenly the pressure was released and the sound of battle faded, leaving a ringing in Paul's ears, and he saw that the enemy was falling back along the entire front. The command to hold position ran down through the ranks. Paul saw a biarchus dragging a soldier who had tried to give chase back into the battle line.

Most of the mist had now lifted, enough that Paul could see across the entire width of the causeway, and several hundred yards down it. The barbarians had taken heavy casualties in their first attack. A few bodies were scattered where they had fallen to arrows and darts, and more were stretched along the battle line. Half a dozen corpses lay heaped on the ground before Paul and his neighbours. He looked quickly at the breathless men around him. Belator was blood-smeared but alive; the master of standards, who had been fighting on Paul's other side, was nowhere to be seen and must have fallen. Two other badly injured men were being carried to the rear. But here, at least, the shield wall had stood firm.

Behind the battle line a mounted messenger came at a gallop from the left flank. Paul called out to him. 'Report, soldier!'

'The left flank holds, senator. Centenarius Gavo reports thirty men lost. On the right flank Centenarius Senecio reports twenty-five men lost.'

'Where's my primicerius?' called Belator. 'Veda! Report!'

Belator's second-in-command pushed his way through the ranks towards them. 'Forty-one dead and injured, tribune, including Doccius.'

'That's almost a hundred men down in the first attack,' said Belator.

Paul's fears had been proved right. The disciplined centre of the city militia had kept the line from breaking, but the flanks, where he had deployed the paramilitary units formed from the bucellarii, were no match for the Attacotti warriors. With those losses it was a miracle they had stood their ground. He turned to Belator. 'We need to redeploy some militia on the flanks.'

'That'll stretch our line too thin.'

Paul knew they needed to hold a fighting front until the iron-clads were in position – but when would that be? It had surely been more than half an hour already. Rufus should be in position by now. 'We have no choice. If we let them outflank us, it's over.'

Belator nodded. 'As you wish, senator. Veda – have Losio send half his century to each flank. Tell him to send his best men to the left.'

The barbarians had withdrawn back into the haze. No doubt they had been given a shock, but they would soon be back. Paul made use of the pause to walk down the battle line with Belator, encouraging the centenarii and their men, and saw for himself how badly some sections had suffered. Men with hastily dressed injuries had returned to the front line, determined to fight on. Several soldiers were moving between the fallen barbarians, checking for any still living and despatching them, while others were removing the British dead and dying from the line and carrying them to the rear. Behind the right flank Paul saw the bodies of bucellarii laid out on the ground, some wearing the blood-stained livery of his family.

A messenger came running from the centre. 'Senator, there's a rider out in front. He wants to talk with you, alone.'

Paul nodded grimly. He returned to the centre and saw the rider, a pale figure in the mist some hundred yards distant. 'Wait here,' he told his men, and walked out alone into the battlefield.

The messenger was the same man to whom he had spoken yesterday. He saw Paul approach, touched a clenched fist to his chest, and said, 'Senator Cironius Agnus Paulus of the Dobunni, King Ailill Tassach sends his respects. He offers you a final chance to prove yourself a man of peace.'

'Remind your king that no honourable man is a man of peace when his country is invaded.'

'Withdraw, Roman, and he swears not to violate your lands or the lands of Corinium.'

'Never.'

The messenger almost laughed in exasperation. 'Roman, you cannot win.' He twisted in his saddle and shouted a few words in Irish back to his own lines. Presently three figures emerged on foot from the fog. Paul saw that they were a pair of Attacotti warriors leading a bound, struggling captive between them.

It was Rufus. He had been stripped of his armour and helmet and was covered from head to toe in mud, but he looked otherwise unharmed. They brought him up to the messenger.

'We found him in a bog. My king offers you his life in return for your surrender.'

Rufus was staring directly at Paul. He shook his head slowly. Paul said, 'No.'

'Very well.' The envoy jumped from his horse and barked a command at the two warriors, who seized Rufus's arms and held them behind his back. He writhed and cursed, but did not have the strength to resist. The envoy stood before him, with one hand reached out to grip his throat, and with the other drew a long, narrow dagger from its sheath.

Paul was frozen. He could not cross the twenty yards between them in time, nor could he call for help. Rufus closed his eyes as the barbarian carefully placed the edge of the blade against his throat.

There was a sudden, sharp *crack*, and the envoy collapsed limply on top of Rufus. The two warriors let go of him and drew their weapons; an instant later one of them was also struck, twisting and falling to the ground. The surviving warrior cried out, spun around in panic, but could see nothing within the circle of mist but Paul, Rufus, the horse and his two dead comrades. By now Paul had unsheathed his sword and was advancing on him. The barbarian hesitated for a moment, considered standing his ground, and then ran.

Paul cut the ropes binding Rufus. A man came running silently out of the mist, a slight, lithe figure. He was unarmoured, wearing a tunic and hooded cloak, and in his right hand was a leather sling.

'Thank you,' said Paul. He pointed at the body of the envoy, lying prone on the damp grass, the rear of his skull smashed. 'His gold is yours to keep – but be swift.'

Pausing only to allow Rufus to grab the sword of the fallen warrior, Paul helped him limp back to their own lines. Once there he took Rufus to the rear and called for some water. 'Tell me what happened.'

'Forgive me,' Rufus said. He was shivering as he sat on the ground, his voice unsteady. 'They ambushed us as we approached from the north. We couldn't see a thing after we left the road, and we ended up trapped in a marsh. They must have been tracking us from the start.'

Paul nodded. 'Any survivors?'

'I don't know. I was captured in the vanguard. The ground was too soft. They were all over us.'

'What about Glevum?'

'We rode by the south gate, but not a word from the sentries. It was like we were invisible.'

Paul gripped his shoulder. 'I want you to return to Corinium.'

'No.'

'You swore an oath.'

'I swore an oath not to join the charge. We never got to make the charge.'

'Then I'll make you swear a new oath. You're in no condition to fight.'

Rufus got awkwardly to his feet. 'I'm not leaving.'

From his tone Paul knew there was no point arguing, and he no longer wanted to. He saw Rufus as he had not before: as a young man of frustrated ambitions who had taken on a military career against his father's wishes, who had spent his few years of service in dull inactivity before crippling himself back into civilian life, and who now had the chance to recapture everything fate had taken from him. He sought purpose and fulfilment. Paul could well understand this. 'All right. Find some armour, go to the right flank. Good luck, Rufus. Fight well.'

Rufus reached out to grip his arm. 'Fight well.'

Paul returned to the centre of the front line. The enemy would soon launch their final attack. This one would be better planned, fiercer. Paul saw the battle unfold in his mind. Despite his precautions, the left flank would be the first to collapse, followed by the right flank; after that the barbarians would encircle the centre and overwhelm them. The line would break and fragment into a messy, crowded slaughter, and somewhere during the fight, perhaps without him even being aware of it, he would be cut down and would die.

He felt the insidious grip of fear tighten around his gut. Perhaps if he believed in an afterlife he might be reconciled more easily to the fact of approaching death. It was not too late to retreat. The road to Corinium was still clear behind them. He might yet live to see tomorrow.

The battle line was reforming without any order being given. The archers reassembled in a skirmish line ahead. Paul watched as soldiers, even those with injuries, stepped back into place. If there was fear or weakness in their eyes, he did not see it: rather, he saw the willingness of men to die for their homes and families.

The fear loosened its grip. Paul was suddenly ashamed that he had even considered retreat in the presence of his brothers. He took his place in the front rank beside Belator.

The battle line waited; time passed; the veil of mist finally rose from the field, burned away by the climbing sun, as the barbarian line started its crawl towards them. Now Paul could see the entire expanse of their army. He wondered whether he would see Talorg, the Pictish butcher-prince who had murdered his friend a lifetime ago, perhaps even test arms against him. But he did not know Talorg by sight, and now he never would. For that they would have to take him alive.

At three hundred yards the archers began to shoot. This time the Attacotti were prepared, and continued their advance, holding their shields high to receive the steady rain of arrows. The archers withdrew to the rear, the battle line readied and hurled their darts, and the barbarians broke into an open charge and came across the last fifty yards like a great thundering wave.

Paul screamed for his men to hold the line, and it was the last time he heard his own voice. The impact this time was harder, relentless, and almost crushed him beneath his own shield; he lost his balance and struggled to regain it, counting on the spearman behind him to keep his attacker back while he found his feet and brought his sword into play. To his right Belator was fighting hard to withstand an enormous, full-bearded warrior who was bringing his axe down in repeated swings on Belator's shield, each time sending chunks of splintered wood flying. Paul saw that a quick thrust would bring his blade into the axeman's naked flank, but his own assailant would not give him the chance. He could already feel the shield wall breaking as the centre buckled. The weight of the attack was too great. With desperate effort he lunged high with his shield, stunning the barbarian and striking him clean through the stomach, but the man hardly had time to fall before he was replaced.

The attack became a flood. Soon in this torrent of flesh and steel there was hardly room to swing a sword, nor space to plant a foot without standing on a torso or limb, and no time to think. Men were being pierced and cut, sliced open like animals, everywhere Paul looked. He fell, and this time could not rise, but lay on his back, propped on the bodies of the fallen, their blood seeping through his clothes, and he kept his shield close while he slashed and stabbed the figures crowding about him, lunging at their feet and naked shins where he could not reach higher. He abandoned himself to blind instinct. He would not stop, would not surrender. Death could swallow him whole and he would rip its throat to shreds as he went down.

A moment came when Paul saw a savage directly above him, his face´looming down from the light of the heavens. He was young and sandy-haired, hardly even a man; his eyes were a bright, gleaming blue, the same as Eachna's, and across his chin was a reluctant spread of stubble, a first wispy attempt to grow a beard that reminded Paul somehow of Victor. This was a strange moment to remember such a thing, Paul thought, a heartbeat before a left-arm reflex raised his shield to deflect the falling blow.

He waited behind his shield, eyes closed, tensed for the impact to shudder his arm, but it did not come.

Very slowly he lowered his shield. The savage had disappeared, leaving only the great, clear vault of the sky. Paul craned his neck to either side. Heaps of bodies surrounded him. Fatigue flooded through his body. Stiffly he climbed to his feet, keeping hold of his sword and shield. A pair of hands took hold of him, helping him balance as the blood rushed to his head. It was Belator, still alive. Others from the militia were around them, some standing, some trying to rise or squirming where they lay. The groans and weeping of the wounded seemed to rise from the earth itself, like the blood that squelched beneath Paul's boots.

The barbarians had gone. They were fleeing back across the battlefield. Yet they had surely already won. Why had they broken away?

Belator saw the confusion in Paul's eyes, and pointed to the sky beyond the enemy camp. 'There.'

Now Paul saw the columns of smoke: not the wispy grey of cooking fires this time, but a thick black colour; and not from the enemy camp, but from the river beyond, much further away. The columns were so many that they rose and merged into a single great cloud. The colour, Paul realised, was from the pitch used to waterproof boats. Someone had set the Attacotti fleet alight.

'Glevum?' asked Belator.

'Whoever it is, this is our last chance. Summon every man who can still walk. Quickly!'

There was no time to organise or count the surviving troops. The cornicen was still alive, and the draco standard of the city militia was still intact, its bearer wounded in the shoulder but able to carry it. Belator had the emergency assembly sounded in front of what had been the battle line. Soon a few score men had gathered, with luck enough for a counter-attack; Rufus was nowhere to be seen, nor did Paul see any men from that flank, but there was no time to wait. He stood before the ragged survivors of his army and raised his blade high. 'On me!'

His men followed him at a slow run. It was a mile to the river, a fair distance for men already exhausted by battle, but Paul drew on his deepest reserve of willpower to overcome the pain. He trusted that his men would not flag as long as he had the strength to lead. He led them deliberately around the edge of the rise at the far end of the causeway, avoiding the enemy camp, and headed directly for the nearest bend of the river, where the line of moored boats began.

As he came nearer, Paul saw that most of the fleet was now burning. Scattered crowds of barbarians were running across the flat, sodden fields to the ships, but it was far too late.

And they were expected. Along the river line, arrayed in the shadow of the black smoke, was a fresh force of Roman troops. It looked like almost a full cohort, with wings of cavalry on the flanks. These were not the Glevum militia, but regulars.

Paul came to a stop, as much from amazement as to catch his breath.

Belator was right behind him. 'Where the hell did they come from?'

'Christ knows,' said Paul. 'Draw up the men here.'

At this point the Sabrina slowed and took a broad sweep, forming a sheltered crook half a mile wide where the pirates had moored their boats – and in which they were now trapped. Ahead of them and to either side was the river; between them and what was left of their fleet was the new Roman force; behind them Paul could now close the box. He cast his eye over his hastily assembling battle line. Some men were still arriving. He reckoned a quarter of his force was left. From what he could tell there were still close to a thousand barbarians, which gave the enemy an advantage of numbers. But they were in chaos, with neither the training nor the leadership to deal with what was about to happen.

'Sound the advance!'

With a punctuated drone from the buccina, Paul's men began to march. When they came down to the lower ground and the flat, soft meadowland astride the river, Paul could no longer discern the movements of the enemy, except that they were still huddled together. Five hundred yards from the enemy line Paul set the pace to a fast march. Many of the militia were not drilled for such manoeuvres and their cadence was shambolic, but the biarchi held the line well enough.

Ahead they heard the first battle sounds, a distant hum of voices and clashing weapons. The new forces had engaged the barbarians. Paul had almost reached within arrowshot when the

Attacotti left flank seemed to break off and drift south; first a few scattered men, then small packs, then finally the entire flank collapsed. As the barbarians dispersed, Roman light cavalry surged through them, herding and cutting them down.

Fifty yards from the enemy, Paul drew his sword in the signal to charge, and screamed: 'For the emperor!'

The cornicen dropped back and sounded one long, deafening blast that was quickly drowned out by the roar of the troops. There was no finesse and little discipline to this charge; the barbarians, already wavering and ready to break, could do no more than form loose pockets, which were quickly enveloped.

The momentum carried Paul and his men deep into the enemy formation. For a terrifying instant he found himself almost surrounded by long-haired, white bodies, but in their faces he saw a terror greater than his own, the seeds of panic and confusion best nurtured with violence, and so, with his men on his heels, he cried out in fury and rushed on. He slashed at every sight of enemy flesh, hardly noticing whether he killed or maimed or missed altogether, until there were no more barbarians to kill and he was faced instead by the first ranks of the new Roman troops.

They stared at him, keeping their shields raised as though he were a madman. He stood before them, panting, and realised that he had somehow lost his shield during the charge. His sword was bloodied to the hilt. Around him the ground was littered with the dead. The enemy line was broken. It was snowing black ash, flecks of canvas from the burning sails.

Paul noticed Belator not far away. Their eyes met, and they laughed, though Paul was not sure why. At that moment the very fact of his breathing seemed absurd.

An officer from the regulars approached. He eyed Paul warily. 'Primicerius Marcus Cara of the Sixth Cohort of Lingones.'

Paul raised his sword in a casual salute. 'Senator Cironius Agnus Paulus, acting commander of the civil garrison of Corinium. Forgive me, primicerius, but I didn't think any regulars were left this side of the country. Where's your tribune?'

'That's a good question. We were supposed to be getting a new one a week ago. He never arrived.'

'Then where have you come from?'

The officer jabbed his thumb over his shoulder, towards the mountains of the west. 'The iron mines.'

'Good Christ in Heaven!' came a fresh voice. Paul looked up to see a horseman trotting towards him through the wreckage of battle. He did not recognise him at first, only noticing that he was well into middle age but bore himself with the easy strength of a much younger man, and that apart from his helmet and sword belt he was not wearing a military uniform. He stopped, climbed from the saddle, and came to Paul with both hands outstretched. 'Come, nephew, it's been only a few years!'

Realisation had barely hit Paul before his uncle took him in a suffocating embrace that lifted his heels from the ground.

'Uncle Pertinax?'

His uncle released him. 'Your father would be proud of you! What a fight!' Pertinax took his arm and led him across the battlefield. Surrounded by death and detritus, the air thick with the toxic stench of burning pitch, Pertinax was as relaxed as though they were taking a stroll through a summertime garden. 'We'll take a good haul of slaves and hostages from this. Some of them have fled north, more south, but we'll see how far they get without their boats, eh? We captured a Pictish prince alive. We'll make him sing like a bird before the day's out.'

'Where did you come from? We thought you were in Glevum.'

Pertinax spat into the grass. 'Hah! I told them: surrender if you like. Not while there's a breath left in my body will these savages get a scrap of my land. There's my old cohort over by Ariconium, I said, sitting on their arses outside iron pits or guarding wagon trains – no kind of work for real soldiers! They know me; some of the old boys are still in the ranks. So let's go and find them and teach these Attacotti a good lesson!' He waved his hand. 'Pissing in the wind. But I thought, to hell with them. I'll go myself if I have to, so I did. It's a good job the council got some practice grovelling to Attacotti kings – now it can grovel to *me*.'

Paul, who had always found his uncle overbearing, tried not to find fault with him today. They walked along the riverbank, looking at the charred and smoking skeletons of the Attacottian fleet, and Paul listened to Pertinax talk about victory and glory, and how the stuck-up councillors of Glevum would have to listen to him now that he had an army at his back. Paul was not sure whether or not his uncle was joking. But then they came to where the Romans had gathered the prisoners, and were binding their necks and wrists with rope from their own boats. One skinny, half-naked prisoner was being kept separate from the rest, flanked by two soldiers, and Pertinax led Paul to him.

'Here,' said Pertinax proudly, 'is Prince Talorg mac Keocher of the Pictish folk.'

Talorg raised his face to look at Paul. It was the sandy-haired youth who had almost killed him on the battle line. At first Paul could not believe this was the feared Pictish prince; he was almost comically slight, with skinny shoulders and a child-like face trying desperately to look old beyond its years. But as Paul held his gaze, he recognised the arrogant spark of royalty in his eyes, and a savage coldness. These eyes, he thought, had been among the last to see Victor alive. Perhaps Talorg himself had performed the sacrifice.

'Quite a prize,' muttered Pertinax. 'Hasn't said a word since we caught him trying to cut out his own guts. We're not sure if he understands us.' He leaned close to Talorg and pronounced clearly, 'You'll have a royal parade through Glevum – in chains!'

Pertinax and the soldiers laughed. Paul did not. He knew he deserved most of the credit for the victory. He had managed to win over the council of Corinium, and had confronted the barbarians with a weaker force, and had fought almost to the death, whereas Pertinax had scarcely muddied the hem of his cloak. Most of all he wanted Talorg for his own. He could conjure good practical reasons for this: such an important prisoner should be kept at the provincial seat of power, which was Corinium, not

Glevum. Paul, as a member of the senatorial class, was his uncle's social and political superior, and he had every right to demand possession of a royal hostage.

But the true reason, he knew, was Victor. He sensed that having Victor's killer within his power would satisfy some deep need.

Paul asked to have Talorg. When his uncle resisted, Paul started to demand, and quickly grew impatient. This was not a squabble he needed. He was coughing up cinders from the smoke, he needed fresh air, and now, with the haze of battle gradually lifting, he felt a familiar emptiness envelop him. In the end they compromised: his uncle would have Talorg in Glevum for three days, and then send him unharmed to Corinium.

Paul walked with Belator and the remainder of his men away from the battlefield. Let Pertinax keep the pomp and glory; let Pertinax have the privilege of stripping the enemy camp and returning the pirate booty to its rightful owners. Paul longed not for parades but to count his losses, to find Rufus – if he still lived – and bring him home to Amanda, and most of all to be with his wife.

XXX

There is a kind of river of things passing into being,
And Time is a violent torrent. For no sooner is each seen,
Than it has been carried away, and another is being carried by,
And that too will be carried away.

Marcus Aurelius, *Meditations*

This was the first time Eachna had seen Silvanicum from the hill across the river. She stood in the shade of an oak tree, and through a faint shimmer of heat she looked at the villa basking in the July sun, its walls a glaring white between the brown of the grass and the thick green of the valley trees. The slope below it was half reaped, the stubble dotted with piles of hay, and teams of peasants enjoyed their midday break down at the riverbank. Even from this distance Eachna caught the occasional sound of laughter, or the vivid splash of someone jumping into the water of the Colona.

Two weeks had passed since the battle of Glevum. Eachna remembered standing with Amanda by the side of the road outside Corinium and watching the army return. She remembered the moment of horror when she had seen the vanguard of tribune Belator approach with the standard and hornplayer, followed by the first batch of chained captives, but no Paul, and the terrible thought that he had fallen, even though the report of his victory had already been brought to them; and the relief when Belator saw them and shouted that Paul was at the rear.

They had waited for the army to march by, until finally among the stragglers and the wounded they saw Paul. He was on foot, walking with Julian and Alypius alongside a cart loaded with the lame. He had already removed his armour, and but for his filthy senatorial tunic he might have passed for any soldier of the ranks. On the wagon was Rufus, who had taken an injury to his leg, bad but not fatal. Amanda ran into the road and almost knocked Paul over with a hug before clambering inelegantly over the side of the wagon, where, to the great amusement of the other injured men, she threw herself on Rufus.

Paul had come to Eachna. She would never forget that moment.

As they had walked into the city she had asked him why he had removed his armour, and he had replied, 'I was made a general to defeat the barbarians. We defeated them. Now I'm a general no more.' She walked by his side as the army paraded into Corinium and its throngs of rejoicing citizens.

His first duty, Paul had said, was to give his father the funeral he deserved. But even after the funeral, many days passed before Paul could escape from the city council and their adoration. With the aid of Alypius, Silvius Fronto and more donations of land, he had persuaded them to organise a larger and better equipped militia for every city and town in the province. Corinium had been saved, but the rest of Britannia had not. News still came that the northern country was being overrun by Picts and deserting soldiers turning to brigandage, and there were rumours of Saxon raids on the south coast. It was said that if the empire did not send help soon, Londinium itself might be threatened.

'Eachna?'

At the sound of Paul's voice she turned. He was still standing a few yards up the meadow with the others. The six of them had all ridden up here together, she and Paul, Amanda and Rufus, Julian and Patricia, to enjoy the sun and the precious peace while they could. Now it looked like Rufus and Amanda were preparing to leave.

Eachna returned to the group, where Amanda kissed her. 'Goodbye, sister. Rufus is taking me back to Silvanicum. He needs to visit the villa Caecina.'

'Technically it still belongs to my father,' Rufus said, and shrugged. 'Someone has to look after it in the meantime, so it may as well be me. Looks like I'm becoming a gentleman farmer after all.'

After promising Eachna that they would read together that evening, Amanda left with Rufus. Eachna watched them go fondly. For the last fortnight Amanda had besieged Eachna with questions about her past, about her memories of home and the fables of Hibernia. Eachna, in turn, had learned much from Amanda about how the wife of a senator was expected to behave. Though much of the etiquette baffled or amused her, she was enjoying the company.

'We should be heading back, too,' Julian said to Patricia.

She nodded regretfully. 'We promised Father and Mother we'd return home today before dusk. In her last letter Mother actually said she was missing us. Imagine that!'

'Is your father at the villa?' asked Paul.

'He's still in Glevum,' said Julian. 'Putting the council to rights. He's expecting to be elected magistrate next year. Saviour of the city, captor of Prince Talorg.'

Paul laughed briefly, unable to hide a trace of bitterness. 'Tell the conqueror to hurry up and send me the prince like he promised. I was expecting him over a week ago.'

'We'll tell him, cousin.' Julian smiled and shook Paul's hand, then kissed Eachna. 'Christ be with you, sister. I'll see you again shortly.'

Soon Paul and Eachna were alone. Neither wanted to return to the villa quite yet. They had found little time to themselves over the past fortnight. Eachna took Paul by the hand and led him to the shadow of the oak tree, where they sat on the soft grass and looked down to the villa. They saw Amanda and Rufus approaching the bridge over the river, riding side by side, Julian and Patricia some distance behind.

'When you have Talorg, what will you do with him?' Eachna asked. She knew that Talorg and his warband had killed Paul's friend in the northern forest. Whenever Talorg had been mentioned over the past fortnight, a strange darkness had come over Paul's expression, and it worried her.

'I don't know yet,' he said. 'Talk to him, when I'm ready.' He dragged his hand idly through a clump of grass, teasing the blades between his fingers. 'There's enough to do here for now, anyway.'

'Maybe we should go down to the river and help them make hay.'

She had meant it as a joke, and he laughed, but she could sense him considering the idea and finding some appeal in it. Free from the city, all Paul seemed to talk about now was the estate: how they had lost many days of labour during the panic of the invasion at such a busy time of year, how much was to be done in the lean weeks before the harvest with haymaking, shearing and the weeding of the crops. Of course he did it to distract himself from other things: from Talorg, from the uncertainty of what Agrius Leo was scheming in Gallia, from what the months ahead would bring.

Perhaps Eachna would one day grow weary of listening to him, but not yet. He could talk about farming for the next fifty years if it kept his thoughts away from politics.

Together they sat beneath the tree, comfortable in the cool air. When he lay on his back, stretching out his limbs with a contented sigh, she lay beside him with her head on his chest. He tucked his arms around her. Clouds of war might hover on the horizon, their thunder a distant rumble, but here, at least, and for now, the sky was clear and blue.

Acknowledgements

Thanks first of all to family, for being family – to Mum and Dad, to Ren, Abi and Gem, to Noel, and especially to Edmund, my earliest and wisest critic and advisor. If there's a secret centre to this novel, they are it, even if they don't know it. It took a long time before I found the nerve to announce my creative writing ambitions to the world outside the clan, and so those friends whom I told deserve thanks for their encouragement – most of all Craig, Anna, Suzanne, Hsin-Chi, Ross and Aleisha, and even Alex, who hates Romans. Over the years I've been fortunate also to have teachers who inspired both a love of writing and a love of the past; for the latter in particular Mary Garrison deserves heartfelt thanks. Helen Foxhall Forbes was very kind to cast her expert eye over the Old English in chapter XI, and didn't even complain about the awful anachronism of having fourth-century Saxons speaking it. The quote from Marcus Aurelius at the start of chapter XXX is from the 1946 translation by A. S. L. Farquharson. Finally: starting a novel is one thing, completing it another, and getting it published something else entirely. Without the tireless enthusiasm of Jim and the rest of the team at United Agents you would not be reading these words at all, and without Nick and Laura, my fantastic editors at Hodder and Stoughton, the book would be far less than what it is. Thanks to all.

Historical Note

On historical fiction

A ll of the main characters and events in this book are necessarily fictional. While the fourth-century empire is relatively
well documented in general, our sources rarely have much to say
about Britain. The soldier and historian Ammianus Marcellinus
offers a few frustratingly brief glimpses of events in Britain around
the middle of the century. Otherwise, we rely on archaeology to
fill out the picture: but it is in the nature of archaeology that this
picture is impressionistic and ill-defined.

This does, at least, leave the novelist with lots of freedom to
invent the detail. Ammianus tells us that there was a serious
barbarian invasion of Britain in 367, but his account is brief and
his details incidental. He does not tell us where this took place,
or exactly how, and so I had the pleasure of imagining it myself.
In the aftermath of the invasion there was a rebellion led by an
influential Pannonian exile named Valentinus – but again, we
know little about this. His complicity in the barbarian invasion
is entirely my invention.

In general, however, I have tried to stay close to the few facts
we have, clinging to them as a drowning sailor might cling to
every scrap of floating wood within reach. Virtually every location
in the book is based on a real place. We have clear archaeological
evidence that a series of villas along the river Avon east of Bath
(Aquae Sulis) were burned by raiders at this time, and thus Fuscina
leads her destitute household in rags to Cirencester (Corinium).
Historical figures make occasional appearances, and each appearance is at least *theoretically* possible, if unlikely. Hesperius is the

son of the famous Gallic poet Ausonius, whose family did have vague connections to Britain, although we have no evidence that either father or son ever visited. Indeed Ausonius, judging from some of his epigrams, held Britons in snobbish disdain.

Most important for me was to capture the mood of the time, as best we can discern it from what traces remain, to make it live through imagined human experience, thereby to achieve a deeper truth than the question of did-it-happen or did-it-not. The tensions between Christianity and paganism, between rich and poor, between loyalty to a higher cause and the eternal cause of self-interest, after all, were no less alive in this period than in periods that drown in documentation. By way of illustration, below I have attempted to describe some features of the age so that the reader might see where the historical fact underlies the fiction.

Late Roman government

Late Roman government is a large and complex area of academic study, but two main points are worth mentioning here. First, from the late third century onwards there was an increasingly stark distinction drawn between civilian and military government, which had formerly been much more closely entwined. Second, at the same time the civilian bureaucracy was massively expanded as provinces were divided and sub-divided, offices and positions multiplied, and new layers of officials and clerks invented at every level of government.

Society became increasingly polarised between civilian and military: the old senatorial elite was steadily de-militarised and 'softened', while the army became increasingly open to men from rustic frontier provinces, or even from beyond the empire itself, who lacked the traditional qualities of educated and cultured men but could potentially rise through the ranks to positions of great influence. This was especially true during the reign of Emperor Valentinian (364–375), a tough career general who loathed the aristocracy and was raised to the purple on the back of his military reputation.

As a novelist, I am most interested in the impact that such drastic changes in the nature of government had on everyday life. Paul's father Agnus, for example, being a member of a thoroughly civilian aristocracy, has few contacts in the military beyond his wife's brother-in-law Pertinax, and resents the inaccessibility of the army-dominated imperial court. We also encounter several instances in the book, the tribunes Bauto and Drogo and the duke Fullobaudes among them, of 'barbarians' who have managed to attain command positions within the Roman army, positions that in earlier centuries had been filled by the Roman equestrian and senatorial classes.

At the same time, the increasing number of bureaucrats was a symptom of the empire tightening its grip over the provinces. Before the late third century the empire was essentially composed of a galaxy of small city-states, over which the emperor exercised a relatively light hand: the city councils were structured according to Roman principles and paid Roman taxes, but they also operated with a fair degree of autonomy.

In the late empire this changed. We can take Cirencester as an example. Previously it had merely been the 'cantonal' capital of the Dobunnic tribe, with the nearest representatives of imperial government in Londinium, the capital of Britannia Superior. When Britain was divided from two provinces into four, Cirencester, now capital of Britannia Prima, received its own imperial government office. Archaeologists have discovered that the Roman forum of Cirencester, the main public space of the city and the location of the tribal government, was physically divided in half during the fourth century, and this may reflect the arrival of the imperial governor with his own staff. From now on, tribal and imperial government existed cheek by jowl in the heart of the city. High-ranking officials from across the empire, Gauls and Italians, Greeks and Syrians, walked the streets of the city, lived in sumptuous townhouses and became entwined in local political life. On the one hand, this did present direct access to imperial power to important provincials such as Agnus, and new career opportunities for the more ambitious locals; on the other hand, the intrusion of imperial government into local affairs no doubt caused widespread resentment among those unable to take advantage of it.

The late Roman army

The late Roman army was very different in organisation from the classic legions of the early empire. From the late third century there existed a broad division between frontier garrisons, the so-called *limitanei* (from Latin *limes*, 'frontier'), and troops of the field army, known as the *comitatenses* (literally meaning 'companions'). The latter were better paid and equipped, and formed the mobile forces typically used for campaigning, although frontier garrisons could also be called on for this purpose.

While the overall size of the army increased, late Roman regiments were also smaller, and thus more tactically flexible, than the old and cumbersome 6,000-strong legions. Field army infantry regiments appear to have numbered about 1000 men, cavalry regiments perhaps 500. Most frontier regiments, infantry and cavalry, numbered 500 men; some, such as Paul's First Tungrian Cohort based at Housesteads, were larger, around 750 men. Some of the old legions still existed within this new structure, likely reduced in size from former times: we know, for instance, that during the fourth century the Sixth Legion was still based in York, as it had been since the second century. The above numbers of course only represent paper strength, and are based on a great deal of supposition.

It seems that there was no significant field army presence in Britain at the time of the Barbarian Conspiracy; they had likely been withdrawn over the previous two years to help deal with barbarian invasions in Gaul. We do know that there were at least two high military commanders present in Britain: Nectaridus, count of the maritime region (*comes maritimi tractus*), in charge of naval forces and coastal forts; and Fullobaudes (sometimes spelled Fullofaudes), duke of the British provinces (*dux Britanniarum*), who commanded the *limitanei* in the north. Ammianus Marcellinus records that the barbarian invasion of 367 led to the death of the former and the capture or death of the latter. The provinces must have been extremely exposed once these commanders were lost and the frontier defences failed.

It is likely that the fortified towns and cities of Britain were normally garrisoned by detachments from the frontier garrisons or field army, and we know that the compulsory billeting of troops in ordinary households was deeply unpopular across the empire. When these troops were needed elsewhere, however, the cities must have had some means of maintaining order. Despite the lack of clear evidence on the matter I have therefore envisaged the existence of urban light militias, which could be raised by the civic councils of each tribal canton. Thus after the withdrawal of its regular garrison, Cirencester is still not entirely undefended, and it is this militia, supplemented by the paramilitary *bucellarii*, which forms the core of Paul's defensive force. *Bucellarii* literally means 'biscuit-eaters'; it was a term used to describe the armed retainers of aristocratic households.

I have used Latin terms in anglicised form for the higher military ranks (hence 'count' for *comes*, 'duke' for *dux*, and 'tribune' for *tribunus*), but for the less well-known titles of junior officers and lower ranks I have retained the original Latin form. Here I offer a brief explanation of the late Roman ranking system, limited to the ranks mentioned in this book. For certain ranks, including *ducenarius* and *centenarius*, we know very little of what they involved beyond where they fell in the rank structure. I have included the Latin plural forms in parentheses.

Tribune/prefect – commander of a regiment
Primicerius (primicerii) – second-in-command to the tribune
Campidoctor (campidoctores) – drill master, a high-ranking NCO
Centenarius (centenarii) – roughly equivalent to the earlier centurion, commanding 80–100 men
Biarchus (biarchi) – commander of an eight-man squad
Semissalis (semissales) – second-in-command to the biarchus
Pedes (pedites) – unranked infantryman

Senators and equestrians

Another major social change of the late empire was the expansion of the senatorial class beyond the ancient senate in Rome itself. By now the Roman senate was largely irrelevant as a political body outside Rome, but senatorial status still carried high social prestige, not to mention legal and financial benefits. During the fourth century, especially from the reign of Valentinian onwards, it was possible to acquire senatorial status not only through birth, but by holding certain high offices in the imperial administration. The result was that many wealthy, career-minded citizens throughout the western provinces were raised to the senatorial class. This was certainly the case in Gaul. There are no known *parvenu* British senatorial families, but it is quite possible that at least a handful existed, as I have imagined in this book with the Cironii.

Such was the expansion of the senatorial class in the late empire that senatorial status itself became devalued. Human nature being what it is, this led to the creation of grades *within* the senatorial class, to distinguish greater and lesser senators. The grading system appears to have developed somewhat organically during the fourth century, and was official by the 370s. The top senatorial rank of *inlustris* was reserved for the very highest officials of the empire. The most important provinces were controlled by consul-governors, who held the rank *clarissimus*, the lowest senatorial grade. Regular provincial governorships came with the rank *perfectissimus*, the highest equestrian grade. The senatorial and equestrian ranks are listed here in descending order, along with the rough English translations I have used in the novel.

Senatorial ranks:
   inlustris (illustrious)
   spectabilis (outstanding)
   clarissimus (most esteemed)
Equestrian ranks:
   perfectissimus (most perfect)
   ducenarius
   centenarius
   egregius (distinguished)

Religion

When the emperor Constantine converted to Christianity and made it an official religion of the empire in 313, he set in motion a century of tumultuous change. The empire did convert to Christianity, but not quickly or easily. The years 361 to 363 saw the short reign of the pagan Emperor Julian, remembered by Christian posterity as 'the Apostate', who made a naive and ultimately thwarted attempt to reverse the conversion process. Emperor Valentinian was a Christian of the military school, practical-minded and tolerant, but after him came emperors much less willing to compromise with those whom the church called *pagani*, a derisory term that literally means 'those from the country', i.e. unsophisticated rustics (think 'hillbillies' or 'country bumpkins').

As usual, evidence for religion in Britain at this time is slight. There were certainly British bishops, as we have records of some of them attending church councils on the continent, and where there are shepherds there must be flocks. Archaeology also makes clear that Christianity was spreading among the villa-owning classes, and it was likely beginning to trickle down to the population at large. But in the middle of the century it was still very possible to be wealthy, influential, and pagan. The temple of Nodens at Lydney on the Severn Estuary was refurbished around this time, as described in the novel, along with other rural pagan temples. A governor named Lucius Septimius did indeed restore a column to Jupiter in Cirencester during the fourth century, and the inscribed base of this column can be seen in Cirencester's Corinium Museum:

> To Jupiter, Best and Greatest, His Perfection Lucius Septimius, *vir perfectissimus*, governor of Britannia Prima, restored [this column], being a citizen of Rheims. Septimius, governor of the First Province, restores [this] statue and column, erected under the old religion.

The inscription is conventionally dated by archaeologists to the reign of Julian, but it could plausibly date from the reign of a Christian emperor. Pagans could still hold high imperial office for years after Julian, and provincial governors did not always toe the official line.

Finally, there is the matter of Ludo's tentative mission of conversion to the barbarian peoples beyond the Wall. This is pure fiction. We know, however, that some Picts and Irish were being converted in the early fifth century by Christian missionaries, and these missions possibly had precedents closer to home. The Venerable Bede, writing three centuries later, records some hazy traditions of a church founded by Saint Ninian at Whithorn in Galloway in the fourth or fifth century, and I imagine Ludo's activity as a precursor to this.

Characters and Places

Agrii

Agrius Leo, equestrian
Pupilla, his wife
Rufus, his son
*Lucius Septimius, his cousin, governor of Britannia Prima

Other characters (in order of appearance)

Victor, soldier of Vercovicium
Eachna, an escaped Irish slave girl
Ludo, bishop of Luguvalium
Braxus, biarchus of Vercovicium
Bauto, a Frank, tribune of Vercovicium
Caratoc, biarchus of Trimontium
Gregory, bishop of Londinium
*Potitus, priest at Luguvalium
Martin, bishop of Corinium
Silvius Fronto, equestrian, city councillor of Corinium
Drogo, a Frank, tribune of Mediobogdum
*Fullobaudes, an Alemann, duke of the British provinces
Kunaric, primicerius of Mediobogdum
*Decimius Hilarianus Hesperius, a young Gallic nobleman
Fuscina, sister-in-law of Agnus
Porcius and Atius, magistrates of Corinium
Belator, tribune of the Corinium militia
Talorg, a Pictish prince

Places, with modern equivalents

Aquae Sulis	Bath
Calleva	Silchester
Corinium	Cirencester
Cunetio	Mildenhall
Deva	Chester
Eboracum	York

Galava	Ambleside (Cumbria)
Glanoventa	Ravenglass (Cumbria)
Glevum	Gloucester
Isca	Caerleon
Londinium	London
Lugdunum	Lyon
Luguvalium .	Carlisle
Mediobogdum	Hardknott Roman fort (Cumbria)
Remis	Rheims
Rutupiae	Richborough
Sabrina	River Severn
Salinae (the saltworks)	Droitwich
Silvanicum	Chedworth Roman villa (Gloucestershire)
Temple of Nodens	Lydney Roman temple (Gloucestershire)
Treveris	Trier
Trimontium	Eildon Hills
Venta Belgarum	Winchester
Venta Silurum	Caerwent
Vercovicium	Housesteads Roman fort
Viriconium	Wroxeter
White Hen House	Great Witcombe Roman villa (Gloucestershire)

HISTORY LIVES
at Hodder

From Anya Seton and Mary Stewart to Thomas Keneally and Robyn Young, Hodder & Stoughton has an illustrious tradition of publishing bestselling and prize-winning authors whose novels span the centuries, from ancient Rome to the Tudor Court, revolutionary Paris to the Second World War.

———

Want to learn how an author researches battle scenes?

Discover history from a female perspective?

Find out what it's like to walk Hadrian's Wall in full Roman dress?

Visit us today at **HISTORY LIVES** for exclusive author features, first chapter previews, book trailers, author videos, event listings and competitions.